A Royal Ruckus

(Book V of The Osten Chronicles)

Author: Daniel Thorman

ISBN: 978-1-963913-28-6

Imprint: Native Publishers, The

The Osten Chronicles

Dedicated to:

Roger Anderson

CHAPTER ONE

The Almoner

PICKERING: Have you no morals, man?
DOOLITTLE: Can't afford them,
Governor. Neither could you if you was
as poor as me.

~ George Bernard Shaw ~
(Pygmalion, Act 2)

They say that all roads lead to Fairglen. And though it's true that Osten's capital is indeed the kingdom's hub for commerce and culture, it is equally true that roads run in both directions. It was therefore just as valid to say that all roads lead *away* from Fairglen. But you certainly wouldn't know it based on today's traffic.

I steered my trusty mount along the winding road that would lead eventually to the city's edge. The last marker I'd passed had proudly proclaimed the fair city lay only a few modest leagues farther on. The evening sun warmed my shoulders. Spring was certainly well advanced. And soon the lazy days of summer would commence. Not that I would be left alone to enjoy their tranquil comfort. My lady's latest missive was edged with an urgency she was seldom wont to express. No. My duty was clear. I must rush to her side at once or be forsworn.

It was late. And as much as I longed for a hot meal and the comfort of human companionship, I knew that entering the city at night was probably a bad idea. Rather than seeking some accommodating inne, 'twere better to make a final camp here at the outskirts and arrive there fresh in the morning. Nestled amid the farmsteads of western Fairglen, this rolling stretch of hillside was likely the last bit of wilderness I'd find. It should do nicely enough.

I'd chosen this back road specifically to avoid the fuss and bother currently cluttering the king's highway. Patrols there were frequent, and a lone traveler was always the subject of extra scrutiny. It wasn't that I had anything to hide. I just wanted a final bit of quiet time before entering the thick of things. Though the grand celebration was still a good month off, I needed to be on hand and available to fulfill my oaths during all the preliminary festivities. My lady was depending on me.

I shortened the reins and dismounted near a bend in the trail,

"Well done, Gypsy," I praised.

Her ears straightened, and she emitted a brief snort from her long muzzle in reply.

As I loosened the saddle strap, she leaned in toward me and hung her head to munch at a weed that grew beside the trail. The mule was a gentle soul who had served me faithfully ever since I'd hired her at the caravansary. The folks there were more accustomed to outfitting entire caravans at once, but the timing of my arrival required that I set off alone. On the morrow, I would locate the merchant stables to reclaim the bulk of my deposit before seeking lodgings of my own.

After attending to Gypsy's needs and picketing her for the night. I built a small fire and spread my bedroll beside it. I opted not to erect my tent. The sky was clear enough. I settled myself and considered the circumstances that had brought me here.

It had started with a letter from Megan; always a happy event. It had arrived by griffin at the conclave. Was it a mere fortnight ago?

I'd been well aware that Prince Henry was soon to be made a crowned prince sometime this coming summer. The conclave had been all abuzz with gossip about the event. All the high nobility would descend upon the capital like a swarm of blade moths, there to renew their oaths and vie for the crown's favor. I'd met the prince just this past season near Eagle's Keep. There, he'd been traveling incognito on his grand tour of the kingdom. He'd seemed a decent enough chap in his guise as Kendrick.

According to Megan's letter, the date for the coronation had been set to coincide with the prince's eighteenth birthday on the twentieth day of June. My baron, Vincent Arenson Lord Westarbor, would be in attendance, as would his entire family. Leading up to the main event, there were to be a series of lesser galas celebrating the nobility of the kingdom and introducing their children to the assembled peerage.

Of particular interest was the debutante ball that would mark Megan's emergence into high society. As her protector, my attendance was mandatory. It was considered unlucky (and uncouth) for a young lady to attend such an event without her protector at her side. To hear them speak of it, one might think it possible for a noble-born lady to actually *die* from such an embarrassment.

Once I'd explained the situation, Mistress Julia had been most understanding. She granted me leave from my training and even provided me with a small purse to help fund the endeavor. And so I'd ridden ever since, intent on arriving at Megan's side to fulfill my obligations. I wasn't too clear on exactly what role a protector played in these proceedings. But I was certain the girl would soon explain.

As I settled back, I felt a familiar rumbling from within. Rockytop was stirring, preparing to assume his nighttime vigil. Closing my eyes, I steadied my breathing and envisioned my inner hill. And there he was, his solid presence filling me with a sense of peace.

"So, brother. It's to be yet another night outdoors, is it?" he rumbled.

"The last for a while, I should think," I replied.

It was generally considered foolhardy to sleep alone outside. Who knew what creatures of the night might be tempted to prey on a helpless man? But since raising my homunculus, I felt well guarded enough. Surely, Rockytop would alert me should any danger approach. Still, a little extra precaution mightn't go amiss. So I silently recited my evening prayer.

> Matthew, Mark, Luke and John,
> Bless this bed I lie upon.
> Four corners to my bed.
> Four angels round my head;
> One to watch and one to pray,
> And two to bear my soul away.

The Black Paternoster was a bedtime rhyme taught to all the children of my village. It was supposed to calm their fears and let sleep take them more readily. It had always amused me to think that the last two angels were there in case the first two didn't do their job very well. Also, my soul must be quite heavy with sin since it took the two of them.

"Sleep well, Brother," chuckled Rocky.

***

My restful night just wasn't to be. I awoke to the rumbling din that was my homunculus' silent shout of warning.

"Awaken, brother, and beware. A man approaches whose stealthy tread speaks not of good intentions!"

I opened my eyes a crack. The night was still and black. And the fire had burned its way on down to embers. From its muted orange glow, I could scarce discern things three feet from my face.

I listened, but heard naught.

Only by my earth sense could I feel the faint footfalls that had so alarmed my inner self. They were creeping ever nearer.

"Visio tenebris," I sub-vocalized, calling forth my darksight.

It still felt strange invoking spells as a geomancer. Whereas beforetimes I had envisioned my magic as vines, this draw came straight from my inner hill. I imagined flinty chips sheering off it and snapping into place behind my eyelids. Still, they did the trick quite well enough.

And by my eldritch sight, I peered into the night and spied the stooped down figure skulking toward me. I considered my father's sword, which lay at my side. Though its presence was a comfort, it was largely just for show. I could snatch it up. What then?

Instead, I reached deep within and readied a spell I'd lately been wanting to try.

The figure dashed forth to snatch up my pack from by the fire where it lay. He scooped it up and wheeled about then quickly began to race away.

Sitting up with narrowed eyes, I swiftly let my magic fly. From the ground directly beneath the cad, two earthen arms erupted. They grabbed his ankles and held him fast, tripping him up. He fell over with an explosive out-rush of breath. And as he lay struggling, from the ground emerged two more arms to wrap about his chest as well, pinning him there, helpless. 'Terreno tenaci' had worked even better than I'd imagined it might.

I looked around carefully. Thieves were oft known to run in packs. But the fellow seemed to be quite alone.

Turning back to the villain, I incanted once again. 'Flammas auget,' I said. And though pyromancy was not my forte, the flames of my once-diminished campfire increased, roaring up in a mighty column. Backlit by its flames, I surveyed my captive. His eyes had grown wide with terror.

But what was this? He was a mere boy, no older than eleven, if I was any judge. By his shabby clothing, he was a peasant lad. (And by his sour smell, he had wet himself as well.)

"Please don't kill me!" he pleaded.

I calmly walked over and retrieved my pack. Had he made off with it, I'd have had a difficult time. My bob (bugger out bag) had an enchanted pocket, allowing it to store a much greater volume of equipment than one could readily carry otherwise. And in it were stored many of my most precious possessions.

"What's your name, boy?" I demanded.

"Why should I tell you?" he asked sullenly. "You're just gonna turn me in."

"If I don't kill you. Probably. Yeah."

He gulped.

"It's Toby," he said more respectfully. "Tobias Antonio Moss."

"And where do you live, Toby?"

"Well nowadays, I live in the refugee camp, just t'other side of the hill. I'm from Gretchford Gulch, originally. That's down in E.K. But we had to leave there on account of all the monsters. Can you get this dirt off me? I can't hardly breathe proper."

"In a minute," I snapped.

In truth, the effort of maintaining the spell was fast consuming my store of magic. I looked up and pretended to track something hovering in the air. Plucking it between a thumb and forefinger, I brought it before my nose and 'examined' it closely.

"This will do quite nicely, I should think," said I.

Then, stepping over to the trapped boy, I placed it gently against his ear. He squirmed violently within his earthy bonds.

"Here now! What's that you just done?"

"That, Toby, was a Lorédonian ear-moth," I fibbed. "It won't harm you in any way. But now, if you try to run, I shall be able to find you wherever you go. Now, I'm going to release you, but you'd better sit still and answer the rest of my questions."

I wished I'd had Royland's ability to read people. The boy's fright had swiftly given way to a calculating calm. He seemed to be weighing his words most carefully and noting my reactions. I couldn't tell whether he honestly regretted his misdeed or only that he'd been caught. I suspected the latter. Still, there was something both pathetic and endearing about the lad's circumstances and his plucky spirit. I hoped it wasn't all just an act.

Despite the hour, I saw no way to return to my rest. With some misgivings, I released the spell that bound the boy and awaited his response.

He sat up, eyeing me with suspicion.

"What now?" he asked, rather cheekily, I thought.

"Now we'll go and have a talk with your father, I think."

"Good luck with that, then. He's been marched off to work in the king's stone mine; he has. Ain't seen him in more'n a fortnight."

"Your mother, then," I insisted.

At this, his face fell.

"Aww. You wouldn't want to go worrying me poor mum, would you? I can see by your woolies you're an important man, and you even have the gift to boot. Surely you got better things to be getting on with."

I did indeed. But it was everyone's responsibility to discipline the young when they went astray. Elsewise we'd have anarchy. So, despite my pressing need, I rejected his suggestion. I would make time to see this rapscallion taken to account. He stared mournfully at me as I began saddling Gypsy.

I retrieved a lantern from my pack and lit it from the spent coals of the depleted fire. The fire spell had burnt nearly everything to ash. Returning to the mule, I freed her from her picket.

"Get on," I said.

"Me?"

"Who else?" I grunted.

By my lantern's light, I'd noted the child's boots were in a woeful state of disrepair, their tattered remnants worn nearly through. I recalled the kindness the prince had extended to me when I'd been hobbled by my injury. It was a kindness I had promised to repay. Pay it forward, I thought. And it felt right.

I helped the lad to scramble up. Stepping to the fore, lantern in hand, I led the way up over the rise.

***

A league or so later, I spotted the camp. It was just up the trail to the north. The sky was brightening in the east, and in the pre-dawn light I could make out the telltale glimmer of campfires. I opened the void pocket of my bob and slid the lit lantern inside. I knew the fire would be promptly extinguished. (There was no air in that void.)

I turned to the boy astride the mule.

"Is this the place? Not much to look at."

"We do our best," he mumbled in reply. "Leastways the best they'll let us."

Approaching closer, I began to make out structures of a sort. A sprawling cluster of tents stretched off into the distance. Interspersed among them were some boxy structures of questionable wooden construction. The hodge-podge village looked unsanitary. This notion was confirmed when moving closer still, I caught the smell.

"Where in this mess, Toby Tony Moss, do you lay your head at night? That is, when you're not out accosting strangers to pilfer their belongings?

"It's the bede-house just three past the red tent." He said, pointing.

"Don't they have almshouses in the city?" I asked.

"They do, mister. But them that they has filled up long ago with deservin' poor from the city. More recent arrivals are stuck out here. Say, what's your name, anyway?"

"You may call me Journeyman Harper."

As we wove our way through the maze that was the camp, we drew many a curious look from its sullen, bedraggled denizens. When I stared back, most averted their gazes. One spat. As we drew up before this 'bede-house,' Tobias sprang down and moved to its 'door.' It was a slapdash affair that appeared to have been cobbled together from old farm carts. Doubtless, these were the very carts that had transported the refugees here.

"Ma!" he cried. "We got a visitor!"

I looked for a post on which to tie Gypsy's leads but found no such amenity present. I settled upon a stub of an old axle casing which jutted out from the clumsy residence.

A woman soon arrived at the threshold.

She was not so old, but her face had a careworn look. Her lips bore a frown, and her eyes flew wide as she looked me up and down.

"Where've you *been* Toby? You had me worried *sick*. And who is *this*, might I ask that you've brought?"

"I was out hunting squirrels on Donovan's Rise. I fell and hurt my foot. This here kind gentleman patched me up and gave me a lift back home. Ma, this is Journeyman Harper. Journeyman, my ma, Nora Moss."

This rapid exchange caught me quite by surprise. Not a stutter betrayed him as he uttered his lies. His glib presentation had twisted the facts. And yet, how could I gainsay him now without seeming impolite? I pondered on just what to say as Nora hugged the boy tight.

She turned grateful eyes up at me and said: "I thank thee, mister, from the bottom of my heart."

"Come sit by our fire! You must be tired, travelin' through the night. I'm brewing some tea for Toby and me. It'd honor our house if you'd join us. We haven't much to offer. But visitors is rare. 'Tis a long-held tradition among our folk. What we have, we share. Go wash up, Tobias. And bring some dinnerware!"

The boy rushed off before I could even think of declining.

I followed Goody Moss to the open fire pit that graced her home's side yard. Above it hung an old tea kettle from a hook between two sticks. Around it lay some massive logs arranged to form crude benches. I took my seat on one of these and watched as the woman scraped flint over steel, shedding sparks atop a bird's nest of kindling. This soon emitted a puff of smoke and began to blacken. Blowing gently, she spread the smoke until all at once it flared up into a yellow lick of flame. This soon spread to burn more intensely as she added sticks atop it.

It was fun to watch it done in the old-fashioned way for once.

Toby soon arrived, bearing a tray of mugs.

"So who's this then?" demanded an old codger, who had taken a seat across from me.

He was scraggly and unkempt, and his rheumy eyes were squinted my way.

"This is Journeyman Harper, Ce. He helped my boy out of a tight spot."

"Eh?" said the old man in confusion.

I added some sonomancy to my voice and sent it directly to the old gentleman's failing ears.

"I'm Lucas Harper, goodman. A mage of the conclave. And whom do I have the honor of addressing?"

The old man smiled.

"Ah... Cesar. Cesar Hollander."

"A mage?" said Nora, turning to the boy. "You didn't tell me he was a mage."

"Sure," said Toby, handing out the mugs. "He can do loads of stuff."

And so we sipped at our tea as we exchanged our stories. Nora and her husband, Aaron Moss, had been farmers in the southwestern E.K. until the troubles had erupted there. They hoped to return one day, as it was no kind of life here. It amused me that the husband's name was almost the reverse of 'Nora.' Together they might form a palindrome. Who ever coined that word, anyway? Why isn't 'palindrome' itself spelled the same backwards as forward? One would think the wordsmith could have made it more self-descriptive - something like 'palinilap' or perhaps 'emordrome.' But I digress, as I so often do...

Cesar had been a rancher back in the day, but he was clearly too old and worn for any kind of work now. Thus, when the lord mayor of Fairglen had been rounding up the 'undeserving poor' to form work crews, Cesar had been given a pass. Aaron worked at the quarry, chiseling and shaping stones for building projects. His 'wage' for such efforts was used to support the settlement here, and no end was in sight for the former farmer.

And then there was Toby, quite a handful at present, and bound for the same fate as his father one day. Or perhaps for prison... unless something changed in his life.

It was then I conceived my plan. I was a mage, practically a noble. Mages could have servants. As a journeyman, I'd had no need for such up until now. Mistress Julia's household staff could perform whatever menial tasks I required. And in truth, I was rather self-sufficient in that regard. But as an itinerant mage at the capital, I would surely need someone to assist me with various errands and the like. From my wages, I could afford to hire a servant of my own. Toby seemed clever enough and would soon grasp the essentials.

Perhaps I should be more discerning than to choose a known liar and would-be thief. But I also recalled Taylor Allen's recounting of his own childhood years. His narrow escape from poverty and an ill-spent life were thanks to one kindly man who'd taken an interest in him. With his father away, Toby needed a stern hand to help guide him into the light.

I'd heard a story once of a boy and his father walking along a beach where thousands of starfish had been stranded by the tide. They were all slowly dying in the sun. The boy picked one up and threw it back into the sea. He did this several more times. 'Look, son,' said the father. 'There are many thousands of these things consigned to their sorry fate. What you're doing won't really make a difference.' The boy bent over and picked up another starfish. Throwing it into the sea, he said: 'It will for *that* one.'

I'd always liked that story. Toby could be *my* starfish. I made my offer as we sipped at our tea.

"You seem nice, mister Harper, but I don't know..." said Nora. "You ain't one of those men who... fancy young boys, is ya?"

"Certainly not!" I replied.

And soon the deal was struck.

***

"Again I must thank thee, mister," Nora sighed. Honest work is devilish hard to come by out here. What with all the tenancies bein' full up and all. Though it be only temporary, it'll do my Toby good to have aught to fill his days. He's been so restless of late."

No kidding. The woman had sent the lad back into the bede-house to gather his few belongings.

It was then we heard the dawn bell chiming from off in the distance. The sun was only just peeking over the eastern horizon, bathing the camp in its clear, golden rays. And by this revealing radiance, the ramshackle nature of our surroundings was once again made plain.

More people of the camp were stirring. Many emerged blinkingly from within their shabby dwellings. Their bent backs straightened and their gazes drifted north. I sensed anticipation in the muttering of the crowd. I wondered what had so aroused them. I didn't have to wonder for long.

"Best we claim our place in line," Nora prompted Ce. "I wonder what her beneficence will send us today?"

"I hope there's more than last time," replied the old gentleman, standing with some difficulty. "I ain't complaining, mind you. 'Tis kind of her ladyship to send us aught at all."

"You'll excuse us, journeyman," said Nora, turning to me. "Cesar and I must go collect our alms. I'll help to guide him over there. His eyesight isn't what it once was. I need to see to it he gets his share. I trust you'll take good care of that dear boy of mine and keep him from mischief and harm. I'll see you on Sunday then, per our agreement. Till then, I'll be missing him fiercely."

And out strode Toby, looking excited. Nora's face was a mixture of sadness and hope as she folded her arms around Toby once more, nearly smothering the lad in her heartfelt embrace.

"You be good now and mind mister Harper," she said.

With that, she turned and guided old Cesar away.

"Well, get on," I said, once his mother had gone.

The boy climbed up on the mule. He sat there in thoughtful silence. Taking up Gypsy's leads, I steered her toward the roadway, where a crowd was beginning to gather.

"Who is this lady of whom your mother spoke?"

"That would be the good Lady Castleberry, journeyman. Should I call you 'master' now or what?"

"Journeyman will do quite nicely," I replied. "It wouldn't do to cause misunderstanding of my rank. I take it this Lady Castleberry is the one responsible for sending alms to the camp?"

"That she is, journeyman. Every morning without fail. It ain't much but some scraps of clothing and days old bread. But at least she's doing *something.* The Almoner in the city hardly ever sticks his nose out beyond the wall. Without Lady 'C,' ma says we'd be hard pressed to keep body and soul together."

The country lane that led from the camp soon joined the king's highway. Where it did, sat a dilapidated old well. Its cap lay askew atop a jagged opening and moss grew heavy o'er its lip. From this vantage, I could better make out the city wall and its gates. Rolling out from behind them was a large wagon hauled by a team of oxen. It was flanked by a contingent of armored men. They were mounted and wore the livery of the city guard, a stylized black dragon on a vert field. I'd oft seen their like on patrol hereabouts.

I led the mule well off the road and paused to witness the proceedings.

As the wagon rumbled past, a man seated beside its driver began ringing a brass hand bell and calling out an announcement that was quite unnecessary.

"Alms! Alms!" he shouted in a sing-song voice.

The wagon's bed contained barrels, boxes, and baskets of various shapes and sizes.

"What's in the kegs?" I asked the boy.

"Fresh water for drinking," he said in reply.

The dust kicked up by the passage of the cart took a minute to settle back down. By the time it had, we were back on our way, heading for the gates. They were farther away than I'd imagined. As we approached them, I estimated the city's curtain wall must stand at least thirty feet high, and the arched gateway must've towered ten feet above even that. The gates framed an opening wide enough for two wagons to pass abreast. Their hinges must perforce be strong indeed to bear such massive weights.

At this early an hour, there was little foot traffic. But I guided Gypsy and my new charge to stand at the rear of some farm wagons queued up to seek admittance. There were few questions and no challenges as the soldiers passed them through. When our turn came, a bored man at arms simply asked for our names and what business we might be about. I told him I was a mage of the conclave invited here by Lord Westarbor and that Toby was my servant.

"Good day, then, sir mage. Welcome to Fairglen."

Beyond the gates I could see the city's sprawl. There were people everywhere I looked, already up and about their business. Three great avenues fanned out, flanked by buildings of every description. The central of these was the widest. From a signpost nearby, I marked it was sensibly known as 'Broadway.' Fairglen was obviously far grander a metropolis than ever I'd imagined. I had some idea of places I must go, but had nary a clue how to find them.

***

The sun hung low as we trudged our weary way down the narrow lane toward the Wayfarers Rest. It had been a long and frustrating day. I'd barely put a dent in the tasks I'd hoped to complete. Returning Gypsy to the trader's guild had been straightforward enough, once I'd figured out how to navigate the streets. Unlike in Meadowfork, when one encountered someone coming from the opposite direction, it was customary here to pass by them on the left.

We'd also had the good fortune to stumble upon a cordwainer's shop where I bought an adequate pair of boots for my young charge. They were sturdy and fit him well, but their price set me back a pretty penny (six pretty pennies, to be more precise). I'd been in no mood to wear out my tongue haggling or to seek alternatives. So I parted with the unreasonable sum and chalked it up to necessity.

For his part, Toby remained mostly quiet, taking in his new surroundings. He would glance at me hopefully when we encountered an eatery, but held his tongue when I passed them by. Eventually, I'd relented and purchased a couple of hot crossed buns from a street vendor who'd assured us they were 'straight from the bakery!' I didn't fancy the dense, salted rye. And I doubted the stuff had seen the inside of a bakery for a week at least. It took a goodly draw from my waterskin to finally

15

choke one down. But Toby didn't seem to mind. I noticed the boy ate only half of his, squirreling the rest away.

"Aren't you tired, journeyman?" he once asked.

"What? You mean because I was awakened in the middle of the night by a thief with designs on my property?"

"Awww. Here and I'd thought we'd gotten past all that," he bemoaned.

Perhaps I was being unfair. I'd already used my wakefulness spell twice to banish my weariness. And Toby had been up for at least as long as I.

When I'd asked around, I was informed that many of the better local inns were all booked up, owing to the upcoming festivities. Rather than chance finding no vacancies, I'd made my way instead to Cheapside, where it was rumored there were still plenty of rooms to let. I wasn't yet ready to announce my presence to any of the gentry here - not without first getting cleaned up and adopting the local fashion. I'd learned my lesson at Conclave. How much worse to be seen as under-dressed here at the kingdom's capital? For tonight, I sought only some clean sheets, a pleasant meal and a warm bath.

Beneath a painted placard which featured a crescent moon, the door was wedged open a crack by a loose cobblestone lying at its base. Opening it still further, we were greeted by a warm rush of air and the boisterous sounds of merriment from within. The patrons sat in the common room at tables here and there. A cheerful blaze graced the hearth. I made my way to the barman's station with Toby at my heels.

"What can I get you today, good sir?" asked the man who tended bar. "The special of the house is a Dwarven stout brought down last week from Echo Hills. It's guaranteed to curl your beard or to grow it out if you're lackin' one."

"Have you a room to let?"

"For how long would you be wanting such, goodman?"

"For tonight, at the very least, perhaps for longer, depending. Perhaps as long as a week.

"A room with two beds is two pence for the night. For three pence, you get supper as well. For a full week's stay, I could make you a deal. Call it a round shilling for the whole seven days."

He'd certainly rattled that off quickly.

"Any chance of getting a bath drawn tonight? I've been on the road for weeks now, and I'm afraid I've gotten rather gamey."

The man frowned.

"A bit late in the day for that."

Looking us up and down, he reconsidered.

"I'll see what I can do. A bath is tuppence extra. Cash in advance."

I untied my coin purse and counted out five pence.

"Room number six at the top of the stairs. Settle your things and be down no later than the seventh bell. Kitchen's closed after that."

As I moved toward the stairwell, Toby plucked at my sleeve to draw my attention. I'd have to break him of such familiarity if he was to be my manservant. But there would be time later for lessons in decorum.

"Are we going to eat? Again?" he hissed.

The pitiful crust of bread he'd stashed away earlier made better sense in the light of this question. The lad probably hadn't eaten a decent meal in a good long while.

"Of course, Toby. You'll need your strength if you are to serve me. As your master, I'll see to it you are adequately clothed and fed. In return, I ask only for your loyalty and obedience."

On reaching our room, he stepped ahead of me and held its door ajar. Inwardly, I applauded his initiative, but I made no outward sign of pleasure at this unnecessary act.

The room was modest. It was scarcely as large as the broom closet in Mistress Julia's estate. Still, it was clean enough and would be private, a tall step up from sleeping in the common room. All of my belongings were in my bob, which I didn't intend to leave here. Toby had only a small duffel bag, which he carefully rested atop one of the straw mattresses. Thus, after a hasty inspection, I considered our 'things' to be settled. I was preparing to return to the common room for the promised supper when the lad spoke up once more.

"Master... journeyman?"

"What is it, Toby?"

"I reckon you did me a fine turn when you spared my ma the heartache she'd a had for me. And taking me on as a servant after was... well... unexpected."

He paused, turning away. Silhouetted in the light from the doorway, I marked him shifting nervously from foot to foot. I waited, sensing he had something more on his mind. Finally, he broke the uneasy silence.

"I guess I just want to say thanks... and to let you know I won't run off or steal from you. I'll serve you the best I *can*. Just *see* if I won't."

His solemn vow was spoken as fervently as that of any knight fresh from a vigil. It made me glad. But I also recalled how easily the lad could twist the truth. He might just be telling me what I wanted to hear. Only time would tell whether the boy was sincere. I hoped in my heart that he was.

"... and... journeyman?"

"Yes?"

"Can you please take that lory-don moth from out of my ear now? It's been itching something fierce, and I fear it might be laying its eggs in there!"

***

"Good morn to you, brother. I trust the night's rest has restored your vitality?"

"Mmmmph," I muttered into my pillow.

"A soft bed has left you listless, I see. Rouse yourself and face the day. 'Tis long past time I departed."

With my eyes still tightly closed, I delved within. Though almost awake now, I was loath to stir.

My inner hill swam into focus. I lay at his base in this vision. And above me, the genial face looking down seemed somehow more chipper than his typical flinty frown.

"I'd've let you sleep longer," Rockytop said. "But you told me last night we have much to accomplish today. Your young charge is up and dressed already and has been so for a while. He seems fidgety and uncertain."

"Have you any thoughts about the matters we discussed?" I asked of the hill in my mind.

As my homunculus, Rockytop was actually a manifestation of my own inner thoughts. As such, he often mulled over the events of the day and things I'd unconsciously noticed. Sometimes, he put things together that I'd not had time to properly consider. These surprising revelations could on occasion reveal to me things I never knew I even knew. Today, however, he had nothing of the sort to offer.

He closed his eyes, and his brow descended, trailing behind it an avalanche of loose rubble. This spread o'er his features, solidified, and left me lying there alone.

Once I was up and prepared for the day, Toby and I were off. After our baths of the prior night, I felt (and smelled) more human again. We'd even befouled the water, washing out our dirty clothing once we had scrubbed ourselves clean. I had donned a finer outfit from the mobile wardrobe that was my bob.

Toby had a tougher time of it, not having many items of apparel to his name. I gave him some small clothes and an old doublet of mine. They were a bit over-sized, but at least they were dry. His old leggings would have to do. Dressed in this manner, he looked even smaller. My doublet served him as both a shirt and a short skirt. I drew it in at the waist with a bit of rope I had.

"Where to first, my master?"

"The barber, I'm thinking, Tobias," said I.

"I dare say your hair *is* a mite overlong for a man. I didn't want to remark on such. I figured mages might just always wear it that way."

The daytime traffic was picking up when we shuffled down the lane. According to the innkeeper, there was a barber just down Fleet Street, above the meat pie shop. We navigated the city streets, already beginning to bustle with passers-by of every description. We spotted the pole striped red and white hanging beside the shop in question, proclaiming the man inside to be a barber by profession. We crossed the lane, climbed the stairs, and entered.

A portly man sat in the chair whose head was as bald as an egg. I was certain he hadn't come here for a trim. Beneath a bristling upturned mustache, a foamy white substance was spread o'er his cheeks and chin. The barber stood, his razor flashing, staring down at him.

"Have a seat," he told me, without so much as glancing up. "I'll be with you in a trice."

Toward the front of the shop were some lesser stools. I settled on one and bade Toby to do the same.

"And who might you be, young man, who has come to my humble shop?"

"I am Lucas Harper, goodman, a journeyman mage of the conclave. I came here with my footman for a haircut and a shave."

I watched with interest as the barber (whom I would come to know as Ben), scraped away the lather with deft flicks of his blade. I winced as he slashed at the old man's throat with strokes so swift I shuddered with chagrin. But his hand was steady and his skill was such that he didn't break the skin. Soon the old fellow was waddling off clean-shaven and smelling sweet from the barber's musky tonic.

"So, Lucas, is it?" said the man, dusting off the chair. "What kind of cut do you have in mind? I mark you've a full head of hair, at least. That gives us lots of options."

"I was hoping you could suggest something..."

I went on to explain that I was to escort the Lady Megan at her debutante ball and several other activities leading up to the prince's coronation. I required something suitable for that sort of occasion.

The man stared at me aghast. Had I said something wrong?

"I'm afraid I can't help you," the barber explained once he'd regained his composure. "I'm a simple man of Cheapside. Styling a nobleman's hair for such lofty events is well above my station. Some stylists in the high quarter specialize in that trade. The barber's guild would toss me right out if they found I'd been mucking about in such business. You honor me, sir, but best you seek higher up in society to smarten up your coiffure."

"Well, I confess I never knew the rules were so rigid. I'm from somewhat humble origins myself, as it happens. It's only by my gift that I've been lately elevated. Your candor and scruples do you much credit. Rather than deprive you of my custom today, I'll still have that shave, if you will."

The man set to work at once. Before long, my chin was as smooth as a baby's bum and my purse a tuppence lighter. He even combed out my overlong hair and tied it back in a loose braid.

"I take it a servant's hair is fair game?" I asked the barber while indicating Toby.

Nodding, the man took up scissors and comb, and Toby stepped up in the chair.

As he groomed my young servant, I used the opportunity to collect a few locks of his hair from the sweepings. Should it ever become needful, I knew a useful locating spell that required such. (And I thought it best to prepare.) At least there weren't any leeches this time.

***

Clean and freshly groomed, we strode down the avenue on my next mission of import. I needed to determine whether Baron Westarbor and his entourage had yet arrived. Benjamin (the barber) had recommended we ask the merchant bankers. He reasoned that any man of means would likely make a stop there to obtain funds from his account. The clerks there kept records of such transactions.

Regrettably, this was on the remote end of town opposite Cheapside, in a district adjacent to the High Quarter itself. To get there, we'd need to backtrack a bit and then proceed down Broadway past Cathedral Square. I was never good at directions, but this seemed straightforward enough. And all it would cost me was a bit of shoe leather.

Broadway Avenue was the chief thoroughfare of Fairglen. It ran through the lower city from the main gates all the way up to the lesser gates that separated High Quarter and the royal palace grounds. Along its length were many of the iconic features of the Fair City. It would be a fine day to take in the sights. It struck me again just how many souls called Fairglen home as block after city block we marched our way along. Leastways, it was easy to track our progress. Unlike the arteries running north to south, the cross-streets were all numbered. I was told there were more than a hundred of these, beginning with First Avenue back by the Gates.

I wiled away my time teaching Toby his Reman numerals. At XL Avenue, he balked.

"El!" he exclaimed. "Why'd they have to go and bring another letter into it? Wouldn't X-X-X-X do just as well?"

"It's to keep the numbers from getting too long, Toby. You'll thank me by the time we get to 'C.'"

The lad merely rolled his eyes in reply.

At the corner of XLII Street was a huge and glamorous stone building I'd heard mentioned once before. Enormous brass letters atop its roof declared it to be "The Silverlight Grand Theater." This was the very venue at which Manchester the Jester claimed he'd performed. The musicians of our caravan, too, had spoken wistfully of the noble Fairglen landmark. Purportedly, the king himself oft gave his patronage to this majestic cultural edifice. A placard hung out above the street, surrounded by glittering lights that smacked strongly of enchantment. I would later learn it was termed a 'marquee.' The large lettering upon it read: 'Tonight's Feature: MEDEA by Euripides.' It had been a long hike thus far. Perhaps an hour had already passed. So I paused to rest and gawk at the spectacle. I should have known better.

Immediately, we were approached by a man in a toga with a sword belted onto his side. I could tell by the way his scabbard flapped about that it bore not the weight of an actual blade.

"Beautiful, isn't it?" he crooned on his approach.

"You mean the theater?" I asked rhetorically. "Yes; it's quite a stunning sight."

"I can tell just by looking at you that you're a connoisseur of the thespian's art, a friend of the theater, as it were."

"And what if I am?" I replied neutrally.

"I simply thought you might be a fellow who'd appreciate a *rare* opportunity. You may be new in town. Correct me if I'm wrong. But everyone hereabout knows these showings are all booked up several months in advance. But I've got a better deal to offer. The story of Medea and her descent into wickedness, love and vengeance can raise your hackles this very night, my friend."

"Oh? How so?"

"My company," he said triumphantly, "the Forty-fifth Street Irregulars happen to be performing an off-Broadway production of this very same play. The good news for you is that a few tickets are still available for a lucky and discerning man and his... son? Best of all, the price I can offer for such tickets is but half that charged by the Silverlight here. Such a bargain won't last for long.

As tempting as it was to hear the poetry of Euripedes butchered and botched by this amateur and his group of untalented wannabe cohorts, I thought I should give it a pass. The man could be sincere, but I suspected there might not even *be* such a performance. Either way, I didn't care.

This must have shown on my face (a longtime curse of my open nature).

Seeing his sale slipping away, the man moved closer and sought to forestall my rejection. Turning to Toby, he quickly spoke over me in a husky voice full of wonder.

"I'll wager *you'd* like to see all the pretty costumes and hear a scary story - watch it play out before your very eyes?"

I was hard pressed to stifle my laughter when Toby Moss answered the man.

"If you mean the towel you're wearing, I must say I've seen prettier before. Mister, my *life's* been a scary story. And no gang of jesters hoppin' about in funny robes is gonna lighten my burden none.

The man looked over to catch my eye in a final silent plea.

"You heard the lad," I answered. "No thank you, sirrah."

"Toby, let's go."

Soon he was scanning the crowded street for someone else to accost. He was muttering something under his breath that I couldn't quite make out.

A few steps farther along the road, Tobias turned to me and asked: "Journeyman, what's a Philistine?"

We paused not long after that to enjoy a midday meal before renewing our trek.

Farther on we sighted the barracks, a large blocky building of stone. It was all crenelated and topped with flapping banners.

It housed the garrison of the city under the duke's command. The king ruled over all, of course, but he maintained his own soldiers, an elite force known as the royal guard. Each of them was said to be worth ten ordinary soldiers, and it was rumored that even his knights feared them.

Across from the barracks there was a tower. High above the streets, it rose. It was the famed Black Tower of Fairglen, where only the most dangerous of criminals were held. Murderers awaited trial there. And longer-term inmates dwelt there in misery to regret their sins. These were the ones the church thought might redeem themselves. We hoped that some of these despicable men could, by God's grace, be made 'spicable' again.

Every block from there on up held wonders for our eyes. The closer we approached to the center of power, the more opulent our surroundings became.

At LXXXV Street, an iron-wrought fence began. It spanned a full four city blocks. Cathedral Square, they called it. It was so grand that we couldn't see the whole of it. What we *could* see from the fence was stunning enough. Beyond a formal garden space, we spied the coliseum. It was there in that gigantic amphitheater Prince Henry would be crowned. Hovering behind it, I could make out the spire of the cathedral. As they were completing some renovations on it, much of it was shrouded by scaffolding and tarpaulins.

I understood that beyond even that lay the possible papal palace of his apocryphal holiness, Antipope Pius IV. But that was a conundrum I refused to consider just then. Simply reading about the man and his predecessors made my head spin. Instead, I nudged Toby, and we continued on our way. The merchant bank should lie just up ahead.

And indeed, it did.

***

"Next," said the teller in whose line I stood. "The accounts clerk is available now."

I was soon seated comfortably in a high-backed chair across a table from the man. Between us lay a ledger, quill and ink, and a sturdy box, the contents of which were a mystery to me. The man extended an ink-stained hand.

"You may call me Cedric," said the clerk. "And how may the Bank of St. Matthew be of service to you today?"

He was certainly pleasant for a moneylender. Not at all what I'd been expecting. Although I supposed he was used to dealing with upper-class gentlemen who'd entrusted him with their financial affairs. It probably paid to be polite. I took his hand and gave it a good, firm shake.

"I am Lucas Harper, a mage of the conclave on temporary leave from my duties there. My master told me she would transfer a portion of her stipend to be deposited here. From this account, she assured me I could withdraw my weekly wage."

I was uncertain precisely how such business was conducted, but Cedric was nodding along as though it were a familiar story.

"What is your master's name?"

"She is known as Mistress Julia."

"What is her full name, sir?" he clarified.

"Among her people, she is named Puquabeth Chosha Julia," I replied.

"An Elf?" he guessed, somewhat taken aback. "I'll need to go and check on that. Wait here."

When the man returned, he was toting a thick ledger with many loose pages. He plunked it down on the table and began leafing through it. It was filled with columns of numbers neatly lined up beneath headings that might have been names. So swiftly he surveyed them that I could scarcely blink before he'd moved on to the next.

His finger soon alighted on an entry he'd somehow discerned from the others.

"Ah, here we are," he said with a grin.

He took up a loose scrap of parchment I had thought to be a bookmark of some sort. When he turned it sideways and squinted at it, I realized it must be a pigeon-borne message that had preceded me here. Returning to his scrutiny of the columns of numbers, he muttered for a time as if to himself. Looking up once more, his eyes locked with mine, and he made a most startling query.

"What is Miss Sholeena's surname, then?" he asked.

"Uh, well..." I stuttered, unsure why he wanted to know. "It's 'Blorlafarglish,' but I don't see how that's relevant.

"Ah, good," he said, leaning back in his chair. "I believe you are who you purport to be. You must ask for Cedric Monroe on future occasions. Henceforth, you'll deal with me exclusively. According to your master's instructions, you may draw a wage each week from her account. Two shillings, threepence and a farthing is the weekly amount. You may claim this sum each Friday. Several weeks have passed since these instructions were received. Do you wish to collect the balance now?"

He paused, staring pointedly at me.

"Can I just leave it here to grow?" I asked.

"Certainly, sir. Would you like to open an account of your own? That would certainly make things simpler. Your wage could be deposited there regularly as we tidy up accounts each week."

"What all would that entail?"

"There's an initial and annual accounting fee of a groat. Paper isn't cheap. We would require you to maintain a balance of at least a crown. Elsewise, there's a surcharge of tuppence a week. We'd need to get your signature, so we could compare it with any written instructions. We'll also be needing a lock of your hair."

That last requirement seemed strange until I recalled there were several spells to verify a person's identity using such. I believe Master Chadwick placed a strand of someone's hair into molten wax before enchanting it to seal a missive.

"In that case," said I, "sign me up."

I reached into my bob and withdrew from it an iron strong-box brimming with coins of various denominations. Cedric blinked. I counted out five shillings to meet the one-crown minimum. I made several more stacks until there were twenty more.

"I understand you can forward letters of credit to other cities of Osten. I need to make a full pound available to a colleague of mine at Eagle's Keep."

"Certainly, sir," said Cedric, scooping up the stacks. "To whom shall it be delivered?"

"It needs to go to a Brother Parvus at Eagle's Keep itself. He can typically be found on tier four within the monastic library there. It's somewhat urgent, so dispatch it by griffin post. You can deduct the cost for this from my account."

After collecting my signature and other sundries and making a few notations in his ledger, Cedric sighed in satisfaction.

"Do you need aught else?"

"In fact, I do," I answered. "I came to the city at the invitation of Lord Westarbor. I was hoping you could tell me whether his lordship has yet arrived."

"Westarbor, did you say? That would be Goodman Wahl's account. I'll see if he's available for a consultation."

According to Goodman Wahl, a senior account manager here at the bank, there had indeed been a recent withdrawal from the Westarbor account. But it had been made by a lackey who'd ridden ahead to make arrangements for the baron's stay. The baron himself wasn't due to arrive for another week, at least.

This uplifted my spirits a bit. It granted me more time to prepare myself for the events to come. I collected Toby from where he loafed by the door, and we made ready for the long hike back to Cheapside. It was well past midday, which meant it'd be dark before we reached the Wayfarer's Rest. I hoped we'd make it there before the kitchen closed.

In fact, we'd only made it as far as XLII Street before the sun set. I could see the marquee of the Silverlight flashing in the distance. Broadway bore less traffic than it had in the hectic daytime hours. The lamplighters were out, and one by one the streetlights flared to life. Toby had been silent for a while. The poor little guy was likely worn out. I turned to him to strike up a conversation.

"They say the lantern lights are bright on Broadway, almost as though there's magic in the air."

After a thoughtful silence, he responded.

"Yeah. But when you're walkin' down that street and you ain't had enough to eat..."

I considered how the lavish surroundings must seem from Toby's point of view.

"I get it." I said with sympathy, "It kinda seems unfair."

And all at once, my perspective changed. The Fair City now seemed incongruously named.

An Interlude at Sea

The sea was angry; it was. The little fishing skiff I'd commandeered rocked sharply from side to side as it bucked and heaved atop the waves. My joints ached as I turned the crank to hoist the net I'd cast. The net grew heavy as it cleared the choppy waves. It would be a fine catch; it would. Good.

This far out to sea, there was not another sail in sight. And only the sun up in the sky offered any clue to where land might lie. I was far to the east of Osten, with the sun still at my back; so far-off I was barely in the bay. Surely, my pursuers wouldn't venture out so deep. 'Tis here that legend had it more substantial dangers lay.

Strange creatures of the depths were said to claim these seas as theirs and might drag intruders down to drown within their watery lairs. The pirates of the Indigo Isles were said to ply these waters as well. Lawless men. Fleeing the king's justice. Desperate men thinking they've got nothing left to lose. I came here hopin' to find just such men. I'd teach 'em different; I would. However desperate a man's straights, he still owned his livin' soul And I'd threaten such to draw them to my cause.

I felt it then, a trickle.

The fish flappin' in the net began to cease their useless squirming. Their dream of freedom in the deep blue was a fancy fading fast. Hangin' there in open air with straining gills and vacant stares, they stilled as each choked out its very last. One by one, they began to expire with silent screams that only I could hear. For want of their breath, they were claimed by death. He was a fellow with whom I was intimately familiar, having felt his bony grip myself before. And as each expired, its petty life snuffed out, I welcomed its essence into my private cemetery.

The net hung there and gradually stilled throughout the afternoon. The sea, too, had calmed a bit, and the deck took on a gentler sway. And still I sat absorbing it all and considering what came next for old Truman.

Such a pitiful meal it was. Not nearly the life force I craved. But such would need to nourish me as I planned. I couldn't believe that a gift such as mine wasn't meant to pursue a far loftier ambition.

If the kingdom won't have me, perhaps I should carve out a little empire of my own. It should be an attainable goal for a man who refuses to die. But I'd need help to enact a strategy so grand. And time; lots of time. All that was for another day; it was. For now, I need content myself with the ocean's costive offerings, sustaining me for but yet another day.

I inhaled the bitter aroma of decay. The fish had taken on a pallid cast and had begun already to waste away. The sun was under the yardarm by now. And the rotting chum that hung in the net had given me all the life force it contained. I pulled the gaff hook and let the line unwind. Down fell the net as the crank spun madly, lowerin' my catch back into the mouth of the sea from whence it came. The net spread wide, finally freeing its captives to bob about, belly-up upon the churning waves. They spread out in a ghastly mass, floating there and free at last.

The smell of death was strong enough for others to perceive. In this way, the sharks were like brothers to me. I sighted their fins upon the sea, angling toward my erstwhile catch with jaws spread open wide. And from their frenzied feeding, many were left bleeding. As they fought for scraps whose souls had fled, the white-capped waves were stained with red. They spun and whirled in a dance of death to rival any battle. And the beauty of their motion as they thrashed upon the ocean near wrung a tear from my unbeating heart.

It was beautiful; it was.

CHAPTER TWO

The Quarryman

"There will always be rocks in the road
ahead of us. They will be stumbling blocks
or stepping stones; it all depends on how
you use them."

~ *Friedrich Nietzsche* ~

"Are you ready yet, Tobias?"

"I will be in a minute, Journeyman."

"Well hurry up," I admonished. "Time and tide wait for no man."

The boy finished tying closed his small duffel and glanced over in puzzlement. I could practically hear his unspoken question: 'What's the tides got to do with anything?' I'd picked up the maritime adage from a former student of mine at Conclave whose odd turn of speech arose from having once served as a cabin boy.

Baron Westarbor was still *en route*. So over the past several days, Toby and I had been enjoying the freedom to explore the city more thoroughly. We still avoided the high quarter and its genteel inhabitants. Nor had I purchased any stylish clothing or other finery as yet. I was fairly certain Megan would have some very specific requirements in that regard. I presently wore my plainest outfit in anticipation of the day to come. Today was Sunday, and it would start with a visit with Toby's mother.

"What did the stable master charge you for the mule?" I asked.

"He offered it for threepence a day with eight shillings upfront, but I talked him down to two on the day if I left the full ten shillings for a deposit."

I could easily check on that. It was the first time I'd trusted Tobias with so large a sum. I stifled a grin. Toby hated numbers. But if you put a pound sign in front of them, he suddenly became a prodigy. We'd soon see whether he'd selected a sturdy beast. I hoped that as a farmer's lad, Toby possessed a good horse sense.

"Very astute," I replied.

"What do we need the mule for, anyway? The camp's not a half mile outside the gates, after all."

"Not *we*, Tobias," I replied. "After I deliver you to your mother's loving arms, I have some business of my own to conduct."

And with that, we were off.

The mule Toby had selected was a fine animal, if a bit headstrong. I approved. He was a john mule named Feckless, purportedly for the way he liked to lounge about. Nonetheless, he eagerly hove to once I'd mounted.

I steered him at a gentle walk, and Toby trailed after. We cleared the gates and ambled the short distance to the camp, where our arrival caused a bit of a stir. We were soon surrounded by a gang of wide-eyed youngsters who had gathered at the encampment's edge.

Most were gawking at my charge, sparing me only a few wary glances.

"'E looks like a little prince, 'e does," jeered one lad, pointing and sniggering.

"A right proper little toady," added another.

Despite their taunting demeanors, their barbs seemed good-natured enough. And I looked on with bemusement as the ridicule continued. From the semi-insulting epithets, I soon surmised they were secretly envious of Tobias. This notion was confirmed when the boy himself burst out laughing.

"How *you* been, Enoch?" asked Toby, stepping up to the first lad. "Any luck stalking them squirrels you been after?"

"I've been getting better with my sling," he replied, "but them squirrels is right twitchy little devils. Not much meat on their bones neither, as it turns out. They's hardly worth my efforts."

It was like I wasn't even *there*. I sensed that by these children I was perceived as an adult, and therefore sat invisible behind the fence of their inattention. Adults were to be heeded only when they made some sort of fuss. It hadn't been so very long since I'd stood on the other side of that fence.

"I brought you something," said Toby, untying the straps on his duffel.

The children crowded closer as Toby extracted a small cloth-wrapped bundle.

"Here's some sugar buns I nicked at the inn."

Hardly 'nicked,' I thought. I'd seen the boy tucking them away from his meals over the past several days. I'd assumed he meant to eat them later. In a trice, the buns were distributed and vanished as if by magic. Soon the cluster of urchins were licking their fingers with delight. Then Tobias brought out his old boots, the tattered ones. Handing them to Enoch, he said: 'See if anyone can use these. I've got me a finer pair now.' I found myself strangely moved by the gesture. Evidently, the lad lived by his mother's creed of 'what we have, we share.'

"It ain't much, but I've been busy of late," said Toby blushingly.

"Listen to him!" chimed in a freckled fellow on the left. "And what's kept milord so busy, then, *of late*?"

"*Manners*, Tobias," chided Nora, stalking up to the rear of the unruly mob.

They were startled as their inattention fence was breeched by her scolding tone.

"'Tis courteous first to see your guest settled before running off at the mouth with your cronies."

But despite her jolly banter, the woman was smiling at her son, a loving smile that outshone the harsh words she'd just spoken.

"Ah... yes," replied the blushing boy, staring up at me. "I hadn't seen these blokes in a while and quite forgot myself."

"Not a problem," I quipped with a wink. "It seems that *they* remembered you well enough."

So on to the Bede house, I rode, trailing a procession of inquisitive youngsters. Sigh. When had I gotten so old as to even use that word?

I promptly settled accounts with Nora. Toby's weekly wage was tuppence and three farthings. This was a bit light for a manservant, more on the order of what a maid servant was paid. Just *feeding* the boy had cost more than that. I'd considered increasing it somewhat, but this was the proper amount for the service rendered. And I didn't want this arrangement to be perceived as unadulterated charity lest the boy's pride should suffer. As it was, his chest puffed out as he witnessed his mother receive the paltry sum.

"Run along now, and enjoy your day off," said Nora to the boy.

She didn't need to tell him twice. Soon he was off with his mates, enjoying a game they'd invented. It involved rolling an old barrel hoop around the camp using a set of sticks.

"Lord above, just look at that child of mine!" exclaimed Nora in a wistful tone. "Will you join me for a cuppa, mister Harper?"

"I thank you for the kind offer, missus," I replied, "but I'm afraid I must decline. I've something else in mind for the remainder of my day. Look for me later this evening. I'll be by to collect the boy then."

"As you would have it, then. May the good Lord watch over you and lay his blessings on your efforts."

I mounted and trotted off. Not a hundred paces beyond the camp I encountered Toby and his clique still rolling their hoop about.

"Oy! Journeyman!" one cried out. "Toby here says you got the gift. Any truth to that? Work us some magic!"

Master Chadwick had often told me that magic was only for serious business and not for just showing off. But despite his sage advice, I decided that this one time couldn't hurt.

Smiling, I drew Feckless to a halt and sought my 'spacium gyrabit' mindset. The hoop halted in mid-roll, startling the boy who'd been running alongside it with a stick. It then rose slowly into the air and began to gyrate madly on its vertical axis. This spin increased until all one could make out was a blurry sphere.

The boys stared dumbstruck as the hovering sphere slowed, resolved itself into a ring once more, and fell at last to lie flat upon the ground.

"Like I said," Toby remarked smugly, "he can do loads of stuff."

***

Geography was one of many topics I'd studied at the conclave. The duchy of Fairglen is a squarish province that lies directly in the kingdom's center. If Osten were a great game of tic-tac-toe, Fairglen would be its center spot. Fairglen, the city, stands just north of its middle at the confluence of two mighty rivers.

The Khazalid Ilur flows down from the north from out of the Echo Hills. I believe the name means something like 'big wide mountain river' in Dwarven. Many barges ply the Khazalid Ilur conducting trade with that race. The Everclear runs from west to east, its far-off headwaters originating somewhere in the Unchartable Lands. It cuts across Stein Barony in Northford, where it becomes known as the Quaboshiqua for a time. In Deerfield Duchy it veers somewhat southward and enters the Whispering Woods, only to emerge here in Fairglen, passing just south of the city.

After joining with the Khazalid Ilur, the Everclear runs all the way to the eastern seaboard, bisecting the kingdom entirely. It pours out into the Indigo Bay, freshening the water for miles beyond the shore. I understand this poses quite a hazard for sailors who might suddenly find their crafts less buoyant in such waters. A heavily laden vessel might sink straight down! All that aside, I assumed riding southward on the king's highway would soon find me at the river's bank. And so it did.

Where the road met the Everclear, there was no bridge. Instead, a long stone pier jutted out into the flowing river. It was so broad and solid that the word 'pier' was insufficient to describe the massive landing. I understood it was termed a 'jetty.' Ferrymen plied their trade to bring passengers and goods across in a continuous cycle of docking and shoving back off. But also, I spied a heavy barge moored to its eastern pylons. This was what I'd come to find.

Even now, I watched men off-loading blocks of stone from that barge and stowing them into the bed of a heavy wagon. Several similar wagons were lined up behind, awaiting their turns.

"Ho there!" I shouted to the porters on my approach.

The men had just finished sliding a heavy block up onto the wagon's bed. One of them wiped his hands on his thighs and turned to regard me while his fellows adjusted the load. He looked pleased at the excuse to take a break.

"What'cher want then, goodman?"

"Is this boat returning to the quarry anytime soon?"

"Naw. It took most of the night to tow her up here. We won't be drifting back down till late this afternoon, I expect."

"You worked your team all night?"

"All night and all day too, mister. A second team's already restin' up downriver. The cathedral's still behind schedule and the Lord High Architect is all in a tizzy over it; he is. Archbishop's been down on his neck over the whole sorry affair. I reckon if you want to get to the quarry, your best bet is to trot on down the tow road and you'll come on it quick enough."

I thanked the man and returned to the road. Down below, nearer to the river's bank, was this tow road of which he'd spoken. It was a muddy strip running just alongside the river. Resting there was the draft team that had lugged the barge upriver. They were eight of the largest horses I'd ever seen. I'd later learn the big shaggy brutes were called 'percherons,' and alongside any one of them, my Feckless would look like naught but a newborn colt.

I'd driven wagons for long hours before, but was still fairly new at sitting a saddle. Nevertheless, I urged my mount up to a reckless (for me) canter. And as the miles slid by we wended our way alongside the Everclear. The steady clop of hoofbeats and the sun shining brightly in my face caused my mind to wander. It took me back to my days with the caravan.

I knew a team of horses pulling a load could walk about four miles in an hour. At a canter, Feckless and I moved at three or four times that pace. If the barge had been hauled for 'most of the night,' call it ten hours? Hmm...I would expect to arrive well before midday. And so I did.

Where the tow road ended, I spied a long causeway running from the river up to an enormous rock formation. It thrust up from the earth like the fist of a titan. Along its face, tiny men labored. And at its base were gathered even more.

I reined in my lathered steed, who gratefully shortened his stride. Dismounting, I led him on foot. We first went down to the river, where I let him drink his fill. I could see from here where the barge must dock. A path of beaten down earth led to an abutment at the river's edge. This seemed like a nice spot. After giving Feckless a rubdown, I'd go see to my business.

***

Not long thereafter, I spied a group of mounted men on a swift approach. They were trotting toward me in standard six-pack formation, with two in the lead and the other four trailing after. They drew up a few yards from where I knelt currying the mud from Feckless' fetlocks. They rode horses nearly as large as the percherons that towed the barge, and all were armed to the teeth.

"You there," asked the one on the left. "What business have you at the king's quarry?"

"I come on a mission of mercy," I replied, standing to face him.

This seemed to baffle the man. He bore the green livery of the duke's soldiers, and a rank insignia I now recognized to be that of a sergeant. Roy had lent me a book on military history since our prior excursion into the marshes.

"Will you take me to whoever is in charge?"

"The quarry master is quite busy," he replied stiffly. "You will explain your presence here. And if it is to my satisfaction, we will escort you to the field office, where the foreman might deign to have words with you."

"Very well then, sergeant," I replied, stuffing my brush back into my bob. "I understand there's a man here who hasn't seen his family in more than three weeks. He's a free man whose only crime was seeking refuge here from the depredations in the south. Aaron Moss is his name. I come to ask for his release for a time that he may visit his wife and child."

"Only that?" asked the sergeant with surprise. "What's this vagrant to you?"

"A symbol, sergeant. A small injustice that gnaws at our kingdom's heart. I would have words with this foreman of yours."

40

The man stared at me dubiously. Though my clothing was that of a tradesman at best, I think he sensed from my words and manner of speech that I might just be above his station. Master Pete had once demonstrated how one might most effectively talk to soldiers. I smiled when he decided to pass this troublesome pest farther up his line of command. I could see it on his face as he dismounted.

"Corporal, secure that animal. We don't want to tempt any of the prisoners or conscripts here with the hope of escape."

"You," he commanded. "Come with me."

As the second man took up Feckless' leads, I fell into step beside the first. The four others trailed behind, still astride their beasts.

"What may I call you, sergeant?" I snapped.

"Uh. I'm Sergeant Davis, Simon Davis, first regiment of Fairglen, second battalion."

"You may call me Journeyman Harper."

"A journeyman of what profession, might I ask?"

"Well, I'm not certain it's a formal profession, *per se*. It's more of a calling, really. I'm a mage. We work directly for the king."

This seemed to have the desired impact on the man. His brow knit as he spared me a sidelong glance. A worried look haunted his face as we trod on toward a large shack resting farther up the causeway.

"Tell me, then, Sergeant Davis," I said, "what kind of man is this foreman of yours?"

"A short one," muttered a man in the rear.

"Pipe down Louie," commanded Sergeant Davis. "And be more respectful of the fellow in charge."

"To answer your question, sir mage," he said, turning to me. "He's a dwarf sent down from Echo Hills. No one knows mining like the dwarves. But I suspect you're asking more about his temperament. It's a fiery one; I'm afraid. Stoneheart's under a lot of pressure right now. He's like a little teakettle just about to go off. I'd watch my step if I were you."

"You call him stone-heart?"

"It's his name. God's truth. Javertimus Stoneheart. But yeah, it does seem to suit him."

At the shack, the sergeant stepped up and hammered on the door. We stood in silence for a time before he was forced to knock again. Poised to do so a third time, the sergeant flinched when the door was suddenly flung wide.

"What is it?" bellowed the bearded man, who stood no taller than my chest.

His eyes were squinted into the morning sun, and a sour grimace tightened his lips.

"This fellow arrived from Fairglen, demanding to see the man in charge. He claims he works for the king, so we brought him here, your excellency."

The dwarf turned his sleepy eyes to peer my way, looking no less annoyed.

"If he's from the king, then I'm a ballerina," he snorted. "Take him away. Throw him in the river if he refuses to go."

"A moment, sir," I asserted, balling up my fist.

I dredged up a smattering of therianthropy to harden it, then held it forth, braced for the impact.

"I am Lucas Harper of Meadowfork. May I have the given and clan name of the stouthearted fellow I'm addressing?"

He stared at my fist, bemused. Even if they knew the custom, not many humans who valued their digits would dare to fist bump with a dwarf.

"Javertimus I be, of the Stoneheart clan," he grumbled. "Make light of it at thine own peril!"

And hauling back, he took aim and smashed into my fist with a powerful, wide-knuckled jab. I felt it all the way up to my shoulder and I feared my elbow would ne'er be the same. But I spotted a glint of respect from the man as he rubbed at the back of his hand.

"Sergeant, you may have done right this time. I'll hear this fellow out. Return to your watch post while I ascertain what his business with me might be."

Once the soldiers had departed, Javertimus invited me in and offered a rickety chair.

"So then, what would you have of me, Lucas who serves the king?"

He listened patiently while I explained once again the holiday I sought for Aaron. He appeared to consider for a time and then shared his decision.

"If I let him go on your say so, then others will get the idea it's okay to lie about on every seventh day. There'd be resentment. And the schedule would fall even farther behind. No, sir. I can't have it. I *won't* have it."

"You do your clan name honor, sir. For stony is your heart, if for the mere crime of vagrancy you'd keep a family split apart. Vagrancy is just a term that would make a crime of merely standing about, doing no wrong. How about this, then? I'll take the man's place that he may enjoy this one day and night in his family's warm embrace. He'll return to you tomorrow, fresh and rested and no harm done."

"What know you of stone work, boy?" said the foreman. "Though he's no dwarf, conscript Moss is at least somewhat competent in chiseling out the granite blocks. I can't spare the man."

"What I know might surprise you. Give me a chance."

I held his gaze steadily. I could tell the man was intrigued, and a smile played upon his lips as he rubbed at his bruised knuckles. I think he had some notion of showing me my place. And soon, he did.

***

The foreman led me farther up the causeway. We passed a pit where men in leg irons were pounding away at rocks with sledgehammers and breaking them into a pale grey powder. I would later learn that this 'limestone' was brought here from a lesser quarry farther upriver. It was reduced by the unskilled laborers here. The powder was to be baked in a kiln and used to make mortar to set between stones to affix them in place.

Farther along, I finally encountered Toby's father. He stood at one end of a row of granite slabs that had been brought down from the mountain. There were six of these enormous slabs lined up one behind another like the wagons of a caravan. Even now, another such approached. It was being rolled down toward us on a set of logs shepherded by a gang of conscripts. When a log would roll out from behind the massive slab, a pair of men would tow it free and hustle up to place it under the front. They looked a bit silly, prancing about their craggy burden like ants tending their queen. It finally came to rest at the rear, and the logs were retrieved from beneath it. The weary men turned and trudged back uphill.

At the head of the line of stones stood Aaron and two others. I could tell the man holding the chisel was Toby's father, because the other two were in leg irons. All the men were shirtless, and mud caked their skin. All looked to be well-muscled, albeit a bit on the lean side. They looked up from their task when they saw the foreman and me drawing nigh.

"Continue," said the dwarf in a voice of command. "We wish to observe your technique."

Aaron placed his chisel against the face of the slab, gripping it firmly with both hands. The man beside him brought a sledgehammer down to strike its head with a ringing sound. A fist-sized piece of granite sheered off from the stone they were working, leaving a smooth spot in its wake. The third man deftly darted in, snatching up the flake. This he tossed on a pile of stones growing there beside him as Aaron sought a new purchase for his chisel's blade.

They repeated this dance a few times more, each time carving out a broader, flat area upon the stone. Periodically,

Aaron would take a measurement using a piece of string with a series of black marks upon it. Every so often, he would hold a strange L-shaped piece of wood against the stone's surface.

It didn't take a genius to recognize he was trying to cut out a regular rectangular block like I'd seen being loaded on the wagon at the jetty. In fact, there were several such neatly stacked nearby. What did amaze me was the finicky and tedious nature of the endeavor and the bewildering variety of wedges, chisels, and drills required for the task. Not fifteen minutes later, Aaron set his chisel down. Grimacing, Aaron said:

"Now this one too is worn down dull. I'll need a sharper one again. Here, Harry, run this back to the camp blacksmith for sharpening and fetch me another."

The man who'd been clearing the shards hustled off to do so. There was no actual 'running' involved, hobbled as he was by the leg irons. For Harry was no conscript. Rather, he was a prisoner, sentenced to this labor for some past misdeed. Aaron sat down, and the tall fellow beside him passed him a waterskin after taking a drink himself.

"While we're all having a little break," sneered the dwarf who stood beside me, "I believe introductions are in order. Gentlemen, this is Lucas, a boy who serves the king. He seems to have taken a fancy to your family, conscript Moss. He believes he can do your job for you, so you can enjoy a holiday and spend a proper night with your pretty wife. I'm inclined to let him have a try. Lucas, this sterling fellow, who'll be swinging a hammer at your hands, is Jon Valden. Best you hold her steady and keep your thumbs and fingers tucked out of sight."

I took it from the dwarf's demented smile he thought this a fine joke. When Harry returned, Javertimus took the chisel and placed it in my hand. Aaron stared at me quizzically. I stepped over to the stack of cut blocks and sized one up carefully.

"It's the big one over there," said the dwarf, helpfully.

But I wouldn't let his japes distract me from my task. I walked up to the slab from which the team had been carving and placed my temple to the stone.

"Rockytop, are you there?"

"I am here, brother," whispered my other self.

With our mind, we delved into the stone, exploring its weaknesses and dis-joining some of the stubborn spars. It was a jumble of feldspar, quartz and muscovite held together by a mixture of many other minerals. We traversed the maze of irregular shapes and worked our will upon them.

"Brother," said Rocky after a time, "there is an angry little man asking us if we are asleep. Are we?"

I increased my breathing and ended the fugue, coming back to myself bit by bit. The others were all staring at me oddly. I lifted the chisel with deliberation and placed it far back from the face of the stone.

"Right here, I think, is the proper spot."

This elicited a sneer of contempt from the dwarf, who harrumphed and smoothed his mustache.

"Strike, Jon Valden. I trust in your aim. A tap is all it should take."

With a doleful look and a shake of his head, the man did as I had bidden him. He struck lightly with narrowed eyes. When the hammer fell, the chisel bit more deeply than one would expect. And sliding out from that granite slab fell a rectangular block of the desired size.

The foreman stood frozen for only a moment, then tugged at his beard and spoke.

"You're a stone-conner. Who'd have figured? My schedule could be saved!"

"A geomancer, actually," I replied. "I take it we have a deal, then?"

"What?" said the dwarf, startled from his reverie. "... oh... that... of course, of course."

At this, he turned to Aaron Moss, his flinty eyes alive with calculation.

"Conscript Moss, you are freed from your duties for the remainder of the day. Make your way home with my blessing. I'll inform the guards straightaway. Lucas here can fill in for you. Take your own sweet time, and we'll see you on the morrow."

Rather than answering his foreman, Aaron turned to me instead. He quirked a grin.

"I don't know why you're doing this or what I've done to deserve it. But it's appreciated. I owe you one, mister."

And with that, he was off, led away by Stoneheart himself, who'd been so opposed to his leaving.

Jon rested his hammer on its head in the pit in which we stood. I hadn't heard the big man speak as yet. I wondered what he made of all this. Jon turned to me, his expression grim.

"That was beautiful, what you done for him."

And so began one of the longest days of my life.

***

Stone after stone, I separated. That dwarf was determined to squeeze every last drop of magic from me. He'd trotted up the hill to direct even more slabs our way. In truth, John and Harry had little to do. But I insisted they were needed, and they were thankful for the lighter load. My head was aching from my efforts as I pressed it once again to the seventh slab. Just three more to go, I thought wearily.

The sun was nearly down, painting the clouds of the western horizon in glorious shades of orange and pink. Harry informed me they'd normally be picking up their tools by now. But the greedy dwarf who ran the dig had urged us to finish all ten. Even now, he had men positioning poles around our pit. And lanterns were being hung thereon. A deal was a deal; I supposed, but this seemed rather excessive.

My stomach rumbled. The midday meal had been a small portion of salted pork and pottage. This was a stew consisting of some unidentifiable root vegetables boiled nearly to paste and hastily gulped from tin cups. The tasteless stuff stuck with you for a while, but it had *been* a while, and then some.

The barge had returned and now lay moored to the abutment. I'd learned its name was "The Queen Henrietta" in honor of the former king's second wife. She sat low in the water now. Javertimus seemed hellbent on sinking the poor thing with all the stone blocks we'd produced. I'd hoped to catch a ride back upriver on her, because Aaron had taken my mule. But once again, the foreman frustrated my plans.

"You said you would take conscript Moss' shift," he said. "If you're a man of your word, you'll work for me until the man returns. As you can see, we've a bit of a backlog, as the lumberjacks are wont to say."

"Enough," I declared. "This shift is over when the sun no longer sheds its light. We've already done the work of a dozen crews and more. If I am to stay, then I must have some proper rest at least. Show me where the men sleep. By morning's light I'll resume my efforts more effectively."

He didn't argue. By this, I suspected we'd already made up the shortfall, perhaps even putting him ahead of schedule. With a simple nod, he indicated I was to follow. I left the other men to collect all the tools, having no clue what was to be done with them myself.

As I lay me down, a chilling thought crept into the back of my mind. What if Aaron never returned? I hardly knew the man. What if he simply gathered up his family and set off for parts unknown? Javertimus would certainly insist on the letter of the law. How long might I be bound here by my word? Had I been too trusting? Was my altruism too hasty?

"Peace, brother" rumbled Rockytop, emerging from the depths to soothe my frightened musings.

"Though he might have good reason to do as you fear, Goodman Moss won't abandon us to languish here. We'd do better to worry some ill might befall him. But even in such a case, your vow to the Lady Megan would soon take precedence over even your given word.

Ah, yes, I thought as I drifted off to sleep. It was good to have such a trump card handy.

I groaned as in the morning I approached our station. During the night, our fiendish foreman had managed to have three more slabs rolled up behind the others. Jon and Harry were just setting up, and the barge was no longer to be seen. I stretched my back and dug right in. Now that I'd found the rhythm of it and was fully rested; it didn't seem so bad.

After Mistress Julia had returned to the conclave, she'd taught us many interesting uses for our magic. Among the more challenging techniques was diversification. That's where a journeyman broadened his or her gift to encompass other disciplines apart from his affinity. I'd been instructed in the rudiments of fire magic, sound, light and shadow, and all manner of effects that other mages could achieve. To earn full mastery, one had to be versatile. In my case, I also had to learn geomancy from the ground up, as it were, being relatively new even to my own primary affinity.

My weakest discipline was aeromancy. Stone didn't readily lend itself to manipulating air currents. I had trouble summoning a breeze strong enough to disturb a candle flame. What I was doing now, however, rested squarely in my wheelhouse. As a result, it required only a small expenditure of magic to achieve the needed outcome. Rockytop could even assist me. True, shaping stone was slower and more difficult than earth, clay, or sand, but I could literally do it in my sleep. So, block after block, I carved from the slabs until my magic was all but spent. It was approaching midday when fatigue finally began to overtake me.

I was working on the fourth slab of the day when I felt a terrible grinding and wrenching from within.

"Rocky?" I asked in alarm. "What was that? Is aught amiss? Are you hurt in some way?"

"Not me, brother," he growled in reply. "It came from deep below. You wait here and I'll go check."

Strong arms soon gripped my shoulders, and Jon ushered me over to a stone block on which to rest. Harry passed me the waterskin.

"What's wrong?" he asked."You look like a dragon done flew over your grave."

"Give me a minute," I replied after taking a swig.

The wrenching feeling hadn't abated. In fact, It seemed to swell. It reminded me of that time last winter, when Oberon's spire had fallen. It was an unrelenting ache, like a tooth that needed pulling.

"Brother," reported Rockytop, whose voice was somehow more distant, "I think I know what's wrong."

"The digging on the cliffs above have angered the mountain spirit. It will soon erupt in some fashion. Woe indeed to any who are near it."

"Are you saying this miniature mountain contains an oread?"

There was silence for a moment.

"I think not," my homunculus replied. "It's more like an echo of one that once *was*. I can't explain any better. But the cliffs are unsafe."

"Can we make it stop? Soothe it somehow?"

"We cannot, brother. The process is already underway."

I leapt to my feet and dashed down the slope. To the foreman's shack, I ran.

***

I called out the foreman and warned him of the danger I suspected.

Skeptical at first, he questioned me most thoroughly. In the end, my arguments convinced him. He had seen with his own eyes that my affinity for stone was genuine. And being a dwarf, he had a healthy fear of when stonework went amiss. He returned within his field office. From it, he retrieved a hollow ox horn, which he raised up to his lips.

He blasted out a mighty note that grated on my ears. It rolled like thunder and echoed back. He sounded it repeatedly in this fashion, at even intervals a dozen times at least. I covered my ears lest they should burst from the awful sound.

In the distance, I could see the effect this soon had on the workmen. It was like when one kicked over an anthill and the ants all came boiling out. They scrambled down, clearing the cliff and filling the area below it. Soon they were moving toward us en mass in a hasty but orderly retreat from their various tasks.

The guardsmen were the first to arrive to discover what the matter was. Astride their beasts, they clattered up to where we stood. They were led by a grim-faced Sergeant Davis.

"Is this merely a drill, or has something gone awry?"

Looking over at me thoughtfully, the dwarf considered his words.

"Young Lucas here has made a prediction. I've decided to heed his warning. Something is awry indeed. I feel it in my bones."

"Your orders, then, excellency"

"Line them up and count them out and make sure all are present. I wouldn't put it past some of these louts to use a dire calamity to cover an escape attempt. Then lock them all in the bunkhouse."

"See to it, corporal," said the sergeant. "What then?"

"Send a detachment to secure all tools and have the quartermaster give an accounting of them. You know as well as I how easily leg irons can be defeated should any be mislaid."

"It shall be done."

As the men rode off to carry out their orders, I felt the pressure build still further. It made me want to flee. I sat down on the ground, and the dwarf looked down at me.

"Aye," he said. "Even I can feel it now. A slight trembling signal of what's coming. And a sound so low it must be made by the lips of the earth herself."

I was glad for the confirmation. Gladder still the men would all be safe. I'd have felt pretty silly had this feeling in my gut been merely the result of a bad bowl of pottage.

An hour we waited as the sun passed midday, and still no disaster had befallen us. Aaron Moss had arrived on Feckless, so technically I was free to go. Javertimus let him join us rather than be locked in the overcrowded bunkhouse. He wasn't a prisoner, after all, and had demonstrated his trustworthiness by returning. He and I, the foreman and the sergeant, all sat waiting and watching. The dwarf was getting irascible, though, and had begun to doubt my claim. If I'd disrupted the camp and nothing came of it, he'd happily let me take the blame. Not for the first time, he glared sternly over at me. This time, I met his gaze squarely.

"Stone is patient," I reminded him.

"Aye," he agreed reluctantly.

And then it happened. I felt a sudden release. The face of the cliff just crumbled away. Sitting so far distant, there was no sound at all at first. Just a silent rockfall running down and trailing great clods of earth. From where this waterfall of stone struck the ground at the base of the hill arose a plume of dust growing broader and broader still. Rising up, it obscured our vision of the ongoing dire collapse. It grew even larger, churning forth to place more ground in its stricture. A cacophony then ensued when the sound caught up to the picture.

It was a groaning, cracking sound as the face of the mountain was sundered. There followed a faint rumbling, increasing as the landslide neared. And the ground on which I sat began to shake in sympathy. My earth sense was ringing like a bell. Rocky was cowering beneath his hill. I'd ne'er felt so fearsome a trembling since the witch had leveled the mill.

And then the dust swept over us, thickening the air. It deposited many grains of grit on our clothing and in our hair. But from that foul brown breeze, none took any actual harm. Only our sight was overcome. Not a pebble rolled this far. And soon enough, the swirling eddies began to settle and disperse. Although a summer breeze sent much of it wafting away, a pale brown haze lingered stubbornly near the ground, giving the quiet scene an eerie, indefinite quality.

The whole event had likely taken fewer than ten minutes. The dwarf stood up and dusted himself off.

"Lucas," he said, "your warning was most timely. Every man in that bunkhouse likely owes his life to you. And imagine the harm to my own reputation had my workforce been obliterated. I find myself therefore beholden to you. Ask me what you will, and if it lies within my power, I will grant it. For the Stonehearts all be men of honor, and such a debt must be repaid."

I too stood. Looking down at the formerly haughty foreman, I considered.

"For myself, I desire only two wagon loads of loose rubble and eight sacks of your baked, powdered lime. I would like them delivered to the refugee camp outside the city's gates."

"Only that?" ask Javertimus, standing straighter as a wry grin twisted his lips. "We've lime aplenty as it happens and can spare so paltry an amount. As to the rubble, look ye about. We'll be weeks clearing all of this detritus out. Done and done, sir."

"Is your honor bought so cheaply, then? There is one more boon I require. And this one is more dear."

"Oh?" he said with narrowed eyes.

Sensing my mood, the dwarf became more wary, and the smile fled his face as he listened on.

"Henceforth, all conscripts who labor here and are not imprisoned for some crime will be given leave one day each week. Every Sunday, without fail, you will transport them back to their kin. On Monday at dawn, you may collect them to resume their work for you."

Javertimus looked affronted. And generosity warred with his greed. His cheeks and forehead reddened as anger colored his countenance. Sergeant Davis had been right. The dwarf's fiery temper did put one in mind of a tea kettle about to boil.

"You ask too much, sir mage. You overstep unfairly. You make a mockery of my kind and humble offer. Who are you to make such a preposterous demand?"

Aaron Moss stared at us, wide-eyed. The sergeant's face was deadpan. I let the silence stretch out a bit before answering the man.

"Is it too much for saving your entire workforce to release some for one day in seven? Perhaps things are different among the dwarves, but we humans need our rest. It is said that even the creator above observed a day of leisure."

"As to who I am," I continued more thoughtfully, "your king granted me a title last summer: 'Lucas the Just.' And it is my aim to make myself worthy of it in his service. I deem it a cruelty to work these men so hard. Do I ask too much for the simple service I did you? Perhaps. Nonetheless, it is my price. And shame be upon the Stoneheart clan if you refuse to pay it."

The dwarf paused. He swallowed hard and finally nodded.

"And some better food wouldn't go amiss either," I put in for good measure as I turned and stalked away.

CHAPTER THREE

The Guildmaster

"There is no limit to the amount of good you
can do if you don't care who gets the credit."
~ Ronald Reagan ~

We sat breaking our fast in the common room, Toby and I. The excited boy was still regaling me with details about his father's visit.

"... then he took me all the way down to the river. We watched the ferrymen taking people across and stones being unloaded onto the jetty. Ma even made us a picnic lunch."

His excited jabber came between mouthfuls of the scrambled eggs he was shoveling down.

"I'm glad you had a pleasant day," I remarked.

"Pleasant don't describe the half of it, master. You should'a seen ma's face when he came trotting up on that old mule. It was epic; it was. I just don't ken though why women have to shed so many tears when they's happy about something."

"Women's ways are a mystery, Toby. Get used to it."

I only picked at my food. Though it was quite good, I just didn't have the zest for it I usually did. As the boy prattled on about this and that, I was thinking about the upcoming celebrations and dreading the fuss and bother they'd entail. My musings were interrupted when a man near the window leapt to his feet and issued a startling announcement to the room at large.

"Crownies!" he declared. "Two of 'em! They're tying up out front and lookin' this way."

This sparked a murmuring among the other guests. And I noticed several of the more unsavory types scattering coins on their tables and making swiftly for the back door. Though unfamiliar with the term, I doubted the man was referring to the duke's patrolmen, who were known to drop by on occasion, never eliciting such a stir. I stared toward the entryway to see what had everyone so agitated.

A man soon entered. He was draped in black chain mail of an elegant cut. Rather than shining, it seemed to absorb the light that fell upon it, blending into the surrounding shadows. The man himself was solidly built, but not over-muscled. And from his belt hung the scabbard of a long blade that seemed to flow with his strides as though it were a part of his body. Everything about the man screamed of danger, despite the placid look upon his neatly shaven face.

He scanned the silent room. When his eyes fell upon me, they stared unblinkingly for a moment, and he approached.

"Are you Lucas Harper, a mage of the conclave?"

"I am he," said I amiably.

"You are to gather your things and come with me."

He managed to make it sound almost polite. But from this soft-spoken, gentle command, it was clear he expected to be heeded at once. Very well, I could match his civil tone.

"May I ask what it is you want of me and where you would have me go?"

His jaw clenched.

"I will tell you, sir mage, but not here," he said in an even tone.

I rose to my feet. All eyes of the breakfast crowd were turned my way. But most of the other patrons seemed to be trying to shrink into their seats. From this, I took it my would-be abductor was some personage of authority. Though he bore no insignia of rank, the chest plate of his armor was emblazoned with a dim golden circlet so dark as to almost escape one's notice. I hefted my bob from off the floor and slung it over one shoulder.

"Let my servant collect his things, and we'll be ready to go."

The man glanced down at Toby, who seemed as apprehensive and mystified as I. At the man's nod, Toby leapt up and scrambled for the stairwell. We waited in silence for him to return.

Outside, I saw another man outfitted just as the first. He was holding the reins of two sleek black horses. The beasts were smaller than the horses ridden by most knights but elegant of line. Atop high arched necks and sloping shoulders, their smallish heads had broad brows and overlarge eyes and nostrils. I was no judge of horseflesh, but I'd hazard a guess these were built for speed.

"What may I call you, sir?" I asked as the man led us toward his cohort.

The mere presence of these men had cleared the street out in front of the inn.

Still, he made no reply.

From down the lane emerged a strange carriage. It was drawn by two bay horses similar in breed to the ones the 'crownies' were riding. The carriage itself was somewhat longer than was typical and lacked any windows. It put me in mind of a hearse. Atop it sat two men on the driver's bench, one of whom held a serviceable-looking crossbow at the ready. It drew up before us, and my escort opened its door.

Shrugging, I stepped up into its cab, followed by Toby and the man with whom I'd spoken. Inside, the vehicle was well-appointed. I slid across the upholstered bench to make room for the others. If this was to be my final ride, at least I was going out in style. I heard the clatter of the wheels as the carriage rocked into motion.

"You may call me Guardsman Willis," said our abductor, finally loosening his tongue.

"And where are we going, guardsman?"

"The royal palace," he replied tersely. "You have been summoned."

"Why?"

"That's really not for me to say, sir. I was simply instructed to retrieve you. I did overhear talk about your using the king's name in some recent dealings you had at the quarry. But I'm not certain that's the whole of it."

Toby sat glancing in amazement between the two of us.

I couldn't blame him. I was no less astonished myself. Whoever had summoned us to the royal palace must be an important person indeed. I supposed I *had* mentioned the king once or twice. As a mage, I *was* under his direct command. I hoped this wouldn't be misconstrued as a fraudulent claim on his authority. It was Javertimus, after all, who had kept asserting I 'worked for the crown.' I simply hadn't corrected the man.

Silence reclaimed the windowless cab as we clattered toward our destination. My half-eaten breakfast sat uneasily in my stomach as the minutes ticked on. Things could be worse. I'd been half convinced we were bound for the Black Tower when first I'd been 'retrieved.' It was a lesson I'd had to learn several times over and now was relearning once again. In Osten, you never knew *what* direction your day might take.

***

When the carriage finally halted, we were rousted out like drunkards from a tavern. Before my eyes could adjust to the bright light, we were surrounded on all sides by royal guardsmen and hustled toward a rear entrance of an enormous stone building. I caught the impression of impeccably sculpted hedge rows and a lush garden space while being ushered inside. There followed a hasty trek through some rather well-appointed hallways so posh as to be awe-inspiring, had I time to examine the portraits and intriguing wall hangings.

Ere long, we arrived at a set of brass doors emblazoned with a stylized rendering of a dragon reared up and breathing fire. Flanking it were two more royal guardsmen, looking as sober as our escorts.

"Is this the one?" asked the tall fellow on the left.

The other was peering at me through a familiar ocular device.

"Hand. Breast pocket. Mind seems clear," he reported in some kind of verbal shorthand.

The other only grunted in reply and nodded stiffly.

Guardsman Willis, however, reached into my breast pocket and promptly withdrew my wand, while using his other hand to relieve me of my backpack.

"You'll have to leave these here; I'm afraid."

To the other man, he nodded.

"Confirmed. This is Lucas Harper. The boy is his servant. Courtesy dictated he be permitted to accompany him."

"The perimeter is secure. They are to be let in directly."

At this, the man stepped aside and shoved open one of the doors. As it swung inward on silent hinges, its gilded panels caught and reflected the light of flames. The dragon's eyes gleamed wickedly, and my mage sight detected a faint enchantment whose nature I couldn't quite discern.

"Lucas Harper and his servant have arrived, highness," intoned the man with the ocular. "We have conveyed them here per your orders. They await your pleasure."

"Enter and approach," said a familiar voice from within.

My shoulders immediately relaxed. I don't know what I was expecting, but the presence of the prince allayed many of my fears.

On entering the hall, we were marched up its center aisle toward Prince Henry, who was alone and seated in a high-backed chair. He looked much the same as he had at our last encounter, the one where he had revealed his true nature. When we arrived a dozen paces distant, each of the guards flanking us fell in unison to one knee. But their wary eyes remained fixed on Toby and me. Uncertain of royal protocol, I fell back on an old maxim: 'When in Fairglen...' I fell to my knees as well, as did Toby a moment later.

After a suitable pause, the prince spoke again.

"You may rise," he said.

"And you guardsmen may depart," he commanded. "This is to be a private audience."

Guardsman Willis seemed perplexed by this, but upon rising to his feet and after only a brief hesitation, he responded.

"As your highness wishes."

At this, he turned on his heel and marched from the hall with the other men in tow, adding: "We'll be just outside should your highness *require* anything."

As the door was secured behind the retreating men, the prince turned an assessing eye my way.

"He's getting a bit cheeky, that one."

By this time, Toby and I had also regained our feet and stood pondering on how to proceed. Prince Henry didn't leave us waiting for long.

"Let us retire to the grand hearth that we may conduct our interview in better comfort."

He indicated an area off to our right where a roaring blaze crackled noisily. Before it, sat several plush armchairs and an ornate, cushioned divan. I stared about in wonder. Everything around the room seemed larger than was necessary. It made me feel like a small child in relation to its grandeur. The room was themed in purple and gold, colors denied even to the nobility. And everywhere I looked rested priceless appointments and glittering relics. One that caught my eye was a statue of a she-wolf with twin boys suckling at her teats. These must be Romulus and Remus, the two who were said to have founded Reme. Prince Henry led the way, while Toby and I trailed after in a daze.

The prince took his seat in one of the large chairs. Turning to me, he said: "I grant you permission to sit in our presence."

I sat.

A moment later, Toby hopped up into one of the chairs as well. The prince stared at him and blinked, startled that a servant would be so presumptuous. Shaking his head and overlooking this behavior, Henry directed his attention back to me.

"I recall writing you a letter wherein I said and I quote: 'If ever you are in Fairglen, feel free to call upon me.' You've been here six days already. Why have you not done so? Is a royal audience not to your liking?"

I did indeed recall the missive in question. And he knew to the day when I had arrived. How to phrase my response?

"Well, I didn't want to presume on your highness' kind offer, especially during such hectic times."

Nodding, Henry finally got to the point of the summons.

"It seems you've found aught to keep you busy anyway, Lucas. Word has reached us that the king's quarry is in a shamble."

"That wasn't my fault. I only warned of the --"

"We are aware," interrupted the prince. "Moreover, it seems that a certain stony-hearted dwarf with a reputation as a harsh task-master has suddenly gone soft on his workers. It is said that by order of the king, he will grant them a weekly respite from their labors and has even requisitioned better food to sustain them."

"Well, I never actually said I was speaking with the king's authority - only that as a mage, I work for him directly. The rest was taken all out of context."

At this, the prince smiled.

"Knowing you, I thought it must be something of the sort. Verily, his majesty is rather *pleased* at how it all turned out. Now he can take credit for having dispatched someone to sort out that mess at the quarry. A large shipment of stone blocks has recently arrived at Cathedral Square. This has put the renovations back on track. Thanks to you, the cathedral's new facade will shine like new on coronation day. The lord high architect is singing your praises to the bell tower, and the archbishop is looking into the workmen's miraculous escape from harm. There may even be a *sainthood* in it for you."

"I sincerely *hope* not, your highness. As your highness is no doubt aware, the extraordinary gifts we mages possess are not deemed saintly in nature. The doctrine of justification holds that salvation is a gift from God granted to those who have faith, not merely some aberrant and inexplicable talent."

"Be that as it may, from among the people, there has arisen a muttering. From the back streets and alleyways of Cheapside right up to these very walls they whisper. Some claim that one has come among them who will right all wrongs and rectify the kingdom's inequities. The name on their lips is Lucas the Just."

Here we go *again*, I thought. Despite my best efforts to remain unnoticed, why did everything I touch turn into fodder for wagging tongues? As if reading my thoughts, the prince went on to say:

"Naturally, you should realize that even such momentary fame will draw detractors. You should hear the grumblings from the mason's guild about the quality work done by our 'unskilled labor' at the quarry. They threatened a boycott until father explained this was the result of magic. He assured them it was merely a temporary measure and that all would soon revert to the *status quo*. We trust this is so?"

"I don't intend to slave away at the quarry any longer, your highness, if that's what you mean."

"Good. Then we have an accord."

He drummed his fingers on the arm of his chair as he considered me once again.

"You know, Lucas, you're getting quite the reputation around the kingdom as a heart breaker."

What?

"Me, my lord? I think you mean my cousin..."

He began counting on his fingers.

"Well, if you think about it, there was the witch's heart, shattered. The heart of the swamp, crushed. And now Stoneheart brought low. We've half a mind to grant you this as a second title. It is well within our powers as a prince,"

"I beg your highness to heed the other half of your mind and refrain from it. Megan would never *forgive* me."

"Ah, yes. The Lady Megan. We've heard much about her. We look forward to making *that* good lady's acquaintance."

The conversation was settling down. The prince seemed relaxed and in a bit of a jovial mood. It seemed I wouldn't be hauled away to the black tower after all. Could it be he even viewed me as a friend? From this, I found the courage to pose a question of my own.

"Since your highness is so well informed, do you know when Westarbor and his entourage might arrive?"

"That's difficult to say. Father received word by pigeon that he's been mysteriously delayed yet again. He's being rather tight-lipped about precisely why. It is our hope they'll arrive by the middle of next week. It would be a pity if the girl missed the debutante ball next Friday. It's the season opener; don't you know? And such things require time to prepare. We wish them godspeed."

I *didn't* know, actually. But I sensed my time with the prince was growing short. I think Toby sensed it too. The lad had remained respectfully silent throughout the interview, just as I had instructed him. I could tell from his face and his squirming manner, however, he was bursting to ask a question of his own. It was a bit distracting. Again, as if reading my mind, the prince turned to Toby and addressed him directly.

"We can't help but notice your young servant has aught he would say. Indulge our curiosity and tell us what's on your mind, boy."

Toby gulped and spared me a sidelong glance. I nodded encouragingly in response.

"Well, your greatness, it's just I mark you keep sayin' we, us, and our when referring to yourself. Is there two of you in there somehow, or is this some proper way of speaking I ain't learned of yet?"

"*That?* It's just that when in my audience chamber, I have to use the 'royal we.'

"Well," said Toby, blushing furiously, "I'm certain milord can quick find a chamber pot for that need. We can wait."

The prince stared at my servant deadpan. I was biting my tongue and hoping against hope to keep a snicker from erupting to give a further insult to my prince. I'll never know how Henry may have responded, for just then there came a knock at the doors, one of which swept inward a crack.

"We do not wish to be disturbed," said Henry over one shoulder.

"This can't wait, brother dear."

And in strode another man wearing hunting attire. Brushing past the royal guards, he made his way toward where we sat. He was a large man, broad of shoulder but narrow at the waist. He bore a placid smile, and his eyebrows met in the middle to form a continuous line above both his eyes. He was carrying before him a silver coffer about the size of a loaf of bread. It looked weighty.

Henry sighed.

"These are the new proofs, fresh from the royal mint. Father wants to get your approval immediately. And who might we be granting an audience today?"

"This is Lucas of Meadowfork and his servant. Lucas, my brother prince, Richard."

"An honor," said I, sliding from my seat to kneel before the man.

Without giving us another thought, Prince Richard opened the lid of his coffer and held it out for Henry to examine. Within it were scattered a few coins. I couldn't see very much around Richard's broad backside, but when Henry held one up, it appeared to be a shiny new silver shilling. The reverse side featured the dragon symbol of the realm. Flipping it about, Henry held it out toward me that I might mark the obverse side. On this was depicted a portrait of Prince Henry himself.

"What do you think, Lucas?" asked the prince. "Oh, and you may now rise and resume your seat."

Doing so, I quipped: "It's a striking likeness, highness."

"I think so as well," he confirmed.

"Egads," mumbled Toby in wonder. "He's got his own money..."

"You amuse me, boy," said the prince to the pauper. "You may keep this one."

He flipped the coin toward my servant, who snatched it eagerly from out of the air.

"We're having more than a thousand of these struck to commemorate my coronation. Each invited guest will be given one and the remainder will be scattered to the crowd as largess."

"I take it," said Prince Richard, "that this round is acceptable?"

"Indeed. Extend our compliments to the moneyers and tell them they may now proceed with their crafting."

When the man failed to leave, Henry stood.

"Yes? Is there aught else?"

"Father wants you to go and talk to the masons again straightaway. They're all riled up and need to be soothed. They've formed a muster in Cathedral square and are refusing to work until we meet with them. The king believes this an apt exercise for your diplomatic skills."

Henry sighed again. I guess heavy hangs even the head that's *soon* to wear the crown.

"Very well, brother. I'll gather a contingent of the royal guard and go see what they're demanding now."

"I take it you won't be joining me on the hunt, then?"

"No. Go have fun with your... killing things."

Turning to me, the prince asked: "Care to come with?"

The question struck me as odd. In my experience, nobles rarely asked anything apart from opinions of their close advisers. They commanded or made bald statements. Still, as I may have played a part in instigating this conundrum, perhaps I could be of some service. I also wouldn't mind a tour of Cathedral Square. As he'd given me the option, I answered in the only way that made sense.

"If my lord wishes it, I would be most honored to accompany him."

"Very good. Give us a moment. We need to use the 'royal wee' and then we can be off."

***

I pressed my hand against the low ceiling of the carriage in which we rode.

"Aurea lux mollis," I incanted.

When I withdrew my hand, it left a glowing imprint which shed a soft yellow light, brightening the cab's interior.

"Better, your highness?" I asked.

"Much," Prince Henry replied. "I have often had occasion to curse the designers of these wretched rolling windowless coffins.

Toby grinned.

"It'll fade in an hour or so, sire. If you'd like, I could perhaps produce a permanent one. I'm getting much better at enchantment."

"We shall keep it in mind, but this should suffice for now."

"We've cleared the upper gates, highness," reported a muffled voice from above as we lurched into motion once more. "Ten more minutes should see us at the target destination."

"Something else puzzles me, Lucas."

"What troubles your highness?"

"Our informants told us of several loads of stone that were delivered to the refugee encampment. But the sacks of lime are nowhere to be seen. Would you care to enlighten us?"

Informants, I assumed, was a polite word for 'spies.' The king's spy network, the brotherhood of the board, was renowned throughout Osten for their ability to pose as people from any walk of life and blend into the background. I wondered who at the quarry could have overheard my dealings with the foreman. One of the guardsmen, perhaps?

"That's easily explained, highness. I put them here in my bob for safekeeping, and so they'd stay dry."

"Ah, yes. That wondrous knapsack of yours. We should have guessed."

He peered at my pack which rested on the back-facing seat next to Tobias.

"I know of many nobles and even royals who would pay handsomely for such a handy item. Hmm. Quite coincidentally, you may have heard I have a birthday coming up soon..."

"I have something else in mind for that, your highness," I demurred with a sly grin.

"Oh? What is it?"

"I don't want to ruin the surprise. You'll simply have to wait and see."

As we rolled along, the prince and I chatted about this and that. It was almost as though I had my old friend Kendrick back. I discovered last autumn the prince was a surprisingly clever actor himself. Even Royland hadn't caught him out when he'd posed as mere low nobility. He might even be as skilled as Megan, who could feign any emotion at the drop of a hat. It had me wondering whether this was the prince's true persona or just another mask he was choosing to wear today.

But when the carriage came again to a halt, the prince's face hardened. With an uplifted chin and a stern demeanor, he became royalty once more. Though my mage sight never wavered, I could practically feel his aura of command filling the space surrounding us.

"Highness, we have arrived," the coachman reported. "Give us another few minutes to secure the site properly."

We sat in silence for several minutes more. It seemed that once Henry put on his game face, he preferred to remain prepared.

***

The carriage door finally opened to reveal a double row of royal guardsmen. They faced outward to either side to form a narrow aisle down which we were ushered. Toby and I followed the prince toward a pavilion tent. It had likely been erected for the sole purpose of these talks.

Not much was visible beyond the guardsmen's cordon, save for the cathedral looming above. No workmen labored on the scaffolds. And from them, loose tarpaulins fluttered gently, stirred by a summer breeze. It was another cloudless sky and the midday sun shone down on the heated flagstones we trod.

We passed into the pint-sized canvas fortress surrounded by the royal guard. Above it proudly flew the regal banner of Osten. It struck me just how far in life I'd come. If you'd asked me three years earlier what I'd be doing now, never could that humble miller's son have foreseen it. 'Consorting with royalty at the kingdom's capital' wouldn't have been his first guess, nor, in fact, his hundredth.

The tent was more like a mobile palace. Its interior was lavish and grand. And a long table graced its center where two men stood arguing.

The first was obviously a nobleman. He wore a long brocaded gown of silk whose patterns made my eyes water. Over this lay a surcoat emblazoned with some sort of coat of arms on its left breast pocket. Perched atop his wizened head was a broad-brimmed floppy hat. And in a flagrant display of wealth, the man was festooned with sparkling rings, ornate buckles, brooches and the like. About his neck hung his chain of office, marking him as the lord high architect.

The other man stood shouting at the nobleman; his hands splayed out on the table before him. In stark contrast to the nobleman's opulence, he wore a simple tunic of tan. Over this, an old worn brown leather apron flapped as he barked out his complaints. No jewelry had he, save for a small silver pin on his sweat-stained cap in the shape of a mason's square.

"...the king promised us that no more dwarfs would be hired to take our place. The one is bad enough! Any more would snatch the food from the very mouths of our children. The mason's guild won't stand for it, I say. And so say we all."

"I assure you, Goodman Bennet," sputtered the indignant lord. "No more dwarves have been employed at the quarry."

"That's *Guildmaster* Bennet to you, Sir Lawrence," he all but bellowed. "Or shall I call you Archibald? And then how do you explain all them perfect stone blocks?"

"Now see here, Guildmaster..." began Sir Lawrence.

He paused in mid-retort with his finger thrust toward his adversary. He had spotted the prince approaching, as did the other man but a moment later. Both men paused, swept the hats from off their heads, and swiftly bent the knee. After a suitable pause, the prince released them.

"Rise. We have come to hear of what delays our project."

Whereupon both men began to speak at once.

"Silence. Let us be seated, gentlemen, and I shall hear each of you in turn."

After they'd complied, the prince seated himself at what was now the table's head. When Toby also made as though to sit, I caught him by the collar and hauled him back. We retreated a step to observe.

"We shall begin with you, guildmaster," Henry announced.

Nodding his head in my direction, the mason asked: "Who's this, then, highness?"

"A special adviser, Lucas of Meadowfork. Pay him no mind. To business. I thought my father had cleared these matters up. Why have you placed this worksite under a stint?"

"Well, it's like I was tellin' Archie here, highness. Them stones is near perfect - no rework necessary."

"Then just slide them into place, you ignorant ninny," muttered the architect in a fit of pique.

"Peace," interjected the prince. "Name-calling is unproductive," he admonished them both.

"But our lord architect makes a good point," he continued. "Why is it a problem that the stone blocks are so well-wrought?"

"It's like I just said, sire. We of the guild are proud of our work. The cathedral is a monument to our craft. We won't have outsiders steal our thunder out from under us. Not on my watch, anyway. But we're businessmen as well, we are. The men of our guild are relying on this project for the wages to feed our families."

Mixed metaphors notwithstanding, it was an impassioned plea. The prince seemed to consider this for a long moment.

"Perhaps it would be best if I could see one of these stones for *myself*. Run and fetch me one."

With a glint of triumph in his eye, the man leapt up to do so.

"Yes, highness. You'll soon see it for yourself."

When he'd gone, Henry turned to the other man, the architect.

"Fear not, old friend. we'll soon have them back on task."

"I hope so, your highness. It's been a most bothersome day butting heads with that old goat."

Turning to me, the man asked, 'Did I hear right? You're from Meadowfork? Do you perchance know a fellow named Javier Lewis?'

"Indeed I do, Sir Lawrence," said I. "He's our artillator. He helped my father build the mill and worked on several other projects for my baron."

"He's far more than that, lad. The man's a genius. You should see the innovations he added to the palace while he was here. Fortifications I'd never dreamed of and little traps and other details in the labyrinth beneath... "

The man trailed off when he espied Prince Henry glaring at him sternly.

The awkward silence that followed was soon filled by the tromp of heavy boots. The guildmaster had returned, followed by two men hefting a familiar granite block between them. Several royal guardsmen accompanied the detail. We made way so the men could place their burden on the table before us. I prayed silently the table was sturdy enough for so heavy a load. My prayer turned out to be either successful or unnecessary.

"You see, your highness?" groused the guildmaster. "This block is clearly of the highest quality. If dwarfs didn't do it, then who? The sneaky little buggers didn't even bother to leave their maker's mark - doubtless so as to hide their involvement in encroachin' on guild prerogatives. Well, we won't place a stone without no maker's mark, so say I."

"So say we all," chanted the guildmaster and the other two masons in unison.

Prince Henry nodded respectfully at the men in silent acknowledgment of their demand. He then glanced my way and arched his eyebrows. It was clearly an invitation to enter the fray. I screwed up my courage and waded right in.

"It was no dwarf who cut that stone," I declared. "It was I who did so."

The men peered at me skeptically for a beat, then began laughing aloud. The prince let this run on a bit before interrupting their reverie.

"*Show* them, Lucas."

And so I did.

Pressing my forehead to the block, I roused Rockytop and told him what I wanted. It would be much simpler than carving out this block originally. Still, it would likely take a few minutes. To stall for time, I righted myself and addressed the men while still resting one hand on the stone.

"You men need not fear for your livelihoods. I only helped at the quarry for a short while. As an early birthday gift for my prince, I thought to help get them caught up. Then your project could be brought to fruition in time for his coronation. I apologize for my shortsightedness. I didn't realize I was stepping on anyone's toes. I am a geomancer from the conclave. And I assure you, the king keeps us quite busy with important tasks for the kingdom."

"*It's ready, brother,*" whispered Rocky.

With a gentle tap, I parted the block into two equal halves. The split in the middle was just as smooth and even as the rest of the stone.

"As to the maker's mark," I continued, "will this do?"

I brushed at the corners of each block, then blew on them to eject a flurry of gray dust. This revealed a stylish 'LH' identical to the one I used to seal my missives.

"You must be *that* Lucas," said one of the dumbfounded masons, "Lucas the *Just*."

Guildmaster Bennet appeared no less amazed than his men, but he soon frowned and shared the unpleasant news.

"Regrettably, that mark ain't valid."

"Explain," ordered the prince.

"Only a guild member of journeyman rank or above can register a maker's mark."

"Well... you're the guild-master, aren't you?" I pressed. "Induct me then."

The man paused to consider.

"I can sponsor you for membership, aye. I can even be your master, so you can apprentice under me. But you can't be made a journeyman without havin' your masterpiece approved. The rules can only bend so far."

Really? He was going to hold everything up on a technicality? But wait...

"Actually," said I, "I have just such a project in mind. Have you enough of the old stones to use until Sunday?"

Discussions continued for another hour or so. I swore my apprentice pledge to Guildmaster Bennet on the spot. Luckily, it didn't conflict in the least with my vows to the conclave. With the prince's backing and some helpful advice from the lord high architect, I was able to get my idea approved by the taciturn mason. Success was by no means assured, but I would do my utmost to make this the shortest apprenticeship Fairglen had ever seen.

"Well," said my new master, "I suppose I'll get the fellas off their keesters and back on the job. The masons of Fairglen are ready to work. So say I."

"So say we all!"

Toby nudged me.

"Oh. Er... So say we all," I belatedly added.

"I've another load ready, Lucas."

His words reverberated up from the depths below with eerie resonant echoes. They brought me out of my communion with the stone, trying to recall who I was. 'Lucas,' the voice had named me. Ah...yes, that was indeed my name. And there was a 'load' ready. I sprang to my feet and hustled over to the well.

My hand squelched in the slimy moss which had overgrown its jagged lip. Above me stood the sturdy framework supporting the winch. It was a heavy model I'd borrowed from the construction site - not the more modest version which would one day haul up buckets of water. That was still being crafted by the carpenter's guild.

"How's it looking, Aaron?" I hollered down.

I marked the hollow sound of my own voice as it rang down the stone cylinder and rebounded from the bottom.

"Dark," returned the disembodied voice. "You might want to send down a few more of those glowing handprints you make."

"Alright, but I mean, is the rubble nearly cleared?"

"Hard to tell with all the slimy muck it's buried in, but I think so."

I took a reading from the rope that wound about the winch. According to the knots, the platform rested more than seventy feet below. As this had once been a functioning well, it was not so surprising. Architect Lawrence had estimated the water table typically lay very near this same depth depending on the season and how much rainfall there'd been.

What *was* surprising was how much muck had accumulated at the bottom since it had been abandoned. The encampment where the refugees squatted had once been a farm tenancy serviced by this very well. The new city wall had lopped off a portion of its fields, and even more had been given up as a servitude to the rerouted king's highway. What remained was not useful as a working tenancy and had lain fallow until the arrival of its latest crop - the refugees. It was a crop that would *also* need water to grow and thrive.

"Alright, stand back," I said. "I'll haul her up."

To either side of the wellhead stood the sturdy support beams of the winch. Between them rested a heavy log wound about with hempen rope. There was a large crank on the right side, which I didn't intend to use.

"Spacium gyrabit," I chanted while spinning my forefinger in circles.

Not many mages had the knack for this spell. It was my special talent. I was a winder, a mage specially attuned to the turning force of the earth. As such, I could make things spin about with far more ease than most, even when pitted against powerful opposing forces. Some other mages could perform this spell, but it caused in them a debilitating dizziness and nausea to which I was all but immune.

The winch turned, winding the rope onto the log and drawing up the load of stones from the bottom. I could have done it quicker, but I was focused more on a smooth ascent. I didn't want to cause anything to fall on Aaron below. Soon, the boxy platform rose above the lip of the well. It was heaped high with mud-encrusted stones. These had fallen from the lining of the shaft or from the partial collapse of its rim. I moved the bar to lock the winch firmly in place.

As I offloaded the stones, I mentally reviewed our progress to date. Earlier, I had examined the shaft, finding it sturdy enough. I'd had to patch it in a few spots where it seemed a bit unsteady. But this was short work for a geomancer with some loose stones and a bit of mortar. At the bottom, however, I found to my dismay the well would need to be cleared and re-dug somewhat. I wanted to add a good ten feet to its depth to insure proper function. I could have done it myself. But it was Sunday already. My time was growing short. So, I'd ambushed Aaron at the bede-house to conscript his assistance.

Remembering to place several fresh glowing handprints on the platform's rim, I unlocked the winch and began unwinding it.

"Lowering it back down now!" I hollered.

"Understood-ood," Aaron replied.

Before the echoes of his voice had faded, he spoke up again.

"Remind me," he groused, "why I'm devoting my day off digging at the bottom of a dreary, dank hole instead of enjoying my family like the others."

"You said you owed me one, Conscript Moss." I replied in a gruff imitation of a certain dwarf.

"I did say that; didn't I-I-I? Silly me. I'll know better next time!"

When the rope went slack, I returned to the lumpy slab that lay nearby. There were two such. Each was a large slice of granite, the pitted surfaces of which were uneven. It had taken Toby and I most of the day yesterday to select and retrieve them from amid the rubble Javertimus was clearing from the hillside's collapse. The dwarf hadn't charged me for the stones, but transporting them had been a different matter. The boons he'd given me had cleared all debts, and we were beginning anew. Though it lightened my purse to have them lugged upriver on the Queen Henrietta, it was a price I was willing to pay.

I'd never sculpted stone before, unless one counted the simple practice exercises Mistress Julia had put me through. I lay myself down beside one and delved once more within it. It was similar to work I'd done on topiary bushes. A skilled gardener I'd known in Meadowfork once taught me that the shapes he imparted to the hedgerows were already present. He merely removed the extra bits to reveal them.

Why then was it proving so difficult to shape these as I desired? The fountain at the conclave featured a trio of mermaids atop a great shell. It was sculpted from a single piece by a geomancer just like me. Granted, it was his masterwork. But it proved such a thing was possible. I had a similar theme in mind. I think it was only inspiration that I lacked.

Then came a stirring, not from my mind but from within my heart. I envisioned what I wanted, and a fuzzy outline formed. The arms should be raised above her head, and her hands positioned to hold her burden aloft. Add a bit more bend to the elbows. Add a bit more spread to her wings. One foot resting squarely on the ground. The other resting atop a stone. This would cause her long flowing gown to fold thusly where it draped over her knee...

"I've another load ready, Lucas," came the shout from without. "This one's all muck and silt."

Who was Lucas? Oh. Me. I stood to my feet as the vision faded and hustled back to the well.

"I'm up to my ankles in muck down here, and the water's risen to my knees."

"Hold on, Aaron. I'll see what I can do."

Now that Aaron was below the water table, I knew the hole would keep filling up. That was the whole point of a well, after all. Fortunately, this wouldn't happen all at once. The water would seep in relentlessly from the surrounding soil. But we (and by that, I meant Aaron) could keep digging if we (see previous clarification) could only stay ahead of it.

It was time to incentivize the secondary crew. After hauling the boxy platform up once again, I scattered its contents using my gift. Gobs of silty muck were hurled to splatter as far away as I could toss them. Then I sent the spotless platform back to my unenthusiastic excavator.

"Oy! Enoch!" I hollered.

I knew the children had been watching me. They hovered nearly out of sight to see what the mad sorcerer was up to. I was certain my recent round of flinging muck about hadn't gone unnoticed. Soon the boy in question stood forth along with several others, Toby among them.

"Sumpthin' you need, Journeyman?"

"Come over here, sprat. I've a job for you."

The boy warily approached. I indicated some buckets I had neatly stacked nearby. Several coils of rope lay there beside them.

"Round up a crew and start drawing up water from the well. I'll pay you a farthing for each full bucket you bail out of it. As he presently works for me, Toby will keep the tally. He'll decide how much each of you has earned. Is this acceptable?"

As expected, they eagerly hove to.

Suffice it to say that by day's end, the hole was dug to my satisfaction. I kept to my multifarious pursuits while my soggy spelunker completed his task and reemerged at last. My damp digger in the dark had ambled off as an arid idler again.

As to the statues, I had one firmly in mind. Some larger chunks had already fallen away. Alone once more, I pondered it. It lay there, roughly man-shaped and ready for the final mystical refinement. But I was weary. The wakefulness spell I'd learned as an apprentice restored my body's energy. But I sensed a deeper depletion of my soul.

Well, I'd pushed through worse before.

The masters of the guild would arrive tomorrow, and I needed something wonderful to show them. As with all such endeavors I attempted, I would try my best.

Digging deep (as it were), I lay down once more and released a calming breath. As the last of the sun's rays caressed the scene, I envisioned the most beautiful face I could imagine. The wings must have feathers. The feathers must each have barbs radiating out from their shafts. The face must bear a beatific smile. Each fold of the garment should flow like cloth. Each finger should be well-defined, with nails and natural lines. She happily bears her burden. From within her, goodness shines.

In an explosion of dust and splintery shards, the final vision was realized.

My eyes snapped open, and I sat up beside her with a burst of heartfelt satisfaction. Made solid, she was even more beautiful than I had envisioned. From her curving lines, the shadows fell, accentuating each gentle roll of her robe. But when I beheld the face, my heart near leapt from my chest. It was the Lady Megan staring sightlessly into the darkening sky. A perfect replica. And the stone somehow managed to convey a warmth that only love could stir.

Had I unconsciously wrought her image while contemplating angelic bliss? And speaking of unconscious, where was Rockytop during all of this? I sought my inner hill. There he was, smiling up at me.

"I didn't speak, my brother, because I didn't need to. We were fused together for a time. It is a skill few journeymen can manage, and a step toward mastery. Artistry like we have wrought is the product of both the conscious and unconscious mind. Logical calculation must blend with deep feeling and unspoken desires."

"Here and I'd thought you were just taking a holiday."

I looked over at the second slab and shuddered.

"I don't know if I've got another one in me, Rockytop."

"Nonsense, brother. Now that we've done it once, we can simply reverse the pattern for the other side."

I was relieved to hear this, but it felt wrong somehow. The two angels shouldn't be identical. It would diminish them both. It was then I felt the furtive footfalls approaching. Turning, I spied Toby walking out toward where I sat. He was straining his eyes in the failing light.

"Oy! Master Harper. Are you out here still?"

I withdrew the lantern from my pack and lit it. And as Toby continued to amble my way, I marked the lad held a tray. On reaching me, he nearly dropped it. He was staring slack-jawed at my latest creation, and his words failed him for a time.

"Did you make that?" he finally asked.

I smiled and nodded wearily.

"I've heard tell of angels, master, but you'd best be careful with her. The real ones are gonna be jealous of that one."

"What's on the tray?" I asked.

"Oh. Yeah. My mum and dad and the others are all sittin' round the fire, tellin' stories and jokes and such. Then ma got to fretting over how you hadn't eaten today. Leastways, we didn't think so. So she sent me out to bring you this."

On the tray were some hard bread and cheese, a wrinkly apple and a mug of hot tea. Knowing Nora, this was the very finest she had to give. I had some better food in my pack, but nothing to match the warmth I felt when munching that old apple.

And in a flash, I had my answer. I set the tray aside. Toby stared in fascination as I scooted over to the other slab. Rockytop went silent. Alright, I thought. No sense reinventing the catapult. I produced the same image I had wrought upon its twin, then reversed it as my homunculus had suggested. Now thicken it a bit and shorten the hair. And now came the more demanding part. I grappled with my weariness as I reached yet again for my elusive art. The face. It would be completely different, but just as loving and caring, Like she wanted to hug you close and enfold you with her wings. Her eyes shine with pride and she bears her burden uncomplaining. She's all but crying tears of mirth.

I felt the mighty release as my vision was once again made manifest.

Covered in dust and splinters of stone, I sat up quickly to survey her. Toby turned and ran from me, stumbling toward the camp.

"Ma!" he cried. "Come see. Come see. You'll never believe what my master done made!"

I now had my two gin poles in the form of stone angels. They would stand to either side of the wellhead, holding up the headframe winch. Their outspread wings would also help support the well cover. The first one was Megan, staring adoringly like a lover. The second was Nora Moss, offering the love of a mother. I would definitely drink from *that* well.

***

Ouch!

I awoke beneath a warm blanket to a jabbing pain in my side. I'd been dreaming two angels had come to take my soul. 'One to watch and one to pray...' - *ouch!*

"I'm sorry, Master, but you told me not to let you sleep past first light."

"Toby?" I croaked.

"Yes, master?"

"By my authority as lord of this blanket, I do hereby release thee from thy obligations and dismiss thee from my service forthwith."

"Here now, master. I know you don't *mean* that. I'm only wakin' ya cause you *told* me to."

I peered out through slitted eyes. I was lying on the hard ground covered by an old horse blanket with my head propped up on my rolled up surcoat. The sun had yet to mount the sky, but the morning birds were chirping. How long had I slept? Several hours at least, but it felt like mere minutes. I silently chanted 'manent vigilate,' my wakefulness spell. This cleared the cobwebs from my head somewhat. But these were soon replaced by a dull, throbbing ache.

The city gates will open at the dawn bell, and the guild masters will arrive soon thereafter. It had taken nearly all night to fashion the wellhead once I'd knocked down the remnant of the prior one. I had painstakingly carved and laid course after course of masonry. Each block was fitted so closely to its neighbors that hardly any mortar was required. Rather than laying simple courses, these were arranged in a complex zig-zag pattern which fit together like a puzzle. They interlocked with and buttressed my stone angels, who stood embedded into either side. Their upraised hands were ready to accept the headframe winch.

"You're right, Toby. Please pardon your grumpy old master."

I threw off the blanket, heaved myself up, and staggered toward the well. From its rim stared Megan, her eyes beckoning me thither. I walked over to stand beside her comforting presence. Bending down, I gripped the rope and began hauling up the bucket. Toby rushed over to help, taking up the slack and winding it into a neat coil behind me.

Last night, I scattered several handfuls of lime dust into the well to purify it. We'd soon see how much of the silt had settled. When the bucket arrived, the results proved disappointing. It held a murky yellowish-brown liquid with a bit of a milky-white cast. I knew it would eventually settle, and the water would run clear, but I had hoped for a more immediate cleansing.

Ah. 'Well.'

Perhaps the few hours of sleep I'd snatched had replenished my magic enough to hasten the process along. I was no water mage, but Sholeena had taught me a useful spell that should do the trick.

"Aquam claram!" I howled down the shaft, giving it all I had.

To my mage sight, it looked as though a stream of foggy vapors issued from my hands to drift lazily downward. I waited a few minutes, then emptied the bucket and drew it up again.

Ha! Got it in one! The bucket came up filled with cool, clear, sweet-tasting aqua pura.

The radiant sun peeked above the horizon. And from the distant steeple rang the tolling of the dawn. Something was missing. Something I had meant to do. What was it? Oh, yes. The name! It had come to me in an epiphany just before sleep had overcome me. I'll do it in the morning; I had thought. It had seemed a brilliant plan at the time. But now here I stood with time running out and all of my magic spent.

"Alms! Alms!" I heard as the wagon went clattering past.

And in the distance, I spied a group of men on foot emerging from the gate. Doubtless, they were my fellow guildsmen, come to critique my work.

I felt empty. I suspected it would be a long time ere I could engage in such artistry again. Not only did it rapidly use up my magic, but it left me feeling hollow inside and greatly slowed the rate at which I recovered. I had only one more card to play.

I withdrew my wand. I hadn't used it much since my verdumancy had been stripped away. I could barely freshen a wilted bloom with the power I wielded today. But once upon a time, it had allowed me to siphon energy from plants. Imbued as it was with fairy magic, perhaps my wand would allow me to do so again. My verdant field had been lost. But alongside Rockytop, I had since developed a window-garden-sized plot, a small remnant of what once was. I called it my vestigial verdumancy. I opened a conduit from this to my depleted inner hill.

I invoked the wand, surprised that I still remembered how to do it, and sent a root-like tendril plunging into the ground before me. There was a tingle; then a trickle. It was working. It *was*. All too slowly, my earth power was filling, just as water seeped into a well. Meanwhile, the plant life all around me wilted and withered as I drank my fill. It couldn't be helped.

I saw Toby flapping my surcoat about, to shake off the mud and stone dust.

"Hurry, master, they're practically here!"

What I had now would have to suffice. Staring at the wall of the well head in the spot between its angels, I engraved a single word. 'REFUGE,' it read.

Then I turned to greet the approaching men just as Toby thrust my surcoat into my hands. Where the devil had my boots gotten, anyway?

"Hello apprentice," said Master Bennet from the head of the imposing gathering of masters.

He looked me up and down with a critical eye as I hastily tugged my doublet straighter.

"Forgive my appearance, master," said I. "I was lost within my work."

It was the unvarnished truth and no excuse.

"What's to forgive? A mason *should* look like that after a hard day on the job. You do your guild proud with the sweat of your brow. We're no namby-pamby nobles with our noses stuck up in the air. We masons ain't afraid to get our hands dirty; say I."

"So say we all!"

This time I remembered to join in on cue, and smiles were exchanged all around.

"Now, to the serious business of evaluatin' your work. Is that the piece just behind you?"

"It is."

"Care to tell us about it?"

"I prefer to let it speak for itself."

There was a murmur of approval among the masons. Score one for Lucas; I thought.

"Good man," said the guildmaster. "No one likes a Chatty Charlie. Get on with your inspection, men, while I question my apprentice."

To me he said, "I mark you laid out the wellhead stones in a herringbone pattern. What made you choose that?"

"Um. I didn't know it had a name. I first saw such a pattern on a cobblestone walkway at Conclave and marked it was rather striking."

The guildmaster chewed his lip and shook his head disapprovingly.

"You should always consider function first and visual impact second. I'm docking you a point for that."

"Well, they do lock together rather neatly, reinforcing one another when laid in that V-shape. They firmly lock the angels in place."

"Too late. Let's go see these angels of yours."

The other men were all clustered around the statues. When Master Bennet rounded the well and sighted Megan, he drew up short.

"By the rood!" he exclaimed. "This one sings to my very soul."

He moved around to the Nora side.

"As does this one, but on a different note. I never knew granite could stir such feelings."

When he looked at me, I saw wonder in his eyes, and from it knew the girls had made my case.

"We need to confer on this at once! I call the guild council to order. Lucas, go and stand over there out of ear shot. You ain't privy to our dealings just yet."

"Yes, master," I replied.

Toby came sidling up beside me.

"Journeyman?"

"Yes Toby?"

"If he's *your* master, and you're *my* master, what should I *call* him? Is he my *grand*-master?"

"No, Toby. That's something else entirely. You are to call him Guildmaster Bennet."

I welcomed the distraction because the overlong conference was gnawing at my nerves. They seemed to be splitting into two groups and arguing about something. Assuredly I had passed; hadn't I? The conference finally broke up, and Guildmaster Bennet waved me over. He was smiling - so there was *that*.

"Welcome to the outer circle, Journeyman Harper. I'm certain you'll be making some fine contributions to our distinguished guild."

At this, he pinned a small silver brooch to my mud-stained doublet while the other men all chanted:

All hail the Journeyman, wise and skilled!

Working hard to be a credit to his guild.

Trowels the mortar. Sculpts the stone.

Working toward a mastery of his own.

Sigh. Cheerful though they were, I dreaded having to learn all these chants. I hope they had a book or something.

It was then that Master Bennet pulled me quietly aside.

"Perhaps it is time we discussed your apprenticeship fee, Lucas."

What?

"What's an apprenticeship fee, master?"

"Well, I should have collected it up front, but with you bein' friends with the prince and all, I figured you were good for it. It's the fee a new apprentice pays his master for all the time and training. It varies from master to master, but as a highly sought-after fellow, I generally charge two gold crowns."

"But I apprenticed under you for barely three days. I took up none of your time and received no training whatsoever."

"Aye. But it's the principle of the thing; don't you know? If I give you a free ride, then what's to stop my next apprentice from calling me out and getting all sullen-like?"

"Simply tell them you'll waive the fee if they can advance to journeyman status in less than a week."

"You drive a hard bargain, lad, but rules are rules. If you want to keep your pin, you'll settle up your apprentice fee. I'll make it easy on you and lower my fee to one gold crown. Split the difference; half is fair."

I thought half was still *unfair*. It was more than what I made in a fortnight. But it was likely true that other families had to save up, hoping to apprentice their eager young lads to a skilled master. So, to keep the peace, I nodded.

"Good then. Next, let's discuss your journeyman's dues."

What?

"To share in the guild's many benefits," he continued, "each journeyman contributes two shillings a month, payable upfront."

That was nearly a quarter of my stipend.

"But you know I'll be leaving here after the coronation later this very month. What *then?*"

"Well, you can quit the guild at any time, but don't think you can just come waltzing back in after such an insult. Perhaps you might start a new chapter at this conclave of yours; be its charter member. We can discuss it later."

How did I ever get mixed up in this mess? Again I nodded.

"Is that all?"

"You are, of course, aware there's a journeyman's tax of one in ten on any stonework you engage in?"

At least that wouldn't be a problem. Up until now, I'd only offered my services for free. And I didn't intend to be making my living as a stonemason, after all.

"Of course," I replied.

"One more thing."

What *now?*

"Would you care to make a donation to the guild beneficence fund? The beneficence fund helps out when a member gets laid up and is unable to work for a time. You'll have the satisfaction of knowing your brother masons and their families are well looked after."

"I'll think about it."

"You do that. I'm not sensing your community spirit here, Lucas. Well, I guess it's time we broke up this little shin-dig. You've got sixteen tons of granite blocks to mark, after all. You'd best get right at it, lad. We won't place no stone without no maker's mark."

Though by this point, I lacked the focus to work through the quadruple negative, I got the general gist. Feeling lightheaded, I stepped in a daze toward the gates. Sleep would have to wait. So far, I wasn't seeing many upsides. I now knew what Bennet had meant about the 'fine contributions' I'd be making to the guild. But at least I'd gotten something I wanted out of it too.

With a free source of clean water, sanitation at the refugee camp would improve. And I'd spoken to Aaron and his fellow conscripts about erecting a few permanent structures using the stones and remaining mortar. What would come of it? Who could say? But I liked leaving things a little better than I found them.

"Wait, master!" shouted Tobias, running up and proffering me my boots.

An Interlude at Sea

Raising up and lowering the net to satisfy my hunger had become a daily ritual; it had. It was a peculiar sort of fishing practiced only by me. I dubbed it 'catch and release.' For nearly a week, I bobbed there on the water before they snapped at the bait. The captain's corpse I rode within was, by then, in a terrible state. Even his own mother wouldn't recognize him now. His distended, bloated belly had all but burst my belt. I kept it buckled tight to prevent my innards from oozing out, at least no more than they already had.

So when I spied sails and a black flag approached, I greeted the sight with relief. I looked forward to a fitter corpse and a more seaworthy craft. She was a galleon measuring perhaps sixty feet from upcurved bow to stern. Her square sails hanging from three great masts caught the wind to move her. Her oars weren't even in play.

Lined up along the railing were dozens of well-armed men. I beheld bowmen among them, but no volley issued forth. They were saving their arrows, for what resistance could a tiny fishing skiff mount? They'd count on sheer intimidation to board me and have a look about. The treasures I had might surprise them, not that they'd take them from me.

On closer approach, the pirates hurled grapnels, and still I made no move to resist them. I *welcomed* a boarding party of these ignoble men. I merely smiled and waited as they swiftly reeled me in. As the first of the men swung over on ropes and landed on my deck, they seemed startled I wasn't cowering or begging for my life. I didn't beg for life. I took it as my due.

"You there!" said the swarthy man, approaching with his cutlass drawn. "Lie on the deck face down or I'll carve you a necklace of blood."

How very colorful; I thought. It sparked the imagination. It was a pity I couldn't answer him in kind. For my tongue had swollen and begun already to protrude. No intelligible speech could I utter. I'd have to bargain with them in the language that such men understood. I brandished my dagger menacingly, and the pirate's eyes widened with startlement.

They say if a shark comes after you, you should swim straight at it. It may be your only chance. Within its tiny mind, this might stir a note of caution. Quite often, it will veer away because prey simply didn't behave that way. Unlike a shark this uninvited guest of mine considered his odds to be greater than they were. He began laughing and came at me, a decision he'd soon regret.

The outcome was predictable up to a point. My dagger was easily brushed aside and the cutlass laid me open wide. But even as my putrescent guts spilled out upon the deck, I offered the man a ghastly smile. With the small hidden knife in my other hand, I had made a cut on his forearm; I had. Just a prick, but that was all it needed.

I slid to the deck to lay among my own entrails, struggling to retain control of my eviscerated host. In truth, the pirate had gutted me like a fish. Still I watched as my would-be murderer swooned. Two of his mates ran over to check on him. Good. The poison was acting swiftly, and he was soon foaming at the mouth. Pain racked the man for several minutes more. He was a hardy one; he was.

And then it happened.

When he finally gave up the ghost, I felt that thrill of exhilaration, the one for which I longed. I fled my prior host and entered the still-warm corpse I craved. My magic center sang and thrummed from the influx of life on which I'd supped. I took up my cutlass and leapt to my feet, running the surprised helpers through. The hunters had become the hunted, and I watched them bleeding out with glee. Before long, I'd have two more spares, and nothing could now stop *me*.

CHAPTER FOUR

The Debutante

"It's tough to make predictions, especially about the future."

~ Yogi Berra ~

"Cheapside?" remarked the archer, his sardonic smile stretching wide.

"Well, the prince offered to put us up in the palace," said Toby, "but my master and I had some work to finish up here first."

As Taylor began to suspect this was no jest, his grin of amusement sputtered out like an oil lamp burning the last dregs of its fuel.

"You're serious!" he softly exclaimed.

His brow lowered in puzzlement at my curt nod of confirmation, and the scar below his right eye reddened.

I savored a rare bit of meat that accompanied today's fare. The smell of sausage wafting about the common room had summoned a crowd that filled all vacant stools. The sizzle from the kitchen beyond served as a backdrop to the clatter of cutlery and the soft chatter of the contented diners. Rubbing at his chin, the archer continued in a low tone.

"As I was saying, the baron sent me to collect you. I admit to some surprise at first learning your whereabouts. According to the beggar's guild, 'Lucas the Just' has been carving a path of devastation all across Fairglen. And you're chums with the prince now?"

"They's thick as thieves; doubt me not," Toby put in earnestly around a mouthful.

At this, the archer laughed and slapped at his thigh, causing the breakfast crowd to turn our way. They'd been shooting us surreptitious glances ever since Taylor had entered. But his outburst gave them an excuse to drop all pretense.

"Wait," I said. "The beggars have a guild? How on earth do they collect dues?"

"In the usual way, I suppose," Taylor replied. "While it's true that beggars solicit alms on the street, their main source of income is selling information to the city's more affluent. They're always on the lookout for some tasty tidbit they might parlay into an actual meal."

More spies, I thought. I would never look at a beggar quite the same way again. Still, I suppose one has to make the most of what one's given in life.

"Are you going to eat that?" asked Taylor, reaching for Toby's sugar bun.

This nearly earned the astonished archer a fork in the hand as the pastry in question rapidly vanished into my servant's knapsack.

"Watch yourself, runt!"

I suppressed a snigger as I finished my own sweet roll, chewed and swallowed.

"I'll thank you not to disparage my servant, Goodman, nor to deprive him of his cherished sustenance. Let me settle up with the innkeeper, and we'll be ready to go."

"Well, hurry up. If I don't return you soon, there's a certain young lady who'll birch my buttocks - and not in the good way. She's been frantic enough over our late arrival."

"Frantic? Megan?"

"Well, nothing ever cracks that veneer of calm she manages to maintain. But the baron felt it. He told me he had to stifle a wince whenever their eyes met. And her frequent questions about our progress made for a most unsettling ride through the countryside. It's no secret she'd prefer more time to adequately prepare for her debut."

The prince had also mentioned something of the sort. I wondered what could be so pressing as to upset even *Megan*.

"What delayed you, anyway?"

Taylor scowled.

"State secret," he muttered.

"*Fine*," I acquiesced, sliding my chair back. "Toby, go make sure we've gotten everything out of our room."

With that, I headed for the barman's station to settle up with Cliff.

Through the window, I spied the carriage resting just outside. In the bright morning light, its fixtures gleamed and the wheels and cab were spotless under a fresh coat of paint. I could scarcely believe it was the same vehicle that had conveyed Royland, Taylor and me halfway to Conclave. It had obviously been refitted and gussied up to impress the gentry of the capital. It was good of his lordship to send his beloved coach to 'retrieve' me yet again.

Toby and I, with our things all packed, were ready to depart. And a grin tugged at the corners of my mouth at the thought of renewing old acquaintances from home - one in particular.

"You're certainly looking chipper today, mister Harper," said Cliff at my approach. "Going uptown again, are we?"

"Yep. This time, however, it's for good; I'm afraid."

He polished at a glass he'd just rinsed out and sighed. The light from the other glasses sent a playful myriad of colored specs bobbing about on the man's apron. It reminded me of Royland's magic.

"Bigger and better things, eh? Well, if you get tired of them nobles and their toadies, you come right back here and we'll put you up."

"The room's cleared out. I know there's still a couple nights left on the week..."

"I suppose I could refund you a groat."

"No. Keep it," I said quickly. "I simply meant it's free for you to let out again. And tell that wife of yours breakfast was smashing."

"Alrighty then. Gonna miss your mug around here. Give our regards to Broadway."

Taylor climbed up to the driver's bench and we were soon bumping along the bustling boulevard. Toby and I sat within. The not-so-fresh city air tousled my hair as it flew in through open windows. The ride was just as smooth as I recalled. Javier had fitted the baron's carriage with an experimental set of springs where it attached to the axle casings. This absorbed the buffeting that might otherwise have been inflicted upon our dainty derrières.

"This is better than the prince's carriage, master!" Toby exclaimed. "You can see all the sights from up here."

And what sights they were. We passed what I suspected was a bordello on XXX street. Painted ladies waved at us from its upper balcony.

After passing out of that unseemly district, we spied another group of ladies emerging from a salon. They were dressed to the nines in what I assumed was the current fashion. Each sported long white gloves and held lacy parasols to shade them from the morning sun. Their flowing gowns complimented their slender figures, and tight bodices emphasized... well... emphasized.

I turned to Tobias, who was watching them like an owl.

"All the maidens seem most fair, on Broadway," I remarked.

"It makes me glum to mark their attributes," he began in an odd rhythm.

"'Cause how d'you find a maiden willing, when you've not got a single shilling?"

"...Nor coin enough to even shine your boots."

"Where'd you *get* such a notion, Tobias?" I scolded. "You're *far* too young to be having thoughts about willing maidens. And I can certainly obtain the services of a bootblack, should such a need arise."

"It's just something a man was singing back at the camp, master. He wants to be a bard."

"Well, stay *away* from *that* man, Toby. What's his name?"

"I dunno. He's moved on already. Just some drifter..."

***

Well past Cathedral Square, our coach had turned onto a long stone-lined entrance to its manor house. It was just off XCV Avenue. This close to the High Quarter, estates were typically owned by the low nobility or, perhaps, by a pretentious, wealthy merchant. Taylor had told me that the Arensons had been invited to stay here by his lordship, Count Edmund Camburn, an old family friend.

From across the room, her wide-eyed gaze drew me straight in. Megan was seated in the lavish sunroom of the Camburn estate. Behind her stood Lynette, fussing with my lady's hair. Those long black tresses shone with the reflected light of the high chandelier. I was grinning ear to ear as the herald who'd greeted us at the door announced our presence.

Megan stood.

"Thank you, Beaumont," she said with a nod of dismissal.

She cast an assessing glance my way as the man withdrew before gracing me with a smile of her own.

"You came," she remarked unnecessarily. "Not that I ever doubted you, but I understand mages are subject to the whims of their masters."

Relief was evident on the girl's face. Mischief danced in her eyes as she extended her hand toward me. My cheeks reddened as I took it gently between my thumb and forefinger, inclining my head respectfully.

Megan was no longer the girl of fourteen I'd once known. The baron's daughter had blossomed into a rare beauty fully come into her womanhood. I could scarcely reconcile her current appearance with the more juvenile version I'd held in my heart for these past several years.

"Who's this then?" asked Lynette, indicating Toby.

Megan's petite handmaiden had stepped between us, quite ruining the mood.

"Ah..." I replied intelligently. "Just a little starfish I picked up from the beach.

Lynette looked confused, but Megan grinned impishly. It was she who had told me the story originally.

"You've taken on a servant?" inquired Megan.

"Yes. This is my servant, Tobias Antonio Moss. Toby, allow me to present Lady Megan Arenson and her companion, Lynette Powel of Somerset."

"That's quite a mouthful, I daresay," observed Megan. "I believe the king's page is named Toby. To avoid confusion, I think it best we refer to you simply as 'Tam.'"

"That's me," the boy muttered. "Too poor to own even my own name."

"Cheer up, Tam," I said laughingly. "And show our lady more respect. So where's Constance?"

Megan pouted.

"Father allowed me only one companion on this trip. It nearly broke my heart to choose, but Lynette's skills will assuredly be needed. Constance is, at present, vacationing at her father's estate and consoling herself among her beloved equines there."

"Worse still," Lynette groused. "His lordship allowed us only one trunk each in which to pack essentials. You try stuffing ballgowns into a single coffer among all your other necessities. It will shame my lady to wear the same gown on more than one occasion. All to make room for that accursed --"

"Ahem."

Megan was giving Lynette a sharp look and scolding her with her eyes. Megan's eyes could do that. I wish I didn't know personally how it felt to be on the receiving end. Following the awkward exchange, Megan indicated Toby again.

"So I take it," she said, "this is your attempt at dressing Tam properly?"

"Well, I just sort of lent him a few things," I murmured. "I was waiting for your advice on the matter."

"Naturally," she sighed. "And I would deem it for the best if time weren't so pressing. What have you been doing here while we were delayed?"

"This and that." I responded cagily.

"Men are useless," she remarked.

The way she said it belied the harshness of the words, and the glint of amusement in her eyes softened them even further. I tried for a change of topic.

"Speaking of men, when do you expect them back?"

On greeting us at the door, Beaumont had informed me Baron Westarbor and the two lances that accompanied him had joined the count on a hunt. Only the ladies and the servants of the manor remained.

"They set out early and shan't likely return until this evening. They were invited by Lord Stapleton and will be feasting in his hall afterward. However, we can't afford to wait for them. Time is too precious. You and I have an appointment at Sir Arthur's ballroom. While we're occupied there, Lynette can sort out your servant's attire."

"Why are we going to a ballroom?" I asked.

For the first time, Megan looked irritated.

"This is my debut, Lucas. Were you not aware we are to perform an inaugural dance for the event? You *can* dance; *can't* you?"

I cast my gaze down at the sunroom's polished floorboards and scuffed my toe upon one.

"Well, sort of."

"That response lacks confidence. I repeat: men are useless."

This time, I feared she might mean it.

"Don't worry, Lucas," said Lynette in a rare moment of charity. "Look who you'll be escorting. All eyes will be on her. And I will gladly take Tam here on a little shopping trip. About ten shillings ought to suffice for an initial wardrobe."

She held out her hand, palm up.

"So much?" I asked.

"Of course," put in Megan. "Just wait until we start in on *you*. Courtly attire for a person of your rank will require a much greater outlay, not to mention the makeover you so *desperately* need. That ponytail is *most* unflattering."

My poor purse, I thought. No. My soon-to-be poor purse, I hastily revised as I counted out the coins.

***

There was an acrid scent in the air as we strolled down the windswept lane. Despite its bright beginnings, the day had grown overcast. Gripping my arm, Megan began tugging at me, obviously eager to arrive ere the skies opened up. I picked up my pace a bit, but held us to a dignified stride. Castle House was just ahead, and its portico looked to be a welcoming shelter from the downpour to come.

Sooner than I expected, I felt a drop. It struck me on the cheek just as Megan glared over with impatience.

I merely grinned and waggled my eyebrows.

I had slogged through many a drencher in my day, but for once I was prepared. My first master had been a water mage, after all. I'd seen him amble through worse, only to emerge as dry as an over-baked biscuit. The trick, I'd discovered, was to walk between the drops.

So, as others about us began scuttling off to find shelter, I sought my magic's source. With a silent intonation of 'inter guttas,' I began deflecting the pestersome bullets from above. We strode on at a regal pace, heedless of the despoiling drizzle.

Megan smiled.

We were soon working our way past a small group that had taken cover beneath the portico and engaging its bell pull. A deep-sounding chime rang out from within.

"May I help you, sir?" said the chap who answered the door.

"Yes," said Megan, taking charge. "We're here for our lesson in the dance."

"Are you expected?" asked the man with a hint of hesitation.

"Yes," Megan repeated. "Our reservation was made months ago. You should find it under the name Westarbor."

"Come ahead then, milady."

The man stepped aside to let us pass. He was a young fellow dressed as a servant, but seemed more dapper than most. The clean cut of his garb flattered a slender physique, and his lush brown hair was combed to perfection. He swiftly closed and latched the door once we'd passed within. This put an abrupt end to the brisk breeze which blew across the tiled entryway floor.

"Ballroom's just this way. Follow me, please."

We followed the young man down a hallway toward an arched set of open double doors. I heard the sound of raised voices from just beyond its threshold.

"... know who I *am?* I am Duchess Farax's *daughter*, for pity's sake, and a baroness in my *own* right. One would think allowances would be made."

"We are aware, your ladyship. The Baroness De Kuttleston, if I'm not mistaken. Nonetheless, the ballroom has been booked and payment accepted. Perhaps we can accommodate her ladyship tomorrow. There's an opening for an hour at one --"

"Unacceptable. I've a dress fitting tomorrow at *LaShalt's*. Mayhap instead, this client of yours would be willing to give up his spot for the leading debutante of the season. We shall ask him when he arrives."

It was into the lull that briefly followed that our young guide chose to thrust his head within and announce us.

"Westarbor's arrived, Sir Arthur. She and her partner are ready for their lesson."

"Show them in, Jonathan," sputtered the middle-aged man the lady had been berating.

He was of average height, with his hair slicked back from a receding hairline. He looked even more dapper than his servant. His loose-fitting clothing was of the finest quality with creases as sharp as knives. Sir Arthur was, without a doubt, a scion of the upper-crust. And there was something energetic about the man.

We stood in a vaulted hall with ceilings so high as to defy a leaping ogre's reach. Despite the overcast sky, the room was well lit. The pale mockery of daylight filtered in through a series of tall, narrow, stained-glass windows. These cast their dim reflections on the highly polished wood of the dance floor. In addition, the chandeliers hanging high above had been lit. There was also the low glow of the candles centered on each table about the periphery.

"Ah," said he, "Would you be the Lady Megan then?"

At her nod, he went on to ask: "And is this fine gentleman to be your dance partner?"

"Yes, good sir, he is Lucas Harper, my escort and protector."

"Hold on for just a moment, Megan dear. I am Lady Katherine de Kuttleston, and this is my escort, Sir Roger Hammerstein of Holbrook. We've come here today to brush up on our *basse danse*. It has a tricky duple meter. I intend using it for my introduction to the peerage this Friday. I'm *certain* you wouldn't mind if I take your slot? I could make it worth your while."

Megan took a moment to size Katherine up. Not so much as a flicker of annoyance showed on her face, and her body language remained relaxed and demure throughout the diatribe. I could only imagine how Megan truly felt about the arrogant woman before us - so great was her control.

Katherine was youthful for a baroness. The title was likely honorary due to her status as daughter to a duchess. She was attractive, as most men reckoned such things. Her flawless skin had likely only rarely seen the sun. And her trim figure was draped in a tailor's rhapsodic fantasy. The elegant gown was beyond description. That said, it was yellow. The man beside her was a knight. His manner of dress and the way he carried himself left no doubt of it. And yet he stood silent.

"Lady Kuttleston," Megan began, lowering her gaze. "It grieves my heart to reject your fine offer, whatever it may be. For I, too, am a debutante slated for the very venue you describe. Long have I awaited my chance to practice under the tutelage of Sir Arthur here. There are no grand ballrooms in the small barony whence I came. Surely, your ladyship won't begrudge me the chance to learn at least the bare essentials so as not to dishonor my homeland?"

"I will reimburse you twice what you paid Sir Arthur to quit your claim. I hear he has another brief opening on the morrow."

"Alas," said Megan, "I expect my protector and I shall need the full afternoon and much of tomorrow to practice. Please surrender the floor, so we may begin our lesson."

This time, Megan put some grit in her response, and if I had a tail, it would now be firmly tucked between my legs. However did she manage to convey such icy malice in that calm, polite voice? I suppose it arose the same way one got to the Silverlight Grand - practice and more practice... Nodding stiffly, Lady Katherine and her knight withdrew. Casting a glance back, she addressed Sir Arthur.

"Have that servant of yours bring us a refreshment. I trust it's not too much to ask that we be allowed to sit here in what passes for comfort until this beastly drizzle subsides?"

"Not at all, your ladyship."

At Arthur's nod, the boy rushed off.

"And rouse the musicians," he hollered after. "Inform them break time is over and Sir Arthur Murray requires their immediate presence!"

Thus began our lesson. At its start, I was somewhat daunted. For her debut, Megan had chosen 'the pavane', a slow and stately dance characterized by elegant and graceful movements. I'd never heard of the thing, but Megan assured me it was all the rage among the younger nobility. In it, couples moved in a formal, measured, and dignified manner around the dance floor. It seemed straightforward enough when Sir Arthur demonstrated, but my feet just couldn't quite get it right.

"Chin up, my boy," admonished the knight (and he meant it literally). "And extend your leading arm somewhat more. Ah, here come our hired vielle players. Overpriced, if you ask me. Too late a night at the tavern, lads?"

And into the room strode a man I knew, followed by two others. I laughed on sighting him.

"Liam!" I exclaimed.

The minstrel looked me up and down for a moment in confusion before responding.

"Lucas?" he queried.

"None other," said I, beckoning him over.

When I'd last seen Liam, he'd been a member of the team of minstrels who traveled about with Master Ross' caravan, the Tomcats.

"Megan, this is Liam Gordon, a fiddler of my acquaintance. Liam, this is the lady Megan Arenson of Westarbor. I think I may have mentioned her."

"Only about a hundred times. I'm truly charmed, milady. Lucas here didn't do you proper justice. Lucas, these here are my mates, the ones I told you about. The fellow on the left is Jules, and on the right there is Renny."

"I thought you three split up," I said.

"We're back together *now*. We were all hired to play at the coronation and what not. We thought it an agreeable time to launch the Fiddlers Three grand reunion tour. Boys, this here is Lucas, the crazy kid who was walkin' through the snow barefooted and bustin' up the ground. Where's that skinny cousin of yours? Is he around here too?"

"No. Royland is back at the conclave. He --"

"Enough," snapped Sir Arthur. "I'm not paying you lot to stand about socializing. Get set up to practice the pavane. The young lady debuts in two days."

I suddenly had an idea. As the musicians tuned up, I explained what I intended to Megan and Sir Arthur. Finding both to be agreeable, I sat and began unlacing my boots.

A few minutes later, I was following Sir Arthur around the dance floor. I placed my feet down precisely where he had trod. The pavane snaked us all around with little flourishes here and there, but eventually concluded before the central chair. It was placed roughly where we thought the king might be seated at the ball. With each step, I chanted 'aurea lux mollis' and called upon my magic. It was exhausting.

Looking back, I was elated to note a trail of glowing footprints. I'd never thought to channel my magic through my feet before, except for that one time Liam had mentioned. The musicians were chatting amiably, pointing and laughing.

"Ingenious," exclaimed Sir Arthur on noting the display. "A pity they'll last for only an hour or so."

"Perhaps not," contended Megan. "Elsewise, you'd have to limit your teaching to this single set of steps."

"I suppose," said the man wistfully. "Perhaps I could lay down a set of... Ah. But let us return to the purpose of your visit. Maestros, strike up the pavane!"

After that, it became a lot easier. Megan was an ideal dance partner, as it turned out. Being an empath, she could sense my intentions instantly, as long as we touched or maintained eye contact. She even followed any mistakes I made, mitigating them and helping to steer me back on course.

About midway through, a dark cloud lifted. When the rain had mostly let up, Lady Katherine and her knight finally departed. By the end of the lesson, we could reliably perform the pavane to Sir Arthur's exacting standards. I felt certain we could give a credible performance on Friday. Moreover, our kindly instructor had remarked favorably on our improved spirits. Megan fed on my joy for the dance; and I on hers. Though I'd been dreading the lesson, I was now somewhat sad to see it end.

***

Soft moonlight filtered down through the gently waving branches above. There was a crisp freshness in the air courtesy of the recent rainfall, and fireflies flitted about. Though the fey mark on the back of my hand remained unlit, I could almost imagine fairies dancing in the idyllic grove behind the Camburn estate.

The men had returned from their hunt as evinced by the occasional bouts of raucous laughter that drifted over from the Stapleton estate. This was home to Sir Charles Stapleton, whom I'd met down in the E.K. escorting the prince. The servants said one could always tell when the hunt returned by the boisterous baying of the hounds. The elder Stapleton, father to Sir Charles, kept extensive kennels. His great gray brutes were half wolf by the look of them. And lord help anyone who wandered onto his grounds uninvited.

I sat beside the Camburn well reflecting on the day. I had a new appreciation for wells, and this one was 'well wrought,' as it were. Though lacking my fanciful additions, the masonry was sound. Instead of simple courses of stone, the wellhead was ringed by seemingly uneven courses which nonetheless resolved into a smooth, level circle at its top. The whole effect was enchantingly natural-looking. I marveled at the precision with which the stones were placed. Some were square or even vertical, but never repetitive and always serving to form a coherent whole.

Life should be like that.

My legs twitched from the unaccustomed strain I'd put them through this afternoon. I had thought I was in good shape, but dancing, it seemed, called on entirely different muscles than one typically used. Probably, I'd have leg cramps throughout the night and some stiffness in the morning. It called to mind my sword drills with Taylor Allen. And it struck me I'd best begin wearing mine again tomorrow. My body would need time to reacquaint itself with this important status symbol should I need to wear it at the upcoming celebrations.

Sigh.

Who built this bloody well, anyway? I knew one way to find out.

"Rockytop?" I whispered.

A soft, grinding rumble ensued. I slowed my breathing and waited. Stone is patient.

"Yes, brother?" came the sleepy reply.

"Do you see any maker's marks on this stonework?"

"Hmm. Let us see..."

Our minds joined, and we delved into the sandstone blocks. It was difficult to see through the gritty stuff, but... ah-ha! There's one. It was a highly stylized letter 'L' that appeared to have a sort of fish hook joined to its back. We had a vague sense we'd seen something like it before, but we couldn't recall exactly when or where. Perhaps the guildsmen would know. I should get *something* for the two shillings I'd shelled out in dues this month.

I was interrupted when soft footfalls approached me from behind. It was all but impossible to sneak up on a geomancer over bare earth.

"Who's there?" I demanded of the night.

"Shh, be quiet!" she hissed.

"Lynette?"

She sat beside me with a package cradled in her arms.

When Megan and I had returned from our lesson, we had found Lynette and a fully outfitted Toby... er 'Tam'. The lad looked adorable in his stylish new attire. But he was somewhat grumpy. Evidently, 'adorable' wasn't the look he was going for, and he chafed at Megan's cooing. *I* think she did it on purpose. When I'd asked Lynette for an accounting, she'd brushed me off. 'Later,' she had said. Now here she was with some mysterious package.

"Do you know what tomorrow is, Lucas?"

"Yes," I affirmed. "It's generally the day following the present one."

She stuck out her bottom lip and blew a wayward strand of her hair upward in exasperation.

"Seriously?"

"I know it's Megan's birthday. Her sixteenth, in fact. Toby and I walked the whole length of Portobello Road, and nothing suitable leaped out at me. I thought I'd take her around and let her pick out something she likes."

"No," said Lynette emphatically. "That's not how it's done. It has to be from you. I *thought* you might let her down, so when I went shopping today I bought these. That's why there's no change. I even had to pitch in a bit myself."

I was touched by this.

"Let me know how much, and I'll cover it. What are they?"

I hadn't ever noticed just how lovely Lynette was. Her star was too often eclipsed by a certain raven-locked beauty we knew. But smiling there in the moonlight she looked captivating indeed. She opened the box and withdrew from it a pair of turn shoes. They were pointed, and the fine leather from which they were made was a shimmering blue exactly matching the color of Megan's eyes.

"She likes shoes," remarked Lynette with a wink.

I wanted to hug the girl, but in this setting, I deemed such an action untoward. So instead, I settled on a mumbled thank you. Lynette could be my personal shopper *any* time. But I sensed from her pursed lips and stiff posture she had aught else on her mind.

"What is it?" I whispered, not bothering to elaborate.

"Lucas..? Be careful with her. I know she seems strong, but there's more going on here than you know."

And on that mysterious note, she stood and padded softly off. I recalled the advice I had once given Toby.

"Get used to it," I muttered.

***

I had made it a habit of always carrying my own bob. But when we set out, Megan assured me that was more *properly* a task for a servant. A man of my station should walk about unencumbered. Therefore, with many a misgiving, I handed my satchel over to Toby. Despite the immoderate amount of gear I stowed within it and in defiance of physics, my bob didn't weigh very much. I suppose violating such rules was the quintessential essence of magery.

As to my being unencumbered, try explaining that to my sword belt. I had strapped it on this morning, determined to relearn the proper way to move with four pounds of steel hanging from my side. It was a work in progress.

"So, exactly how much will fit in this 'bob' of yours?" asked Megan.

"I'm not entirely certain. I sense there's a limit, but I've yet to test it fully. Already, I need to use a minor locating spell just to retrieve things from among all the clutter."

We were walking up the lane, Megan, Lynette, Toby and I, We'd already passed through the lesser gates and into the high quarter. The exclusive shops and salons bordering Century Avenue served the needs of the upper nobility and even *royal* patrons. I felt out of place, mages being unofficially ranked as lower nobility. But as a baron's daughter, Megan was within her rights (albeit barely) to tread these noble lanes. And we others had the good fortune to be part of her retinue.

"You say there's no air within," continued Megan, perplexed. "Why then, when you open it, does it not suck in all the air from around itself?"

"I've often wondered about that myself, my lady. The airless void my fellow mage discovered seems to be filled with some sort of aether rather than a true vacuum. The pressure within is about the same as the atmosphere without. Hence, when I open it, I see only the things I've placed within it bobbing about in a stew of mist."

"All that jibber-jabber aside, master," tossed in Tobias, "should I be afraid it might bite me?"

I heard Lynette's laugher from where she too trudged along behind us.

"I think my lady's interest lies in how many dresses might be stuffed inside the thing," she observed.

Megan nodded, her eyes sparkling.

We soon split up agreeing to meet back at an upscale eatery we had spotted near the gate. Megan was headed to a clothier for the final fitting of her new gown, attended by Lynette. While there, she would attempt to find me a suit that matched and obtain for me an afternoon fitting. This was no mean feat during the hectic days leading up to the galas. But I had confidence in my lady's capabilities in dealing with people. Her persuasiveness and persistence were legendary.

Toby and I, meanwhile, would seek out a styling salon. I had learned this was how the aristocracy referred to their barber shops. But it was deemed 'barbarous' to refer to them thus, as though cutting a common man's hair was a lesser occupation entirely. They didn't even advertise using the familiar striped pole to which I was accustomed. We finally found one by its placard. It bore the image of a pair of scissors.

Clean-shaven and with our hair now stylishly groomed, we went to meet Megan for the midday meal. Toby looked quite dapper with his pageboy cut, while I had opted for one they called 'The Bob'. My hair was barely chin length all around and parted down the middle. At least I lacked the ponytail which Megan had so despised. Approaching the restaurant, we spied the ladies out front speaking to a man in a white shirt with a tiny mustache.

"...But the patio is all but empty, good sir. Surely you can offer us seating. There will only be two more joining us."

"I am sorry madame, but without a reservation, this is quite impossible."

"Is aught amiss, my lady?" I asked, ambling up to the dispute.

Megan turned weary eyes my way.

"This gentleman was just explaining to me that seating here is by reservation only."

"Ah," I said, not really understanding the problem. "Then we'd like to make a reservation."

The man smiled. Actually, it more resembled a smirk to my eye.

"Very good, sir. And for what day would you like to reserve a table? Might I suggest next Thursday? We have several openings then."

Just then, a man came bustling out of the doorway. He was groomed impeccably and carried quite a few extra pounds on his well-dressed frame. He leaned in and began whispering urgently to the first man, who soon went scuttling off. He then turned to me and smiled broadly.

"Welcome to the Regal Repast, good sir. I am its Maître d', Monsieur Harding. But you may call me Oliver. And what is you pleasure today?"

"We've come for a midday meal and to soak in your fine ambiance," I returned, catching the spirit. "Could you spare the four of us a table on the patio here?"

"But of course! Will this one suffice?"

I looked over at Megan.

"This will do nicely," she said.

"Very good, Sir Harper. Our special of the day is a wine-soaked and buttered brown trout. Your waiter will arrive tout suite. Happy dining!"

He brought his fingers sharply up to his pursed lips to make a little popping sound, turned, and was gone. I had marked his use of my last name, though we'd not been introduced. Just what was going on here? I puzzled on it as I pulled back Megan's chair. Moments later, the first man reappeared with bread and a crock of butter. After he'd taken our order and hustled back inside, Megan turned suspicious eyes my way.

"Have you come here before?" she inquired.

"No," I replied. "And I find the restaurateurs' abrupt turnabout quite odd.

"The way I figure it," said Toby around a mouthful of bread. "That matador fellow, mister kissy-fingers, was reminding the snooty one that they needed our coin."

Lynette burst out laughing. This caused blotches of red to appear on the pale skin of her neck and cheeks.

"Tam," she said after she'd settled down a bit, "I don't know whether to correct your manners or to submit your application as court jester at the palace."

"Either way," said Megan, "the man did seem to know of you somehow, Lucas. Just what have you been getting up to?"

"Oh... this and that," I replied with nonchalance.

"Perhaps now," I went on to say, "would be a good time for your birthday surprise."

I reached over to where Toby had settled my bob, withdrew the package, and set it before her. When she opened it, her eyes lit up.

"They're gorgeous!" she exclaimed. "Thank you, Lynette!"

What?

"But..." I sputtered.

"Nice try, Lucas," said Megan with a sigh. "There are downsides to my talent to perceive the feelings of others. Not the least of these is my inability to be truly surprised any more - save perhaps by father on occasion. Lucas forgot, and my loyal companion tried to make it right. Nevertheless, the shoes are lovely. 'A' for effort. Thank you both."

And, raising a fluted glass, she upended it and quaffed its contents.

It was then I felt Rockytop come surging up from below. He touched my mind and memories came swirling to the fore.

"Remember now, my brother," he rumbled. "I've kept your secret well. 'Tis time for you to recollect and finally to tell."

I wandered backward down the halls of my mind to several days ago. I'd finished marking all the stone blocks and was informing the prince of my success. In thanks, he offered me a seating at the Silverlight Grand Theater. His family had a balcony box reserved for the entirety of the season which they only used on occasion. They'd all seen the current production already. When accepting, I'd chosen tonight, the evening of Megan's birthday.

But how could I keep such a secret from Megan's keen perception? The answer I'd contrived was as elegant as it was devious. Having a homunculus, I entrusted it to him, burying it deep within my own unconscious mind. In short, I suppose I really *had* forgotten.

"What just happened?" asked Megan, staring over at me sharply.

I smiled.

"It is almost time for your *true* birthday gift, my lady."

She sensed my joy without a doubt. Her eyes went misty, and the impish grin I so loved to elicit was tugging at the corners of her lips.

"Let's conclude our shopping and other business here. We're ready for tomorrow's debut. Tonight, the four of us shall relax and enjoy a night out on the town. I'm told it isn't a proper visit to Fairglen without taking in a show. I've secured admission to a theatrical performance I've heard is all the rage. And they mean that both figuratively *and* literally."

***

The street lanterns had not yet been lit when we passed beneath the glittering marquee. Megan and I made a nice matched set, adorned in our freshly fitted garb. Our group entered the theater to join the dense crowd in the outer lobby. It was just as grand as its name would suggest. Many people stood queued up before the ticket takers, but the ushers weren't seating anyone just yet. Others simply stood about greeting old friends or chatting cheerfully with their family members and colleagues. I sensed anticipation as the hour for the performance drew nigh.

Having no tickets, we moved toward the wall and considered how to proceed. I was scanning the crowd, hoping to find someone to tell us where we should go, when my eyes

112

alighted on a familiar pair. Lady Katherine stood arm in arm with her knight protector, Sir Hammerstein. And the two were looking our way.

"Megan, darling," she said as the two drew near, "I didn't figure you for an enthusiast of the theater, coming as you do from that provincial barony of *yours*."

Her gown was even more flamboyant than the one she'd worn at our previous encounter, and her smile was just as false.

"I heard there might be a truly wicked woman on display here tonight," said Megan suggestively. "I refer to *Medea*, of course."

"Of course. However did you come by tickets, my dear? The Medea's been sold out for ever so long."

"Well, we don't actually have *tickets*," I put in. "We were hoping to speak with an usher..."

At this, the lady's smile broadened and took on a nasty edge.

"Oh, that's just *precious*. By all means, let us summon an usher then, shall we?"

She raised her hand and waved it about to draw attention our way. Soon, a fellow in a dark cloak was making his way toward us. It took me a moment to banish the notion that the 'SGT' on his badge stood for 'sergeant.' More likely, these were simply the initials of the theater.

"Welcome, honored guests, to the Silverlight, where Medea's tragedy unfolds. How may I assist you this eve?"

"We are here by special invitation and were wondering where we should go."

"What's your name, good fellow?"

"Lucas Harper."

"Ah! We've been expecting you. How many in your group?"

"Myself and these three others."

"Follow me sir, your balcony awaits. The royal package includes wine of your choice. Shall I send a bottle up?"

"That would be splendid," said Megan as the usher guided us to a roped-off stairwell nearby.

I glanced back when I realized Toby was missing. He was standing before the baroness, who was looking rather unwell.

"Thank you for your kind assistance, milady," he said, executing a curt little bow.

Sir Hammerstein looked apprehensive, his eyes flitting this way and that.

"*I* taught him that," whispered Lynette, hiding a smile.

Soon we were in the king's royal box, high above the milling throng. Our view of the play would be excellent, and the acoustics were such that we could hear the curtains rustle on the stage below. We sat upon cushioned benches and even had a small table for refreshments and the like. I shared a bench with Megan. Toby and Lynette occupied the bench to our rear. The murmuring crowd below invited and enabled a private discourse.

"However did you do it, Lucas?" my lady asked.

"What? Obtain these seats? Or keep you unaware of their existence? A good magician never reveals his secrets."

After a pause, she remarked: "I suppose I'll have to tickle it out of Tam later."

"My lady had better mean that only figuratively," I said with mock severity.

Megan had an unfair advantage. She'd once told me she herself hadn't been tickled since her fifth birthday due to her talent. As she explained it, you can't tickle *yourself* because you are always expecting it. Try it sometime. It's true enough. Since by touch, Megan experienced the feelings of others, this included expecting and anticipating any touch upon her person. It was a little sad (but fun to think about...)

She turned her blue eyes upon me.

"I'm supposed to be making contacts and forging new alliances for Westarbor. The Arensons have enough enemies. Am I evil for so enjoying Lady Katherine's dismay? She's just so..."

"Annoying? Arrogant? Irksome?"

"Yes. All of those things."

"It would be nice if everyone were a friend, Megan, but some people are just incapable of reciprocating. If the woman acts uncivilly toward you, give yourself the right to dislike her. Treat her fairly, but don't be a doormat."

"It's just..." she began, "sometimes I wish I could heed what my heart is telling me, in spite of what I know is the more rational course. Do you think I should do so?

"I expect we're just about to witness one man's vision of why that might be a bad idea. But your decisions are your own. You have a *kind* heart, my lady. Know that I will support you in whatever it decides."

She lay her hand over mine where it rested on the bench. The warmth of her touch sent a shiver up my arm.

"Thank you," she said. "You make for an adequate confessor."

"Say ten hail Mary's and all will be forgiven. Now hush, the play is starting."

The curtain went up to reveal a woman. She stood before a house with Greek-looking columns. It was an impressive set piece. Thus, she began:

"Pray to whatever gods you know, for I have reached a point where I must dare all or abandon hope of safety..."

The play went on to depict the woman's descent into madness and vengeance and culminated in atrocities I wouldn't wish on even the dark druids. When the final curtain fell, we vigorously applauded the actors for their compelling portrayal of these horrific events. So deeply were they rooted in their roles that Megan claimed she could actually feel a murderous intent radiating up from below. Lynette suggested this might merely have been Lady Katherine glaring back up at us.

It was with a deep sense of regret that we finally relinquished the royal box. As we departed, I spied a fellow I supposed to be a stagehand. He was lurking in the shadows at the hallway's end. Dressed all in black, he wore a decorative mask covering his entire face. It was the mask of Helios, the sun god, who had spirited Medea away at the end of the play. Why was a stagehand haunting the balcony entrance area? Was this part of the show? I had heard that characters from performances sometimes approached wealthy patrons afterward, seeking small donations for a favored charity.

"Excuse me, sirrah! You in the mask!" I challenged, "What business are you about?"

The man stiffened. And before I could take another step, he silently vanished beyond a blackout drape. It could have been my imagination. I'd only caught a glimpse. But when the man had fled, I could have sworn he held a loaded crossbow at the ready. My heart raced, and a shiver ran down my spine as the fine hairs on the back of my neck prickled. I kept my eyes on the spot where the man had disappeared as I directed my companions toward the exit. Thankfully, this lay in quite the opposite direction.

***

We all sat around the long table at the Camburn estate. I had hired one of the horse-drawn carriages lined up at the theater's entrance. The four of us had ridden in style the fifty-three blocks along the well-lighted street before being deposited back here safe and sound. On our arrival, we found the house in an unsettled state. The servants were arrayed in a double row, which formed an aisle from the front doorway to the main banquet hall.

"Happy birthday, Miss Megan," they had all cheered in unison.

The feast that awaited us was attended by Baron Westarbor, Lady Westarbor, and all of their men. I'd finally met Count Camburn and was able to thank him personally for hosting us here. The two lances that had accompanied the baron had been that of his son, Sir Trenton, and that of Sir Nolan.

I knew most of the members of Sir Trenton's lance quite well. His squire, Derrick, was a friend. There was Taylor Allen, of course, and their cook, Connor Dawson. The newest member was Grindal Cain. He'd come into Trenton's service more recently as a replacement for Kyle Digby. Kyle had been slain by a giant spider before my very eyes. I still wished there'd been something I could have done to save him. I remembered Grindal from the several nights I'd spent with the Cain family when the goblins were invading. The boy hadn't spoken much. Some of that was because he'd been a wild boar during most of that time. Still, Sir Trenton assured me the lad's tracking skills were top notch. This was high praise indeed, given the source.

The group had all dined earlier, but stacked up before us lay the elegant porcelain plates from the count's buttery. Beyond them stood a three-tiered cake atop which sixteen candles burned.

I hadn't seen the baron and his men since my arrival. After the hunt, they'd all joined Lord Stapleton for feasting and drinking long into the night. None had yet aroused themselves this morning when Megan and I had again set off. It was good to see their cheerful faces and to recall that earlier time I'd dwelt among them. After Megan had blown out the candles and the cake had been thoroughly vanquished, we settled into companionable discourse. It was then when Grindal approached me.

"Uh... howdy," he said.

"Howdy *yourself*," I returned.

He had the same thickset build most of the Cain men sported. One might even call him 'portly' if one hadn't wrestled with his cousin once upon a time. I recalled eating dirt on that occasion. With his curly brown hair, his resemblance to Gregor was remarkable. Beneath those faded overalls was likely more muscle than one would expect.

"I never did get the chance to thank you, Mister Harper, for breakin' the curse on our clan. We's much obliged. I just wanted you to know that if there's ever a chance to do you a good turn, you can count on a Cain."

With that he promptly shuffled off toward where Trenton and the others sat, for the baron was ringing his glass, preparing to make a toast. As the chatter subsided, we all turned to regard him. He began softly, as if overcome by emotion, and his eyes seemed to stare into the distance.

"Sixteen years ago this day," he began, "Chamille and I were blessed with a second child. From the moment we first beheld her, she became the owner of our hearts. Thus it is, and always should be for a father and mother."

The baron looked lovingly at his wife, who nodded her agreement. A quietude had descended on the guests as all ears strained to hear, and the flickering candlelight reflected from the baron's raised flute. He then continued, and as he did, his voice arose to take on the timbre of conviction.

"But for more than a decade and a half since, she has grown and matured into a lovely young lady of which our family can be rightly proud. Lo, have I watched her and been amazed by her countless acts of charity. By this, she has won over many other hearts. There isn't a man or woman among my subjects who would fail to acknowledge our Megan's goodly graces. All remember her comforting the sick during the siege, and none can forget her leadership at the dovecote!"

"And now she is of marriageable age - every father's nightmare. For many suitors will doubtless swarm to this rare flower who is our daughter. And we shall have to select from among them one who is worthy of her hand. I often wonder if such a person even exists, but I certainly hope he does. And thankfully, I've my knights to deal with the others.

"But life marches on, and we must all find our peace with what is to be. Arise, Megan. Come to your mother and me."

Megan stood and did so.

"Happy birthday, darling child," said her mother, presenting to her a strand of glittering gemstones.

"To Megan!" exclaimed the baron.

"To Megan!" we replied.

Megan smiled and glanced down along the table.

"It's beautiful," said Megan, holding up the necklace.

"Oh. It's just an old strand of topaz my mother used to wear. We thought it would look pretty at your debut."

"Not the necklace," Megan declared. "I meant father's sentiment."

All in the hall joined in laughter at her jest.

All in all, it had been a marvelous day. Much had gone our way. But fate was a fickle mistress. She might even now be planning our undoing. We stayed and chatted for a while but soon begged the forgiveness of the other guests. The hour was late, and we had big things to accomplish on the morrow. So we turned in early to rest up and greet the day refreshed.

***

The royal palace ballroom was grand. There was no other word that could describe it. It made Sir Arthur's studio seem like a quaint little nook by comparison. The dance floor itself was similar in size, but the areas for the audience were much larger. There was even a second tier above, overlooking the dance floor. From the rafters beyond even this, hung a massive iron-wrought chandelier that shone with the light of more than a hundred candles, presently lit. It was spectacular.

We had all arrived early, the debutantes and their escorts, and the empty hall had echoed with our footfalls. We were to receive final instructions about the order of events. There were only three other couples aside from Megan and me. There were Lady Katherine and Sir Hammerstein, whom we'd already had the distinct displeasure of meeting.

Next, there was Lady Nimble, the daughter of a baron from Freemark. Her escort was a tall, muscular fellow she'd introduced only as "Titus." Lady Nimble was dressed in a poofy little pink skirt that revealed a shocking amount of her long, well-muscled calves and thighs. In a sideways nod to modesty, these were covered (barely) by stretchy stockings that ran from her heelless, soft leather shoes all the way up to the hem of her inadequate skirt and beyond. Under a sparkling bodice, she wore no shirt. She sat there, sleeveless, a shocking testament to the state of affairs down in Freemark.

Finally came Lady Felicity MacLaren of Dalriada. I had never seen a female dwarf before. Some doubted they even existed and put forth a theory that the dwarves reproduced by growing their young from underneath their beards. Yet there she sat, alongside her escort, Malcolm Sinclair MacDuff. Lady Felicity had arrived surrounded by a delegation of her kindred, who had traveled here from her homeland in Echo Hills.

Of the seven dwarves who had accompanied her, only her escort had been allowed to join us at our table. On promise of their good behavior, and after securing their war axes with peace knots, the other six were permitted early admittance. It wouldn't do to give insult to their influential thane. They milled about a table near the front of the hall, regretting that no ale was being served yet.

"Under no circumstances are you to approach the king except at the very end of your performance. And then it is to be only the debutante herself. Is this understood?"

We all nodded.

"Do not speak unless the king bids you to do so and keep your responses succinct and to the point. If you have any further questions, you may direct them to the master of ceremonies. He's the fellow in the red sash just over there. The doors will open in about a half hour, and the guests will begin to arrive."

After the man finally finished his wearisome briefing, He left us to our own devices. To break the moody silence, Megan addressed the elephant in the room. Not that the girl was at all rotund - quite the opposite. Lady Nimble was, in fact, rather lanky.

"That's an interesting dress you've chosen, Lady Nimble. Has it some cultural significance among your people?"

The lady had the good grace to blush.

"My father insisted on it. Great freedom of movement is required for the dance I intend. And you may call me Jackie, Lady Megan, is it?"

"Speaking of dresses, my dear," interrupted Lady Katherine, "isn't that the same one I saw you wearing at the theater last night?"

Katherine was draped in yet another elegant gown from her apparently endless collection.

"It is," Megan affirmed. "As it's new, I needed to break it in a bit to make sure the fitting would hold up to the rigors of my debut."

"Speaking of new," Katherine added, "I see you're wearing some new jewelry as well. That must have set your father back at least three pigs and a goat."

Sir Hammerstein frowned at this and stared over at us in silent apology. The knight looked miserable. Perhaps there was still a bit of chivalry in the man. He plainly knew his lady's words strayed far from the code. But then the dwarf spoke up - Lady Felicity's escort, Malcolm.

"My lady here and I are wearin' the traditional tartan of the MacLaren clan."

The dwarf stood, proudly displaying his colors. They were a riot of grayish stripes checkered upon a pale blue field, further separated by thin stripes of yellow and red. I understood the pleated skirt he wore was called a 'kilt' and was deemed appropriate for men. It was akin to but not quite the same as the women's skirt worn by his silent partner.

The dwarven maid seemed retiring and shy. This could be because women were more sheltered in Dwarven society, but I suspected she came by it honestly. Her father, Ewan, was said to be bashful.

Lady Katherine stared at Megan for a bit longer but finally gave up. Megan was ignoring her and staring off in another direction.

"I think I'll go freshen up," she announced. "Sir Roger, go and ask that master of ceremonies fellow where a lady might attend to her necessities."

As the two stalked off, Lady Nimble grinned.

"I hope she gets lost on the way back," she remarked.

"She's awful, isn't she?" Megan agreed.

"A right unpleasant troll, she be," said Felicity, piping up for the first time.

In a voice as smooth as butter and as sweet as honeysuckle, she continued.

"And your dress is lovely, Megan dear. My apologies to the rest of ye. In our clan, we're taught to shun such a one."

So. Not so timid after all, I thought. Megan and Jackie exchanged a sinister look.

"Oooh, let's try it," said Jackie. "I wonder how long 'Lady Katie' can stand to be ignored."

"Eeeaaahh," said Malcolm, stretching and yawning as he resumed his seat. "I'm sleepy. Wake me when the thing starts."

***

As the guests filed in and claimed tables, they were greeted by the herald. I found it odd that such high-born personages weren't being announced. I supposed that among the peerage, everyone knew everyone else. Why wear out the herald's tongue on such frivolous pomp? When the Westarbors arrived, Megan nudged me and pointed them out at a table near the rear. Sir Trenton and Sir Nolan sat on either side of them, attended by their squires. The baron himself was attended by his page, Ronnie Turner, and Lady Westarbor was served by Grindal Cain. I almost failed to recognize him in the elegant attire he now wore.

All the while, the debutantes kept to their plan of excluding Lady Katherine from our discourse. When she would make a comment, the rest of us would simply ignore it and continue our conversation as if she hadn't spoken. When she caught on, she grew quite irate. She turned to her knight and began muttering a stream of invective. The man grimaced and began shaking his head woefully. In a polite voice, he gently reproached her.

"Settle down, my lady, and focus on your task. It matters not that others seek to rile you. Maintain your composure lest the peerage think you mad."

But despite his attempt to calm her, the lady grew apoplectic. Half-rising from her seat, she shrieked back at him.

"I AM NOT MAD! MY SUSPICIONS ARE REAL! EVERY-ONE IS CONSPIRING AGAINST ME!"

A hush descended upon the hall as many of the guests turned to witness the disturbance.

Lady Katherine was suddenly aghast. Realizing her error, she took command of her voice and hissed at us.

"All of you will rue the day you embarrassed the Baroness de Kuttleston."

At this, she turned on her heel and fled the hall, followed by her reluctant knight. Perhaps it had been unwise to goad her so. Who knew the young lady had so little self control? I think we all felt bad about the incident. But what could we do to make amends now?

It was at this time that the herald strode up to the platform before the musicians, bearing a wooden staff. I'd seen its like before. At the conclave, the mages have an enchanted cane called the speaker's staff. At our meetings, it is used to amplify the voice of a speaker. It figured that the king would commission one for his own events.

"Ladies and gentlemen of the peerage," he began in a sonorous voice that filled the hall. "All will now rise to greet the king and his royal retinue! I am honored to present his majesty, King Raymond Osten III, goodly monarch of our realm!"

At this, the musicians struck up a stirring martial melody, and the sovereign in question graced us with his presence. He was accompanied by his wife, two sons, and six members of his royal guard. They filed in to take up seats in the center of the hall, just at the edge of the dance floor. The king looked most regal indeed with his crown and mantle of office. Standing there, I gawked at the spectacle with all the others. After a bit, the king signaled the herald, who made to speak again.

"You may resume your seats."

"His Majesty bids you welcome. We are gathered here tonight to introduce to you some young ladies of the kingdom who have recently come into their majorities. This season's debutantes are four accomplished young women of noble lineage who exemplify the courtly graces to which all should aspire."

Well, three at least, I thought.

"She's the daughter of Baron Nicolás Nimble of Navarra. I present to you Jacquelyn Beatrice Nimble, who'll be performing: 'The Dance of the Sugarplum Fairy!'"

Jackie had already made her way onto the floor. Earlier, we'd drawn lots for the order of our presentation, and Jackie had lost. At least *I* hadn't wanted to go first. As luck would have it, Megan and I were the very last in the program, directly after Lady Katie, if she ever came back.

Jackie stood beside Titus. And though she was rather tall herself, the man seemed to tower over her lanky frame.

The music rose slowly. It was a light and airy melody composed primarily of a harp and some woodwinds at first. These lent an ethereal quality to the rhythm that slowly built upon them. Jackie's arms fluttered upward, and she began striking and holding various graceful poses, demonstrating her strength and flexibility.

Titus didn't do much. He mostly just stood there. Jackie was using him as a platform from which she would lean this way and that. I wished that I had *his* job rather than the more active role Megan intended for *me*. Then the girl began to stroll about the floor on her toes with fluid arm movements and incredible poise. This must be that new style of dance they call ballet. The outfit she wore now made more sense. Whatever it was, she did it well. Her movements matched the music so well that she seemed to be one with it. My heart raced as though I were dancing along with her.

As the music intensified, she began a series of graceful hops and whirling twirls that were quite dazzling to the viewer. At one point, the toe of her foot nearly touched the back of her head, so flexible was she. To watch it, one might think the girl was made of taffy.

But what was this? The lighting on the dance floor suddenly wavered, and a horrible screeching sound was heard from above. I tore my bewildered gaze from the girl to glance up. To my horror, the chandelier was all atilt and threatening to break free of its moorings! With a sudden rattle, it made good on this threat. With a deep hollow boom followed by a myriad of clattering sounds, the massive iron construct came crashing down right in the center of the floor, scattering candles all around. I gasped. The smell of candle wax grew strong even as the room's lighting diminished by half.

Jackie had been directly below when the rope gave way, but to everyone's surprise, the girl leapt aside in the final moment. She tucked into a roll only to spring back up in a defiant, graceful pose. The music had come to a screeching halt. Some in the audience cried out in alarm, and a general muttering arose. But despite all the chaos, a look of determination crossed the girl's face. She stared at the musicians and made a beckoning motion with her hand. My eyes widened with surprise.

After a moment of shock and disbelief, the panicked musicians resumed their piece. Jackie began once again the steps of her interrupted performance. Slowly at first, but with rising confidence, she adapted her routine to account for the wreckage of the chandelier and other obstacles. Her twirling and hopping resumed, adding even more dignity to her dance by overcoming these challenges. When she came upon a candle (many of which were still alight), she would veer around it or sometimes hop over. And all the while, she matched her art to the music. It was hypnotic. I doubted I would have recovered *half* as quickly had I been dealt so wicked a surprise.

As the music neared its final refrain, Jackie pirouetted all the way to the right side of the floor. Then, in a brilliant bit of improvisation, she enacted a swift set of leaps and bounds directly toward her chief impediment. With a final great leap, she cleared the hurdle and was caught by the waiting arms of her massive sidekick.

Titus lifted the girl up onto one brawny shoulder and turned to face the audience. She inclined her head and blew us all a kiss. What poise. What flare! Titus then set her down gently, and the girl made her shaky way over to where the king sat, a look of wonder upon his face. She awaited his ruling.

"Spectacular," said the astonished monarch, handing her a rose.

The ballroom thundered with applause for many minutes afterward. It made me proud even to *witness* such a triumph. When the adulation had finally died down, the herald called for everyone's attention.

"There will be a brief intermission while this mess is tidied up and to assess any danger to the royal family from the unsoundness of this venue. By order of the royal guard, none of you may leave your seats until the danger can be assessed. The ball will resume anon. Until then, we ask for your patience."

As my heartbeat slowed and my thoughts began to clear, I considered all I had just witnessed. Where was Katherine during all of this? Had she not only recently sworn vengeance on the lot of us?

***

By the time the wreckage had been cleared away and the puddles of wax had been scraped from the floor, Lady Katherine and Sir Roger had returned. Apart from a somewhat stiff comportment, the lady was calm and composed withal. This abruptly changed when we were confronted by two members of the royal guard. They wore the black chain mail that marked them as such, and there was no peace knot affixed to their scabbards. Each of the two had the lean, well-muscled build common to their brethren and moved with the fluid ease of a cat.

"It is our understanding," said the leading guardsman, coming to a halt before our table, "that some of you were unaccounted for during the incident."

"I was freshening up," Lady Katherine put forth. "And Roger here was consoling me."

The guardsman focused on her and narrowed his dark eyes.

"Some witnesses claim you exchanged angry words before stalking off in a huff. I must ask you, madam, have you a blade on your person?"

"Just a small knife to defend my virtue in case I am ever accosted," she replied haughtily.

"Let me see this knife."

She produced it. It was a tiny thing cleverly concealed among the pins that held her hair in place.

"Whatever is the meaning of this guardsman...?"

The guardsman glanced toward his silent partner, who nodded.

"You may call me Guardsman Freelander, and this is my associate, Guardsman Lovitt. As to our purpose, it is to assure his majesty's safety and that of the royal heirs. Our investigation has discovered that the rope used to lower the chandelier was cut as if by a blade."

"And you suspect that I may have..."

"Outrageous!" exclaimed Sir Hammerstein.

But before he could rise from his seat, the second guardsman was looming above him with a hand on his shoulder to hold him in place.

"Gentle, sir knight," he said. "Let's not do anything to upset the other guests. Was there anyone else with you who might vouch for your innocence?"

There was a pause.

"*I'll* vouch for them," said Megan.

What?

"You were with them?" asked Lovitt.

"No."

"Then explain, please, miss."

She sighed.

"Perhaps you are aware of the Arenson family talent?"

"We are aware."

"Then believe me when I affirm that Lady Katherine was genuinely shocked to hear you might suspect her of the deed. And Sir Roger is truly indignant about such suspicions. I would know were it otherwise."

Again, the man signaled his partner with a simple nod. And after a moment, Guardsman Freelander spoke again.

"Very well, madam, you are cleared of suspicion. But I'm keeping this," he said, indicating the knife.

And though they left us in peace, Lady Katherine continued to sulk. We tried to draw her out with gentle words of reassurance, but she proved inconsolable.

"They doubt a lady of station. But of course they believe *her* straight away," she said amid other dark mutterings.

Before long, the herald was mounting the stage once more with the speaker's staff in hand.

"We are ready to resume," he announced. "Next up is the daughter of Ewan MacLaren, the distinguished Thane of the Citadel Deep. Lady Felicity will be performing a traditional dance of her people to a tune they call 'If Thou'lt Play Me Fair, Play.'"

By this time, Felicity and Malcom had moved to the center of the dance floor. Another of their kinsmen, Finlay by name, had crossed to the musicians' platform and taken up a strange backpack with a set of horns poking out from its top. He looked to be happy as he strapped it on in front of himself and took a shorter horn between his teeth. The five remaining dwarves at their table all leaned forward expectantly.

When the music began, I didn't know quite what to make of it. It sounded like Finlay was strangling a bunch of cats in his bag, with a live goat thrown in as well. They wailed and blatted out a stuttering introduction. But then, from among this cacophony, I perceived a piping melody of sorts. It had a strange six-count beat that became better emphasized when the drummer joined in.

It was at this point, Lady Felicity and Malcolm began to move. Their legs began stepping to the rhythm of the piece. But whereas Malcolm raised his hands above his head, waved them about, and clapped occasionally, Felicity did not. Instead, she used hers to fan out her skirts to either side and held her arms rigid.

The steps became more varied, lively, and interesting as the song progressed. It was mesmerizing to watch. At first, the two stood side by side, and their steps were identical and synchronized. I felt my own toe tapping out the rhythm in sympathy, and the strange bag didn't sound so screechy anymore. The dwarves at their table had begun clapping their hands and clomping their feet, pausing only to toss down an ale occasionally. They had had an entire keg delivered to their table and were tapping it frequently.

Then Felicity and her partner turned to face one another. As they did, their high steps mirrored each other, still in perfect sync. The joy on their smiling faces was clear as they circled about, at last coming to rest facing us. With a formal bow and a curtsy, they ended the dance. As the audience applauded a job well done, none cheered louder than the dwarves at table one. They whistled and pounded their table until some tankards were upended.

Felicity bowed before the king, who graced her with a single word.

"Delightful," he said as he handed her a rose.

***

I was worried. How were Megan and I ever to match the skills we'd seen on display thus far? I feared our dance might bore the crowd to tears. Sensing my mood, Megan elbowed my ribs playfully.

"Soldier on, Lucas," said Megan, her confidence undeterred. "The pavane is quite popular. It's quiet elegance will make a nice contrast to the more energetic debuts and end the evening on a pleasant, traditional note."

Even now, Lady Katherine and her escort were striding out onto the dance floor. They didn't stop in the middle, however. Instead, they continued on directly up to the stage and were speaking to the herald. He, in turn, was having some last-minute words with the musicians as the couple returned.

"Third up, gentlemen and ladies, we have the daughter of her grace, Lady Cynthia, Duchess of Farax. Please welcome Lady Katherine de Kuttleston and her distinguished escort, who will perform for us the pavane!"

When his words finally registered in my disbelieving brain, it felt as though a spike had been driven into my heart.

"Why that spiteful little minx," murmured Megan with balled fists.

With an effort I could only imagine, she reasserted her control, banishing the color that had arisen on her cheeks. In stoic calm, she watched as her rival enacted the first movement of the dance she had so carefully selected. Much to our chagrin, Katherine and Roger turned out to be very skilled dancers indeed. They strutted around the floor like peacocks, each movement elegant and refined. Their faces were masks of hauteur as they strode about, hand in hand, to the delicate strains of the chamber music.

In truth, the baroness was in her element with this fashionable dance of aristocrats. She was clearly enjoying the dance. And sadly for us, the audience couldn't perceive that her joy was tainted and empowered by malice. They saw only that she was joyful.

I could see the rapt faces of the crowd as they followed the duo's every subtle movement, and smiles abounded when the two executed the clever steps I had learned from Sir Arthur just two days past. What were we to do? We could at best match their performance, but the crowd would certainly grow bored and see it as derivative. Or worse, they could laugh at our pale imitation of the stately procession we were witnessing.

When, all too soon, the infuriating procession neared its end, and the last strains of the music faded, the pair turned to the audience. Smiling sweetly, Lady Katherine gave them a low curtsy on the final note. I began to panic. And though seemingly calm, I knew my lady's mood reflected my own.

Katherine approached the king. He was smiling.

"It's good to see a traditional dance. Well done, my dear."

She grinned at us as she approached the table with her rose.

"You're up," she mocked. "Break a leg, sweetie."

Megan arose. Silently, I offered her my arm. Stepping mechanically toward the floor felt like marching to the gallows, but we persevered. We would strive to do our utmost to uphold the honor of Westarbor.

The herald made his way toward the stage, but ere he could reach it, he was intercepted by Grindal Cain. Their exchange quickly escalated into a heated struggle over the staff. The king's guards rose from their seats, prepared to intervene, but a few whispered words from Prince Henry forestalled their advance.

Having wrestled with a Cain before, I didn't favor the herald's chances of success. True to my expectations, Grindal's stubbornness prevailed, and he triumphantly carried the staff toward where the musicians sat. Murmurs spread among the onlookers as the lad from Westarbor whispered to Liam Gordon and the others. Megan and I stood there, perplexed.

"HELLO FOLKS!" the boy proclaimed. "Lord above, this thing is loud."

Silence greeted his words.

"How're you all feelin' tonight?"

Silence.

"How about them debutantes?"

A smattering of applause.

"Yeah. Give it up."

More applause.

"Have you ever been to a hoedown?"

Confused muttering.

"Well, I bet your tenants have. All across the land, people gather in town squares or cleared-out barns to celebrate the happy times in life. And if you haven't been to one, you're in for a treat tonight. Yeah, boy."

The king's expression turned dubious, as if weighing whether to silence the insolent intruder. I think only Grindal's affiliation with Westarbor had stayed his hand thus far. The boy's blue tabard was plain enough to see. Grindal began tapping his foot to set a beat and speaking more rhythmically.

"It's easy and it's fun. So just sit right back while Megan and Lucas show you how it's done!

What?

To a sudden drumbeat, Liam leapt up with his vielle tucked under his chin, bowing out a lively, high-pitched melody.

Dee-di-di-dee-dee! Daddle-daddle-doo. Dee-di-di-dee-dee! Daddle-daddle-doo.

Jules joined in a lower key.

Daaa-diddle-dum-dum Daaa-diddle-dum-dum Dum-dum-dum-dum Diddle-daddle-do!

When Renny joined in, the music transformed into a complex back-and-forth, a continuous duple meter arrangement very familiar to me. *I'd* been to hoedowns! Every kid in Westarbor had. It was *easy*; you simply followed the caller's instructions and laughed at any mistakes you made.

Frightened but now curious, I began to tap the heel of my boot to the boards of the floor in time to the music's call. Catching my eye, Megan did the same.

"Come on now, let's start right in. Bow to your partner. Let's begin."

I bowed, as did Megan.

"Circle left, then circle right. Bring her in close and hold her tight."

Stepping in time to the music, we circled one another. With her eyes locked with mine, the girl was able to mirror my movements very precisely. Those blue eyes widened when I took her about the waist, placed a hand on the small of her back, and drew her to me.

"Don't be shy. There's plenty more. Waltz around the dancing floor."

With my left hand clasped in Megan's right, we swayed in a wide arc across the front. All the while, the fiddlers kept up their lively and energetic performance. This could work, I thought. It was simple and familiar, yet it had a joyful quality that just might transcend social boundaries. For the first time since we began, Megan quirked a grin. I was acutely aware of her hand on my right shoulder and the clean scent of her hair where it nearly brushed my cheek. It was intimate, the way we moved in concert. Grindal let the music run on for a while before calling out the next move.

"Let's all help 'em keep the beat. Clap your hands and stomp your feet! (You knooow you want to.)"

We continued gliding and swaying, our arc now taking us around the back. I knew this latest instruction was directed at the audience. But would they understand? I needn't have worried. The dwarves at table one had taken a keen interest in our dance. They caught the spirit at once and began clapping their hands together in time to the music. The clomping of their heavy boots resounded through the hall, as if challenging the courtly nobles to match them. And no knight worth his salt would ever shy away from such a challenge.

"Sashay left, then do-si-do!"

Wait. That was only half a couplet. Weren't there usually two?

Nevertheless, I linked elbows with Megan and executed the maneuver before Grindal dropped the other shoe.

"Chicken in the bread pan, pickin' out dough!"

What? Really? Well, why not? We were in this far, after all. I began to flap my elbows and chicken-walk across the floor, with Megan pacing dutifully beside me. There was some laughter from the gathered nobles, but it seemed good-natured and not at all scornful.

As we continued the ridiculous maneuver, the dwarves at table one got up to some antics of their own. Two of them were practicing a do-si-do. Another two stood up on their stools and knocked their large pewter tankards together with a clunking sound, spilling ale over their rims. They then threw their heads back and drank deeply. Despite my bent-over posture, it was hard to miss this amusing behavior. It almost caused me to misstep.

"Promenade like a spotted cow; even the king is clappin' now!"

It was a risk, trying to command his majesty like that. But as a good caller, Grindal had doubtless noticed the king's head bobbing along to the lively beat. So, as Megan placed her hands on my hips and we paraded across the floor like a four-legged animal, King Raymond Osten the Third raised his hands and added to the acclaim.

"Moo!" shouted one of the dwarves.

After several more maneuvers, I was breathing heavily. I hoped Grindal had marked this. We had trusted the boy thus far, and I sensed from the crowd's unwavering clapping and laughter that they were enjoying it as well. But there were limits.

"Music's fine, you'll all agree. GIVE IT UP NOW for the FIDDLERS THREE!"

The rhythmic clapping broke into a cacophonous roar as the crowd poured out their agreement. There was some whistling and an impromptu declaration of love shouted by an overexcited damsel near the back.

"We love you, Renny!"

"This here shindig now is done. Hope you folks has had some fun. Like a mill wheel in the spring, twirl her around to face the king!"

Then I got a notion. As we closed the distance to the throne in the final moments of the song, it occurred to me that we might as well finish with a proper flourish. Megan was staring trustingly into my eyes, so I was all but certain she would glean what I intended. She quirked a smile and nodded.

I pulled her in close, took her hand, and spun her out under my extended arm.

Spacium gyrabit, I silently intoned.

Releasing her, I drew upon my magic to keep her upright and guide her toward her amazed monarch.

Megan went whirling away like a dervish, balanced on one foot with her head thrown back. A smile of glee graced her upturned face. Her skirt flared out from her waist, and her long black tresses splayed out as she spun about. Her impromptu pirouette finally concluded, depositing the girl panting at the king's feet.

I lowered my head as I stood there, exhausted.

A hush fell over the hall.

"Marvelous," said the king.

This one word benediction brought a tear of joy to Megan's flushed face as he kissed her forehead and handed her a rose.

***

After this, the ball progressed smoothly. A cheerful atmosphere ensued as the band struck up a series of more traditional tunes and other couples took to the floor. Escorted by the royal guard, the king and his entourage soon departed. I'd have liked to have heard Prince Henry's impressions of the debuts, but I understood the royals wouldn't be available until the prince's own ball later in the season.

I escorted Megan back to the Westarbor table, where a bevy of would be suitors were already lined up to offer their congratulations and to beseech her father for a dance with the lady. The baron greeted each one with the deference due their stations and began the delicate task of thinning the herd. As her escort and protector, I thought I might have some role in helping to schedule my lady's evening. But I soon found I was quite mistaken in this. Baron Westarbor was well-prepared to handle the onslaught. Not only did he seem to know all the noblemen on sight, but he also shared Megan's gift to divine a person's true heart. Moreover, his diplomatic skills were well up to the task. Trenton, too, stood nearby, greeting his social equals and exchanging pleasantries. Doubtless, he was here to learn aught more of the social arts and to guard his sister's honor. I soon found myself politely edged out of the fray.

I feared it would be quite some time ere Megan might be free. So I decided to wander among the crowd and have a look about. At some other tables, similar crowds of hopefuls had gathered, congratulating two of the other debutantes. Only Lady MacLaren seemed immune to the debutante fever that had infected the young gentry of the capital. She was visited by some well-wishers who applauded her performance. But mostly, these were older couples and people curious about the dwarves and their culture.

I saw some others that I knew. There was Baron Murphy of Deerfield, chatting with his duke. And *there* was Duke Gaulle of Eagle's Keep, the one who'd had me arrested by his inquisition. Ah, those were the days. I veered sharply aside when I spotted Baron Downham and his son, Sir Eric. At his father's behest, the young man had administered a beating to me in my one and only sword fight. And though we'd used only wooden practice blades, my ribs ached just thinking about it.

Then I spied Baron Stein and his lady wife. He sat staring morosely into the distance, guarded by several of his loyal knights. The baron and his wife had been kind to me when our caravan had become snowbound at their castle. They had offered us refuge and entertained us there until the roads could be cleared. I knew that the good baron was suffering from a progressive malady that robbed him of his memory and awareness. All knew that his wife, Lady Wilhelmine, was the one who actually ran Barony Stein. On a good day, Lord Stein was very clever and congenial withal, but the good days were growing ever more scarce. I was surprised the Steins had even come.

But then I remembered the gossip. It was rumored that the king might use this occasion to finally appoint a new Duke of Northford. Baron Westarbor and Baron Downham were seen as the leading contenders. But whichever way it worked out, all the barons of Northford Province would need to be present to swear fealty to their newly arisen duke. I began to make my way toward the Stein table when I became distracted.

It would seem the debutantes hadn't monopolized quite all the local admirers. I spied a gang of giggling adolescent girls who appeared to be following me around. They were glancing my way and whispering to one another behind gloved hands. I was being stalked! Soon, one broke away from the pack to head in my direction. She approached boldly enough, but then seemed hesitant and uncertain. I turned to face her fully.

"Yes, miss?" I offered. "Is there aught I can do for you?"

"I saw your dance," she stammered. "It was quite... lively."

"Thank you, I think," said I.

She clasped her hands behind her back, and color rose to her cheeks.

"I would dance with you," she blurted, "if you were to *ask* me, that is."

I could tell by her tremulous lower lip that the girl would be crushed should I reject her. Beyond her stood her friends, eagerly awaiting the outcome. I extended my hand, palm upward, and placed the other over my heart.

"It would be my honor, young lady, if you would grace me with a dance. Will you?"

The sudden smile that lit her young face warmed my heart to witness. She cast a swift glance back toward her confederates, then placed her hand in mine. I led her toward the dance floor, followed by her curious peers. We waited for the current song to end. Thankfully, it was followed by a sober piece, a waltz with no rigid pattern.

I clasped her right hand in my left and placed my other on her willowy waist, taking care to keep a courtly distance between us.

"You're Lucas, right? Lucas the Just?"

"You have the advantage over me. I didn't catch *your* name, miss."

"Oh, it's Sarah, Sarah Hawkins. But you can call me Sadie; everyone does."

I didn't recognize the surname. As we gently swayed across the floor, I noticed someone watching us.

"So, Sadie," I said, guiding her around so she could view the dame. "Is that your governess yonder - the one in the blue and white striped gown? She seems to be watching us quite intently."

The woman looked too old to be the girl's mother.

"What? Ah... no, Sir Lucas. That's the Lady Castleberry, widow of the Marquis. Everyone knows *that*. But you're right. She does seem to be enjoying our dance with us."

Curious, I thought. The music was entering its final measures, and the girl in my arms looked up expectantly.

"Are you going to spin me like you did the Lady Megan? I told Arabella that you would."

Hmph. So *that* was their game, was it?

"Such promises must be kept, my good Lady Hawkins. But only this one time. If you're sure then?"

She nodded.

"Give Arabella my regards."

With that, I spun the girl toward her envious fellows, using my magic yet again. She went whirling off to arrive dizzy but laughing in their midst. While her friends peppered the girl with questions, I made good my escape. I made my way toward where the old matron sat watching. It was time for some introductions.

As I approached her table, a man stood up to bar my way. He was a heavyset fellow with a trim goatee who eyed me with suspicion.

"May I help you, sirrah?" he said.

From the way his nostrils flared, I doubted his offer of help was genuine.

"A young lady of my recent acquaintance told me this is the Castleberry table. I would like to extend my fond regards and best wishes to the lady of your distinguished house."

"Peace, nephew. Let him approach."

The man winced like a scolded hound and silently withdrew.

"I've heard of you, young man. Come, have a seat. Let us become acquainted. Lucas the Just, is it not?"

"Just Lucas to you, madam. Your ladyship would laugh to hear of how I first came by that title."

"Do tell."

"Well, you see, there was this dryad..."

I went on to relate the mix-up and several other adventures I'd had. It turned out the old girl was a dowager marchioness, that is to say, the widow of a marquis. Her late husband had once held title to several counties in the duchy of Fairglen. On his passing, the day-to-day ruling of these reverted to their respective counts or barons. But Victoria still held considerable sway in the court of King Raymond. The generous woman was a well-known patron of many charitable projects. The latest of these was the plight of the refugees dwelling outside the city's walls. As a like-minded fellow, I thought I might make common cause with her in this.

However, whenever I sought to broach the topic, the cagey old woman would steer the conversation off on some other tangent. Her nephew, Howard, by now seemed comfortable with my presence. Initially, he'd been suspicious that I might have come with my hat in hand, seeking to prey on the good lady's charitable nature. Many did so. But now he seemed satisfied that my intentions were honorable. We watched Megan and the others dance with a parade of eager young nobles while Lady Castleberry filled me in on their families and backgrounds. It was very informative.

"Well," she said at last, "It is time for Howard to take me home. The hour grows late for these old bones."

There was a pause.

"Here, young man," she whispered, "is where a gentleman must protest and spin some audacious fib about a lady's immunity to the ravages of time."

I rose from my seat.

"I would rather say more truly that a woman ages like a fine wine, losing the sharpness of youth, but growing in wisdom and complexity."

"I find such honesty refreshing, Lucas. It makes the compliment all the sweeter."

"Blame it on my dance partner, your ladyship. Lady Megan never lets me get by with a fib."

Rising to her feet, the former marchioness offered me her hand, and I took it gently.

"I am most pleased to have made your acquaintance, sir mage. Feel free to call upon me at Castleberry Hall. There are some matters we should discuss."

From my earlier dealings with the prince, I understood this to be more of a command than an invitation.

"I will certainly do so, Madam, at my earliest convenience."

As she and her nephew departed, I wondered just what the old dowager had in mind. It was clear she hadn't wanted to discuss the refugees - at least not here.

Most of the rest of the evening passed in a blur (and I wish I meant that only figuratively).

It started innocently enough. I stopped by the MacLaren table to congratulate Felicity and to thank the dwarves for their robust support during my and Megan's debut. Lady Felicity and her seven protectors were a fun group.

We were soon dancing and drinking to the lively tunes of the band. They taught me some of their Highland steps. I, in turn, showed them some magic. I used my vestigial verdumancy to freshen Felicity's rose. This not only perked up its bloom but also caused little rootlets to grow out from the bottom of its stem. I told her if she kept it moist and gave it some sunlight, it might take root in the soil of her homeland. The "Royal Crimson" was a special cultivar grown exclusively by the king's rosarian. Its blooms were a captivating blend of vibrant hues, alternating between salmon pink and the crimson that was its namesake. Felicity's father, Ewen, seemed touched by this gesture.

"How can I reward ye, Sir Lucas? The smile on me daughter's face is worth to me a hill of gold."

The man couldn't be serious, could he? By then, I was getting loopy from all the ale I'd consumed. Just what did they put in those kegs, anyway? So I said the first thing that came to mind.

"Buy me a beer, and we'll call it quits."

All the dwarves laughed uproariously at this, and the Thane thumped me hard on the back. I was certain I'd feel that quite keenly tomorrow, but for now, I just gave him a sloppy grin.

"I like you, lad!" declared Laird MacLaren. "If it wasn't for your whiskerless chin, I might think ye be half dwarf yourself. If ever you come to the Citadel Deep, be sure to stop by for a measure. We'll show you wonders beyond your ken and take you down to the Sunken Grotto. That's where me daughter will likely be planting the thing."

There was yet *another* appointment to remember.

"Rockytop?" I thought with my head awhirl.

"Understood, brother," said he. "We will make sure we recall it. But it's past time you headed to bed. Rest now. Let slumber wash over you, and I shall take charge in your stead."

CHAPTER FIVE

The Servant

"I have made an important discovery... that
alcohol, taken in sufficient quantities,
produces all the effects of intoxication."

~ Winston Churchill ~

It was boring since my master had gone and left me here.
Beforetimes, at least I had Ronnie Turner to hang around with.
He was a mite over-serious, being the baron's page and all, but
at least he wasn't so stuffy as all them adults. He was off with
his own master now. The baron and his wife got to bring their
servants, and the two knights had their squires. So why couldn't
my master or his lady bring servants too? I suppose I was glad
enough to be shed of them fancy costumes Miss Lynette had
been dressing me up in, but I woulda at least liked to see what
all the fuss was about. No, I didn't know who Debbie's aunt was,
and now I likely never would - not bein' invited to her ball and all.

So, here I stood in the manor's front lane with nothing but
time on my hands. The night was awfully quiet, like it sometimes
gets in the summer. I saw fireflies blinking here and there, but

143

I'd learned not to be afraid of these ones. They couldn't actually burn you like the ones from down in the south. I tracked one hovering nearby and caught it in my hand, being careful not to crush it. I spread my palm and watched it climb up my thumb. Soon, it was drifting off and shedding light from its backside on occasion. I much preferred this type.

I looked over at the carriage house. It was funny. I hadn't actually seen it opened up as yet. The baron's carriage, Count Camburn's carriage and even his wagon too, was all left out in the open most nights. Them wide double doors always stayed closed shut. And now I saw a light from inside it. It was curious. Was I curious? Sure was. I'd been warned not to pry. But I bet no one would be the wiser if I was to amble over and have a peek. What could it hurt?

I was fixing to do just that when I heard them. It was a gang of men laughing and singing off-key, their voices getting closer and louder.

"Quiet down, lads; let's not wake the whole house," I heard from out near the road.

Before long, I saw, by the light of the moon, a procession of men creepin' down the manor lane. They was no taller than me but wider by far, and they sported great beards from their chins. They had quieted a mite, but still was quite noisy. And rolling up behind them was the biggest barrel I'd ever seen. Even lyin' on its side, it was too tall for a bull to mount. What on earth was they up to?

Just then, one of the doors to the carriage house creaked open a mite, and a blonde-headed woman peeked out. The light I'd seen from inside flooded out onto the carriageway and sharpened the features of the dwarves. The one in the lead shielded his eyes and came to a stop.

From the house, there came a shout. And as the front door flew wide, I saw a bunch of the baron's men stepping out into the night. The carriage house door creaked closed again, and the lanterns of the men took charge of the scene. It was just too much to take in all at once.

"Who approaches House Camburn in the dead of night, with bushy beards and bearing no light? Have you business with the count or the baron, perhaps? Move along, then. They're at the ball. And we've no patience for the antics of you merry little chaps."

The leading dwarf grimaced. A second dwarf answered, stepping up from behind. He was grumpy.

"Have a care, goodman, and know to your woe that you address a thane! He is Laird of the Citadel Deep, Ewen MacLaren by name."

The man with the lantern moved closer. It was Taylor Allen, that archer fellow who'd tried to steal my food. He bowed low before the first dwarf, who I thought might be this Ewen. The dwarf tugged at his beard and addressed him.

"We've come only to return one of your own. The moon provides light aplenty for the eyes of us dwarves, living as we do surrounded by stone. And we know very well what the lords of this manor are about this happy night, having just come from the ball ourselves."

"Oh?" said Taylor, standing back up. "How fared our lady Megan?"

"'Tis a long story, that. But the king was well pleased. He honored her with a rose. And my Felicity nearly shone with delight when he handed her the same. All the debutantes did passing fair. Truly, Osten's got talent. But we've come here on another matter."

"You mentioned one of our own?"

"Aye, bring him out, men!"

From behind the massive oaken keg stepped two more dwarves. Sprawled between them was my master, with his arms slung over their brawny shoulders and his feet dragging out behind.

"Master!" I cried out.

"This one has the heart of a dwarf, but maybe not the stomach to match. The lad was dancing with the ladies and spinnin' them all about. He got a wee bit carried away wi' the revelry, and we thought we should see him safely home. He was quite affable before being laid low by a snootful. It's nothing a good night's rest and a bangin' headache in the morning can't work through. So, we'll leave him in your care, goodman, and be on about our 'merry little antics.'"

Taylor put on a sideways smile, like he was halfway sorry over something.

The two dwarves who were carrying my master poured him into a puddle on the pavers, being careful not to crack him on his head.

"What's with the tun?" asked the archer, jabbing a thumb at the colossal keg.

"Och, 'tis a private matter between Lucas and me. A MacLaren always makes good on his oaths. It's the beer I owe him. When he awakens, you tell him that."

***

Long after dawn, there came a knock on our bedchamber door. My poor master was still fast asleep. He lay as if dead beneath the covers we'd tucked him under. Though I was hungry, I feared to rouse him. We'd missed the breakfast bell already. But the hunger in my belly was no stranger to me. In fact, I almost missed the old rascal. Almost. He'd scarce come to visit since I came to live here at Camburn Manor. High on the hog weren't tall enough to half describe the dining these noble folk got up to. I wished in my heart I could share some of this bounty with Ma and Pa and the others.

I crept to the door and listened when the knocking came again.

"Who is it?" I asked of the caller.

"My master is ailing and sleeping still. Best not to disturb him," I said.

"'Tis the lady your drunken master abandoned at the dance. When he wakes, inform him that such a sin won't soon be forgiven."

It hadn't been hard to imagine my master dancing with Lady Meg. From the first time I met her, I could see those two belonged together, like two ticks on a hog's back. She made my master get all goofy like Ma sometimes did Pa. My master had introduced me proper, giving my full name: 'Tobias Antonio Moss,' like I was some important person. 'Tam,' she called me straightaway when she learned I was his servant. I didn't take it bad.

My pa says naming something is a way of claiming ownership over it. By claiming his servant as her own, I reckon she was *really* shimmying closer to *him*.

Well, two could play at that game, I'd thought. I learned from Megan's ma that her middle name is Irene. I'd claim her right *back*, I would. 'Mia,' I'd call her the next time we met. I could hardly wait to spring it on her. She'd probably laugh or go all quiet-like, as she sometimes did. She wasn't prone to scold a fellow like most of those other high-falutin nobles. But I sensed that just now was likely not the proper time.

I opened the door a crack. Standing in the hall was Lady Meg and her lady friend, Lynette. I hadn't often seen the lady frown. It was a fearsome sight, to be sure. I was sad to think she and my master might be on the outs.

"A nasty piece of neglect," I said. "I'll tell him you're most cross, and I'll scold him good and well for the deed once he can hear it proper."

I imagined I could see the smile that hid behind the lady's frown. She reached out her hand and messed up my hair like I was a favored pet.

"You do that, Tam. Lynette and I will be shopping for new hats. I suppose we'll have to beg an escort from Trenton or one of the others. Is Lucas truly unwell?"

This last was said with concern. I thought I'd better lay it on thick to help my master's case.

"Oh," said I, "I'm certain he'll wake in an *awful* lot of pain. Them dwarves done worked him over good with their celebratin' ways. You should see the blackening bruises up and down my master's back. All purple they is, and *angry* too."

It was all true enough, if a bit overblown. I'd learned early on not to lie to Lady Meg. She could cut a tall tale right down to its roots. But it was then when the lady's icy frown finally started to melt.

"It serves him right, I suppose. Whatever was he thinking, drinking with the dwarves? Tell him... well... tell him to get better soon. We shall require a proper escort to Lady Ashbourne's banquet three days hence. Take care of him, Tam."

"I'll let him know it, Mia," said I as I eased the door all the way shut.

Timing was everything. I'd be out of her reach by the time she worked it out. I padded back over to Lucas, still lying there like a log.

"That was well done," he suddenly said, his eyes snapping open full wide.

"You're *awake!*" I exclaimed. "Were you faking? You had us worried, master."

"Not really, Tam," he answered, "Your master slumbers still. You have the righteous honor of addressing his inner hill."

Oh. I thought. It was that *other* fellow. The one that only came out at night and rarely spoke to me. Lucas sometimes talked in his sleep. He called himself 'Rockytop' at such times. I'd kept mum about it because folks thought ill of them who talked with themselves. At the camp, I'd known several such, and usually they was a bit off kilter. I'd thought at first the prince was such a one from all his we's and ours. But my master assured me it wasn't so.

"Rocky Top, is it, then?" I asked him.

"That's me, little servant. I'm still in control, though the sun rises high in the east. 'Tis almost time to rouse Lucas and return to the strata beneath."

"Why is it," I asked in wonder, "that you so often rhyme when you speak?"

"Perhaps my brother and I share the heart of a poet. Is it such an answer you seek?"

All that and a sense of humor to boot, I thought.

"Well, it was nice talking to you, mister Top. Go ahead and wake my master."

"This body of ours has suffered abuse. Go fetch us a pitcher of water and a glass. His thirst will be great when we wake him here. And a chamber pot, too, will be needed, I fear."

I rushed off to comply.

***

Once my master was tidied up and in a fitter state, he made his way to the kitchen. He was still in a sorry way. I told him about Lady Meg's visit, but this seemed only to make him sadder still. We was met in the kitchen by Connor Dawson, who was brewing a kettle over the fire in the oven. He was one of Sir Trenton's men-at-arms, the one who cooked for 'em.

"Here's our wayward reveler, finally emerged from his cozy cocoon," sang the cheerful man. "Good morn to you, Lucas. We heard about your jolly exploits of yesterday eve. And how are we feeling this fine morning?"

"Mizzerbalanga," my master replied, shuffling over to a chair.

"I thought that might be the case," said Connor, with a wicked grin on his lips.

He lowered the trammel from which the kettle was hanging. Taking it up with a pothook, he poured some black tea from it to fill a mug, which he set before my master. A bitter odor came off it that weren't like no tea I'd ever smelled before. The man cocked his head and shared a little ditty.

"Let it be a lesson to all who dare partake,
In the laughter of the evening,
there are choices that we make.
Think twice before imbibing, lest it strike you like a viper.
Remember, in the morning, 'twill be time to pay the piper."

"What's this?" asked my master, sniffing at his mug.

"It's another fine gift from the dwarves to all the inebriated world. They call it 'Caff.' Drink up, son. It's good for what ails you."

After taking a sip, my master made a face like he'd just been poisoned.

"Ick, what's in it?"

"There's a kind of bean they grow high up in the mountains. They dry them up and roast them before grinding them up to make this. They brew a similar drink down in Freemark, adding a little hair of the dog. *They* call it 'café olé.' But the dwarves swear that their mountain-grown is the richest kind.

"Well, it's certainly the bitterest kind," my master put in grumpily.

"Some people add a drop of honey or a bit of cream to reduce the sharpness, but I prefer mine black. It's not so bad once you get used to it."

At this, he poured another mug for himself.

I'd been thinking of asking to try some, but I gave up on that idea right quick. I wasn't sure which kind was which, but I didn't want to risk drinking something with dog hair in it.

"What is that god-awful racket?" said my master, setting down his mug.

"Oh, that?" said Connor. "The knights and their squires are sparring out back. Sir Nolan thought it meet to resume their morning regimen. Wouldn't want to get flabby from too much fine living and feasting.

"And the barking and baying?"

"Lord Stapleton's hounds seem to have taken exception to the unaccustomed activity."

"Well, I wish it would stop. My head can't take much more."

I'd been hearing a ringing clatter, and some dogs was soundin' off nearly non-stop. I knew my hearing was sharper than most, but it didn't seem so loud to me. Certainly nothing to complain so about. My master was clearly out of sorts. Maybe I could take his mind off it.

"What are we doing today, master?"

"Once I've finished this vile dwarven concoction, I plan to visit the merchant bankers again. Between the guild fees and all of Megan's shopping trips, I've run through the coins in my strongbox far quicker than I'd planned. I need to reassess the state of my finances. Then we'll circle around and try a visit to Lady Castleberry. I'm curious about what *she* wants."

"Well, don't plan on a carriage ride, Lucas. Both are out at present," said Connor.

My master groaned.

Not long after, we was setting out. It was nearly midday by the time my master had collected himself sufficient to take to the cobbles. As we stepped out into the yard, my master drew up short. He'd spied that enormous barrel layin' in the lane.

"What's this?" he exclaimed with a puzzled frown.

He'd been frowning a lot lately.

I quick explained about the visit from the dwarves on the prior night when they brought him home from the ball.

"... Thane Ewen said it was the beer he'd promised you." I said in conclusion.

My master stared at the thing for a full minute, and his down-turned lips crept up a smidge.

He snorted.

"I remember bits and snatches of that," he muttered. "It's likely just the thane's attempt at a grand jest, but perhaps not. Maybe I should have asked for that hill of gold after all."

***

We was lucky to make it to the merchant bank while they was still admitting callers. Bein' as it was Saturday, the

151

merchants would be closing her up early. Friday was payday for most folks, so there was a thick crowd queued up in front of the moneylenders. My master steered us straight toward the shorter line of folks seeking an account manager. It wasn't long before he was let in to see Mister Cedric. Just like the last time we was here, I lingered in the doorway.

"Was that Lucas the Just?" said one fellow to another.

Bein' a lowly servant, I'd learned that most folks tended to overlook me like I wasn't even there. Add that to my sharp hearing, and I found it easy to get a leg up on all kinds of gossip. I stared off in another direction and began cleaning my nails. They even more ignored a person who looked to be busy.

"I think you're right, Finn. I heard they're calling him the heartbreaker now," said the other man in a quiet voice. "He was charmin' all the ladies last night, young and old alike."

Another fellow turned around to join in their hushed speech.

"They quite adore him down in Cheapside. They say he trots about all humble-like on a mule, righting wrongs and whatnot.

"'Tis said he has the prince's ear. He and his lady were even seen sittin' in the royal box t'other night, pretty as you might please."

"That's nothing. I heard he won a drinking contest with seven dwarves. Seven! And to hear my missus tell it, they rewarded him with a whole tun of Stonehammer Stout. She and her ladies saw them rolling it up the road right out in front of our house."

I was hard-pressed not to laugh. I was sure my master wouldn't reckon that a win.

"They say he's a mage, but I dunno. He wears that sword at his hip. And it ain't no fancy blade like them nobles all be sportin'. It looks to be a serviceable piece.

"Well, I heard..."

"Toby? Come in here. I have need of my bob."

I unslung the pack and ducked inside.

My master was sitting at the small table. Mister Cedric sat facing him with a big book laid open wide between them.

"I assure you, sir. There's no mistake," he said.

"But it's only been a couple weeks since my last visit," said my master. "How can it have grown that much since then? My stipend is little more than a few shillings."

"True," said the clerk, running a finger down the page of numbers, "but there was a large deposit this past week from the royal coffers. Here it is: eight pounds, sixteen shillings for 'shaping and delivery of masonry blocks.'"

My master's eyes grew wide as he marked the entry. I couldn't rightly blame him. My own legs felt wobbly at the thought.

There wasn't even a coin big enough to make a pound. It took a whole bunch of little ones. Since there was twenty shillings in a pound, and twelve pence made a shilling, it would take, well... a lot of pence to make a whole pound.

After Cedric stepped him through it, my master settled down a mite. According to the clerk, the going rate for carving them stone blocks was a bit over eight pence apiece. My master had somehow made and marked more'n two hundred and some odd a couple weeks ago.

"Alright," said my master, squarin' off with the clerk yet again, "I suppose I owe some of it to the mason's guild. The journeyman's tax is one in ten."

"Would you like that deposited directly into their account?"

"Yes, please."

"I'll need your written instruction to do so," said Cedric, passing my master a quill.

"I believe it is also customary to tithe one tenth of one's earnings to the church. Can we transfer a like amount to them?"

"You are most generous, sir. Not all do so. The Church of

Fairglen, however, prefers to receive coins. I can prepare a complimentary tithing bag with that amount, which you may deliver personally."

My master was indeed most generous, I thought. On stumbling into a bit of good fortune, I marked he was quick to spread it around before even thinking of his own needs. He drew out his strongbox from the pack I bore for him. In it, he placed his tithing bag and a bunch of other shilling coins.

Stuffed back inside of his bob, this wouldn't weigh very much on my back. But it weighed awful heavy on my mind. If Ma saved my wages for six whole weeks, she'd barely have a full shilling (well, two if you add in the one the prince gave me for free). I doubt my master would even know if one of his shillings was to go missing.

My face heated and my stomach soured as I had the wicked thought. He might not know, but *I* would know. I felt again the shame at how we two first met. I thought at the time that nicking something from a stranger who had more than his share wasn't so great a sin - that it was just survival. After coming to know my master, though, it occurred to me how wrong-headed I'd been. It was something my ma had tried to teach me, with a hickory switch like as not. I think she'd be glad the lesson finally took.

"Are you alright, Toby? You look a little green."

"Hmm? Uh... It's just a little stuffy in here, master. Are we ready to go, then?"

My master thanked Mister Cedric, and we were soon on our way.

***

Castleberry Hall was a big old manor house way up in the high quarter. We were met at its front door by an old fellow claiming to be the porter. From his scrawny looks, I didn't suppose he'd be too successful at luggin' heavy loads about. Maybe her ladyship kept him on outta pity. He asked us if we was expected, and my master assured him we were, giving his name and such.

"And what is the purpose of your visit, sir mage?"

He was awfully nosy for someone who moved stuff about.

"I made her ladyship's acquaintance at the ball yesterday eve," said my master. "She expressed an interest in continuing our discussion and invited me to call upon her here."

"Wait here, and I shall ascertain whether my lady might be willing to receive you."

It wasn't very long before the man returned.

"Lady Castleberry would be delighted to receive you, sir mage. She is enjoying her garden at present and has instructed me to guide you there. It's just this way."

We followed the fellow through a mostly empty house as big as a castle. All about was paintings and wall rugs with pictures of knights fighting dragons and the like. I saw a lady maid with a feather duster cleaning an old suit of armor near a long set of stairs leading up. She stepped aside and stared down at the floor to let us pass by.

Passing into a side room, we came to some doors that was propped wide open. Through them, I could see a flagstone patio bordered by a riot of greenery. Beds of flowers sat in orderly rows, stretching off into the distance. All kinds, they was. And there at the patio's edge stood an old woman with pruning shears in hand, trimming at a rose arbor. She was elegantly dressed underneath the old apron with smudges of dirt.

That porter fellow stepped out onto the flagstones, followed by my master. The lady turned to face us.

"Wexley," she said, "go and have the kitchen staff bring us a refreshment."

"What do you think, Sir Lucas?" she asked. "Does this strike the right balance?"

"I presume your ladyship is going for an espalier," he replied. "Might I suggest a few more thinning cuts and a bit more crown reduction?"

The old woman's smile lines deepened. She set her shears to one side atop the garden wall.

"I see you know your onions, young man."

I didn't see no onions. My master once tried to explain to me a type of speech where one thing was likened to another. I reckoned the woman was really still talking about her flowers.

"Actually, I'm more interested in *these*."

Growin' all along the wall were vines with little yellow blossoms. And hanging from them was a bunch of round green apples, some of which was turning red.

"Quite decorative, aren't they? It's too bad they're poisonous."

"That's a common misconception, your ladyship. It dates all the way back to Reman times. The Reman nobles called them poison love apples, claiming that eating them would eventually kill you."

"And they were wrong?" she asked.

"No," my master sighed, "they were right after a fashion."

The lady looked confused.

"The Remans often took their meals on plates crafted from pewter. The acidic tomatoes would leech lead from the dishes, and it was this that slew their nobles."

My master cradled one of these tomatoes in his palm, and I watched it ripen to a bright crimson before my eyes.

"It's a shame they got such a nasty reputation," he went on to say. "They're harmless and quite tasty. They lend a pleasant, tangy flavor to stews and the like."

Plucking it from the vine, he bit into the round red thing. Lady Castleberry approached us, still smiling.

"You've convinced me. I shall have to try one. But the word is properly pronounced to-MAH-to."

"No," insisted my master. "The correct pronunciation is to-MAY-to."

She glared at my master stubbornly for a moment, then seemed to give up.

"Let us agree to disagree," she said. "You say tomayto, and I'll say tomahto. Let us waste no further time in a petty dispute over the naming of a vegetable."

Lucas grinned.

"Technically, your ladyship, it's a fruit..."

I reckoned that in a battle of wits, my master was better armed than most. By a stroke of luck, food arrived before they could take to bickering again. A servant brought a platter over to a dainty little table by the house. There was a tea service and some little tea cakes that set my mouth to watering. I'd missed breakfast, after all.

Then I remembered my proper role. I rushed over to hold the chair out for her ladyship, then wandered over to stand silent behind my master while the servant poured.

"I understand you recruited your servant at the refugee camp, Sir Lucas. Is this so?"

"Yes, your ladyship. Toby is the son of refugees."

She looked me up and down.

"He looks like he could use a refreshment himself. Lucille, take this young man back with you to the kitchen. Find him something to eat."

"Yes, milady," said the maid.

She bobbed a little curtsy, turned, and led the way back into the house. I followed her down several hallways filled with more curious things until, at last, we arrived at the kitchen. Lucille showed me to a cozy little nook in the corner and brought me a flagon of milk and some more a them tea cakes. The kitchen was warm and filled with the smell of cinnamon and other spices. Two other servants were rolling out dough and filling some pie pans, pinching em tight around their edges.

"You. Boy," said one of them. "Was that Lucas the Just you came in with?"

"Yes, miss. He's my master."

"Is it true he slew a whole goblin hoard up north a few years back?"

"Well, I ain't been with him all that long, but that sounds like something he might do."

I went on to tell about some of the things my master got up to while the cooks readied their pies for the oven. It was nice here. I was on my second apple tart when Wexley hung his head into the room.

"Your master is preparing to depart," he announced.

It was about time. I'd thought this would only be a short visit, but it seemed like they was talkin' for hours. I shoved the rest of the pastry into my mouth , licked my fingers clean, and hopped up to follow the man.

"I'b cubbig," I was quick to declare.

Out on the patio sat my master and the lady we'd come to visit. A look of surprise crossed my master's face when he turned and saw me coming.

"Done so soon?" he said. "I hope you took the time to chew, Tobias."

"It was kind of you to drop by, sir mage," said Lady Castleberry, snatching his attention back to herself. "You must visit us again soon."

Taking the hint, my master stood from his seat.

"The pleasure was all mine, madam. Your estate is almost as charming as its mistress. I shall gladly return when next my duties permit."

We followed Wexley back to the main entrance and were soon headed back to Camburn Hall. By the sun, I marked it was getting pretty late in the afternoon.

"Master, what was you and the lady talking about all that time?"

"Well, after our dispute about tomatoes, we..."

My master stopped in mid-stride and started rubbing at his chin.

"Well, we... I'd meant to raise a few other topics, but I suppose I never got around to them. We mostly just exchanged pleasantries and shared a bit of local gossip. Perhaps next time we can delve into other matters of more consequence."

At this, he continued down the street, with me following right after.

***

It was finally Sunday, my day off. I made sure to eat a hearty breakfast in the servant's nook in the kitchen. The other servants there helped me make up a basket of tasty treats for Ma, Pa, and the others. I went to meet back up with my master in the front foyer, only to find him squabbling with his lady. Though not overloud, their voices carried a mite as they echoed over the hard tiles of the entryway.

"Lynette and I shall need the carriage for our shopping trip. You'll just have to do without."

"For stars sake, haven't you two done enough shopping? If we walk, it will take half the day for me to bring Toby home for his visit. Your father said --"

"We had hoped you might even escort us this time, seeing as your mind is not too befuddled by spirits today to be of such service."

My master flinched at this and put on the face of a scolded hound.

"I suppose that's fair," he said wistfully. "How about this, then? Come with us. You and Lynette can scout out shops along Broadway, and we can visit them on the way back after dropping Toby off."

159

"It seems a fitting solution," she replied.

"Besides," added my master, "there's something I want you to see."

I was soon climbing to join the two ladies in the baron's fine carriage. They was seated on the back bench, leaving me to sit across from them on the rear-facing seat. Lucas was up top, driving the thing.

"You look so *cute* in your new footman's attire, Tam," spouted Lynette. "I bet the folks back at your camp will be impressed."

Oh, I was sure they'd have a lot to say about the way I was dressed. I tried dressing down this morning, but my master told me I'd better get decked out fancy to please the ladies. I still woulda refused, except he double-dog dared me to. And there was no overcoming the shame of refusing a double-dog dare.

"I can't hardly wait," I lied.

Lady Megan let it pass.

Thankfully, the two was soon ooohin' and ahhin' out of the windows and leaving me alone with my thoughts.

"There's LaShalts," exclaimed Lynette. "I doubt we could afford much there, but I'd love to go in and browse a bit."

"Keep an eye out for other dress shops. We'll need some new gowns for the coronation ball, at least. There should be more room for luggage on the return trip. Father said I could have an additional trunk now that the... you know what won't be taking up so much space."

I took to cleaning my nails again, but there was no fooling Lady Meg. She laid her blue peepers on me and kenned that I was listening. Smiling sweetly, she turned to me.

"Tam," she said, "let us have a look in that bag Lucas is so fond of."

"I dunno," I hedged. "My master is trusting me to keep it safe."

"Oh, I'm sure he wouldn't mind. We just want to see how so much fits inside."

She wiggled her fingers menacingly. I quick edged away from the satchel that lay on the bench beside me.

"Which pocket holds all that gear?"

"It's the big one on the side, the one with the brass buckle," I reported glumly as we bumped along.

At this, the two ladies set to undoing the straps and opened it up to peer inside.

"I see something," said Lynette,

She reached in up to her elbow and fished out a shaft of wood that turned out to be the handle of a shovel. She couldn't even get it all the way out before it bumped against the roof of the coach. With a little laugh, she thrust it back down in.

"How does he *find* anything in here?" Lynette asked of no one in particular.

"He mentioned having to use a minor locating spell to retrieve a specific item," said Lady Meg. I wonder what's in this other pocket."

She looked to me for an answer.

"I only ever saw him pulling things from out of the void pocket. But he said that was a newfangled invention that he didn't fully trust as yet. So he keeps his most precious things, them as he can't afford to part with, in the regular side."

The two ladies' eyes met, and soon they was unlacing the bag proper. I was starting to regret not putting up more of a fight. But I admit to being curious myself about what my master valued so highly. I leaned in with the others as they opened the main section.

Inside, there was only a leather case. It was stuffed full of all kinds of papers and such. Lynette pulled out a wad of these, spreading them out a bit, and Lady Meg went all quiet like.

"Put them back, Lynette," she said in a husky voice. "I know what those are."

"Well, don't leave us in the dark, milady," said the other woman. Tell us, then."

"It appears to be every letter I've ever sent him."

Lynette and I tried to put everything back the way we'd found it. I hoped I'd imitated my master's knots close enough that he wouldn't spot the difference. But Lady Meg stayed staring out the window in silence for a long time after that.

***

"Whoa," I heard from up above.

I swayed back in my seat as the horses drew up. Looking out the window, I saw we'd arrived at the city gates. The guardsmen stood within the great opening, directing wagons in and out. As it was morning, most of em was inward bound farm carts bringing their produce to market. But a few, like us, was headed the other way.

"I'll be jiggered, Wally, if that ain't Lucas the Just," shouted one of the green garbed guards. "And he's got a slick coach now."

Lynette and Megan crowded up beside me to stare out the front-facing window. At the man's shout, some of the wagons had slowed, and folks were craning their necks our way.

"Out to slay a dragon today, Sir Lucas? Or perhaps are you planning to build a hospital for all the widows and orphans of the land?"

I heard my master laugh from up above.

"Nothing so grand today, Clem. Just a quick out and in. Dropping off Tobias at his village."

"Always with the good deeds," said Clem.

"God bless you, sir," added Wally.

The men passed us on through. Folks on some of the inbound wagons took to waving at us, and I could see from my master's shadow on the cobbles that he was waving back.

Where the king's highway met the lane that led to Refuge, there sat a well. It was a lovely sight, all clean and bright, its stones set in a zig-zag pattern. Astride it stood two angels, holding up the roof. Its wooden shakes were cedar, fresh cut, and sparkling with the morning dew. All around it, flowers grew, and before it, knelt a girl. It was not a girl I knew.

Our carriage stopped well shy of it, and Lucas clambered down from the coachman's bench. He opened the door and lowered the folding step so's we could all step out. Lady Meg lit right into him with a question - three, in fact.

"Dragons? Hospitals? Just what have you been getting up to out here?"

"This and... well... that."

This last was said while pointing over at the well he and my pa done built.

He led the way on over, followed by us three. The girl never bothered to look our way. She was still kneeling down before the statue. She wasn't from the camp. Her clothes was a mite too fine for that. No, she was likely a gal from a nearby farm who had come to our well for a blessing. Her head was bowed down, her eyes was tight shut, and her hands was folded in a prayerful way. In front of her lay a shepherd's crook at the feet of a stone angel.

"Oh, my word," mumbled Megan when it became clear that she'd seen that angel's face in the mirror.

At this, the shepherdess finally turned to look up.

"You came!" she shouted. "Glory be. I prayed, and you came!"

Megan looked like the girl had just bit her, but then she calmed herself.

"I think you have me confused with someone else, miss," she put forth. "What were you praying for?"

The girl's eyes got sorrowful at that.

"I've lost my sheep and don't know where to find them. Pa will be ever so cross."

"How on earth did you lose a whole flock of sheep?" asked my master.

"Well, I was taking a head count, and the next thing I knew, I'd fallen asleep. By the time I woke, they'd all strayed off."

"Maybe we can help you look for 'em," I said.

Lynette made a face.

"That's a good idea," said Lucas. "Go round up Enoch and the boys. See if they're willing to help."

"Yes, master," I said.

"Wait," said my master. "On second thought, perhaps there's a better way. I know a spell to locate a person using a lock of their hair. Maybe it could be made to work for sheep."

He turned to the girl.

"Have you any wool?" he asked.

"Yes, sir," she said brightly. We sheared them just the other day. I got nearly three bags full."

"Run and fetch me some - just a few snips."

Once the girl had run off, I saw Lady Meg standing beside her winged twin. She was running a finger over its jaw line and staring at it thoughtfully.

"Who inspired the other one? Should I be jealous?"

"That's my ma," I put in quick to take that off her mind.

"This is what you do in your spare time? Carve stone effigies of people you know and help others?"

"Well," said my master sheepishly, "magic is a funny thing. I was trying to sculpt an angelic face and unwittingly conjured up yours. I... hope you aren't offended? I thought it best that you were made aware. As to helping people, the refugees needed a source of clean water. And someone has to step in and help the incompetent shepherdesses of the world. "Elsewise, where would we get our mutton?"

"Speaking of that," he continued, "'twere best I prepare. It should only take a few minutes once the girl returns."

I ran off to find Enoch and the others. They were gonna want to see this.

When I got back, my master was sitting cross-legged on his spread out cloak with the shepherd's crook resting before him. He sprinkled the fine gray-white hairs on the head of the staff and started chanting some funny words.

"Quaerite mihi ovium," he said over and over.

At first, nothing seemed to happen. But then the hairs blackened, curled into a tight little ball, and sank straight down into the wood. We was mightily impressed. After a time more, his head snapped back, and he sagged forward a bit. I reckoned he was done, but I stayed quiet, just in case.

"Whew. That took a bit more than I thought it would. Let's try it out; shall we?"

He handed the staff to its proper owner and told her to say something that sounded like 'Kwair-itay.'

After a couple of false starts, she got it. And when she did, a little bobbing ball of light came right out from the top of her crook. It went drifting off toward the south. She went walking after it, a happy look on her face.

"You boys go with her and help her round them up. It wouldn't hurt for the farmers and ranchers around here to see you can be useful."

So we went scrambling after - me and the boys, that is. I knew my master would be heading back for the city. And after a long morning of rounding up stray sheep, I returned to the camp I'd once called home. Make no mistake. I enjoyed visiting my folks. But I'd be just as happy to return to my master's side. Nothing was ever simple with him, and you never knew what surprises lay in store when following *him* about.

Another Distressing Interlude at Sea

The boarding party was routed quick, and at my feet, the deck was slick. Its blood-soaked boards were littered with the bodies of the dead. Too late, they tried to disengage, to quell my wrath and thwart my rage. By then, I'd vaulted over to their galleon instead.

It was the third such tub that me and my men had lured in and boarded. I would need a full flotilla for the deeds I had in mind. The hardest part was leaving some of the men alive; it was. For in the ecstasy of killin', I always wanted more. But I still needed sailors to man these crafts. I couldn't make do with just a skeleton crew.

On the windswept sea so far from land, I battled the pirates dread. Winning through their shrinking ranks, I gave no quarter and spared none the sword. The devil was jolly well-pleased with me. For as I slaughtered on with glee, I sent more than a score of souls to hell. Body after body, I wore right through, falling only to rise anew. Never had I feasted quite so well.

I came at last upon the pirate king, the captain of this grand vessel. He wore a fancy hat. And he had an air of command about him as he stood proud beside the wheel that steered the ship.

"I understand," I shouted, leaking blood from the many open wounds I'd taken, "that among your kind, ownership of a vessel goes to him who can take it."

"And keep it, aye," he said, leveling a saber at me.

"Then you know why I cannot spare you. Greetings from your inheritor."

"I'll greet you in hell," were the captain's final words.

When I lopped off the former captain's head, the fight seemed to go right out of all the others.

The pirates needed structure, and I would give 'em that. Once they were properly humbled and had bowed down to my captaincy, I revealed to them my true body. It had slept within the murky hold of the prior ship I'd conquered. From the bowels of that ship arose my finest avatar. Its beastly body stood near nine feet tall, with Luthor's head agrinnin' at its top. They call me the demon of the sea now; they do.

CHAPTER SIX

The Prince

"It is only with the heart that one can
see rightly; what is essential is invisible
to the eye."

~ Antoine de Saint-Exupéry ~

In the week that followed our shopping trip, things slowed down for a bit. But I was to find that this was merely the calm before the storm. The baron had instructed all the suitors they could begin calling on his daughter after a suitable time had passed. In noble-ese, this translated to three days after the debut (more or less). Therefore, after but a three-day reprieve, House Camburn came under siege from a wide variety of gentleman callers bearing poesies and other minor gifts. They were all here to chat with Lady Megan and petition her father for the right to a courtly date with the maid.

Megan greeted each in the sunroom, where they could take refreshment and enjoy a bit of polite conversation. From the baron's frank discussions with my lady afterward, I gathered that none of them thus far stood an actual chance. However, politeness dictated that each be given an opportunity to make his case.

"Enjoy it, Megan," he said as yet another young knight tottered dejectedly down the manor lane, unsatisfied. "Remember, we may need a favor from one of these lords or their fathers one day. Truly, this is the cream of the crop."

Forced to be present as her chaperone, I took exception to the baron's characterization of the young men on several levels. Milk had cream, whereas crops had what? Grain? Ears? Fruits? The baron should've said 'the grain of the crop.' Only they weren't. None of the dullard sons of nobility I'd seen thus far were, in my estimation, worthy of the lady Megan. And don't even get me started on the other fops and pretenders who showed up. To be fair, the baron proved very adept at turning the latter away or quickly convincing them to retreat after but a hasty sortie.

It was a sign of my boredom that I sat here quibbling over metaphors to pass the time as we idled. If I were honest, it wasn't mere boredom that had put the bee in my britches. I recalled the crowd of suitors who had descended on Megan after our debut. I had felt both superfluous and a trifle... jealous? Was that what had driven me so deep into my cups that night?

"Hardly that, father," said Megan. "That last fellow was ancient."

"Lord Pembroke? I included him only because his family has great influence in the copper trade. It strokes his ego to think he's in the running. Besides, forty-three is hardly ancient, my dear. Haven't you heard of a May-December romance?"

"I have when December was at least in the same decade," she shot back with a casual wink. "Why, he could be my father or perhaps even a grandfather if his own children got started early enough."

"Oh, and fathers are *ancient*, are they?" quipped the baron with a raised eyebrow.

"You know what I mean, father," said the lady with a sigh. "Let's try to limit ourselves to more recent... vintages, shall we?"

I took another drink from my mug. The caff had quit emitting steam by then and was cool enough not to burn my lip. Admittedly, I hadn't liked the stuff at first, but it sort of grew on me. Now, I find it to be the best part of waking up.

"The most acceptable thus far was Sir Wulfric, I believe," said the baron. "Should I place him on the short list, then?"

I hated him. In his dance with Megan the other night, Alfred Wulfric held her in far too close an embrace. He'd probably trod all over my lady's feet.

"In truth, he is a rather interesting sort," said Megan with a smile I didn't care for. "Indeed, he asked to escort me to the masquerade next Saturday. Put him down for that. What do you think, Lucas?"

What?

"Oh, um, yes. I'd like him put down."

The baron looked at me strangely. I felt my cheeks grow warm. Turning back to his daughter, he said, "Forget about Sir Thurstan. The man has the manners of a troll."

"You're preaching to the pulpit there, father. He's very forgettable indeed. Scratch him off the list, please."

"Don't you mean 'preaching to the choir?'" the baron inquired.

"No," my lady replied. "That's altogether possible and even likely."

Megan must be as bored as I to engage in such wordplay. It just goes to show that great minds think alike. But I took cold comfort from this because I knew that little, tiny minds also had very similar thoughts. To wit: lemmings. And just as the witless little creatures would follow one another off a cliff, if I wasn't very careful, following my feelings for Megan might lead to disastrous results. After all, what kind of life could I offer her when compared to the wealthy nobles who wished to court her? Oh, I was comfortable enough monetarily, or soon would be. But the life of a mage was hard sometimes.

Intellectually, I had always known that Megan would enter the marriage market. Nobles married for convenience and to form strategic alliances to benefit their houses, ultimately for the betterment of Osten. But still, I held out hope that something different might occur. Once again, Royland had called it correctly. I was smitten. Like all the lovelorn losers in the ballads of the bards, I'd have to make my peace with it and consider only the girl's happiness.

Once again, the baron glanced at me strangely, his penetrating blue eyes so much like his daughter's.

I welcomed the distraction when another young man came skipping up the lane. And by "young," I mean very young. I half expected his mother to come rushing up to retrieve him. Alright. Perhaps not quite so bad as that.

He was dressed in gentleman's attire, and only belatedly did I mark his tabard was styled in royal hues. When he knocked at the front door, both Count Camburn and the baron himself hurried to greet him. The baron returned the boy's respectful bow with a simple nod and waited for him to state his business.

"I am the king's page, Toby, milord, and I come on behalf of his son, the prince."

He looked a bit older than *my* Toby and rather more plump as well. But the mischievous grin he sported put me somewhat in mind of my servant in one of his better moods.

"Have you a message for Lady Megan?" asked the astonished baron.

"No, milord," the lad replied. "His highness, Prince Henry, would like a word with Lucas Harper of Meadowfork. I'm told he's staying here. Is he?"

"I'm Lucas," I squeaked, then coughed roughly.

The lad turned toward me and bowed yet again.

"His highness would like to invite you to afternoon tea, sir mage. 'Twill be an informal affair in the royal audience chamber.

He also said to bring along that manservant of yours, the funny one. "Should I tell the porter to expect you by the third bell?"

Once again, I answered in the only way that made sense.

"Tell his highness we'll be delighted to satisfy his curiosity over what we misfits are about."

"Very good, sir mage; I'll tell him that."

As the page ran off to bring word of our acceptance back to his prince, Baron Westarbor turned baffled eyes my way.

"What was that last part about?"

"Oh. I was just reminding the prince about what he had written me once."

"The prince writes to you?"

"Only that one time, your lordship. He's a very busy man. We prefer long walks together and chatting beside a fire."

***

"Now, Toby, mind your manners and stay quiet when we're with the prince."

"You don't need to tell me three times, master. Twice was one too many."

We sat outside the royal audience hall on a set of benches where petitioners awaited his highness' pleasure. Although we'd arrived at the appointed hour, the porter had informed us that the prince would be delayed by some last-minute business that had come up. As a result, tea would be served "anon."

"Besides," the lad continued, "his greatness --"

"His *highness*," I corrected.

"Yeah, that. He invited me specifically."

I was beginning to regret telling Toby that. I think Henry was amused by my overbold servant, but there were limits, after all. And I took it from the delay that the prince mightn't be alone. I leaned my head back against the wall and let my eyes drift shut.

As the back of my head encountered the cool stones, I felt their solid mass supporting the weight of their brethren above us. Each stone had a story to tell about its creation and later shaping by a mason. They fitted together and worked harmoniously to... It was then that the tinny voices crept into my awareness.

"... Lord Stein taking his medicine?"

"He will be soon. Despite strenuous objections, the royal physician is preparing a tea of rosemary steeped in luminaria leaf."

"You know that stuff will kill him, your highness."

"We are aware. But the man was adamant."

"So, what are your instructions regarding the coastal attacks?"

"Wait and watch. The pirates have never acted so boldly before. Perhaps it will blow over. Lady Cynthia has increased the patrols of our fleet, and the local lords have beefed up the harbor defenses all along the eastern seaboard."

"There's talk that the dead walk among the raiders."

"We've heard such rumors before. Frightened men invent all sorts of demons to explain the motivations of the wicked."

"So we do nothing?"

"No. We gather information and assess the situation. That's your bailiwick, I believe. Now, if that is all, I'm late for an appointment."

"Your afternoon tea with the Harper lad?"

"He's quite wise, Manny, and he is close to Lady Megan of Westarbor."

"I know. I've met him."

There was a pause.

"Be careful with how much you entrust to him, sire. The lad

is ill-suited for keeping secrets. He's loyal enough, but his face can be read like a missive from the town crier. Whatever you do, don't tell him --"

"Master?"

I felt the hand shaking my shoulder as my mind was torn from its trance.

"Master!" Toby hissed in my ear. "Are you asleep? Wake up. The prince could call on us anytime now."

"I'm awake, Toby. I was only meditating."

I leaned forward, rested my elbows on my knees, and my chin on my fists. Assured that I was indeed awake, my servant returned to his relaxed posture beside me on the bench.

"RockyTop?" I mind-whispered.

"Yes, my brother," came the sleepy reply.

"Can you bury the conversation I just overheard and remind me of it after we've left the castle?"

"I believe so, brother."

"And RockyTop? Have you caused me to forget anything else recently?"

If stone could blush, my homunculus would be doing so now.

"If I had, it would have been at your own request. Would you want to dredge it up now, or when you originally asked me to do so?"

Flummoxed, we pondered the matter. Without knowing what it was, how could I decide why I had suppressed the information or if now was a good time to reveal it? I suppose it came down to whether or not I trusted myself.

"Do as I originally asked you, Rocky. Also, go ahead and hide that recent conversation from me."

"Consider it forgotten, brother."

"Consider *what* forgotten?"

"Exactly."

Not long thereafter, we were summoned.

The royal audience chamber was much as I remembered it from our first visit. The afternoon light slanted in from windows high above to cast its warm glow upon the many precious artifacts and strange exhibits of the Osten dynasty. Unlike that previous visit, the prince was already seated before the grand hearth. And he was not alone.

Seated across from the prince was a middle-aged man outfitted in noble garb. His brocaded tan sleeves were festooned with black fleur de lis in a diamond pattern. I couldn't make out much more about the man, as he was seated facing away from me and didn't rise to greet us.

When I'd approached to within six paces from the prince, I bent the knee, and Toby followed suit.

"Rise and approach," said Prince Henry, gesturing with a goblet. "Didn't Toby inform you this was to be an informal audience?"

"But an audience nonetheless, sire," I replied, rising to my feet.

Spread out between the two men was a feast fit for a... well... a prince.

"Be seated and help yourself to a refreshment. Your servant too. What's his name, anyway?"

"It's Toby, your highness," said I.

"But you can call me Tam, your highness, seeing as you got one too many Tobies here in the palace already."

That was... almost acceptable, I thought as Toby executed his curt little bow. Now, if only he didn't talk with his mouth full, we might manage to salvage some dignity during this visit.

"I believe you have already met Lord Manford here, Lucas. Manny was just telling me he had traveled with you through much of Northford Province."

Rounding his chair, I spied the man's face. This Lord Manford was none other than Manchester, the jester. His eyes moved over me assessingly.

"Ta da!" said Manny weakly.

"You don't seem too surprised," he added.

"Well, I knew the jester wasn't all that he seemed. You're in the brotherhood, like Taylor was."

"Did he tell you that?"

"No. Royland worked it out a few weeks after you'd left us."

"I always suspected that rascal had more brains than he was letting on. It's always the quiet ones who notice more than they should. I was sent on a mission by the king to assess and possibly pass summary judgment on a disobedient member of our order. I was relieved to find the man remained loyal to the crown, albeit indirectly so."

"So, should I bow or genuflect or what, your lordship?"

The man spared the prince a glance before replying.

"I think we're well beyond that, Lucas. Curtsy, for all I care. Someone had to fill the vacancy left by the former duke of Fairglen. It's a courtesy title, anyway. The king holds all the power here. I only sit in regency while we groom Prince Richard to fill the role."

"Apologies, then, your *grace*," I said thoughtfully. "You wear so many faces, it can be hard to keep track of them all."

"No higher praise, my boy," he said while lifting his own goblet. "Take a seat, or your food will get cold."

Once Toby and I had seated ourselves and filled our plates with two of everything, I returned to the conversation. Prince Henry was sitting patiently and nibbling at a marzipan sweet shaped like a flower. Manny must indeed have great sway at court to subdue even the prince's royal aura of command. Unsurprisingly, Toby had tucked right in.

"Let me ask you a question, Lucas. Satisfy my curiosity, and I'll cease to disturb your appointment with Henry here."

I marked his casual use of the prince's given name and gave him my full attention.

"What topics did you discuss with Lady Castleberry yesterday evening?"

I stared at him blankly.

"Tomatoes," I replied.

"Only that?" he pressed. "Did she happen to mention the refugees camped beyond our gates?"

"Not that I *recall*."

"And roses, master," added Tobias earnestly while licking his fingers. "Roses, and onions too."

"Well," said Manny, rising and stretching. "I'm told the lady *does* enjoy her garden. I'll leave you to it, then. It was nice to see you again, Lucas, highness. I'll see myself out. Oh, and tell that cousin of yours I've got my eye on him."

And with that, he stalked off.

***

"I think he likes you," said the prince, munching on his marzipan.

Toby looked somber.

I took an eclair from my own plate and examined it.

"He never was very upbeat, even as a jester. As a duke's regent, I think I like him somewhat less. How old is your brother, anyway?"

"Prince Richard is twenty-six."

"But..."

"That would make him my senior. I *know*," he snapped.

"I was going to ask why someone of his years might require a regent."

The prince sighed and lay aside the empty stick.

"Well, he doesn't, actually. Richard came into his majority eight years ago and qualified for the posting as duke. But he's only my *half* brother, you see."

"So he must wait twice as long?"

"Hardly," the prince snorted. "Hey, leave me some of those. I like the yellow ones."

This drew my attention back to Tobias. With a sly sidelong glance toward the prince, my servant was retrieving a handful of tea cakes from bob and returning them to their plate.

"Richard is the result of a dalliance my father had with one of the maidservants before he wed my mother. Richard was already eight years old when I was born."

"So he's a bastard," said Tobias, round-eyed.

I winced. But the prince treated Toby to a simple nod of affirmation and continued.

"Years passed. And when it became clear that no further children by my mother would be forthcoming, father finally acknowledged Richard as his legitimate son and heir. As a child, I was in poor health, and it was uncertain whether I would survive and be capable of ruling the realm."

"I can see why the king might wish to secure the line of succession," I said thoughtfully, "but that still doesn't explain why Richard needs a regent."

"He cannot be raised up to duke until after I am crowned. Otherwise, he would outrank me for a time. And that *cannot* be allowed."

"Why not, your highness. Why can't --"

"Peace, Toby," I interrupted. Apparently, even three reminders was one too few.

Turning toward the prince, I said, "forgive my servant, sire. He doesn't understand that such delicate matters might prove distressing to its subjects."

Henry smiled.

"You're a gallant one, Sir Lucas. But I find no fault in Tam's forthright nature. Quite the opposite. I only state what is incessantly whispered at court. I find it quite refreshing to share my version of these events with someone untainted by such gossip."

"To answer your question, Tam. Some of the nobles would prefer my brother prince don the crown upon my father's passing. They claim it is his right by primogeniture. Others prefer me, citing that as the first legitimate heir, the crown should be mine."

"That sounds like a very perilous situation, your highness," I remarked.

"It's actually far more complicated and nuanced than that, but it's not as bad as you might think for *several* reasons. In the first place, Richard himself has no desire to rule. He prefers to while away his days hunting and fishing and the like. As Duke of Fairglen, he could engage in these pursuits to his heart's content."

"And in the second place, my prince?"

Henry pointed to a space above the grand hearth. Squinting at it, I made out an inscription carved into the stones. It was in the old tongue, with which I was reasonably proficient. I nodded my understanding.

"I see some letters up there," said Tobias. "What do they say?"

"Regnum meum et praecepta mea," replied Henry. "Loosely translated, it means, 'My kingdom; my rules.'"

"It was the motto of Raymond the first. My grandfather had it inscribed here to remind the nobles that the king need not heed their advice, especially in the matter of succession."

"I see," said Toby. "You will be king because your father *wants* you to be."

"So simple a *child* can understand," muttered the prince. "If only the nobles of my court would take the lesson to heart."

Henry stared dolefully at the engraved letters as though they might swallow us all. Why was the prince being so candid with me? Was it merely loneliness and a desire for our company that had compelled our invitation? Surely not. I took a sip of my cooling tea and cleared my throat.

"So, what else is on your highness' mind today?" I prompted.

"Oh, yes. I wanted to inform you that the cathedral renovations are nearly complete. There is to be a grand ribbon cutting ceremony. Since your efforts were so integral to the project's success, I wanted to offer you a place at my side at the event. In your short time here, you've earned quite a reputation. And it would gladden many a heart among our subjects to see Lucas the Just standing beside their prince."

It was an interesting notion. My presence would be seen as a tacit endorsement of Henry. And standing beside a prince of the realm might elevate my own status as well. I didn't mind the former, but had some reservations regarding the latter.

"Your highness honors me too greatly. Surely, you have other more worthy advisers and notables. I will gladly stand among such if your highness wishes it."

"We do."

I noticed that Henry was plural again, a certain sign I'd displeased him somehow. As if on cue, Toby piped up again.

"Highness? Where can a fellow attend to his necessaries around here?"

Smirking, the prince pointed and replied, "The royal wee is just over there."

Toby tottered off.

"There was another matter I had hoped to breach with you today, Lucas. This one is of a more personal nature."

That caught my attention.

"Speak on, sire. I can keep a secret."

"We have heard otherwise," he muttered.

"Is it this blue one?" inquired Toby in a raised voice.

"No!" said the prince with a rising note of panic. "That's an antique Grecian urn. The round white one next to it."

"Ah! I see it. No harm done," Toby reported.

Henry turned back toward me.

"It's about that ravishing creature you escorted at the ball. I understand you are close to the lady."

"Megan? I have that honor, your highness. But if I may be so bold, the lady would not like being referred to as a 'creature.'"

"This will become court gossip soon enough, so I will tell you plainly then. I am taken with her. Moreover, my father would regard a match with Westarbor as quite beneficial indeed."

I didn't know just how to feel about that. I knew Henry was a good person. When I was wounded and despite my lowly station, he had given me his horse to ride. Of course, I hadn't known at the time that it was a prince so humbling himself. I knew him then only as my friend, Kendrick. I should be glad that Megan had the attention of a soon-to-be-crowned prince. She would make a glorious queen one day. What, then, was this lump I felt in the pit of my stomach?

"Beneficial how?" I asked, perplexed by my own lack of empathy.

"It is said that the girl can discern the truth within a person. With her by my side, I would always know of any threats or disloyalty from among my courtiers. Is it true she can do that?"

"It is, but has your highness thought this through? She would also know *your* truth. This can be inconvenient at times."

"It's why I sought you out, Lucas. The king sees the potential for a political alliance with Westarbor, perhaps raising him up to be the new duke of Northford. But I must determine whether such a match is palatable. I am unable to show preference for any lady until my ball, where I hope to get to know her and make a favorable impression. Tell me, as a friend, what does the lady like? What *is* the lady like?"

There. He'd said it outright. The F-word. How could I deny my prince the best advice on how to win her? The earnest light in his eyes nearly tore my heart asunder.

"Lady Meg?" said Toby, appearing from around the divan. "She's really nice. She's patient with everyone, even when they might have dropped her clean gloves in a mud puddle. You can't lie to her without her knowing, but sometimes she lets you get away with it if it's for a good reason. She likes flowers and has got a lot of shoes. Oh, and she's a mean tickler."

I swallowed and nodded. Actually, that summed her up pretty well. It lacked only the volumes of poetic praise I would heap upon each point. My lady was kind, courteous, discerning, forgiving, and playful at times. Toby had left out intelligent and beautiful, but those were glaringly apparent.

"Perhaps then, I should woo her with some of Sir Lucas' colorful dance moves?" suggested Henry.

At this, he began flapping his elbows and tossed me a wry smirk. I rolled my eyes and leaned heavily on my forbearance.

"Honesty, sire," I finally answered. "The lady values honesty. If you wish to win her, you need only be your true self. If this doesn't charm her, no gifts or other persuasion will. My advice? Share your feelings openly. You have a kind and noble heart, your highness. Since you are a man of worth, she shall know it at once."

We left Henry brooding in silence beside the great fire. I knew the burden of a kingdom weighed upon his mind. I think he really did view me as a friend, as someone he could talk to. Against the wishes of my own heart, I'd done my best to merit his faith in me. Would I come to regret my advice? Yes and no. I wanted what was best for Megan, and it was her decision to make. But a small, stubborn hope lingered to betray my wish for the prince's happiness.

My bob bulged oddly on Toby's back. I neither knew nor cared what treats he may have filched from our royal benefactor. The prince had once again seemed merely amused by my servant's antics. Lost in thought, I was startled by a familiar rumbling from within.

"Brother," said RockyTop, "you asked me to remind you when we left the castle that someone intends to poison Baron Stein."

What?

***

As we neared House Camburn, I spied a commotion out in its front yard. The knights and their men were scurrying all about and seemed to be stretching out carpet runners upon the lawn. My titanic keg of beer had been rolled off to the side and now stood upright before the carriage house. I hurried forward to see what the matter might be. I was about to ask when I saw Baron Westarbor and Count Camburn striding out from the veranda. Behind them came Connor Dawson, lugging a cask over the rim of which water sloshed at his every hurried step.

"Hello, the house!" I hailed them.

"Ah, Lucas," greeted the baron. "Did everything go well with the prince?"

"As well as might be expected, your lordship. We discussed several matters, some of which I'll leave for his highness himself to explain. What's going on here?"

He stared at me and smiled.

"We're expecting a package delivery. The king has a griffin hostelry in the high quarter, but at our instruction, the messenger will make a stop here first."

Now it all made sense. From up above, the griffin riders needed some sort of marker to know where to alight. At

Conclave, Master Martin had marked his backyard very similarly to what the knights were doing now. The crossed aisle runners would resemble a large letter "X" to a person soaring overhead. I marked that Count Camburn was staring nervously upward and shielding his eyes from the sun.

"Why's everybody lookin' up?" asked Tobias.

I hastily explained.

"Griffins comin' here?" he shouted with elation. "Should we be worried, master?"

"*A* griffin, and no, Toby. They're quite friendly to people as a general rule."

We found a comfortable spot well clear of the landing zone and took to scanning the sky. Then I suddenly remembered. In all the excitement, I'd nearly forgotten the threat to Lord Stein.

"Your Lordship," I muttered so as not to be overheard. "While at the palace, I heard some people making plans to poison Lord Leopold. They plan to spike his tea with luminaria leaf. That stuff is extremely toxic!"

Despite the urgency in my tone, the baron failed to react as I expected. He peered over at me owlishly and blinked. After a moment, he replied in a calm, subdued voice.

"I take it, you came by this knowledge surreptitiously. Were you eavesdropping on the prince, perchance?"

"Not eavesdropping exactly, no. Or maybe yes. I don't know what to call it. But it's true, then? And you knew about it?"

This was perilously close to an accusation, but I just couldn't help myself. The baron sighed and leaned back.

"Lucas, the good lord is not a well man. He is physically fit enough, but his mind drifts in and out, as I am sure you are aware."

"Yes."

The baron looked glum.

"I'm afraid it's more out than in these days. In one of his rare bouts of sanity, he begged us... How can I put it? With the coronation soon to come upon us, it is rumored the king may finally appoint a Duke of Northford. If Lord Stein fails to appear and swear his oath of fealty to the new duke, his lady wife will be ousted from their barony and end her days in penury, beholden to any willing to take her in."

He gave me a moment to absorb this.

"To avoid this fate for her, Leopold seeks to assure he is present and in his right mind when the moment comes. In addition to its lethal side effects, luminaria leaf bestows clarity of mind to him that partakes of it. After the coronation, they plan to administer an antidote quickly. I hope my old friend survives, but he cares not either way. His physicians don't give him good odds of lasting through the winter in any event. With his oath duly sworn, he will assure Wilhelmina's place as a dowager, entitled to live in Barony Stein until the end of her days."

"I understand," I croaked.

"I see you do," the baron replied. "We will speak no more of it. The Steins are entitled to their privacy.

It was then that I heard it - a prolonged and piercing cry from above.

Kee-eeeee-arr!

Looking up, I saw the spread-out wings circling lazily above. A bell began ringing out in a familiar rhythmic manner.

When the beast alighted with a rush of wind and furled its wings, I marked the rider. He wasn't any of the Cunninghams I knew. He was too large to be Drew. He wore the blue livery of Westarbor over loose pants and an overshirt. And on his head, he wore a strange leather helmet, the goggles of which obscured his features. He stowed away his bell and undid the lashings that held his legs in place.

"Packages!" he cheerfully announced in a sing-song voice.

Dismounting, he strode toward us with a satchel slung over one shoulder. I thought I may have seen him somewhere before, but I couldn't, for the life of me, recall when.

His mount, too, stared our way. The beast was enormous. Having encountered Marjory's Wynken myself once, I knew the griffins were normally well-behaved. Only this kept me calm under that predatory glare. Toby slunk behind me to cower in wide-eyed amazement.

Meanwhile, Baron Westarbor had drawn out a fish from Connor's cask. It was slimy and glistening with drops of water, which sparkled in the evening sun. This he handed to Count Camburn, who took it with distaste.

"Just toss it to her, Edmond, and stop being so squeamish," said Baron Westarbor. "It's the traditional way to greet a griffin that's just landed on your lawn. Look. She's awaiting her just reward."

And indeed she was. The griffin crouched low to the ground and half-spread her impressive wings. Her tail was lashing like a cat preparing to pounce, and the quavering count was looking rather pale. It put me in mind of something my uncle Robert once said about courage: "In a game of cat and mouse, there's only one way to win - don't be the mouse!"

The man's toss would have fallen a bit short had the griffin not surged forward to snap it up in her beak. Almost before I could blink, she had turned her round, yellow eye toward the barrel, which Connor hastily set down.

"Greetings, Rupert," said the baron, clapping the man on the shoulder.

Ah. So this was the riding trainer of whom Margery had spoken. Yet another Cain. Evidently, the man had gotten a griffin of his own after all. It had been a couple of years since Margery Cunningham had told us of her escapades. This must be a new griffin, not one of the original three. Griffins were bonded to their riders. Even so, for a new griffin, it had grown awfully big. That must have taken a lot of fish!

A set of gasps and mutterings drew my attention to the street, where a line of spectators had gathered. Passersby were stopping to gawk, and neighbors were emerging to stare in wonder. Tame griffins were quite new. I doubt many in the lower city had ever seen one up close.

"I trust you were able to find your way without difficulty?" the baron asked.

Rupert raised his right forearm, whereon a strange disc was strapped.

"Javier's compass worked like a charm, your lordship. Freda and I had no trouble following the new route. We flew from Conclave to Lorédon, then through Eagle's Keep, and back here with nary a head-scratcher. 'Course the winds was favorable, and the sky was mostly clear."

"Rupert, this is the owner of the estate, Count Edmond Camburn."

"Pleased to make your acquaintance, my lord."

"And this," continued the baron, turning toward me, "is Lucas Harper, a mage from our barony. You may remember him as our miller's son."

Rupert flashed me a toothy grin, recognition slowly dawning on his face.

"I'm mighty glad to *see* you again, Lucas. You've grown quite a bit since that night in the bunker with our women folk. Pa says you battled the witch that cursed our clan and gave her what for! I wish I'd 'a been there to see it. We owe you one for that."

"Then you'll be happy to know that debt has been settled," I modestly replied. "Your brother Grindal saved my bacon not four days ago. In fact, I might owe him one now.

"Good to know."

As if the scene weren't chaotic enough, it was at this time that the carriage house door creaked open and a blonde-headed woman came dashing toward us. She'd matured since

I'd last seen her. So much so that at first I thought I was looking at her mother. But no, it was undoubtedly little Nellie Cunningham. She flung herself at Rupert, who caught her in his arms.

"Whoa there, darlin' I'm glad to see you too. But best I settle my business with the baron first. Is everything alright with Blynken?"

"She's fine; a bit broody, perhaps. Best you keep Freda at a distance. Attend to your business, then, but come and see me straight after. I might have some news to share."

She gave him a quick peck on the cheek, then turned and walked back the way she'd come. The two had been married last spring, if I recall correctly. Megan had written to me about it. Rupert rummaged through his satchel and produced a thick packet of missives, which he handed to the baron.

Frowning at the stack, his lordship muttered, "I hope Gerard isn't pestering everyone with unnecessary nonsense. The last time I left the barony, he had them tallying all the dinnerware."

"Oh, and before I forget," said Rupert, "these are for you."

With that, he thrust another stack of missives *my* way. This was followed by a larger, cloth-wrapped bundle. It was heavy for a book that I knew it to be, near the upper limit of objects the griffin riders would carry. I was thankful it had been included. Had it been shipped by caravan or even by a fast horse messenger, it may have come too late. That was one worry off my mind. I could scarcely wait to unwrap it and have a look.

"Thanks," I replied, and meant it.

"What's in the package, master?" asked Toby.

"I'll tell you later," I told him.

"Aren't you overdue for a lesson in table manners with Miss Lynette? Run along, now. You know how she gets when she's forced to come looking for you."

With a gulp, the lad departed.

The griffin turned a wary eye toward the gawking spectators and chirruped out a stuttering cry. Connor was running out of fish with which to appease her.

"She's beautiful," I remarked to Rupert. "How came you to name her Freda?"

"It's short for 'Freedom's Promise.' I named her that because she represents to me the freedom of the open skies. And it's also in honor of his lordship here. He let me have her from the first hatching to keep a promise made by the Cunninghams before they was sworn into his service. It was right decent of his lordship."

"There's some for you *too*, milord."

At this, he handed several letters to Count Camburn. The older man took them absently, but his eyes never left the griffin.

"Now, if I could just find Sir Trenton and Lady Megan, this old boy would be free to go and see what my wife is wanting."

Why was Nellie staying in the carriage house? I hadn't seen her before this afternoon. Had she been here all along? Rupert had mentioned Blynken. Was *she* in there too? It hadn't occurred to me to wonder why the carriages were left out at night. Perhaps the girl was nursing a sick griffin?

"I believe you'll find Trenton around back with Sir Nolan," said the baron. "And I can pass Megan's messages along to her."

"Much obliged," said Rupert.

After handing the baron several more missives, he sauntered off. The people on the roadway had grown more boisterous and had begun making 'cat calls,' as it were. This seemed to agitate the griffin, who chirruped back at them, only encouraging their bold behavior.

"Vincent, is he just going to leave that silly bird to squat on my front lawn, menacing the neighbors?" asked the count.

"Rest assured, Edmond, the griffins of Westarbor don't stray far from their riders, nor do they bite the hand that feeds them. Perhaps, though, you should disperse the crowd. Our noble birds can get a bit twitchy if they feel penned in."

The count rushed down the lane to do so, and I headed toward the dining room to check up on my servant.

***

I entered the room to find Toby seated at the far end of the long table. Lynette stood to one side just behind him with a water pitcher in hand.

"This one?" asked Toby, holding a two-tined instrument up for display.

"No. Forks are only for serving," said Lynette. "For your meat, you use the spearing knife."

"This one?"

"No. That's a *cutting* knife. Do you see how its edge is serrated?"

"Who would know the difference? A knife's a knife, right master?"

I merely grunted in reply. I could likely benefit from such a lesson myself. In my travels, I had learned that customs could differ greatly from place to place. If there were a standard dining etiquette in Osten, I hadn't figured it out yet. I got by mostly by watching those around me and imitating whatever they did. If anyone ever called me on it, I would simply apologize and remark that I'd been living among the elves and had grown accustomed to their ways.

The table had a lit set of candelabras at each end. Since the overhead chandelier remained unlit, this resulted in two islands of light separated by a sea of shadow. I tossed down my stack of missives on the table's near end and rested my package atop them. I took my seat as the lesson resumed. Before long, their soft voices and the clattering of various accoutrements faded into the background as I unwrapped my book.

It was a beautiful bound work. I ran my fingers gently over the soft leather cover of its bindings. It bore golden letters which read "De Re Publica." I opened it to reveal the pristine pages within. The black ink of the transcribed text contrasted sharply with the pale ivory of its leaves, almost seeming to float above the page. And it exuded the crisp, acrid scent of the oils used to treat the parchment.

I longed to begin reading it right here and now, but I wanted to preserve that experience for its intended recipient. Instead, I simply fanned through a few more pages before closing it.

"What's that?" asked Megan, causing me to start.

The woman had crept up behind me while I was enraptured by my purchase. My mind came swimming back to the present.

"No, Tam," Lynette was saying, "The spoon is for softer foods and soups and the like. And no - that's *not* soup. That's a finger bowl for washing your fingertips after you've handled something messy. Although I'm pretty sure it'll be soup by the time *you're* through with it."

"It's a birthday present for Prince Henry," I replied

"He likes books?"

Megan looked thoughtful as she perched on the lip of a high-backed chair and leaned close to admire the tome.

"He'll enjoy *this* one, I think. When I was down at Eagle's Keep, I ran across some scrolls on political philosophy. It's not my area of study, but the prince is mad for such things. Some of the brothers there at Eagle's Keep copy and illuminate texts, mostly scriptures. I commissioned this translation of Cicero's work into modern-day Ostenian."

"Who was this Cicero?"

"He was a senator in the Reman Republic and a famous orator. He wrote, "De Re Publica" to describe how an ideal republic should operate. In it, he suggests that the people be given more of a voice. His loss was a tragedy for Reme."

"Why? What happened to him?" asked Megan

"Oh. Uh. He was killed. The Reman rulers silenced him because of his radical ideas. Shortly thereafter, Reme became an empire and fell into decline due to poor governance. Kind of sad when you think about it."

"So, you know the prince pretty well then," observed Megan. "What did he want to discuss with you this morning?"

I felt my ears begin to burn. I could never successfully evade my lady's inquiries. My earnest countenance had a tendency to betray me, making me an inadvertent sharer of news. And against Megan's talent for seeking truth, a falsehood stood no chance. I didn't wish to betray my prince's confidence, but it will be court gossip soon enough. Hadn't Henry said as much after suggesting I couldn't keep a secret?

"He... he fancies you," I blurted.

Megan's eyes flew wide.

This hadn't been what she was expecting.

"He said he can't show a preference for any maiden until his ball next month, but that you intrigue him."

"Exact words, Lucas. What were his *exact* words?"

"Hmm... He said: 'I am taken with her.' He went on to say his father approved of such a match."

"Father must hear of this at once. For whatever reason, the prince wants to start this rumor."

What?

"He seemed quite sincere to me."

"Of *course* he did, and it *might* even be true. But there are any number of reasons the royals might wish to stir up the nobles."

"Such as?" I challenged.

"They might wish to make someone else jealous, a likely outcome in any event. Or they might wish to scare off one or more of my other suitors. Didn't it strike you as odd that the prince would issue such a statement in front of Tam, of all people?"

"Hey!" came the inarticulate protest from the table's far end.

"Until his highness makes such a statement directly to father or me, it is suspect."

Rising, she stalked out the door.

It was terrible that nobles had to swim in such treacherous waters, where even a friendly swimmer must be distrusted.

I returned to my letters, selecting one at random.

I was just breaking the seal on Royland's letter when Toby approached. Putting his hand on my forearm, he muttered in a low voice.

"You need to tell her how you *feel* about her, master."

I paused.

Lynette was staring moon-eyed at the both of us from where she stood across the room. One hand rested on her hip.

"Toby. Did I ever tell you what the king said to the chandler?" I asked in an even tone.

"No. I don't think you did."

"Mind your own *beeswax!*"

And scooping up my missives, I stomped from the room.

***

Over the next several days, we were visited by still more gentleman callers, but these began to peter off even as the season moved on. My services as escort were far less frequently needed as various noblemen rushed to fill that role. This left Toby and I somewhat at loose ends. But we always found productive ways to fill our days.

Take today, for example. The last blocks of the cathedral's facade had been laid more than a week ago, and all was in readiness for the prince's grand unveiling. Toby and I had arrived early and were let into Cathedral Square by the wary royal guardsmen. The prince had yet to arrive, but I thought I'd take the opportunity to attend to some other business I'd been neglecting. I headed toward the side of the church, seeking an alternate means of egress, with Toby following after.

The tarps hanging above flapped in the breeze as we stepped into the steeple's shadow. They'd all been joined into a single great banner which draped over the new stonework, obscuring it from our view. From the steeple's spire, a great, thick rope descended. Many colorful ribbons were wound about its girth. The other end was fastened to a stake in the ground just off the walkway leading up to the church itself. Ah. I see. When severed, the rope would free the tarps to flutter down, revealing the new facade.

Rounding the corner, I spied a side entrance. But before we had made much headway toward it, it opened, and a man stepped out. He was an older gent draped in clerical garb. His tall, pointed hat was as red as his other vestments and was mirrored by his sharply pointed white beard. He pulled the door closed and was locking it with an oversized key as we approached. He hung the key and its ring to dangle from a hook on his belt. Peering about, he sighted us and began to shuffle our way. Much to my chagrin, Toby decided to address the man before I could intervene.

"Hello. My master and I was just looking for a church officer. And who might you be, good sir? You look like a cardinal all dressed up in red like that."

I was sure he meant the bird. The man squinted down at my charge.

"You're not far wrong, young man," he answered. "I am, in fact, an archbishop. The red is in honor of Pentecost, but I hope to be made a cardinal soon if his apocryphal holiness deems me worthy. May I ask whom I am addressing?"

I breathed a sigh of relief and jumped in before Toby could concoct some other mischief.

"Apologies, your excellency. My servant is new and hasn't learned to mind his tongue. I am Lucas Harper of Meadowfork, and Toby here is my servant."

His gaze snapped up to meet mine.

"Ah, so you must be this Lucas the Just of whom I've heard. I am Benedict, Archbishop of Fairglen."

He extended his hand palms-down with his fingers curled beneath. Belatedly, I remembered it was customary to kiss the ring of a man so high on the spiritual ladder. I bent and did so.

"I take it you are here for the grand unveiling?" he continued. "Why are you seeking an official of the church?"

Straightening, I replied, "I came into a modest windfall recently. Being new to your city, I was uncertain with whom I could leave my tithe."

"The good Lord smiles upon those who are generous, and he shares his blessings with they who share theirs. I will gladly accept your humble offering on behalf of the Church of Fairglen."

From within my cloak, I retrieved the tithing bag Goodman Cedric had provided and placed it in his extended palm. His eyes widened a bit on noting its weight.

"Well, perhaps this not so humble offering entitles you to the grand tour. I was just heading to the viewing stand, as I assume you are as well. Walk with me, Sir Lucas."

I paced along beside the man as he shuffled back the way we'd come.

"Not really much to see at present," said the man pleasantly. "As you have doubtless already marked, here is the church."

He waved his hand to the side. Then he pointed upward toward the spire.

"And here is the steeple."

"Open the doors...?" I said suggestively.

"Whatever for?" he asked me with a perplexed look. "We can't do that until after the ceremony, in any event."

"Ah... never mind, your excellency," I answered. "My mistake. Um. I think I see someone I must talk with. Thank you for the tour. I'll meet you in the stands shortly. If I may take my leave?"

He nodded.

I hurried toward the grandstand where I'd seen Guildmaster Bennet a moment ago. I caught up to him just as he was taking his seat in the front row.

"Ah, Lucas," he hailed me. "I see you're wearing your pin, as is only proper on this proud day."

I approached and sat beside him.

"Indeed, master. Prince Henry himself graced me with an invitation to honor our accomplishment. I thought it meet to represent our guild at the proceedings."

"Just so," he agreed with a sloppy grin.

Some others were beginning to drift in, and the stands were beginning to fill. Where had Toby gotten, I wondered? Then I spotted him. He was standing before the archbishop. The man was looming over him, and their hands were folded in prayer. They were muttering something back and forth. Were they... praying?

"There's something I've been meaning to ask you, master."

"Oh?"

"There's a maker's mark I saw recently. I think I've seen it somewhere before, but I can't recall just where. I was hoping that as the head of the mason's guild, you might enlighten me."

Just then, Toby inverted his hands, still interlaced in prayer. Reaching up, he wiggled his fingers beneath the archbishop's nose. Before long, his excellency was grinning and nodding vigorously, and I heard him chuckle and exclaim.

"...all the nice people, indeed!"

"What did this mark look like?" asked the guildmaster, confused by my distraction. "Perhaps I might know it."

I bent forward and traced out the lines of the 'L' with the fishhook I'd seen on the stones of the Camburn well. Master Bennet's eyebrows shot up in surprise. He obviously recognized the symbol but remained silent for a moment.

"Well?" I prompted.

"Aye," he finally said. "I've seen that mark before."

I waited for him to continue.

"Lucas, do you know that in all of Osten, there are only six grandmaster masons? And out of all of them, there's only one that's not a dwarf. That there is the mark of grandmaster Lewis. What you call a fishhook is the 'J' of his first name."

"Javier?" I said, surprised by his reverence.

Suddenly, pieces began falling into place. I knew where I'd seen that mark before. Many of the blocks from the rubble of the mill had born a similar mark. I hadn't known what they were at the time. I knew Javier was friends with the dwarves and had done some work for the king here in Fairglen. But I hadn't known he was held in such high esteem by the masons. Perhaps he had worked on the Camburn well as a side-project. Well, mystery solved, I guess.

I was distracted yet again when Toby slid onto the bench beside me.

***

"Master," said Tobias, "I see one of them windowless carriages comin' around the coliseum. I think the prince is here."

I craned my neck around to see what he was talking about. And, indeed, there was the prince's carriage making its way toward us followed by a mob. As special guests of his highness, Toby and I had been let in early, along with a dozen or so other dignitaries. The rest of the gathering crowd had been kept out beyond the fence surrounding Cathedral Square. After making way for the prince's carriage, however, they were now pouring in behind it, intent on staking out a good spot to observe the spectacle.

Everyone looked excited, but among them were several groups who looked angry. Amid the general babble and enthusiastic shouts, I heard some chanting in unison: "Make Fairglen fair again! No more refugees!" What in the world were they going on about? The royal guardsmen were hard pressed to keep the unruly crowd back from the royal coach.

Another group of guardsmen were lined up just at the end of Pilgrims' Walk. They parted to let the carriage through, then closed ranks to deny entry to the mob. Some still stood chanting and jeering, but none risked a direct confrontation with the well-armed guards.

"Shameful, is it not?" said a man sitting to my rear. "You'd think they'd have gotten used to the idea the refugees are here to stay."

"I don't know, said another. They're only looking out for their own interests. If the prince lets the riffraff into the city proper, it puts the laborers' jobs at risk. He should've known better than to be popping off such nonsense at council."

A hush fell over the masses as the carriage door opened. Out stepped Prince Henry in full regalia. The few chants and catcalls from the angry-looking men were soon drowned out by the adulation of the rest of the crowd. From the grandstand on which I sat came a smattering of polite applause. I soon joined in.

One of the royal guardsmen stepped up. It might have been Guardsman Willis. It was hard to tell at this distance. They all looked so much alike. He knelt before his highness, holding an enormous sword flat before him. I'd seen it among the relics in the royal audience hall, hanging high upon the wall. Henry took it. One hand was on the pommel, and his other gripped the center of its blade. Leaning the over-sized weapon upon his shoulder, the young prince turned and marched in my direction.

"Lucas, a word," he said on drawing near.

I scrambled to my feet and hurried forth to comply. The people shuffled uneasily as I strode forth to meet their prince, and a hushed muttering descended as the noonday sun blazed down its warmth.

"I wanted you here that I might ask a small favor of you," Henry muttered.

"Anything, my prince," I said with a bow.

"This," he said, holding out the sword, "is Ultimum Refugium, the sword of Raymond the first."

I glanced down at the weapon. It was nearly as long as the prince was tall, and inset emeralds sparkled from its golden pommel. The blade, however, was all business. Its darkened steel gleamed with deadly promise. And to my mage sight, it shone with an inner light.

"It is more commonly known as 'Last Resort.' It is so named because King Raymond vowed to use it only when all other avenues of diplomacy had been exhausted. The problem is it's heavy. I can barely *lift* the damned thing."

"What would you have of *me*, my prince?"

"I'm told that you mages have a spell that can cut things from a distance. Is this true?"

"Yes. We call it the 'force axe' spell. My cousin and I once used it to sever the main shaft of a mill back in --"

"Save the details for another time," he snapped. "If I can't cleave through that rope with a single blow, it will be taken as an ill omen. People will say I am weak. When the time comes, ready your magic. If the rope fails to separate, you must quietly finish the job."

"Understood, your highness. I will stand ready."

I felt the weight of the many curious eyes peering at me as the prince left me and marched over to the stake. A herald moved up beside him with the speaker's staff in hand.

"People of Fairglen!" the herald began. "You are gathered here today to witness yet another triumph. Aye, a triumph, I say!"

"Our mighty cathedral has undergone a renewal. At the archbishop's request and by the talents of our ingenious masons, the ancient stones of its crumbling facade have been replaced. Let this new facade stir pride in your hearts whenever you look upon it. May it stand as a testament to the talents and resolve of all the citizens of our fair city!"

"I give you Prince Henry, who has sponsored this amazing transformation! Our good prince is wielding the sword of King Raymond, the legendary blade of his ancestors. This is the very blade King Raymond used to subdue the vicious troll, Glarp, winning an alliance with the elves. The moment is nigh. Wait for it... Wait for it..."

And then the bell began to toll. I'd heard the twelve bells of midday chime before, but never from so near to their source. Each time they rang out, I winced as their earsplitting ringing resounded. Despite the rattling of my bones, I focused on my inner hill, readying my magic.

Prince Henry, meanwhile, took the pommel of Last Resort in a two-handed grip and raised it shakily above his head. It was pointing straight up by the time the last bell rang.

Down came the sword with a flash and cleft the rope neatly in twain. The twisted ribbons splayed out from the swiftly rising line as the great canvas fell from above. The noonday sun was brutal as all squinted skyward to see. My first glimpse of the beautiful stone facade was marred by spots dancing before my eyes.

But what was this? As the great canvas tarpaulin crumpled toward the ground, it dragged behind it a rope. And suddenly, the rope did snag and catch. With a jerky shiver, it continued its downward course, but from my vantage, I could just make out a more solid mass that had broken loose from above. It plummeted toward the ground, its shadow growing ever more distinct. Directly beneath it stood my prince, still smiling, unaware. Time seemed to slow.

Had I not already had my magic summoned, I doubt I could have acted so swiftly. Leaping to my feet, I dashed forward lifting my hands above me. "Capturam Petram!" I cried, unleashing all the magic I could muster. I knew from experience that I had no chance of halting the craggy thing's plummet. But experience had also shown me an alternative. Focusing hard, I used my spell to divert the falling stone. With a swift prayer to saint Jude (patron of desperate straits) and a silent apology to the mason's guild, I guided it toward the stairway leading up to the main doors. It was the only clear area I could find. In a flash, an ironclad guardsman tackled his prince aside, covering him with his body just as an explosion of shards came raining down. Fragments of stone and shattered stairs alike now littered the area. I was nearly to where the prince had been standing but moments before, when I heard a clunking sound. And bouncing down from the impact site rolled a roundish ball of granite. I stopped it with my foot, nearly causing my knee to buckle.

As the dust kicked up by the collision began to clear, I heard shouts of alarm from the gathered crowd. They were only just becoming aware that something had gone awry. My heart was hammering within my chest as I stared at the offending object. It was the head of a stone gargoyle leering up at me. I lifted it from the ground, (stars, the thing was *heavy*) and turned to where Prince Henry was just regaining his feet. I employed my magic to lighten the load and handed it to him.

Confused at first, my prince soon collected himself and grinned over at me with appreciation. He hefted the thing in one hand, lifting it high above his head. He then lifted the sword, which I had also lightened, in his other hand and pointed it skyward. Turning to face the crowd, he stood triumphant, as though in defiance of fate herself.

"Hen-ry! Hen-ry! Hen-ry!" the crowd began to chant.

CHAPTER SEVEN

The Rabblerouser

"If the rabble were lopped off at one end
and the aristocrats at the other, all would
be well with the country."

~ *Andrew Johnson* ~

Waking in the predawn light, I sat up in my bed and stretched. The birds were just taking up their morning melody. Though it had been several days already, the riotous events at the cathedral still echoed in my waking mind. I brought my hand up to my cheek. The cut was healing nicely. Its scab was already beginning to flake off. I hadn't even noticed the wound in the chaotic aftermath of the gargoyle's fall. I was told it imparted a roguish charm to my otherwise youthful face.

The people were still talking about their prince's narrow escape from harm, and naturally, I figured most prominently in the exaggerated re-tellings of the event. Some even suggested that Henry and I had actually *caused* the mishap to bolster his popularity. Officially, it was deemed an accident. But I knew the royal guard considered it a purposeful attempt at regicide. Henry

203

had been hustled away to his carriage and returned to the royal palace surrounded by a full phalanx of their wary brethren.

"Go up and question the hunchback who rings the bells," I'd heard one guard remark to another. "Maybe *he* saw something."

Gathering up Toby, I had soon fled the scene and hied me back to the Camburn estate. And here I had remained, uncertain how my newfound notoriety might play out. Nor had anyone heard a peep from the palace since the incident. I wondered what had awakened me at this ungodly hour. I scanned the room. Where was Toby? The lad was absent from his unmade bed near the window.

"I sent him on an errand in the lower city," came a familiar rumbling from within.

I shook off the last of my drowsiness and gathered my wits. This was most strange.

"Rockytop? What errand?"

"Brace yourself, my brother, for the day has now arrived. 'Tis time to share the memories of which you were deprived. The plans we made in secret were most cleverly concealed. Lest to those who might oppose them, they too soon should be revealed."

How long had he spent composing that ominous little ditty? I wondered whether all geomancers had to suffer such smugness from their homunculi or if it was only me.

"Desist with all the drama," I commanded myself, "and just tell me already."

I let my eyes drift shut. At once, my mind seemed to open. And from it emerged a vision from the past. I was seated in sunlight at a small table across from Lady Castleberry. A maid was just pouring us tea. Greenery grew all about us and the Lady was staring at something over my shoulder.

"I understand you recruited your servant at the refugee camp, Sir Lucas. Is this so?"

"Yes, your ladyship. Toby is the son of refugees."

She pursed her lips and said, "He looks like he could use a refreshment *himself*. Lucille, take this young man back with you to the kitchen. Find him something to eat."

"Yes, milady," said the maid.

I watched as my servant followed the maid back into the house.

"Your ladyship is most kind," I remarked.

She sniffed.

"It borders on something I wanted to discuss with you. Tell me, are you aware of the nature of the refugee crisis we face?"

"I've seen their suffering. And I know it is through your own generosity that they are even able to sustain themselves. You are a kind and compassionate woman. I feel that working to--"

"Am I?" she challenged.

"Are you not?"

"With my resources, I could do so much more for them, but this would have dire political consequences for the kingdom."

"How so?"

"Let me lay it out for you, young man. Smile and nod a lot. Even here in my own home, I suspect we are being watched. We must be circumspect if we are to speak of such matters openly."

I nodded. Then belatedly, I smiled.

"The beggars and the labor guilds talk of unfair competition from these needy folks. And some concoct stories that the refugees will spread disease if let in. But the real reason they're kept out of the city is to keep others from following them here.

"For decades, this war has dragged on. The king puts on a brave face, but we in his inner circle know that Duke Gaulle is only holding on by the narrowest of threads. Under the battering of relentless assaults of a kind he can't beat back with a sword, he is near to exhaustion. His resources are scarce, propped up only by the king's treasury.

"Many of his tenants have already fled due to the miserable conditions along our southern border. What do you think would happen if word got back to those who remain that life here was fine and good with food aplenty and work for all?"

I set down my teacup and bit my lower lip.

"Eagle's Keep would fall," I replied. "Not in a glorious battle, but through economic collapse. Ground down and left to the mercy of scavengers."

"And the dark druids would soon be on our doorstep," said the lady with a nod.

"So... you help them," I said, hesitating a bit, "...but you try not to encourage them too greatly?"

"Just so," said the woman.

I was suddenly glad that Toby was absent. He'd always been so quick to praise Lady C's generosity. And now here she sat, calmly explaining why his people must be kept low.

"What does the king think of all this?"

"His majesty is... not the man his grandfather was."

"I once heard those very words before, your ladyship - from an autonomist back at the conclave."

Her face went still. This said something all by itself, though I couldn't grasp just what. Up until now, she'd seemed as lively as a lark at dawn. She nibbled at a biscuit and sat chewing for a bit.

"Would it surprise you to learn that Prince Henry himself is an autonomist?"

I was certain my startled face answered her better than any reply I could have made.

"It does," I finally said aloud.

"Prince Henry is intelligent and wise, a fit monarch for our realm. He realizes that societies evolve, and the people must be given a greater voice in their own governance. If he takes up the scepter, he could be a transformative figure the likes of which Osten has rarely seen."

"I mark milady says 'if.'"

"As with any time of change, there arises a stiff opposition by the status quo. Forces gather to oppose his reign. Some would prefer to see Richard on the throne, thinking he would be easier to manage."

I remembered to nod pleasantly, but I'm certain the pained smile I managed more resembled indigestion.

"You're really quite bad at deception, Sir Lucas. Perhaps I erred when I considered engaging you as an ally."

"That is a fair assessment, your ladyship. But please speak on. I can assure you that no hint of our conversation will betray you by my word or expression. I know a way to forget our entire conversation for a time."

"Thats very intriguing, sir mage. I take it this has aught to do with your magic?"

I nodded and smiled - a genuine smile.

"A test, then," she said unexpectedly. "Forget I said 'Bob White.'"

I summoned RockyTop and made the odd request, then nodded (for some reason).

"Bob," said the lady.

"Bob what?" I asked with consternation.

"That's marvelous. What a handy talent *that* would be at court!"

I didn't know what she was going on about until Rocky reminded me. Then we both had a good laugh about it.

"Well, then, given that," said the lady more soberly, "what I'd like to do is have the refugees seen as human beings rather than political pawns. Unfortunately, my position on the matter is too well-known at court and has proven... unconvincing."

"And how could I help with that?" I asked.

"You already have, to a degree. It's what caught my attention in the first place. It's clear that you champion their cause, and as an outsider, you are free of the constraints that have thus far kept my efforts in check. You are somewhat of a transformative figure *yourself*, Sir Lucas. I find it odd how readily you've endeared yourself to both the highborn and those of lower station alike."

She went on to outline her plan for a 'spontaneous' charitable event to be sponsored by Lucas the Just. It was a clever way to bring the plight of the refugees to the attention of all the good people of Fairglen. I tossed in a few suggestions of my own, and we hammered out the details as we finished with our tea. By then, the sun had drifted lower in the sky. The porter had come out to check on us.

"Wexley," said Victoria, "go and fetch Sir Lucas' servant. Tell him his master is preparing to depart."

After he'd gone, she turned to me, saying, "I shall quietly make all the arrangements, but my hand must not be seen in it."

"Alright," I replied. "You have my permission to use my name in this endeavor."

"And now, Sir Lucas, you must use your trick to forget the entire matter until the morning of the day in question."

It was to be the first Sunday in June. I had insisted on a Sunday because the conscripts at the camp and the city's laborers would all have that day off.

"You got all that, Rocky?" I mind whispered.

"I believe so, brother. Give me a moment. That's quite a large chunk of our awareness."

I felt the icy tendrils probing my thoughts, and recent events began to feel fuzzy and indistinct. I remembered sitting down and Toby heading to the kitchen for a snack... And here he was coming back already.

"Done so soon?" I said. "I hope you took the time to chew, Tobias."

"It was kind of you to drop by, sir mage," said Lady Castleberry. "You must visit us again soon."

Well, we'd scarcely had time enough for a proper conversation, but it was a fine start. Perhaps next time we can delve into matters of more consequence. I stood and smiled at the lady.

"The pleasure was all mine, madam. Your estate is almost as charming as its mistress. I shall gladly return when next my duties permit."

We were following Wexley back into the house when the stream of new memory ceased. I found myself still sitting upright in my bed just as the first rays of sunlight crept over my windowsill. I stood and padded over to the washstand. I splashed some water from the basin onto my face. I'd better get moving. If I recalled correctly, I'd have a big day ahead.

"Well done, Rocky," I whispered.

***

So here I stood in the manor lane, waiting for my servant to arrive. The sun was barely up, and I heard a muted cooing from within the carriage house. The knights were in the backyard, honing their skills with the blade. And Lord Stapleton's hounds were baying, upset by the clatter they made. All in all, it was another lovely summer day in Fairglen.

Then, along the road out front, I spied a procession of men. They wore the common garb of servants. Leading them was a man I'd met. He was Lady Castleberry's servant, Wexley. And beside him strode an earnest young man, chatting merrily with the old fellow. The other six burly men followed.

"Hello, the house!" hailed the younger man. "Is this the place where it starts?"

"If you mean the procession, then yes." I replied, as the two strode onto the lane.

"Well met, Sir Lucas," said Wexley. "The heralds should be by soon. All throughout the city, the messengers fly. Soon our invitation will ring in every ear."

"Well met *yourself*, Wexley. Eager for the day?"

"I'm a trifle nervous about it, to tell the truth, but my mistress assures me that all is in readiness. This young fellow is Gideon. We hired him from the crier's guild. He'll be at your disposal all day. And these other stout young lads are porters. They'll take charge of that oversized ale barrel yonder."

He indicated the upright tun standing before the carriage house.

"Toby thinks that *you're* such a porter," I said with a lob-sided grin as the six men shuffled off.

"Well, yes, I can see why he was confused. The man who grants access to a manor house is a very different sort of porter from what he's used to. He's a funny little chap, your servant."

If he only knew the half of it.

"I'm pleased to meet you, Sir Lucas," said Gideon, in a voice as smooth as butter. "'Tis indeed an honor to work for Lucas the Just, the man who saved our prince."

I was saved from responding by Toby's arrival. He was clopping down the lane on a mule. I recognized Feckless by his lazy gait and the way he tossed his head. Toby had arisen before dawn to retrieve him from the trader's guild. According to Lady Castleberry, my riding on a mule was iconic to my brand, and the citizens of Cheapside would lap it up. Scrambling down from the mule's back and taking up his leads, my servant approached, a happy grin on his cherubic face.

"Speak of the devil, and you see his horns," I muttered over to Wexley.

"Someone been talkin' about *me*, master?" asked Tobias with a squint of suspicion.

"So you acknowledge the devil reference, do you?" I chuckled. "Are your ears burning?"

From their color, if they weren't before, they certainly were now.

"I was just telling Wexley here you'd be along soon. He brought us some porters to help move that tun."

Toby surveyed the men who were straining to tilt the upright barrel over on its side.

"Well,,, " said Toby, resting a hand on Wexley's sleeve. "I reckon them six is strong enough, mister Wexley. No need to strain *yourself*. You done good bringing lots of help."

This set the ordinarily sour-faced porter to hugging his ribs and suppressing a laugh with a pained expression.

"Aw. Don't be sad, said Toby, patting the old man's arm. "Folks gets old, is all. It's just the way of things. You're still useful. And you was wise enough to know your limits."

Before long, the six burly men had the barrel on its side and had rolled it halfway out to the roadway. It was at this time that we heard the bells. The nearest was a brass handbell ringing merrily in the distance. I heard a voice proclaiming to the neighbors the message I'd been expecting. I couldn't quite make out the words, but I knew what they portended.

And strolling down the lane toward us came Sir Wulfric with a bouquet of roses in hand. Noticing all of us in the yard, the man looked somewhat baffled.

"Hail House Camburn," he said. "I've come for my outing with Lady Megan. Is she still so inclined?"

It was then that Megan and her father stepped out onto the veranda. My lady was a vision of loveliness, and my heart nearly caught in my throat to see her so beautifully attired, especially when it was for that scoundrel. The baron cast his gaze around the yard with some confusion.

"I am --"

The bell interrupted Megan's reply. Facing us from out on the roadway was the herald we'd heard from a distance. He had a scroll clutched in his fist and the bell in his other hand. It rang rhythmically for a time before the man repeated his announcement.

"Hear ye, hear ye! Good citizens of Fairglen, lend me your ears! It is with great joy that I declare a wondrous celebration in our midst! On this splendid day, a grand charity event unfurls its banner just beyond our city's gates. None other than our very own hometown hero, Lucas the Just, stands as the noble sponsor of this splendid affair! Cast aside your cares and join the revelry at Lucas the Just's grand benefit ball. Bring forth your appetites, for a sumptuous feast shall grace the tables tonight. Free ale will flow abundantly, accompanied by music and merriment that will warm your heart. A dance of joy, a symphony of laughter, and endless delights await you. There are no barriers, no boundaries, only an open invitation for all to partake. Venture to the gates, and the guardsmen there shall point the way. Be warned, for to absent oneself is to forgo an event that may prove the most splendid of the season! Join us, one and all, in this extraordinary celebration!"

With that, he turned on his heel and marched on.

I felt a hand on my shoulder. Turning, I found it was Lord Westarbor. He was searching my face with his penetrating blue eyes.

"What is all this, Lucas?" he asked. "And why is this the first I've heard of it?"

"Uh... It was a secret, your lordship. In fact, I was only made aware of it *myself* a few hours ago."

His frown deepened, but I met his stern glare unwaveringly. His truth sense must be telling him something clearly at odds with all the preparations.

"I confess I am intrigued," said the baron. "I should like to go myself, but the king has summoned me for a serious negotiation."

"*We* should go," said Megan to her stunned suitor. "That sounds like fun."

"But, my lady, it's not even on the social calendar. I've made arrangements for us to have a stroll about the palace gardens. I'm told the columbines are in full bloom."

"That does sound lovely, Sir Alfred, but this charity ball intrigues me. I'll understand if you still want to walk the gardens. I'm sure I can find another escort."

"Uh. No, my lady," he grumbled. "The point of the walk was to get to spend some time alone together. I'll gladly escort you to this strange mixer if that is your desire."

I decided to take pity on the knight and his stumbling tongue.

"In that case," said I, "I'd like to offer you both a ride there on the wagon."

"Oh? And what wagon might that be, mage?"

"That wagon," I said, gesturing with a flourish.

And prancing up the lane came two white horses. Their harnesses jingled festively with bells, and colorful ribbons were woven into their snow-white manes. They pulled a large, decorated wagon, wherein sat a man. In the wagon's bed, just before the man, was an enormous kettle drum.

"Go and get Lynette," I suggested. "See if she'd like to go as well."

"She'll need time to prepare," warned Megan.

"No," I replied. "It's come as you are. Tell her to hurry."

As she ran off to fetch her boon companion, I smiled. Did I feel sorry about ruining Sir Wulfric's 'time alone together' with Megan? Nope. Not one bit.

***

213

I led the way, followed immediately by six men rolling the gigantic tun of beer. Trailing them came our wagon with its drummer, town crier, and several other passengers waving at the astonished onlookers. I could see Megan's white-gloved hand doing so as we plodded along. I wished I could see her face. I resisted the urge to look back again. When she was seated, I couldn't see her above the tun, anyway. What was this 'serious negotiation' his lordship had with the king? It could be any number of things, but I feared my lady's hand might be among the chits on the bargaining table.

I tightened the reins on Feckless a bit. We'd come upon a rougher stretch of road, and I didn't want to get too far ahead of the men rolling the barrel. We'd learned not to stop for Gideon's announcements, lest the porters lose their momentum. It was hard to start up again with the beer sloshing about within it.

Bum. Bum. Bummmm-ba-Bum

The drum marked time with its hollow booming as we marched toward Broadway Avenue. The drummer was actually quite clever, varying it up now and again. He was no Royland, but then who was? In his letter, my cousin actually managed to make me yearn for all that was happening back at Conclave.

Gunther Brubaker and his wife, Meredith, had finally recovered from their stupor. The pyromancer was back at the foundry, firing up its furnaces. He'd even taken Lloyd on as his new journeyman. My former roommate still couldn't light a fire to save his life, but according to Roy, he'd discovered a new use for his gift. Lloyd could now step into his void, move a few steps, and then step back out again. Thus, even locked doors presented no barrier to Lloyd the Void.

Roy also reported that Mistress Julia had given him his first flying lesson. By his own admission, it hadn't gone very well. Still, I was envious. I would likely never master flight, aeromancy being my weakest discipline.

We neared a small group of nobles gathered at the side of the road. They were watching our curious procession. The drumbeats ceased, and Gideon belted out his verse.

"Don't await an engraved invitation.
It certainly won't be that sort of occasion.
Just come as you are; it isn't that far.
It's for people of any persuasion.

"There'll be dancing, drinking, and feasting for all.
So join us at Lucas' benefit ball.
There'll be music by the Fiddlers Three.
And best of all, the beer is free!"

This sparked a conversation among the onlookers. And while some shook their heads and seemed dubious, several others looked after us curiously. Two even fell into step behind us as the drummer resumed his rhythm. By the time we reached Broadway, we were trailing a dozen or so. I continued my ruminations as we turned southward. There was still quite a long way to go.

Tucked in with Royland's letter, there had been an oval leaf. I think it was from a magnolia tree. It was all dried out and brown. And drawn upon it in black ink was a crescent moon, followed only by the letter "T." I wasn't sure what to make of it at first until I thought of a former student of mine. Terwilliger was a brownie, and as far as I knew, he was the only fairy that could read or write. I remembered his trick with the Foxfire Fungus and supposed I was meant to view the thing under moonlight. Not wanting to wait, I experimented with my light spell until I found a hue that revealed the message. It was so deep purple that it was almost beyond my ability to see it. But it caused the letters on the leaf to glow.

"B CN U soon," it read.

For a fairy, that was quite literate, if still tragically vague.

Once we'd passed Cathedral Square, Gideon was calling out nearly nonstop. Several carriages had joined our ranks, and some of the walkers piled into them. At this point, the message changed somewhat. In addition to the now familiar verses, Gideon began adding the following:

"The simmering cauldron will leave you awestruck.
For dinner tonight will be a potluck.
The hungry we'll feed with this savory porridge,
Sparing them another day of forage.

"So open your hearts to the needs of the needy.
Bring what you have and don't be greedy.
A sack of potatoes; a carrot or two.
Anything you have to toss in the stew."

A group of ladies joined our march, spinning their parasols. A bakery wagon rolled up behind us with the trenchers we'd bought in advance. It was going quite well, I thought. But then, among the excited citizens lined up to catch a glimpse of us, I noticed some were booing us and shaking their fists. I remembered the chants at the prince's unveiling. Some wanted the refugees to depart, and our efforts had raised their ire.

Very well, I'd endure it, I thought. But matters would soon come to a head. My resolve would be sorely tested by protesters blocking the road. We had passed the Silverlight Grand, and had forty more blocks to go, when a solid wall of angry men surged out into the street. With scornful chants and sneering faces, they brought our march to a halt. Some began flinging clods of dirt our way, and I feared that stones might follow. Worst of all, our crier couldn't be heard at all above their shouts.

Many who might have joined us wanted no part of this. They wisely turned and walked away from the conflict that was brewing. Then I heard it. A voice. A single voice shouting out aloud. It was the voice of one woman objecting to the bullies barring our way.

"Let them Pass! Let them pass!" she shrieked.

I smiled as her simple words bestirred the conscience of the crowd.

"LET THEM PASS! LET THEM PASS!" thundered out the masses who were taking up the chant.

Though they now looked quite uncertain and saw how outnumbered they were, the demonstrators failed to yield the street. You cannot reason with hate and fear or tell people what they refuse to hear. I could admire their conviction while despising their methods.

I think Lady Castleberry knew that something like this might happen and had prepared for it. It was then that the black clad horsemen came riding up from behind. They were at least a dozen strong and sat atop their snorting mounts. They were led by a man I knew. He came trotting up beside me and eyed the group before us in a calm and placid manner. On sighting me, he made a strange gesture, clapping his closed left fist against his right breast. The others did the same.

The street went quiet then.

"Greetings, Lucas," said Guardsman Willis. "I heard you were hosting a feast. And since some of us have the day off, we thought we might join you."

"Well, that would be pleasant, guardsman. We were just on our way there now. Join me in the vanguard, that we may talk as we ride."

Further demoralized, the angry men began to slink away.

"So, tell me, Guardsman Willis," I said as I urged Feckless forward, "what was that strange gesture you made on approaching me?"

"Ah, that. We call it the sovereign salute. It is the second highest honor we of the royal guard can award. It is earned by taking a wound while defending the king or one of the royal family."

As we slowly picked up our pace, the demonstrators melted away before us. I lifted my hand to my cheek.

"What? This? It's barely a scratch."

"It counts. Those flying stones could have taken off your head. I was there, remember?"

"Hmm. What's the *highest* honor? Perhaps I can earn that as well."

"I sincerely hope not, Lucas. *That* one is only awarded posthumously."

I grimaced.

The drum resumed its lively marching beat. The barrel rolled. And the town crier wailed out his verses. Somewhere below Thirtieth Street he added several more to the end.

And if you haven't aught to give, do not shy away.
In support of your brothers outside of the walls,
join us and come along anyway.
Bring us your stories, your laughter, your song.
In solidarity, the people are strong.

Bring only yourself. Stand tall and shout.
From the very heart of Cheapside, let your voice ring out.

Refugees, by the grace of God, are people just like you.
With dreams in their hearts
and scars from the many hardships they've won through.
Mothers and fathers cruel fate did condemn.
But your presence will show we still care about them.

It was hard not to get a little choked up. The lad had made an emotional appeal to the better nature of those who dwelt here. I saw dozens of beggars and a few folks one might think unsavory come skulking out to join the throng. I hope there were no pickpockets among them, but I suppose that criminal opportunists need to make a living too.

We poured out through the gates and onto the roadway beyond. As we approached the turnoff, I spied the well. I urged Feckless up to speed and trotted on ahead. As we had discussed, I came to a halt beside the well, turned to face the trailing mob, and waved them on past. The breeze was from the south, bringing the scent of wood-smoke.

I sat upon Feckless, smiling and waving as first the barrel, then carriage after carriage, turned onto the lane toward Refuge. When the decorated wagon arrived, it stopped briefly to let Toby, Lynette, Megan, and Sir Wulfric disembark. I winced as the knight helped my lady down. I thought his hands lingered far too long on her waist.

"So where is this statue you've been going on about?" asked Sir Wulfric.

"It's just there, built into the wellhead," said Megan. "It's the one on the right."

Sir Wulfric stepped past me and stared at the stone angel in question. He paused. Then he peered back at Megan. He did this several times more before rendering his verdict.

"'Tis a passing likeness, my lady, but no rival to your own beauty. Just as the moon can do naught but cast feeble reflections of the sun's radiant glory."

Pee-yew.

The man could certainly conjure up an eloquent turn of phrase. I had but one consolation. If his heart wasn't in it, Megan would see through such flattery like a dewdrop on a leaf, only magnifying any insincerity.

I smiled and waved like a good host as the people paraded past.

Eventually, Sir Wulfric, Lady Megan, and Lynette joined the revelers and continued on to the celebration. This left Toby and me to greet the few stragglers who continued to amble on by. I was about to pack it in and head down the lane myself when I spied a lone figure pushing a cart along the road. She wasn't coming from Fairglen, but rather from the other direction. It was the young shepherdess whose staff I'd enchanted.

"Hey, Bonnie!" shouted Toby as she approached.

"Hello, Toby," she hollered back.

"What's in the cart?" my servant asked.

"Oh," she said, "we heard about the benefit from the heralds. And remembering your kind help last week, my pa thought he could spare some lambs from the spring culling. We home butchered a few, and he sent me on ahead with 'em. He's cleaning up and will drop by after."

"You remember my *master*," said Toby.

"Of course I do," said the girl as she rolled up beside us. "In case I didn't introduce myself before, I'm Bonnie, Bonnie Sheppard. Our spread is just over yonder."

I nodded.

"Well, you can take the mutton down the lane to Refuge. Toby, why don't you help her?" I suggested.

The lad rushed to comply, and soon the two were rolling the cart down the lane. Mounted on Feckless, I followed at a walk. In the distance, I could hear music. It was a bouncy little tune punctuated by occasional bouts of clapping. As we neared the camp, I began to make out the words.

The bakers in their bakery are mixing flour and yeast.
And firing up their ovens, preparin' for the feast.
Their tasty pies and pastries will fill us with delights!
We'll wash 'em down
with ale from the brewery to quell our appetites!
Clappidy-clap! Ka-clap Ka-clap! Cla-clapiddy-clap Ka-clap!

Up ahead, I could see a ring of guests surrounding the wagon. In addition to the drummer who had accompanied us down Broadway, there were a group of other minstrels. Just as promised, the Fiddlers Three sat among them. The singer was operating a strange musical instrument I had never seen before. It resembled a small bellows. It made breathy, reedy sounds as he stretched it out and pressed it back together. I would later learn that he called it a concertina.

The chaplain here is overworked.
He's said three masses already.
And from the drinking this required,
he's lookin' a little unsteady.
I hope that by the feast tonight, we'll all be feelin' as fine.
The vicar is sicker,
but liquor is quicker than sacramental wine!
Clappidy-clap! Ka-clap Ka-clap! Cla-clapiddy-clap Ka-clap!

A lot of laughter accompanied the clapping after this verse. By this time, we'd reached the back of the crowd. The gathered people were swaying to the beat and clapping along. I paused there while Toby and the shepherd girl continued on toward the cook fires.

The children at the maypole -
they laugh and sing and shout.
And taking up their ribbons, go twirling and whirling about.
With a heidy-ho and a heidy-hey, To-lou-ra-lou-ra-ley!
They decorate the campsite, on this auspicious day!
Clappidy-clap! Ka-clap Ka-clap! Cla-clapiddy-clap Ka-clap!
Hurray!

At this, the song ended, and after a brief silence, the excited babble of conversation arose. Beyond the wagon, I spied my gigantic tun of beer, before which a line of guests had formed. Serving them was my old friend Cliff from the Wayfarer's Rest. He had tapped the thing and was dispensing drinks to one and all. Beyond even that, I saw a gigantic stew pot tended by a bevy of cooks. It was even larger than the big cauldron Tilda had used to dye her wool, and savory aromas were already beginning to fill the air. My attention was abruptly drawn back to the wagon when Liam Gordon began to speak.

"There he is, our *host* for this fine event."

He was pointing straight at me, directing the crowd's attention my way.

"I had the honor of knowing him *before* he became Lucas the Just. But even back then, when he was just Lucas, he already had a reputation for heroic deeds. Therefore, let us turn back the hourglass and recall those days when he was just a mere lad from the beleaguered barony of Westarbor!"

At this, the band struck up a tune that had been my bane several years back. It had been composed by Maestro Bok to commemorate the grueling battle with the goblins at Westarbor Keep. In it, the good maestro took extreme liberties with the truth, sometimes abandoning her entirely. At its roots, it bore some resemblance to the events that had transpired, but it ascribed to me all the credit for a victory that was hard won by many.

I held my peace as the introduction played out and Liam himself sang the lyrics. I didn't protest. That would be ungrateful. I waited patiently and tried to look humble for all six stanzas of the beastly thing. With everyone looking expectantly up at me, I thought I should say something.

"Yes. Well. Those were certainly exciting times. I understand Grindal Cain will be calling a square dance later out in the commons yonder. In the mean time, please help yourself to a drink on me. Thank you all for coming."

With a wave and a wink, I turned Feckless around and made for the camp proper.

***

Some of the refugees had come out to help with the festivities or join the crowd from the city, but some seemed reluctant to do so. As I wove my way into their hodge-podge village, I saw them casting suspicious glances toward the gathering. Dismounting I led Feckless toward the bede house where Toby's mother lived. Before I arrived, I spied some familiar figures congregating nearby. I ambled over to see what they were about.

"Thane Ewen!" I greeted on my approach. "What are you lot doing over here?"

The dwarven noble and his men were gathered at the edge of a shallow rectangular pit conferring with Aaron Moss and several other men who worked at the quarry.

"Ah, Sir Lucas," he said. "I was just advising Goodman Moss here on the correct way to lay a foundation. Without good drainage, I fear his project will soon lay in ruins."

"And just why, might I ask, is a dwarf of Echo Hills sticking his nose into the business of masons?"

This last was hollered by Guildmaster Bennet. He was approaching the dig-site from the other direction followed by a gang of his guild mates.

"Well," replied the startled noble, "although masonry is not my profession, we dwarves are known to dabble in all sorts of construction, and we are renowned for our fine stonecraft. Who are you, sir, to question a thane so rudely?"

"Only the guildmaster of the Fairglen masons on whose territory you're encroaching. We'll thank you to leave off telling our people how to lay a proper foundation. So say I."

"So say we all!" chanted the others.

The guildmaster looked over at me sharply, noting I hadn't joined in. Ewen stroked his beard and stared at the masons in challenge.

223

"Were we within yon city's walls, I might suffer your abrasive tone in silence. But as we are without, I am more inclined to view it as the imprudent yapping of a pup on spying a bigger hound. We will share our advice with whom we please. So say *I*."

Grinning, the other dwarves belatedly took up the mocking challenge.

"So say *we* all!"

This was quickly getting out of hand. These groups obviously needed a mediator. What were they quibbling about anyway. While they stood glowering at one another across the pit, I slapped on a happy grin, took a deep breath, and wandered into the fray.

"You fellows are all amazing." I laughed. "Everyone wanting to help! It exemplifies the spirit my benefit was meant to foster. What are you building, Aaron? I'm most curious to know."

"Uh. Well..." he began uncertainly. "It's to be a hospital for our aged and infirm. Autumn's comin' on, and we fear the winter to follow might be a cruel hardship for the less hardy among our folk. With the stones and mortar you gifted us, we thought we'd best make a start at it, seein' as how we only have Sundays to work on it."

The dwarves and the masons looked abashed, reminded of why they were here. Guildmaster Bennet was the first to recover and speak.

"You're right, Journeyman. We was just comin' over to investigate. It's clear our aid is needed. I'll organize a work detail, and have this thing built in a week. The masons of Fairglen all be of charitable hearts and minds."

If I knew the thane, he couldn't let that pass. The pride of Clan MacLaren was now at stake.

"Hmm," he mused while stroking on his beard. "Goodman Moss here told us of another need. His village needs a smokehouse so the scant game the refugees hunt can be preserved for the coming winter. We've still a few weeks before the coronation is upon us. Me and the lads will attend to that. It'll do us good to get our hands dirty again."

"That's mighty big-hearted for such a short little fellow," said the guildmaster with a sardonic smile. "I'm certain your squat little smoking shack will look quite quaint beside our matchless manor."

"It's brave of you to say so," replied Ewen with matching disdain. "The sophomoric stylings of lesser men are oft seen as callow when stood next to any edifice raised by dwarves."

"Sopho-what, now?"

I suppose I was foolish to hope for good-natured cooperation between the two rival groups. But at least they were channeling their animosity along productive lines.

"A contest, then." I loudly declared.

This had everyone's attention.

"I'll return next Sunday at noon to see what you're efforts have wrought. For now, though, gentlemen, go and enjoy the feast. You too, Aaron. It's your day off, after all. No one is to lift a shovel until tomorrow morning. Tonight we feast and celebrate in unity."

With a grumbling agreement, the gathered men disbursed.

***

Aaron and I walked Feckless over to the bede house where I'd first met Nora. Aaron seemed excited about the prospect of getting some help. There was a bounce in his step, and he was whistling. When we arrived, I tied Feckless' leads to the same axle casing where I'd tied Gypsy during my first visit. As I was doing so, Nora came from the side yard wearing an oven mitt in which she held a steaming teakettle.

"How are our guests faring?" Aaron asked her.

"Mister Harper, what a pleasant surprise," she greeted me. "We heard you were sponsoring this party and hoped you might drop by."

Nora looked weary, like she'd missed a night of sleep. But her amiable smile was just as gracious as ever. She turned to Aaron and sighed.

"They're sleeping, mostly. I thought I'd rouse them and see whether they could take a bit of broth. The poor dears took an awful chill the other night."

"Well, we've had a bit of good news, dearest," Aaron reported. "The masons are going to finish the new building for us. They say it'll be up in a week's time."

"That's marvelous news indeed, love."

"Not only that. Those dwarves I was talking to want to help out too. They'll be coming to work on the smokehouse."

Nora's eyes flitted over to me, and her smile twisted up on one side.

"I'm guessing we have a certain fairy godmother to thank for that."

I snorted. Few were aware I'd once been granted that honorary title by the faire folk themselves.

"I may have given them a nudge, madam, but the good folk of Fairglen can be very kind once they are made aware of an injustice. Who are you caring for in the bede house? Is old Caesar feeling ill?"

Nora's smile wavered, and Aaron's shoulders drooped.

"I'm afraid old Caesar is no longer with us," said Aaron. "He passed quietly the other night. We buried him in Potter's Field with the others who have passed."

I'd only met the man once, but he seemed like an amiable old gent. I should really be getting back to see to the banquet, but I felt certain they could manage for a while without me. I needed a moment to settle my thoughts.

"Will you take me there? I'd like to pay my respects."

Aaron and Nora shared a look before he replied.

"Aye. Follow me, Sir Lucas."

As Nora turned and made her way into the bede house, steaming kettle in hand, I followed Aaron. We wended our way through the pitiable tents and out onto the hard-packed ground to the east of the camp. A good distance out from the settlement, I spied the turned up earth. It was a series of rough earthen mounds laid out in a row. At the head of each, crossed sticks thrust up from the ground. Aaron led me to the last of these and removed his hat. I did likewise.

It was too bad Caesar hadn't held out for a week longer. He would have enjoyed the festivities. It was unfair. It wasn't his fault that his ranch had lain in the war-torn lands of the south. And after all the hardships he'd suffered, he'd spent his last days in a refugee camp. I felt he deserved better than a pauper's grave. They all did.

Silently, I turned and retraced my steps back to the site where the hospital was to be built. This couldn't happen soon enough, I thought. But I was here for a different reason at the moment. I rummaged through the building stones and found one that would do. Aaron frowned as I dragged it free from the pile and lifted it onto my shoulder. I thought about the old stonecutter back at Gentle Repose as I trudged back toward the cemetery.

By this time, several others had noticed me. Some followed me out onto the field. Their curious eyes tracked the heavy stone as I handled it with ease. Were it not for my magic, such a burden would be beyond my strength to even lift. Gently, I set it down at the head of old Caesar's final place of rest. I already knew what it should say.

Laying my hands upon the stone, I smoothed its craggy face. I worked my will upon it further, causing graven letters to appear.

CAESAR HOLLANDER

A rancher from

The western E.K.

Sought a better place

And finally found his way.

MCCXXVI

There. That set my heart at ease. The dead should be honored, not lay forgotten. I didn't know any of the others, and I shed no tears for them. But at least this one man would be properly remembered. The others had drawn closer around me, and several were muttering to their less literate brethren the words I had inscribed. They looked at me with wonder, nodded, and silently ambled off. Aaron was the last to depart after nodding to me as well.

There was one man, however, who stood apart from all the rest, looking on from the field's far edge. I could tell from his boots that he was finely dressed beneath his soiled gray cloak. He was a somber, hooded figure, standing tall and all alone. Once the others had gone, he approached me.

"You are Lucas, the one they call the just?"

It was barely a question - more of a statement, really. And in his quiet baritone, I heard a note of sorrow.

"I am he," I replied.

"Belated greetings, then, mage. I had the honor of hosting you once, but I'm afraid I granted you a most unbefitting reception."

My mind reeled at the implications. Could this be Duke Gaulle? I knew he was here at the capital, but I hardly thought a man of his stature would show up at my benefit. I'd seen him at the debutante ball, but I hadn't marked his features. His ducal robes had been enough to identify the lord. Why was he here alone, with no servants and no escort?

"Pardon me, your grace," I said, bowing low. "I didn't recognize you."

"Nay, sir mage," he said bitterly. "The fault is all mine for coming unannounced. And do not bow to me in this of all places, for I do not deserve it."

Studying his aged face set in lines of woe, I noticed he was sighting past me along the row of graves. His somber words were off-putting. Lords rarely uttered anything so resembling an apology. How could I respond? I dare not gainsay a duke of the realm, but to remain silent would tacitly confirm the condemnation. I took hold of my panicked thoughts and waded carefully into these dangerous waters.

"Steady, your grace. Why do you feel unworthy of the deference due your station?"

"I failed them," he whispered. "I failed them all."

"I was angered at first each time a serf abandoned his tenancy without my leave. But I have since come to realize it was I, not they, who failed to fulfill the oath. It is true enough that a ruler is owed the respect and obedience of his people. But he, in turn, is supposed to *protect* his subjects; and therein I was found wanting. For when faced with the horrors the dark druids unleashed upon us, my knights could barely protect *themselves*. The serfs who labored under my yoke deserved a better lord."

I didn't like how he was drifting into the past tense. Had my simple gesture triggered the good lord's bout of melancholy? Or had he already been on the brink of self-castigation? At Sir Trenton's suggestion, I once made a careful study of the knightly code. Perhaps therein lay the language that could soothe his sorrowful mood.

"Take comfort, your grace, for the code does not require success in every venture; only that one embrace its tenets and fulfill them to the best of one's ability. One in particular comes to mind, which your grace must surely heed. The code enjoins us to 'persevere to the end in any enterprise begun.'"

"You say your serfs deserve a better lord? Then *be* a better lord. You can start by forgiving yourself for that which couldn't be overcome. But if your grace still harbors regrets, then it isn't with me that you should share them. Tell the people you think you have wronged, and as good Christian souls, they'll forgive you."

The duke went silent for a long moment then, and his eyes finally swiveled to meet mine. When he spoke, it was with a quiet conviction.

"I think I should like to do as you suggest."

I let out the breath I'd been holding and listened on.

"When I was but a lad," the duke continued, "often would I try to postpone any odious task. At such times, my father would chastise me: 'Where better than here? When better than now?' he would ask. Sir Lucas, will you announce me to the gathered crowd? There is aught I would say to them."

"Of course, your grace, if that is what you wish."

***

I led the way back through the camp to the feast on its western side. The crowd had grown quite a bit and had spread out into the fields beyond. I could scarcely credit that so many people had harkened to our call. Had we depopulated all of Fairglen? But no, the city was enormous. Most of the crowd was well-behaved for now, especially while the royal guardsmen prowled among them. But I wondered what might happen should the tun run dry.

As a full tun held CCLVI gallons (more than two thousand pints), I had calculated it might hold throughout the afternoon against a crowd of nearly two thousand, an unthinkable number of folks. I hadn't reckoned on dwarves in these estimates, however. I frowned at the thought. It was a good thing they were so few in number.

On recognizing me, most of the guests politely parted to make way for us. Many stared curiously at the tall, gray-cloaked figure who stalked at my rear. Still, I was jostled occasionally as some of the overindulging revelers brushed against me. I practiced restraint and clutched my coin purse tightly beneath my cloak. I hoped that Toby was keeping a close watch on my bob rather than ogling the comely young vixen he'd befriended.

We finally arrived at the decorated wagon, whereon the minstrels played. Our timing proved fortuitous, as they were just finishing a piece. I caught Liam's eye and gestured for the music to be stilled. I then ascended the ramp on the back, up to the bandstand proper, followed by my mysterious companion. The people stilled (as much as any crowd ever did), sensing a new surprise.

"Um, hello everyone!" I shouted.

Where was my crier? He would have known how to proceed.

"Hello Lucas!" shouted the crowd.

I took a page from Grindal's book to get them in better spirits.

"How are we all feeling today?" I belted out.

The chaotic roar that followed consisted of no discernible speech, but it seemed lively enough. With a sweeping wave of my hand, I indicated Lord Gaulle, who stood to my right.

"We will have a special guest speaker this morning. Let's all give a hearty welcome to his grace, Lord Phillip Gaulle of Eagle's Keep."

Amid the silence that greeted my words, there was some laughter that quickly trailed off when Lord Gaulle stepped to the fore and shrugged off his hooded cloak. Beneath, he was most definitely attired in noble fashion. Looks of alarm were exchanged. Some cringed as if struck, while others swept the hats from their heads. Then, like a wave upon the sea, the crowd bowed low. I probably should have done a better job of preparing them.

The duke was silent for a time, staring out over the gathered crowd, which was growing by the moment as others joined. If he was nervous, it didn't show. Duke Gaulle was likely a veteran of many a public address.

"People of Fairglen and honored visitors," he began. "I hope you will grant me your forbearance while I clarify a few matters."

"My people know me to be a man of few words. Both in speeches and in swordplay, I go straight to the point. So here it is in a nutshell:

"I would have it known that all who fled and abandoned their tenancies in the duchy of Eagle's Keep without my leave are forthwith granted a general amnesty. It was my duty to protect you, and I hereby acknowledge that I failed in that duty. Therefore, you are not in breach of your oath of tenancy and will not be held to account for such."

His stern declaration had a profound impact on the crowd. They stared about, dumbfounded and amazed. Some openly wept. In a single stroke, Duke Gaulle had lifted the burden of criminality that had weighed on the refugees' souls. The other good folk of Fairglen reeled with the implications. Never had they heard a nobleman admit to error in such an earnest manner. The duke raised a hand and waited for the crowd to still once more.

"Some of you present here today were once tenants on my lands. I regret that my inadequacies have led you to such dire straits. But I wish to inform you that conditions in the E.K. have improved. The border has become more secure. With the loss of their powerful overlord, the threat from the dark druids is greatly diminished. And solutions for the plagues that have ravaged us are even now being employed."

"Bullocks!" came a voice from the crowd.

There was a stir to the right, and I saw a man being shushed by his neighbors. Lord Gaulle cast a sharp gaze in that direction.

"Let him speak!" proclaimed the duke. "What part of my statement do you take issue with, goodman?"

Under the scrutiny of his fellows, the man grew pensive. But he soon found his courage and shouted back.

"We've heard all this malarkey before, your grace. And every time we return to tilling the land, some new horror raises its ugly head. What's being done about them blade moths that destroys an entire crop? We nearly *starved* last summer."

The man was brave. I'd give him that. Or perhaps he was merely fortified by the Stonehammer Stout. There followed a murmuring among the people as some muttered their agreement to their neighbors.

"A fair point," said the duke, surprising all.

"You may have heard that we are now allied with the fairy kingdom. They don't offer us warriors, but Queen Tinatia has stationed a number of her sylphs in the south. They command the winds. And since the blade moths go where the wind takes them, whenever a cloud of those destructive pests arises, it is directed southward, farther on into the marshes."

Emboldened by the duke's amiable and seemingly open dialog, a woman stepped up from the center.

"What about the stranglevines that have been cropping up all over? My best milk cow got caught up in one. The next thing I knew, she'd become a vine-covered creature and was attacking the rest of the herd. That's when *I* packed it in."

The wrinkles in the duke's forehead deepened at this, and he stared down at the woman with sympathy.

"I'm sorry that happened to you, dear lady. We're still working on that one. The source of the stranglevine infestation was scouted out and identified last season by none other than Lucas here. It's where we have the sylphs directing all the blade moths."

A few people began nodding their heads and smiling.

"However," he continued, "those perfidious weeds spread their seeds far and wide, and there are still outbreaks here and there. But a mage from the conclave has struck upon a most promising solution. Zaid Guthrie, I believe, is his name. He has found a variety of turtle that eats the damned things; they thrive on them, actually."

"Turtles?" returned the woman skeptically.

"Indeed," the duke replied. "The roots of the vicious plants can't penetrate the turtle's protective shells. Instead, the turtles graze on *them* with their sharp beaks. Best of all, once an infestation is cleared, I'm told the turtles make quite a tasty stew.

"So you see, where our warriors may have failed us, the creativity and ingenuity of our scholars and allies are gaining the upper hand at last. What Osten needs are more brave souls and willing hands to thwart our enemies' wicked plans. And therefore, I'd like to lay before you an offer. If you feel you are up to the challenge, I offer any here the opportunity to help us reclaim our lost lands and industries. Exciting things are happening in the E.K. (and not all of them are bad)."

"What offer, your grace?" shouted a man from the back.

"You need not decide today. After the coronation, I will be returning to my stronghold. At that time, I will make wagons, fresh seed, and livestock available to anyone who wishes to join me in my sojourn and start anew. There are many prime tenancies ready for occupation. It will be difficult at first. There will be hardships. Only a short growing season remains, but nor will the winter be as harsh as here. Best of all, I'm declaring a tax holiday for all new tenants for the first two years.

"Some of you will doubtless prefer to stay here to build your new community. But to those who accompany me, I pledge to do my utmost to protect you and... *be a better lord*."

He saluted them, turned, and stepped down the ramp behind the wagon.

For a 'man of few words,' the duke could certainly be long-winded. I had to hand it to the old codger. He was actually a very accomplished orator. His initial declaration had captivated the crowd. His frank and earnest discussion of the issues disarmed them. And I think this last rousing bit had actually charmed a few.

I realized that they were all staring at *me*.

"Uh. Carry on!" I shouted, waving my hand about.

I could be pretty smooth when talking face-to-face, but crowds gave me the willies. I turned and retreated down the ramp myself with a little less dignity than had the duke.

***

When I scurried down the ramp, the duke was nowhere in sight. Doubtless, he had already donned his unremarkable cloak and melted into the crowd. I thought his speech had been well received and had given the guests a lot to ponder.

Eyes tracked me, but most of the good people had returned to their cheerful revelry. So, I quietly made my way toward the cooking fire, thinking to discover where Toby might have gotten. On my way there, I heard snatches of a conversation that piqued my interest. Out on the open field to the west sat a ring of youngsters, some of whom appeared to be refugees. They were gathered around a storyteller who held them enthralled.

"... Then the gargoyle came swoopin' down from the steeple with murder in its wicked heart."

The round-eyed children gasped.

"It flew down at Prince Henry with vicious intent; aye, vicious."

He flapped his hands about and turned to face each child in turn.

"And while Prince Henry held it off with his big, long sword, Lucas blew it to flinders with a bolt of magic! Then the prince beheaded the creature and held it up so as to prove it to all the crowd."

"How could he behead it after Lucas blew it apart?" objected an older lad with suspicion.

"Oh, um, it might a been still kickin' a bit," declared the storyteller, "but our prince quick put an end to *that!*"

I shook my head and strode on.

235

Nearing the cauldron, I beheld another happy gathering. Lady Megan, Lynette, and Sir Wulfric were seated on the ground, surrounded by young girls from the camp. All had baskets filled with wildflowers they had gathered. As I watched, Megan was instructing them on how to knot the stems together to form daisy chains. Charmed, I decided to join them.

"Hello, ladies," I hailed them. "I see you've found a worthy way to while away the wait for your midday meal. You'll find in Megan an apt mentor for such endeavors, but the man beside her seems to lack the delicacy required, I daresay."

The girls tittered.

"Perhaps you dare too much, mage," said the knight with seeming equanimity.

I noticed, however, how his fist tightened on the posy he was preparing, further flattening the stems of the nosegay. Megan looked up at me with mild disapproval. I was saved from my lady's scorn by the arrival of two others. Lady Jacquelyn, another debutante, was accompanied by a serious-looking maiden carrying a great wooden bucket. Megan greeted them with delight.

"Jackie!" she hailed. "Girls, this is Lady Jacquelyn Beatrice Nimble, the one I was telling you about."

"The one who jumped over the candlethtickth?" asked one little girl who was missing a front tooth.

Megan stood and brushed at her skirts.

"The very same, Elsie. What are *you* up to, Lady Nimble?"

"Just trying to do our part, Lady Arenson. More fresh water is needed for the stew. It's thickening up nicely. This is my companion, Jillian O'Keefe. We asked the cooks what we could do to help out, and they sent us up to the well to fetch a pail of water."

"You're brave and very nithe," lisped Elsie, offering her a circlet of daisies. "Thith ith for you."

"Well, aren't you a little ray of sunshine?" cooed Jackie, taking up the gift.

After examining it and smiling, Jackie rested it on her head.

"How do I look in a crown?" she asked, striking a regal pose with one hand on her hip and the other raised in a wave.

This gave the girls the giggles again. But soon the two were off on their mission, leaving us to our own pursuits.

Before I could even seat myself to try my own hand at daisy-chaining, my missing servant came dashing toward us, pursued by several guardsmen. They wore the green and black livery of the Duke of Fairglen. And as Toby nimbly dodged through the crowd, the two came stumbling after.

"Make way!" they were shouting, raising quite a ruckus.

"Master!" wailed Tobias, nearly bowling me over in his panic. "You gotta protect me."

He slid behind me just as the guardsmen nearly caught him up.

"Stand aside, sir, and... Sir Lucas?"

"Wally?" I sputtered. "What's going on here?"

The man overcame his startlement and glared menacingly at Toby, who peeked out from around my waist.

"That little rascal is to come with us, Sir Lucas," he said through heaving breaths.

"Why? What has he done? ('now' I did not add)

"Only disrespected the duke regent of Fairglen," reported the other guardsman.

Manny? Was he here too? My little event was certainly turning into a merry melange of who's who.

"Toby," I commanded him. "Surrender yourself to the guardsmen at once. I shall accompany you and have a word with the good lord."

The two guardsmen took my servant by the collar and frogmarched him toward the cauldron. I followed, curious about what offense the lad may have committed.

We found Lord Manford standing by the great cauldron, inspecting the mutton that was sizzling on a spit nearby. He was surrounded by four more men in green standing at attention. Upon noticing our approach, he turned and greeted us.

"Ah. Lucas. *There* you are."

"Your grace," said I, bowing low.

Toby dropped a clumsy curtsy, muttering, "Your greatness."

"There!" shouted Wally. "He done it *again!* Surely you all saw it that time."

"I did indeed," said Manny.

"What the heck was *that*, Toby?" I asked.

The boy looked around at the circle of grim-faced guards and chewed at his lower lip. The earnest words that followed bore no hint of either mockery or accusation.

"I've only met a duke once before, and *he* told us we should curtsy."

I recalled the conversation we'd had at the prince's tea. A grin flirted briefly with Manny's pursed lips before his stern countenance reasserted itself.

"The fault is mine, your grace," I said, "for not instructing my servant in proper etiquette. Although, to be fair, the lad *was* told that this was your preferred greeting. If there is to be a punishment, let me be the one to suffer it."

"Release the boy," said Manny. "It's clear he meant no offense. I shall rely on Sir Lucas to school him in proper manners at his earliest opportunity."

"That is very charitable of your grace. Bow to Lord Manford, Tobias."

Toby bowed low, then turned and ran off.

"Next lesson:" I declared with a grin, "leave-taking without permission."

"Tomatoes, eh?" said Manny, eyeing the several bushels Lady Castleberry had sent along. "I suppose that's code for... all this?"

"Not at all, your grace," I replied.

"You know the king would not have approved of this celebration had he caught wind of it."

"Well, it just sort of happened."

He snorted.

"Nothing of this magnitude 'just sort of happens' without the brotherhood becoming aware of it, Lucas. No. I think you are a puppet, and we both know who's pulling your strings... She will have to answer for this."

The guardsmen looked perplexed. I was glad that, for once, it wasn't only me.

"Well, cheer up, your grace. This is a celebration. Paint on a happy grin. I know your grace knows how to do *that*. And your grace? I would step carefully if I were you. The lady is most formidable."

Yet Another Increasingly Depraved Interlude at Sea

In the stillness of my cabin, I sat there all alone. I felt the gentle rocking and swaying of the deck. And I heard the moans and sobbing from the captives we had taken as my men had their way with them. The villages we'd plundered had filled our holds with tools and foodstuffs aplenty. For the voyage that I planned, we'd need all that and more. I wondered what we'd find upon that distant southern shore.

The king had grown wise to our raids; he had. His fleets patrolled the coast. We were layin' low to the east for now, so as not to risk our boats. So I planned as we lay anchored off the island in the bay. He'd soon become complacent and lower his guard, opening the way. I patiently awaited the day we could shove off from here and return to our provisioning (once the coast was clear).

"Luthor," I whispered.

This conjured up an image of the headmaster. It swirled forth to fill my inner vision. I knew the man's soul had already fled, but speaking to him thus helped me access the damaged mind. I was ever so glad I'd had the foresight to snatch him from his tomb. It was a calculated risk confronting the burial party that day. I only wished I'd had the chance to get at him a mite sooner.

Preserved by the fluids the Stein lad contrived, he was at my disposal now. But sadly, much chaos had already been wrought, for the decomposition of death soon addled a dead man's thoughts. Only fragments of his memory remained.

As a former master of the conclave of the first order, he was quite a prize. There was a lot of knowledge tucked away in this old skull of mine - secret and dangerous knowledge that was banned from all but a few. With time and patience, I could puzzle some things out. Time I had, but patience was a virtue of which I was running short.

"How can I make more of the fluid that keeps this body whole?"

"The boy... new technique... didn't yet share... conclave."

I had figured out the ingredients by working backwards from a small sample. The alchemy was fairly simple. But the necromantic enchantments were anybody's guess.

"What other banned necromantic techniques do we know?"

"Ambu#%$"

"Try again. What was that?"

"Ambulan^#(s &&$% mortui"

The flashes of light and the ache that accompanied this told me I might be pushing too hard. I eased off and calmly put forth:

"That sounds interesting. What does it do?"

"It is used to raise *@$#&%#@ead henchman from #!($ of (*$@cently died."

That was surprisingly clear. A henchman? That might be useful indeed; it might, if only I could ferret out the full technique. Luthor hadn't performed any but the most minor necromantic rituals himself. But he had reviewed everything available in the stone of recall. I'd get it eventually; I would. Just knowin' such a thing was possible put me farther along than I was. I'd take the time to tease out all I could; I would.

I sat back, done for now.

And as my grand flotilla bobbed upon the gentle ocean, I was eager for the day that I could set my plans in motion. Beyond the Black Plagued Marshes to the south, I would set forth, abandoning the disrespectful lands here in the north. And on our arrival, the seed that I envisioned would be sown. A colony I'd plant there, a little kingdom of my own. And through the years, I'd nurture it, growing an empire to rival Reme. Beneath my heel, all the petty kingdoms will bow before my dream. From the valleys, they will shout, and the mountains will answer. All hail! All hail Truman, the mighty necromancer!

But first things first. I had to get there.

I missed breathing. I could still do it, but it lacked the calming effect it had once had on me when I was alive. Instead, I silently counted to ten before resuming my thoughts.

I had no map to the place I sought, but the southern seas were beckoning. I suppose I need find that sublime destination by undead reckoning.

CHAPTER EIGHT

The King

"To be a king and wear a crown is a
thing more glorious to them that see it
than it is pleasant to them that bear it.."

~ Elizabeth I ~

In the week that followed, I was assailed by many a missive.

Most were invitations to a variety of events, but among them were some letters by fathers inviting me to call upon their daughters. It seemed that 'Lucas the Just' was considered eligible and was now deemed noble enough to merit serious attention. Some of the events sounded interesting, but were these *also* thinly veiled overtures of courtship? I'd have to be very careful in responding to each. Some of the surnames were prominent figures I didn't want to offend.

Distrusting my own knowledge of courtly etiquette, I considered asking the baron for help. Lord Westarbor, however, seemed always to be busy managing his own affairs. I shouldn't be surprised. Running a barony from afar was no easy feat. And this while handling the matter of his daughter's suitors and hobnobbing with all manner of nobility here at the capital. No. His lordship couldn't spare any time to sort out my concerns.

Then another possibility struck me. Trenton? Perhaps *he* could advise me. We hadn't spent much time together since I'd come to Camburn Hall. I strode over to my window, which overlooked the back courtyard. And sure enough, there he stood, sparring with Sir Nolan.

"Toby," I said, "bring me my bob. I have a sudden desire for some sword practice."

Once I'd belted on my sword and arrived out back, I saw Sir Nolan and Trenton locked together, hilt to hilt, and struggling for dominance. The larger knight had the weight advantage, but Trenton seemed to be holding his own. Then, suddenly, the younger knight spun out from beneath Sir Nolan's overbearing embrace, rolled forward, stood upright, and smacked his opponent on the backside with the flat of his blade. With an awkward step forward, Sir Nolan halted his inadvertent advance, a look of surprise on his face.

"Well done, lad!" exclaimed Sir Nolan cheerfully between heaving breaths. "I didn't see *that* coming."

"Well, you wouldn't have unless you had eyes on your buttocks," replied Trenton merrily. "I had to win one *eventually*, sir," he added.

By this time, I had walked up to where Derrick Lester and Jay Harvey stood watching. The squires smiled and nodded to me when I approached.

"And who is *this* who would enter the fray?" Sir Nolan said with a wink. "Have you come to challenge the victor?"

"Hardly," I snorted. "I just thought I could use a bit of fresh air and exercise."

"Well, step forward, then. Let us see what you've got."

Reluctantly, I walked up to the two knights, drawing my sword from its scabbard. It was an infantryman's broadsword I'd been gifted by my father. I dropped into my starting stance with the blade extended before me. I'd nearly forgotten how heavy it was.

Sir Trenton walked slowly all around me, scrutinizing my technique.

"Not bad, actually," he remarked.

I used my magic to fortify my arm, a trick I'd learned under Taylor's tutelage.

"Now show us a strike or two."

I swung the heavy blade ahead of me in a stabbing motion. This caused the knights to howl with laughter, which, in turn, set Lord Stapleton's hounds to baying again.

"Derrick," said Sir Trenton, "come and show this whelp the error of such an opening move."

I wanted to protest, but I was honestly interested in what I'd done so wrong. Derrick came over to face me and gave me a shallow bow.

"Engage," said Sir Nolan.

It took about three seconds for me to be parted from my sword (and I sensed that the squire had been taking his time). I was looking down the length of Derrick's blade, with its pointy end at my throat. Shrugging, the squire re-sheathed it and flashed me a sympathetic grin.

"If you're serious, Lucas," said Trenton, "you'll need many more hours of conditioning and instruction before you risk so much as a sparring match. But as you are my sister's protector, it behooves me to offer such guidance. If you'd like, I can spare you a half turn of the glass each morning while we're here."

I didn't know what to say. I had no real desire to become a great swordsman, but the idea of a physical regimen was somewhat attractive, and the knight's offer was very generous.

"I suppose I wouldn't mind that, sir knight, if you can spare the time."

"Pish posh, my boy," said Sir Nolan. "As the newest knight in our retinue, Sir Trenton has yet to earn his spurs as an instructor. He's done a fine job with Derrick here and several members of his lance. But I'll be curious to see how he shall fare with a raw recruit."

And so I stayed, mostly just watching, as the knights put their squires through their paces. Toby soon arrived to sit beside me. We could scarcely follow the heated exchanges of their sparring, and we were both invited to join in the stretches and squats they were forced to endure in-between. Toby thought this was a great game, but I knew my muscles would ache and cramp later. I wasn't used to the torturous drills.

When the knights were packing it in for the morning, I approached Sir Trenton again. He was standing by the well, drenched in sweat, drawing up a bucket with the crank. He was startled when I took charge of the task, causing the winch to spin around far faster than was natural. The bucket arrived, dancing about on the end of its rope near the bemused knight's shoulder.

He took it from its hook, brought it to his lips, and drank. Then, with a contented exhale, he upended it over his head.

"Oh. I'm sorry," said the dripping knight, extending the mostly empty pail toward me. "Did you want some?"

"I can get my own," I demurred. "I wanted to ask your advice on another matter."

"Oh?"

I went on to explain about the invitations I'd received. This seemed to amuse him.

"Let's go have a look at these letters. I ought to leave you to flounder. 'Twould be fitting payment for tipping me into that muddy ditch. But I suspect it would reflect poorly on the honor of Westarbor to allow you to commit social blunders."

"Are you still angry over that?"

His sudden smile was less than comforting.

"Join me here on the training ground at dawn, and I'll let you judge it for yourself."

I followed the soggy Sir Trenton back into the manor house, pensive about what tomorrow might bring. Toby straggled after, his eyes alight with the many questions he yearned to ask.

With Sir Trenton's help, I soon managed to traverse the maze of courtly requests and invitations. According to Trenton, none of the daughters of the nobles actually had hopes of taking up with a mage. They simply wanted an escort to the prince's ball a few weeks hence. And it seemed that 'Lucas the Just' was the flavor of the month. I was viewed only as a bit of arm candy to serve as bait for larger fish. I declined each as politely as I was able.

The invitation to the prince's birthday, however, was a different matter entirely. All of Fairglen would gather in the coliseum, where the prince would be presented and receive gifts from various factions. Afterward, a smaller, more select group had been invited to attend a feast in Prince Henry's honor. My invitation didn't surprise Sir Trenton, though people of my stature were rarely afforded such an honor.

"Perhaps you should visit a few of these noble ladies and see whether you fancy escorting one to the affair. This could earn you the favor of a noble house."

"And the jealousy of several others, who I didn't deign to visit," I returned irritably.

"True," said the knight with a furrowed brow.

"No thank you, then."

"Still, you must escort someone."

"I thought I would be your sister's escort."

He looked at me as if I'd grown two heads, then shook his own head vigorously.

"'Twould be unthinkable for a debutante to be escorted by her own protector so late in the season. The gossips would soon suggest that she had no better option. Nay. Megan will undoubtedly make a careful selection from among her current suitors."

I grimaced.

"Did you know the prince himself has taken a fancy to her?"

"Indeed. Father keeps me apprised. Such matters might have a significant impact on our barony's future."

"Perhaps I could invite Lady Lynette," I ventured. "I imagine she would be thrilled to attend the king's feast at the royal palace."

Trenton frowned, weighing the matter.

"She might be," he mused. But she mightn't thank you for the rumors that would fly among all the high nobility at such an unprecedented choice."

Was there no end to the layers of courtly etiquette that seemed to surround almost anything the nobles ever did? I wish there was a rulebook I could study. When I asked, Trenton merely laughed and told me such things were obvious to anyone who'd grown up around them. Still, I felt as if I stood surrounded by bear traps, just waiting for me to put a toe out of line.

I finally settled on a unique solution. I asked Lady Castleberry whether she had an escort. And although she had intended to tap Howard for this duty once again, she readily agreed to have me in his stead. The wise old woman would benefit from having such a colorful attendant, and she could introduce me around. As an added benefit, I could dance with whomever I pleased. She expected we'd make quite a splash.

So as the season ground on, sparking much gossip, I soon found myself free from further expectations and in a position where no tongues would wag in my direction.

***

The masons all looked up expectantly. The building they had raised was hardly a marvel of modern architecture, but it was clean of line. And given that it had taken them only a week to build it, it appeared sturdy and serviceable enough. Once the roof was thatched, it would make a cozy winter domicile.

The dwarves' smokehouse, on the other hand, had barely even been started. It was a bare outline in the dirt, with only a few cornerstones laid out. Near its center, a rectangular firepit had been dug and lined with stones. Thrusting upward from each corner of the structure-to-be were wooden poles with a series of nails sticking out at even intervals. Ewen MacLaren stood nearby, surveying it and puffing on a pipe.

"Ho there, journeyman," shouted Guildmaster Bennet, stepping over from among the masons.

I swung my leg over Feckless' haunches and dismounted.

"Well met, master," I greeted him. "I see you've finished the almshouse in a single week, just as you promised."

"Aye," he replied. "It was a bit of a rush job, and there are still a few odds and ends to finish up. But all in all, it's come together rather nicely."

After tapping the ashes from the end of his pipe, the dwarven noble strode over to join us.

I rounded on him with a questioning look.

"And where is the smokehouse your lordship's men were going to erect?"

Ewen pointed east with the stem of his pipe, saying, "Over there, for the most part."

Confused, I glanced in the direction he had indicated. I couldn't see anything past the tents that littered the ground nearby, but beyond them, I noticed a thin column of smoke rising skyward.

"You should come have a look, journeyman," muttered Bennet

I grew even more confused. Where was that bravado with which the guildmaster had berated the dwarf just last week? Was there a subdued tone of respect in the mason's voice? As

Ewen nodded and made his way through the clutter, I took Feckless' leads and followed him, with the guildmaster bringing up the rear.

I was soon once again stepping out onto Potter's Field, but there had been changes since my last visit. From the firmly packed ground of the useless bit of land, there arose several new structures. Potter's Field had been so named because the ground was hard clay, unsuitable for farming. Since the earliest of days, such land was typically set aside as a burial place for the deceased.

The near edge of the field was now a muddy pit, in the center of which a dwarf was even now emptying a bucket of water. Three other dwarves tromped around in it with mud plastered on their unshod feet and sloppy grins plastered on their faces. They almost appeared to be dancing, though no tune could be heard.

Beyond the pit stood a series of poles supporting scaffolds of boards on which row after row of bricks lay drying in the sun. Beyond even that, I saw a circular stack of finished bricks rising up to form an open dome nearly ten feet high. A lazy column of smoke rose through a hole at its summit. I would soon learn that this makeshift kiln had been erected on the spot to complete the drying and hardening of the bricks the dwarves were making.

Ewen led me around the pit to an equally makeshift table where the village youths all stood in a line, patting and kneading blobs of raw clay. They were working it like dough and occasionally picking out bits of stone and other impurities. Enoch and the other lads of the village were rolling the finished loaves in piles of ash. At the end of the line stood Finlay. He was peppering the ashy loaves with some kind of crushed sand, stuffing them into rectangular molds, and extruding them onto a pallet like I'd seen on the drying racks.

They looked like they'd been at it for quite some time. And though all were liberally coated in mud and ash, they seemed happy enough with their tasks. I looked over at Ewen and caught his eye.

"I now see what you meant when you said your men would be getting their hands dirty," I quipped.

"Aye," said the dwarf. "It takes days to properly form and dry firebricks. We should soon have enough to start on the smokehouse. It should go up quickly enough after that. Stone is patient."

"So I've heard."

"There's a wise saying of which you humans are fond. It's said one should teach a man to fish rather than to simply give him one. Tomorrow, we'll show them how to lay a straight course and let them finish it on their own."

I looked at the industrious faces of the villagers as they pounded away at the raw clay. I could tell that they wouldn't likely stop after completing the smokehouse now that they knew this trick. I heard the twelve bells of midday chiming off in the distance. This elicited a grunt from Guildmaster Bennet.

"So, journeyman," he prompted me, "who won?"

"Won what?" I asked distractedly.

"It's noon. Who won the contest?"

"Offhand, I'd say it was the refugees, but for the sake of saving face, you may inform our guildmates it was a tie."

Bennet twisted his lips and nodded. The dwarf, too, grinned in approval.

***

In the final weeks leading up to the prince's ball, the city streets became more congested than ever. Hardly a day went by without a new delegation arriving. It was a veritable parade of notables, as every banner in the kingdom was seen marching up Broadway to the high quarter. More dwarves were in evidence since the arrival of Duke Brax Steelaxe of Echo Hills. Elves, too, became a more common sight when the Bright One graced the royal palace with her presence.

Of particular interest to me was the arrival of a contingent from Conclave. Headmaster Balderas and several other masters were hosted by a nobleman just two streets up from House Camburn. I was disappointed that Mistress Julia was not among them. Nevertheless, I contrived to visit them and welcome them to the city.

It seemed like no time at all before the day of the grand celebration was upon us. I arrived at Castleberry Manor and was promptly ushered inside by Wexley. I strode into the main entry hall dressed in a new doublet of blue and white. Her ladyship had been quite specific about the colors, recommending those that complimented the gown she would be wearing. I felt a bit exposed, not having beforetime had the occasion to wear hose. I had been assured this was the style of the season. It was liberating and cool enough for a warm June day, but they still made me feel a bit naughty.

I tugged at my doublet and shifted nervously.

How did women deal with this breezy feeling from below?

Lady Castleberry appeared with a flurry of handmaidens fussing all around her. Her elegant gown was modest, and she walked with a stately dignity that matched the rich grandeur of our surroundings. She wore a butterfly hennin atop her wimple. Its twin points swept back to drape its gauzy veil down over her shoulders. For an older gal, the effect was quite fetching.

In the distance, the bell tolled the hour.

I offered my arm, and Victoria and I strolled outside. Howard was just pulling up into the entry circle. He waved from the window of the family carriage. It was a quaint little buggy as compared to most, suitable for a noble lady to gad about the town. For all that, it was posh. It was painted the bright blue known as azure, and its fittings gleamed. Emblazoned on its door was the white peacock, emblematic of the lady's heraldry. The coachman sitting atop the compact conveyance wore matching livery. His frowning face seemed well-suited to the crisp lines of his jacket and stiff, erect posture. The large white feather sticking up from his cap exactly matched a similar plume thrusting up from the headgear of the single roan mare pulling the thing.

After helping Victoria into the coach, I climbed inside as well. It was cozy, but ample for our modest needs. Soon we were riding out of the gates into the lower city and traversing the dozen blocks to Cathedral Square. The street lamps were festooned with flapping pennants in the royal purple hue and wound about by laurels of spruce and ribbons of gold. There was a sense of expectation in the air as we joined the line of buggies, dropping folks off before the iron-wrought gates.

Howard and I held the surging crowd at bay, clearing a corridor for our venerable charge. On sighting the noblewoman, many made way and doffed their hats respectfully, and we wended our way to the coliseum itself. There, we took our seats amid other excited aristocrats in the very front row of its shaded eastern side. Before me, a stone palisade overlooked a twenty-foot sheer drop to the arena floor below. Behind us, stone benches rose ever higher, affording all a view of the field. Cushions had been provided in our section, for which I was thankful. I wouldn't have fancied tearing my hose on the unpadded stone.

The arena down below was a large oval field where various contests and sporting events were sometimes conducted. At either end stood enormous double doors, each wide enough to let wagons pass through. I could imagine mounted knights riding out through them to joust with one another. Today, these were only slightly ajar, but on one end, a raised platform had been erected where the royal family would be seated. I knew this would be the case because high-backed thrones were even now being arranged upon it.

Near the middle, over against the side opposite us, was another platform on which musicians sat, tuning up. They looked tiny from this distance, and their toots and blats were barely discernible above the hubbub of the growing crowd. Even as I watched, the stands were filling. On the far side of the amphitheater, they crawled like ants to fill nearly every seat. I had thought my little charity event had drawn a large crowd, but it was as nothing compared to the flocks descending on Prince Henry's birthday bash. I was told the coronation next week would be even better attended, but I couldn't imagine how.

Perplexed, I gave up on trying to calculate the coliseum's capacity. Instead, I just settled back to await what was certain to be an amazing spectacle.

***

Surrounded by a wall of babble, my mind drifted from topic to topic in a lazy way. I shook myself and took a short draw from my waterskin. It tasted a bit off. I suppose I'd been spoiled by the taste of the crystal clear water from the Camburn well. It made me wonder. Why had such an esteemed craftsman worked on so humble a project? Had he perhaps done so in his younger days? When I'd asked Lord Camburn about it, he'd only sputtered a bit and promptly changed the subject.

I felt a jab in my side, putting a swift end to my ruminations.

I looked over at the offender. Lady Castleberry, it seemed, had some rather sharp elbows.

"Attend, sir mage," she said with a nod of her head. "It begins."

And indeed, there was motion on the field below. A contingent of royal guardsmen paraded out onto the field. Their black armor stood out sharply against the tan-colored ground. Their deployment was swift and synchronized as they marched in unison, almost like a dance. They circled about in a dazzling display, presenting their swords, then re-sheathing them, at last taking station around the platform where the king would sit.

I felt I should applaud, and many did. This was soon drowned out, however, by a great fanfare of trumpets and the rolling rhythm of the drums. They blared out triumphant, harmonious notes that rose ever higher, ending in a long, sustained chord once the escalation had run its course.

As this was happening, the royal family emerged from the great doors on the field's most southern side. To a rolling drumbeat, they ascended to the platform and claimed their seats, waving all the while. A great cheer erupted from the grandstands. It echoed about us like thunder to wrap the royal family in its greeting.

It was then that the herald strode to the fore. He bore the speaker's staff, and when he spoke, I marveled anew at its efficacy.

"Good citizens of Fairglen, my lords and ladies, honored guests, and all who attend this gathering. King Raymond Osten the third bids you welcome on this the thirteenth day of June."

His words carried to every corner of the coliseum. (The coliseum being round, this was no mean trick.) There was, however, a strange echo, as his words rebounded from the far wall and arrived a split second later than they initially had. It reminded me of when Aaron had been hollering up from the bottom of the well.

"It is a very special day, as I am certain you are all aware. For it was on this day eighteen years ago that good Prince Henry drew his first breath, blessing our kingdom with a royal heir."

He paused to await the applause to follow, and the crowd did not disappoint. Once we'd settled down, he continued.

"His majesty would have it known that Prince Henry, having reached his age of majority, will be crowned one week hence on this very field. I mention this only for the benefit of anyone who may have failed to get the pigeon."

He paused again, and the arena filled with our laughter.

"That will come in due course. Today, however, we have gathered to wish our prince a happy naming day and to afford our nobles the opportunity to present him with heartfelt gifts and tokens of their good wishes. We will begin with her grace, Lady Brighton, the mistress of Lorédon!"

At this point, the great doors at the northern end of the arena slowly swung wide. This revealed several scores of Elven warriors arrayed in five-by-four formations. I lilting melody arose that was like no song I'd ever heard. I was later to learn it was an elven tune sung by a mother when her child selected her *vallahimay*. This happened at around age eighty and was the closest equivalent to when a human reached adulthood. The singer's voice was hauntingly sweet, and though most couldn't follow all of her words, few could miss the strident tone of triumph with just a tinge of sorrow at innocence lost. I could understand most of it, but no translation I could make would do justice to the poetry of the first people.

'The little one who once clung to my side is now a man of his own... '

'In the fullness of time, may the blessings of our mothers see him on his way... '

'May the great deeds that await him never rise above his reach...'

And on it went. And as it did, the warriors took to the field.

As the unseen singer crooned her melody, the warriors came running out to the center of the arena. As one, as if on some silent command, their swords cleared their scabbards. Then things got interesting. I had thought the royal guard had managed an impressive display. But Lady Brighton's aptly named sword dancers whirled like women possessed. They leapt about with an agility I doubted any human could match, all the while avoiding their sisters and falling into the most amazing patterns.

I couldn't understand how they coordinated it all. Perhaps it was governed by the song. They would freeze in place, then suddenly whirl back into motion, only to arrive at a new pattern. A flower would explode into a crescent moon, which would shatter to form a knight's shield. I suspected these symbols too had deeper meanings that eluded me.

By the time the song trailed off, its last lilting notes unresolved, the small company had stilled. Once more, they stood in orderly ranks. Lady Brighton had approached the stage and been handed the staff. The amphitheater had gone silent in breathless anticipation of what the venerable elf might say.

"People of greater Osten," she began. "Long have our people been allied against those who would threaten the peace of our realm. King Raymond has been a most generous liege. In friendship, he has aided us at every turn to thwart the designs of those who send their blights upon us.

"It is our hope that this friendship will continue into the next generation, as it was with his father and his father before that. Our gift to Prince Henry on arising to his majority is the service of this small company of my sword dancers. They will be solely at his command and will undertake any assignment he orders for a period of ten years. Use them wisely, your highness."

A great murmuring ensued, and once again Lady Castleberry's serrated elbow found my ribs.

"This is unprecedented," she muttered to me. "Elven warriors have never directly served a human monarch, even back in the time of Raymond the first."

"It's an incredible gift," I hissed back. "Serving him for an entire decade..."

"Bah," she mused. "Ten years is barely an eye blink to an elf. What's more significant is the trust this implies. This gift will stand strongly in Henry's favor in his bid for the crown. Not only that, those ladies should be of great concern to anyone thinking of harming our prince."

"I saw one fight once," I remarked. "You're not wrong."

The staff was handed back to the herald as Prince Henry's new double-platoon of dervishes went marching back whence they came.

And the ceremony moved on. First the dukes, then countless others of noble rank, were called forth to offer their best wishes to Henry on his naming day. The princely gifts were many and strange. Not all were accompanied by so impressive a display, but many were most memorable.

I laughed when the gift of the conclave was presented. The masters approached the platform, followed by a knight in a full suit of plate mail with a closed helm. The knight came clanking up rather awkwardly, bowed before his majesty, and lifted his visor. Inside, there was... nothing. The 'knight' was, in fact, the gift. The suit had been crafted for the prince by a renowned dwarven armorer working beside the mages at Conclave's foundry. Every piece of it had been forged from the meteoric sky-metal, unique to the area. And the whole thing bore many protective spells. There was even an enchantment to reduce its weight - a princely gift indeed.

After a myriad of marquises, countless counts, and a bevy of barons had all had their turn before the king, one was called that made me sit up and take notice.

"And now it gets interesting," Victoria muttered, sparing my sore ribs for once.

"Baron Guy Lord Downham!" announced the herald.

He was one of the prime contenders to become the next duke of Northford, and I secretly hoped his gift would displease the king. I'd seen the way he governed. No one in his right mind would want to be his vassal. According to Westarbor's operatives, however, Baron Downham had been oozing his way around the capital, greasing the palms of many a lord in his campaign to claim the duchy. The word was that support for him had grown in certain circles.

From the great doors at the arena's northern end emerged a gleaming coach the size of two normal carriages. It was hauled by a full team of four coal-black stallions. It was framed in ebony timber-beams carved to resemble dragons, scales and all. Their ingenious curves framed panels that were Tyrian purple in hue, and the bright brass fittings shone with the luster of gold. When the gaudy thing approached the royals, the coachman reined it in, and Lord Downham stepped out. He was a large bear of a man, topping six feet by half a head again.

I gritted my teeth as he smilingly accepted the speaker's staff and went on to extol the virtues of the wainwrights of his barony. His deep baritone was not unpleasing, but knowing the man, I found it grating. No expense had been spared when fashioning this mighty conveyance befitting his prince. Blah, blah, blah... I was thankful when he finally bowed and returned the staff to the herald. He didn't do humble well.

"Baron Vincent Arenson, Lord Westarbor!" was the next to be called.

And from the northern doors emerged the baron's more modest carriage. It rolled forth in silence, hauled by a single team. It was elegant of line and bobbed along quite agreeably to the mincing steps of the chestnut mares. Westarbor himself sat atop the driver's bench, smiling and waving to the crowd. I wondered what he had up his sleeve.

I wasn't left to wonder for long. When the baron reined in before the royal platform, he unhurriedly climbed down, stepped to the carriage door, and eased it wide, kicking down the folding step. A bright red carpet came rolling out, unwinding its way almost to the platform. And out strode two knights, carrying between them a heavy oaken chest. This they lay on the ground before the royal retinue as the baron retrieved the speaker's staff. The king squinted down at it with mild curiosity.

"My king," began the baron, "as you know, the barony of Westarbor has little coin in its coffers of late. We are working on that. Our wealth is in our people, whose true hearts serve you well."

He paused and bent the knee before continuing.

"But we have had a rather large stroke of good fortune in recent years and feel it is time to share it. Our gift to the prince is this."

Sir Trenton opened the chest. Within it was... hay?

At the baron's nod, Sir Nolan swept off the top layer to reveal an egg the size of a horse's head.

"We would like to offer his highness the freedom of the open sky."

At this, the drummer began pounding his great kettle drum in a stately rhythm.

"As your majesty is aware, a griffin will form a bond only with a single rider, who must be present at its hatching and weaning. The timing was delicate, but we think this will hatch sometime in the next fortnight."

A shadow flitted across the ground, then another. Peering upward, I saw three large griffins with wings outspread circling lazily above. The sun was directly overhead, casting their shadows in the dirt below. A trumpet blasted out a note, and the three responded.

"*Kee-eeeee-arr!*" they sang in unison.

They circled lower, as all watched them in fascination. When each alighted in a semicircle before the platform, the royal guardsmen moved into defensive positions, relaxing somewhat when the riders dismounted.

"All hail Prince Henry!" shouted the baron. "Westarbor salutes you!"

At this, the three griffins bowed low, their beaks nearly scraping the ground. Their wings extended until their wingtips touched. And the riders knelt as well. I'd always known my lord was an excellent showman, but this one took the cake.

The king clapped his hands as a smile spread across his face. And I saw Henry's eyes widen with wonder.

***

It was with a happy grin that I once again entered the royal palace ballroom, this time with a marchioness on my arm. The enormous chamber didn't feel intimidating in the least. I was ready to face the nobles. What's the worst that could happen? Would someone turn me into a pumpkin?

The bandstand was much as I remembered it, and cheerful chamber music was already filling the great hall. On noting us, a herald by the door checked us off his list and loudly announced us to the few people who had already filtered in.

"Her ladyship, the Dowager Marchioness Castleberry, escorted by Lucas the Just, envoy plenipotentiary to the fey and protector of the realm! "

Well, *that* was a new one. When had Henry thought to add *that* audacious appellation? It was better than "heartbreaker," I supposed, but might be hard to live up to. I was getting to be quite a mouthful.

The master of ceremonies was beside us in a trice.

"Your table is just over this way, my lady. We saved you a prime seat just below the high table to the prince's right."

Arm in arm, we followed. As we arrived at our table, I spotted another couple seated just to the right of us. Suddenly, I felt awkward. I nearly forgot to help seat the lady whom I was escorting. Glaring over at me was Lady Katherine, dressed as elegantly as ever. Seated beside her was some nobleman I'd seen before. I couldn't recall the man's name. Baron Somethingorother.

I shouldn't be surprised. As a mere baroness, Lady Katie wasn't ranked very high in her own right, but as the daughter of a duchess, she merited a lofty place on the seating chart. It had to irk her to see me sitting nearer to the high table by virtue of escorting a ranked noble. I seated myself and quickly looked away.

"You seem pensive, Sir Lucas," Victoria remarked. "Cat got your tongue?"

She shot me a knowing smile and a wink. I'd learned that not much escaped the old woman's notice.

"I've heard that felines can be very territorial and unforgiving."

"Um, so they are, my lady," I stammered, taking a moment to regain my wits.

Victoria seemed to revel in my discomfiture, and had shrewdly divined its source.

"Ah... if only I were back in the game, I could send such a prideful creature scampering back to its mother. But I fear my claws have grown a bit dull these days."

I could tell she wanted to banter. When talking of vegetables, I could hold my own, but on the topic of nobles and their intrigues, I was nearly as clueless as Toby. And speaking of Toby, was that the king's page approaching us and waving for my attention? I beckoned for him to approach.

"Ahh... Sir Lucas? Your ladyship?" he said with a courtly bow.

"Yes, Toby?"

"I hate to disturb your evening, sir," he blurted, "but Prince Henry asked me to see whether you could meet with him in the kitchen. There's a private matter he needs sorted out."

"The... kitchen?"

Victoria shot me a wry grin.

"Best not to keep royalty waiting," she admonished me.

"Of course," I said, pushing back my chair. "If my lady will forgive me?"

"I suppose I can find something to pass the time. By all means, depart. What are you waiting for, a royal summons?"

The page was acting twitchy, and I followed him as he hastened away. What could I help with in the kitchen? I wondered. Had the lettuce wilted or something? I hoped it wasn't rats. But even if it was, could a protector of the realm leave his prince in peril? I should think not.

It was then that Lady Katherine's foot shot out, catching me right in the ankle.

Down I crashed to the hardwood floor with a sudden yelp of surprise. Katherine feigned surprise and gathered in her skirts as though I might be trying to peer up them. *Really?* Could the lady be as petty as all *that?* I stifled the unseemly protest that rose unbidden to my lips and struggled to regain my composure. I rose shakily to my knees and wondered if one could actually die of shame as all the nobles of the realm witnessed my clumsiness.

As I straightened, I found Lady Castleberry by my side, reaching down as though to help me up. I doubted that accepting an elderly woman's assistance would make me look any better, but I was surprisingly mistaken.

When I reached for her hand, she clasped mine briefly, but made no effort to haul me to my feet. Instead, she flourished a handkerchief she had pretended to take from my grasp.

"You found it!" she beamed. "Oh, thank you, Sir Lucas! I must have *dropped* it here. How fortunate am I to have such a gallant young man as my escort?"

Lady Katherine rolled her eyes as the other nearby nobles smiled.

"Come, Sir Lucas," added the page, loud enough for all to hear. "The prince is waiting for you."

And after him, I went, striding forth from the hall nursing my salvaged dignity.

***

Prince Henry was indeed back in the kitchen. And surprisingly, I found him in an apron, dusted with flour. He was flattening out dough with a rolling pin and looked very unprincely indeed. Intent on his task, he failed to mark our arrival in the astonishingly small scullery.

"Cook's day off?" I asked.

I couldn't help myself.

Henry flinched and spun around to glare at us. Toby suppressed a yelp, his cheeks puffing out, and swiftly lowered his gaze to the floor. Belatedly, I dropped to one knee.

"Oh get *up*, Lucas. You'll soil your hose."

"What is it your highness needs?" I asked, rising.

"I'm told you mages have a spell to locate a person. Is that true?"

"It is, sire," I answered. "Who do you want located?"

"My brother," snapped the prince. "He should have been here hours ago, but no one can find him. He was supposed to have this pie in the *oven* already."

The prince seemed flustered. I'd never seen this side of him before, and it wasn't just the apron.

"Have you a lock of his hair?"

"What? Why would I... Oh. Is that necessary?"

His face soured.

"I'm afraid so, highness. Say, where are all the other cooks?"

"They're in the *main* kitchen, of course," he said with trepidation. "Richard and I..."

Just then, the door swung open, and in strode the sibling in question. He was tracking mud onto the tiled floor and holding a brace of game birds aloft. I waved my hands around, muttering some nonsense words.

"And *viola*, your highness! My work here is done!"

Toby (the king's page, Toby) slipped out into the hallway and burst out laughing. At least someone thought I was funny. Prince Henry glared at me again, and Richard stared in puzzlement.

"You're late!" Henry accused. "And on this of *all* days."

"I couldn't help it. These little buggers were devilishly hard to find. I was out most of the night, and we still caught barely enough."

I confess, I was growing ever more curious about the odd behavior of the two brothers. I couldn't help myself. I had to ask. Henry had returned to his rolling with a vigor, and Richard had taken to plucking the feathers from his kills.

"Enough for *what?*" I asked.

"They're for father," said Henry, throwing a fresh handful of flour atop his flattened pie crust. "Every year at this time, he grows depressed. Grandma passed away four years ago, on June eleventh. My birthday on the thirteenth always reminds him of it. Lucky me."

"Would that be Queen Henrietta? The one the river barge is named after?"

"The very same," said Henry sadly. "Thank you for coming, Lucas, but we can manage from here. Go back to the party. You wouldn't understand."

"Oh, wouldn't I? It so happens that my own mother died on my birthday. Father always made a game effort, but he was never very convincing when he tried celebrating with me."

"I didn't know," said the prince. "How old were you when your mother passed away?"

"You misunderstand, sire. She died *on* my birthday, that very day."

Henry had just laid the dough into a pan and was trimming away the excess. He stilled.

"My condolences," he muttered.

And even Richard paused in his plucking.

"What can I do to help?" I asked.

The princes shared their story as we prepared the pie for the oven. It was a special family recipe that had been the former queen's favorite. It required two-dozen plump blackbirds. According to the recipe: 'Certainly no fewer and not a pigeon nor a smidgen more.'

King Raymond had been only a boy when his father's passing made him the heir apparent. His mother sat in regency, beloved by all for her gentle but firm rulings. The king had relied heavily on her advice long into his own reign (some said too long). After her loss, Raymond had grown moody and indecisive. But this special dish, prepared by both his sons working together, always reminded him of his mother and her wise counsels. It bolstered his confidence.

I felt honored that these two had trusted me to share in their private pain. And though it wouldn't lessen my own father's grief, helping the king might, in some way, redeem me for having been its cause. The two seemed to sense my need and allowed me to join in. And soon the pie was ready to be baked.

"May I add something more?" I inquired as an impish thought crossed my mind.

"What sort of thing?" asked Richard, warily.

I explained my idea, and, to my surprise, the two readily agreed. I didn't know their father, but they assured me he would revel in the jest.

"Well, I'm going to get cleaned up so as not to be late to my own party," announced Henry.

"I'll watch the pie and join you there when it's ready," Richard declared.

"Then, by your leave, I'd better hurry back to Lady Castleberry, lest she think I've abandoned her. I seem to be gaining a bad reputation for that sort of thing."

***

When I returned to the ballroom, I found that my table was empty. Lady Katherine and her escort were also nowhere in sight. Instead, seated at their table was Lady Castleberry, chatting amiably with the duchess, Lady Cynthia of Farax.

"... the new refugees are in a miserable state," the duchess was saying as she fanned herself coquettishly. "They arrived only this morning by barge, with scarcely more than the clothes on their backs."

The lady's golden tresses were intricately arranged atop her head, piled behind a sparkling tiara studded with gems large enough to choke a rooster. Her face, though more mature, was remarkably similar to that of her daughter. I tried not to dislike her immediately for the familial resemblance.

"New refugees?" I objected softly once I felt it wouldn't be an interruption. "But I thought conditions in the south were improving."

"Pardon me, your grace," I quickly added, bowing low. "We have not been introduced. I am Lucas Harper of Meadowfork."

She held out her hand for me to clasp lightly.

"So you are," she acknowledged in a laughing tone. "The most recent group of unfortunates of which I speak are villagers from Indigo Bay. As I was explaining to Victoria here, there has been a recent spate of pirate raids. They're burning, pillaging,

268

and looting all up and down the coast. The stories the survivors tell are truly sickening."

"That's terrible," I said, and meant it.

"We've turned the fleet out to look for them, but the cowardly beggars seem to have abandoned their usual haunts. Worse still, they're practicing coordinated tactics heretofore unseen from their ilk. They feint in one area with several fast ships, only to arrive in force elsewhere once our ships give pursuit. It's most unsettling. I hear the king may even send his mages to intervene."

I shuffled uncomfortably.

"But that's a worry for another day, Sir Lucas," she said in a lighter tone. "I didn't mean to upset you."

It struck me then how unlike her daughter the lady was. Where was Lady Katherine, anyway? I didn't see her among the few couples out on the dance floor.

"I shall try to set such concerns aside, your grace. Where has Lady Katherine gone, might I ask?"

"Oh," said Victoria with a sly smile. "After you left, I had a nice discussion with her ladyship. The poor little dear wasn't feeling very well afterward. I believe her escort took her out for some fresh air."

The two nobles exchanged a meaningful glance.

"Was Kat being a brat again?" asked the duchess in a flat tone.

Dropping the pretense, Victoria shrugged and answered. "She may have stuck a toe out of line, Cynthia, but she isn't likely to repeat that *particular* offense."

At this, Lady Cynthia set her fan aside. She rested her elbow on the table and her forehead in her palm.

"That girl could test the patience of a saint. I thought giving the child her own barony would settle her down somewhat, but it only seems to have made matters worse. Thank you, Victoria, for seeing to the matter."

Again, I felt uncomfortable. The conversation was drifting into private matters. Was I to become father confessor to all the dukes of the realm? I made a mental note to steer well clear of Steelaxe and Deerfield. Though I wouldn't mind finding out how Lady Brighton was faring. I was especially curious to know how her game of ninepins with the leprechaun was shaping up.

"Think nothing of it," said Victoria consolingly. "It felt good to stretch my claws a bit again. Lucas, why don't you go mingle while I finish my chat with her grace here?"

Although phrased as a question, I recognized a command when I heard one. It was time for this knight to ride off for a while.

"Oh, and Lucas?"

"Yes, my lady?"

"Did you get the prince sorted out?"

"Yes. Both of them, actually."

"Oh?"

"It's a surprise, your ladyship. You'll see."

I left the two women to stare after me curiously as I strode off in search of new adventure.

Despite her high station, Lady Castleberry had insisted we arrive early. This was purportedly to ease me into it a bit more gently. I could certainly see the sense in this. But I was still amazed at how sparsely the ball was attended, even at this late an hour. True, the prince wasn't here, and food wouldn't be served for hours yet. I guess some people just prefer making a grand entrance.

But among the other early birds, I spied someone with whom I'd like to have some words.

Seated at the room's far end were Lady Nimble and the man who was her escort. It was George Meriwether. He had been one of Megan's unsuccessful suitors, one of the few I thought had shown some promise. I believe his family had something to do with the porcelain trade. I approached the two and extended my hand.

"George? George Meriwether? I don't know if you remember me. We met once at the Camburn estate. I'm Lucas --"

He took my hand in a strong grip and placed his other on my shoulder as well.

"Of course I remember you, dear boy! You're the man who saved our prince. Smashing that! Oh ho!"

"Well, I suppose there *was* some smashing involved..."

"And that party you threw outside the city? Splendid, simply splendid! I believe you've met Lady Nimble already. Ah. Of course you have. Debutante ball and all that."

I waited for the man to wind down and tried to get a word in edge wise. He had a strange habit of answering his own questions before I could formulate a response. Cheerful - but strange. We exchanged a few more pleasantries and talked a bit about this and that before I got to the true reason for my visit.

"My Lord Meriwether, when I saw this ravishing beauty you are escorting, I wondered if you would be so gracious as to allow me to dance with her. Provided, of course, the lady agrees."

"Oh, um," he sputtered, looking over at Jackie.

"Are you certain you want to risk it, Sir Lucas?" said Jackie impishly. "You'll recall my last dance in this room was fraught with perils from above. Some claim I am a jinx."

"Then it's a good thing your next foray onto its floor will be with someone known to have experience deflecting falling objects." I quipped in return.

"Besides," I added with my most winning smile, "I have it on good authority that you're brave, and very nithe."

This caused Jackie to laugh aloud, startling her escort, who was hanging on our every word.

"Go ahead and dance with the lad, my lady," he proclaimed generously. "We shall have ample opportunity as the night progresses. I shall mourn your absence until the happy occasion of your return."

And with that, I took the lady's hand and led her out onto the dance floor, sparing but a single glance and a mock shudder toward the new chandelier that hung above it.

I was soon reminded that Lady Nimble was very aptly named. As we waited for a new tune to begin, I confessed I was a neophyte at courtly dance. As an expert, she was quite used to knowing more than her partners and applauded my willingness to give it a try. She quickly explained the basics of a couple's dance called the Saltarello, a fast, leaping dance known for its exuberance and energy.

Fortunately, there were simplified versions of the Saltarello used to instruct unpracticed beginners. When the music started, she eased me into one of these. Although physically demanding, I found the steps, kicks, and leaps to be within my ability, and anyone would look good dancing alongside Lady Nimble. I even summoned the concentration (and breath) to converse during our dance.

"So, how are you faring, Lady Nimble? When last we met, I believe you were on a mission to fetch a pail of water."

"That didn't go very well, I'm afraid."

"Oh?" said I, spinning around to face her and taking up her hand again.

"No. On the way back, a drunken sot ran straight into Jill and me, knocking us both down."

"The fiend!" I exclaimed, imagining his backside as Jackie and I kicked forward. "Was anyone hurt?"

"Only my dignity," she replied as she circled around me.

"Oh. And I broke my crown," she added. "Thankfully, Elsie was kind enough to provide me with another. So, no harm done, I should think. The drunken lout made restitution by retrieving the water himself."

"Did he apologize?"

"Yes. And quite profusely and graciously as well. Elsewise, he wouldn't be my escort this evening."

I grinned at Jackie. She was all that and a clever storyteller to boot.

The herald had been introducing new arrivals so frequently that I had ceased taking notice of them. But as the dance neared its conclusion, he called out one that caused my heart to stir and my head to turn.

"Lord Everette Winthrop, Earl of Hamelinshire, escorting Lady Megan Arenson, daughter of Westarbor, known to some as 'The Lady of the Well.'"

Lady Nimble's soft eyes sought mine, and she gave my hand a gentle squeeze.

"I thank you for the dance, Sir Lucas. I think Lord Meriwether is a trifle reticent. But fear not. I'll loosen him up before the night is through. Go and find your lady of the well."

***

An earl, eh? I don't recall meeting the fellow, but the name Winthrop stirred a vague sense of unease. Wasn't Hamelinshire one of those counties in the far eastern stretches of Deerfield? I was certain I'd passed through it on my trek to the capital. That was it. I remembered thinking at the time how drab and unfriendly the place seemed. Perhaps I should pop over there and introduce myself.

As I made my way around the dance floor toward the table where Megan had settled, I heard Liam announce the next offering. I smiled. It was to be a group dance that would take a while to organize.

Megan's escort was a tall fellow with an upturned, waxed mustache and a small but distinct mole on his left cheek. He had a furtive look about him as his eyes scanned the room. He was saying something to Megan, and I heard the happy, bell-like laughter she sometimes affected when she wished to flatter someone.

My lady turned and smiled when she saw me approaching. When the earl's eyes swiveled to meet mine, his jaw clenched.

"Welcome, my lord," I greeted him. "I believe I have the honor of addressing a Winthrop, if I heard the herald correctly."

"You do, sir. And is 'Lucas the Just' now a member of the prince's welcoming committee? If not, then for what reason do you come seeking such an honor?"

Ouch.

By that, I was made keenly aware that, apart from the servants, I was the only one in the gathering who lacked a title of 'lord' or above. It was a bit off-putting. But although my swordplay lacked any refinement, I was quickly improving in the sport of verbal fencing. I changed tactics and approached my introduction from a less friendly angle.

"Actually, I have come to collect on a debt, your lordship."

"A debt?" he said, incredulous.

Was that a flicker of fear peeking from behind his hauteur?

"Indeed, my lord," I continued. "I believe the lady owes me a pavane, and since they're just queuing up for such, I wondered if it might be an apt time to collect."

I flashed a winning smile and directed my gaze over to Megan. But though his face showed momentary relief, he was soon scowling at me. Megan's face was unreadable.

"You'll forgive me, sir, if I ask the lady to decline," he said with annoyance. "We've only just arrived. 'Tis only polite that I be granted some time with my companion this evening before she is pestered by intrusive attentions. Begone."

Perfectly reasonable, if a bit strongly phrased. *Ouch and touche.* Megan remained quiet and demure. I took from this that she would yield to her escort's preference. Was I being boorish? His harsh rebuff stung far less than her willingness to abide by it in silence.

Someone behind me cleared his throat noisily. I glanced behind, then lowered my gaze to find the king's page looking up expectantly. His gaze was not directed at me, however. He was looking past me at the earl. I stepped awkwardly aside.

"Welcome, my lord and lady, to the prince's royal ball."

"I am beginning to feel most welcome indeed," the earl muttered dryly.

"His highness, Prince Henry, will soon be announced. He sent me ahead to ask whether the lady Megan would do him the honor of joining him in the next dance."

Megan looked at the earl and smiled at him expectantly. Lord Winthrop seemed resigned to his fate. When he replied, he did so in a markedly different tone.

"It would be churlish indeed of me to deny the prince *anything* on this, his special day. If the lady is agreeable, she has my leave to indulge our prince in his desire. I shall wait here, counting the moments until she returns."

Megan gave his hand a little squeeze and was soon following the page over to where the couples were gathering for the pavane.

"His royal highness, Prince Henry!" announced the herald.

All turned to greet the smiling prince, who was bedecked in a dazzling white doublet. It was so heavily embroidered with golden thread and studded with gems that it might almost serve as brigandine armor. On it, two fierce dragons were entwined. Atop this was a diagonal sash in the royal purple with a matching chaperon around his neck.

A cheer went up that seemed as heartfelt as it was deafening, while the prince smiled and waved.

I was happy for Henry, I suppose. But did he have to invite Megan to the one courtly dance that I had actually practiced? I made my way back to my own table, still happy to be here and a bit more humble.

***

Having concluded her discussions with the duchess, Lady Castleberry had retired to our table. We watched the happy couples perform the pavane, led by the prince and Megan. My feet itched to join them, but Victoria had demurred.

"That would make you one for three by my count, young man," she observed.

Whatever else you might say about the aging widow, she certainly had an agile and engaging wit.

"Don't worry," she added consolingly. "I sense your lady friend is hiding deep feelings for you."

"I know Megan cares for me, your ladyship." I groused. "It's the hiding part that nettles me. She's too blasted good at it."

This earned me a wry chuckle from the cunning courtier.

Victoria was a very knowledgeable and astute observer. As we watched the people around us, she shared with me many keen observations accompanied by interesting facts and stories about each. It was a pleasurable way to while away our time as we waited for the feast to commence.

Lady Katherine and her suitor once again occupied the table nearby. Whenever I glanced in that direction, she carefully avoided my gaze. I didn't want to know how Victoria had put a fright in her. I was only glad to be spared more heartache from that direction.

Drinks were finally served, and the revelry ratcheted up a notch. The dance floor swarmed with the kingdom's nobility. Many even stopped over at our table for a word with me or my companion, and Victoria dutifully made introductions. The room had grown a trifle over-warm from the press of the crowd and the warm glow of candles all about. So much so that Victoria took to fanning herself to alleviate the closeness.

And through it all was Henry. The dashing young prince was very attentive to his guests and surprisingly accessible. He visited many tables, and many a maiden that night was thrilled to claim a dance with him. The frolic was interrupted only once, when the king arrived.

When King Raymond was announced, he and his wife proceeded to the high table and claimed the centermost seats. The high-backed chairs to the left and right of them remained empty, reserved for the royal heirs. From our excellent vantage near the table's foot, I could tell the king was glum. He stared listlessly over the crowd and hardly shared two words with the queen. She would occasionally pat his arm and make some remark, but his responses were short (and off-putting, if her face was any gage).

"It's hard to lose a loved one," said Victoria.

"It is," I replied.

"But the princes and I have cooked something up that should uplift his majesty's spirits."

"I doubt that, Lucas. I've seen these bitter moods of his before. He'll be gloomy all evening."

"Have faith," I said, waggling my eyebrows at her.

With the arrival of the king, I saw more of the royal guardsmen. There were at least a dozen I could see arrayed behind the high table, and I suspected there were others positioned throughout the room and on the upper floor above it. They were hard to spot unless you were looking for them. Their dull black chain mail tended to blend with the shadows, and they were even less noticeable given the flamboyant garb of the noble guests.

And finally, the time for the feast was upon us.

I saw Richard more elegantly attired than I'd ever seen him making a bee line toward Henry. The two were soon taking their places to either side of the monarch. They were smiling playfully as servitors laid a large, covered dish directly before their father. Lifting its cover, Richard revealed the pie he'd baked, and Henry presented the king with a large knife. The king gave the pie an indifferent sniff.

Steam rose from the savory pie. Its crust was a perfect golden brown. The dance floor had cleared, and all sat watching their monarch as he cut into it.

The very first enchantment I had ever learned was rather unique. I invented it on a whim to seal my missives to Megan. When she would break the waxen seal, my lady would be treated to birdsong. It had become a private joke between us. So I thought, why not seal the pie?

As the knife pierced the crust, there came a warbling and twittering, as if from a flock of startled birds. The king leaned back, his eyes flying wide. The queen brought her hand up before her mouth. Henry was grinning from ear to ear, and Richard was hugging his sides with laughter.

Setting the knife aside, King Raymond chuckled. Then he clapped his hands together and loudly proclaimed, "By God, what a dainty dish! You two rascals have outdone yourselves!"

Applause broke out among the nobles then, and servitors rushed forth into the jubilant hall bearing the first set of entrées. Soon, we were all served, and fine wine was flowing like water. As the king sectioned his pie, I saw Henry and Richard pointing my way and talking excitedly to him. The king turned his head my way, and when our eyes met, he smiled and nodded. He dispatched a servitor to my table with a large wedge of the delicacy in question.

"I think I've underestimated you once again, Sir Lucas," quipped Lady Castleberry. "You seem to have a way with buttering up the upper crust"

I groaned inwardly. She had delivered a pun worthy of Master Chadwick.

"Even though you doubted me," I replied, "I'll share it with you. It would please me greatly to see my lady eat crow."

"I shall be happy to indulge you, Lucas. But I'll have you know that although crows are black birds, blackbirds are not, in fact, crows."

"I am well aware of the difference, my lady, but I just couldn't come up with any better blackbird banter."

And after tucking into the tasty treat, I sat enjoying the evening with my canny companion until it was time to head home.

CHAPTER NINE

𝔗𝔥𝔢 𝔖𝔲𝔦𝔱𝔬𝔯

"Of the seven deadly sins, only envy
is no fun at all."
~ *Joseph Epstein* ~

Though the day was mild, my shirt clung to me as sweat poured in rivulets down my neck. Trenton had worked me hard in this session. I'd once been informed that men don't sweat. They perspire. And women simply 'glowed.' Such quibbles and euphemisms aside, I was covered in honest sweat.

The dog days of summer were still a few weeks off. I should be gone from here and back to the conclave before they arrived. I didn't fancy a workout in the midst of their swelter. As it was, even Lord Stapleton's hounds seemed to lack the energy to raise an alarm at our early morning drills.

Retrieving a fresh towel from my bob and draping it about my shoulders, I headed back inside. Toby was sleeping in today, and I honestly missed the little devil. I could always count on him to make some ribald remark when we commiserated over Trenton's tiresome training. I hope he had my bath drawn. I was sore in need of a good soak.

I was soon relaxing in a large wooden tub, scrubbing my back and feet with a long-handled brush. The herbal infusions floating on the water's surface bore a medicinal scent. They supposedly promoted good health, but I didn't favor the acrid odor. The steaming tea kettle Toby had brought up from the kitchen barely took the edge off the chill waters he'd lugged up here from the well.

"I hear they sawed that empty beer tun in half at Refuge, master. They're using the two halves as tubs for laundry and the like."

"You don't say," I said distractedly.

"I do say, master," he shot back. "Oh, and the baron wants you down in the sunroom soon. There's to be more callers today."

Frowning, the lad lingered. He made a show of making up our beds and spreading the drapes, brightening our sleeping quarters cum bathhouse. But his unaccustomed silence cast a pall upon the room.

"Something else?" I asked him.

"Um. In the kitchen, I ran into Lady Meg having a light breakfast. She seemed sad."

"How could you tell? The woman is a master at schooling her expressions. I'm certain you were imagining it."

"She doesn't do that around me. And Lynette was hovering all around, like she does when her lady's upset. So, I was wondering when you were gonna tell her how you *feel* about her."

I paused in my scrubbing.

"Toby, I've told you I don't want to talk about that."

"If it's obvious to me, it's a sure bet that she knows it already - and the baron too. But she needs to hear it from *you*. She's given you more'n enough hints."

"What hints?"

"At the theater fr'instance, she told you, 'sometimes I wish I could heed what my heart is telling me, in spite of what I know is the more steady course,' or some such."

What? I remembered her saying that, but the context eluded me.

"And *you* told her you'd support her however she decided. But you're not giving her a *choice!*"

I was flummoxed. Standing from my bath, I stepped out and took up a towel.

"Toby, courtship among the nobility is... complicated."

"I *know,*" he returned hotly. "But she ain't just a noble. She's Lady *Meg!* If you don't fess up, she'll just do what's expected of her. She might anyway, but you don't *know* that. Leastways, *then* she can know it was her own doing. I dare you to tell her."

"Toby, I..."

"Better yet, tell her pa. Tell him you wanna be considered. You're the right age and almost a noble yourself. Be a man. I dare you to do it. I double DOG dare you!"

Without waiting for my response, Toby marched out into the hallway and slammed the door. I stood there with damp hair and a towel wrapped around my waist. I don't think I'd ever seen Toby so passionate. Rather than dismiss his words, I considered them. Was I being a coward? I don't know *what* the baron would do if I admitted having amorous intentions toward his daughter. I doubted he'd have me drawn and quartered.

I pondered it some more and finally arrived at a decision. And the chill that settled upon me had little to do with my current state of undress.

***

When I joined his lordship in the sunroom, his daughter had yet to arrive. I had hoped the moment would be inopportune, but fate seemed set on favoring Toby's dare. As Duke Gaulle had once said, 'When better than now?'

I tried to deepen and slow my breaths to release the tightness in my chest. The baron seemed to sense that something was off. As I screwed up my courage, he laid his hands on his lap and peered over at me attentively.

"Your lordship?" I began, without greeting the man.

"Sit, Lucas, and tell me what's on your mind."

All the words I had prepared simply scattered from my thoughts like a nest of frightened mice upon the pouncing of a cat.

I sat.

"As your lordship is aware, I've been Megan's friend since we met back at Westarbor Keep. During that time, I've come to care deeply for her, and she for me as well."

The baron sat silent, his face a study of indifference. But his intense blue eyes remained locked with mine, belying his dispassionate aloofness. I gulped and hurried on.

"Though the circumstances are somewhat confusing, seeing her here in Fairglen has brought joy back into my life. It's like when the sun emerges on a cloudy day, bringing warmth and clarity. I can't imagine plodding on under a sunless sky without having her in my life."

"Therefore, I must ask you, is there a chance? May I become her suitor? I may lack the lofty pedigree with which others are endowed, but I swear that, as a son-in-law, I would strive to make you proud. And not a day would pass when I wouldn't consider her happiness above my own. She is the true treasure of Westarbor, and I would give her this choice of another kind of life. One day, if she wishes it, can Megan become my wife?"

My heart was beating rapidly as I sat on the edge of my chair. Now, it was up to the baron. Would he grant me my heart's desire or send my hopes spiraling down the drain? The world seemed to pause as he wet his lips and prepared to make an answer. Never before in my life had I felt such an agonizing expectation.

"I shall instruct Megan," he said enigmatically, "to release you from your vow as her protector."

What did it mean? Had I angered his lordship?

"It wouldn't do for one of her suitors to share such a bond with my daughter. It wouldn't be fair to the others."

Royland had once told me that he envied my 'perhaps,' that precious something extra that I enjoyed with Megan. As the meaning of the baron's wonderful words exploded in my mind, it was as if the colors had intensified around me. The world came rushing back into motion as it struck me I'd be keeping my perhaps.

"Normally, I'd ask you about your prospects and whether you had the means to look after her in comfort befitting a woman of her station. All the usual queries. But I think, for the sake of expediency, we can cut past all that. Nor, I think, are you interested in dickering over the dowry, for I can see that isn't your heart's intent."

No, indeed. I hadn't given it a single thought.

"So let's eschew the formalities and simply summarize. You wish to marry my daughter and whisk her away to live with the mages at Conclave. She would remain untitled, but would live in adequate comfort as the wife of a master mage. Grandchildren by your issue would likely have the gift as well, and be ineligible to inherit my lands. I would have to rely on Trenton for heirs."

When he put it that way, I seemed like a suboptimal choice indeed. But I noted he hadn't said no.

"Balanced against these practicalities is what I see in my daughter's eyes whenever she looks upon you. I knew of your feelings, Lucas. How could I not? Like Megan, I must stare people's feelings in the face every day. It's a useful talent, but not one that lends itself well to self-deception. Is there a chance? Can you become her suitor? My answer is yes. The final decision will be hers."

My joy reignited. Now all I need do to keep my perhaps intact was to outshine a prince's charm. Not a problem. Today, nothing seemed impossible.

Sword practice this morning had worn me out. And though I'd been invigorated by the bath and the emotional high I'd been riding on, now I felt fatigue washing over me. There were no words with which to express my gratitude for the baron's decision.

"Thank you, your lordship," I said.

I relied on his talent to fill in the rest.

***

As a geomancer, perhaps I would never experience the thrill of actual flight. But well could I imagine it. For I walked about as though floating on air for much of the following day.

I was told that Megan had been informed, and I ached to know what she made of it. Whenever I encountered her, however, she avoided my gaze and swiftly absented herself from my presence. The only contact we were permitted was through her companion. Lynette showed up in my doorway bearing a brief missive in my lady's florid hand. In it, she released me from my vow as her protector. And though I had expected this, I had imagined a more fulsome letter than the terse proclamation I was served.

"Lynette?" I asked. "How's she taking it?"

Her eyes flashed as she peered up at me from an otherwise downcast gaze.

"That's not for me to say, Sir Lucas," she all but scolded. "My lady's disposition is not a proper topic for her servants to speculate upon."

At this, she whirled about and flounced away.

Toby was all grins when I entrusted to him a letter for the baron requesting a courtly visit with his daughter. The baron's response was as formal as it was prompt. The lady would receive me in the sunroom at three to discuss my intentions. Tea would be served.

I'd seen other hopefuls and knew well the drill. I sent Toby on a quick visit to the Castleberry estate, there to obtain the good lady's advice on what gift might be most likely to find my lady's favor. Meanwhile, I agonized over a note to include. It would be like no other letter I had ever written to Megan. For it would proclaim openly my feelings for her, truths that, ere now, I had hidden even from myself.

Now that I had dared to place myself in the running, I'd better work swiftly to make my case. The note would be important because I didn't trust my tongue under the unwavering regard of those sparkling blue eyes. Fully a dozen rough drafts lay crumpled on the floor before I struck on one that might suffice. This last one would simply have to do. It was harder than I'd imagined, pitching woo.

Dearest Megan,

I have grown since the day you and I first met. I've seen more of the world and its wonders. But nothing I've witnessed ever came close to the simple joy I feel in your presence. They say each soul has its one true mate, its other half, if you will. I believe I have found mine in you.

Already, I lament the loss of the bond we forged some two years past. Was it only so brief a span as that? This was severed only so that I might offer you a greater oath in its stead. One that will heal the longing in my heart and make us whole at last. You know my truth already. I can only hope you feel the same.

You once asked me whether you should heed your heart, and my answer hasn't changed. You have a kind heart, my lady, and I will support you in whatever it decides. The choice is yours, my lady, and I shall respect it. Whether by this I am condemned to walk the land forever, half a man, or, by your choice, I walk in bliss forever more.

Forever your servant (officially or not),

Lucas Harper

When Toby returned, it was with a gorgeous urn of live blooms dug up from Victoria's own gardens. They were an arrangement of gardenias wreathed within a halo of forget-me-not. The message they sent matched my sentiment and would stand out from the roses the others had brought. Secret love, trust, renewal, and hope and remembrance of one another. I was certain Megan would understand, well-schooled as she was in floriography.

When at last all was in readiness, naught remained but the pacing and fretting. The third bell couldn't come quickly enough. Was there anything I was forgetting?

"Calm down, master," said Toby. "You're wearing out the rug."

I tried not to let it bother me. Why was *he* looking so smug?

And when, at last, the hour was nigh, I gathered up my flowers. I deepened my breathing and tried to still my racing thoughts. I'd faced down witches and ogres and worse. I'd battled grim horrors galore. But my heart's palpitation on that short traverse was unmatched... heretofore.

It was bright in the sunroom. The afternoon sun slanted in. As usual, Megan was seated beside her father on the chaise longue. Before them, on a low table, was a tea set, and I could smell the fragrant goodness it contained. Beside this rested a platter of freshly baked oatcakes.

I headed for my usual seat, only to find it already occupied. Sir Nolan sat there nibbling at a biscuit.

"How good of you to come, Sir Lucas," said Megan. "I believe you know my father. And Sir Nolan here is my new knight protector, my former one having moved on to grander pursuits."

Was she kidding? I could never tell. Best to play along and let my lady set the tone. I could either laugh or cry about it afterward.

"Charmed, my lady, your lordship," I said, bowing low.

"Oooh, are those for me?" she asked, indicating the pot I held.

"They are indeed, my lady," said I, playing along.

She bent forward to smell the bouquet as I set it on the table.

"Will you join us for a cup of tea, Sir Harper? 'Tis a most pleasing decoction of chamomile and mint."

"Indeed? Then I would be most pleased to accept my lady's kind offer."

As Megan poured, her father drew my eye.

"Young man, it has come to my attention that you fancy yourself a suitable match for nobility," he growled. "So I must ask you, what is the purpose of your visit here today, and what are your intentions?"

Now I knew they were having me on. I stifled a sudden grin and affected my most dour frown.

"I think I have made my intentions quite clear to your lordship upon our prior meeting. And in case my lord should doubt my sincerity, I've put it in writing for the lady's own perusal. Mark you, the flowers bear a note."

I took up my teacup and sipped at it while the baron served me with a withering gaze from his frosty blue eyes. Meanwhile, as if completely unconcerned, Megan plucked the note from among the gardenias and began reading it. There are times in life when one can actually hear the beating of one's own heart. She looked at me over the parchment with a stare that seared my soul.

"I, too, have a question, Sir Lucas."

"Speak it, my lady, and I shall answer."

Her lips curled up in the impish grin that plucked at the strings of my heart.

"Whatever took you so long?" she breathed.

Thursday. My courtly date with Megan would be Thursday. Not much time remained before the coronation, but I'd managed to snag one of the few remaining openings in my lady's schedule. I'd dispatched Toby to secure a carriage and make the other preparations. I was certain Megan would appreciate the venue I intended.

The problem was that it was only Wednesday. And such was my anticipation that it proved nigh impossible to focus on anything else. I finally settled on a neighborly visit to pass the time and quell my jitters. It had been several years since I'd last spoken with Lord or Lady Stein. Given our proximity and his ever-worsening condition, I feared I mightn't get a better chance.

The Steins and their retinue were being hosted by Lord Darrington, a colleague from Leopold's younger days. They dwelt but two streets over. When I knocked on their door, I was met by Lord Darrington himself. After I had explained my desire for a visit with the Steins, he ushered me inside and dispatched a servant to inquire whether they would receive me. We exchanged pleasantries and made some idle talk as we awaited their response.

"Lady Stein will greet you in the dayroom, Sir Lucas," reported the page on his return. "His lordship will be in attendance as well."

That was an odd way to phrase it. I braced myself for what I might find and followed the boy to this dayroom. Its layout was much like the sunroom back at Camburn Manor. Instead of the low tables, there was a larger, more sturdy-looking one. It was octagonal in shape, with a set of wickerwork chairs surrounding it.

Lady Wilhelmina sat facing the door as I entered. Beside her, wrapped in a shawl, was her husband. The wickerwork chair in which he was seated had wheels affixed to its base. I had never seen the like. It was an ingenious way to help someone unsteady on his feet. But it spoke volumes about his lordship's frailty.

"Well met, Sir Lucas. It was good of you to come. My lord and I have grown dependent on visitors of late."

I bowed to the lady as was proper.

"Your ladyship. Lord Stein," I greeted. "And how are you enjoying your stay in the capital? I saw you at the debutante ball. I meant to stop over then, but I was diverted."

"Well, we're here," she said, absently patting at her husband's hand.

Despite his inexpressive face, Lord Stein seized her hand in his and shifted his gaze her way. Her ladyship seemed surprised by this and smiled at his regard.

"I think he's happy to see you, Lucas. Come have a seat."

I took my place across from them. From within my cloak, I produced the Karnöffel deck I had brought and set it on the table. This caused Lady Stein to roll her eyes. The couple had introduced Royland and me to the game when we'd been snowbound at their castle. I recalled passing many a pleasant hour learning its complexities.

"Ah, Lucas," remarked the baroness, "his lordship is not capable of giving us a proper game just now. He's having one of his non-verbal days, I'm afraid."

However, releasing his wife's hand, Leopold smacked his lips and reached across the table to scoop up the stack of cards. With his eyebrows twitching, he fanned them out and began taking some up to assemble a hand.

"That's alright," I replied. "Some find it soothing just to handle something familiar. For Royland's grandmother, it was her knitting."

"You are most thoughtful, Sir Lucas, and wise beyond your years."

I blushed at the unexpected praise and sought a more agreeable topic as the addled lord scrutinized and rearranged his 'hand.'

"Speaking of kindness, it was most gracious of Lord Darrington to put you up here."

"It was. Of course, my husband and Theo go way back. When I wrote him, he was quick to offer us *noblesse oblige*."

Lord Leopold played a card from his hand. He slapped it down on the table before him and stared first at Wilhelmina and then at me. He pointed at the card to emphasize his play. I stared down at the wickedly grinning, horned devil depicted upon a blood-red background. When played properly, the Teufel card could trump any other in the game, even the pope.

"He's got *me* beat," I said.

"I, too, fold," declared the baroness, playing along.

At this, Leopold bunched up his lips and stared sullenly off to one side.

"So, I heard you've become close with the prince, Lucas. How did that come about?"

"It's a long story, your ladyship," I said, "but when I first met him, he was pretending to be a knight's squire. He showed me a kindness, and I opened my heart to him. I don't think the prince had ever had a sincere friend who had no desire to curry his favor. So, when he later revealed he was the prince, he knew he could trust my intentions. We also share several common interests."

One of which is my intended (I did not add). I welcomed the distraction when Leopold played another card. It was the Herrscher (ruler) card. Perhaps in spite of his aphasia, he was following our conversation and meant it to indicate the prince.

"Henry?" I asked him.

Lord Leopold beamed, then went back to sorting his cards. I turned back toward the baroness.

"What about you? Are you prepared for the coronation?"

A pained expression crossed the lady's face. I could have kicked myself. I'd meant to avoid the topic of Leopold's mad plan to attend the event in his right mind at the risk of his own life. Nor could I hide my sudden scowl at the slip. The lady was too perceptive.

"What have you heard?" she asked tersely.

I sighed, knowing the jig was up. As I hastened to explain my accidental awareness of the scheme, Lord Leopold grew more agitated. He began furiously sorting through the deck. From it, he withdrew the Krone (crown) card and laid it face up over the ruler. Then, atop this stack, he laid another. It depicted a skeletal figure with a scythe. It was the Tod card, the card of death.

"Oh," wailed Wilhelmina, rocking back in her chair.

Seizing her arm, Leopold pointed at his chest with his other hand and started shaking his head in negation. This having failed to console her, he produced a kerchief from the pocket of his vest and offered it to her. This only caused her weeping to intensify.

Soon, Lord Darrington came bursting into the room to see what was amiss. He scowled at the scene, and then more specifically at me.

"I think it is time that you take your leave, Sir Lucas. 'Tis obvious that Leopold has become overexcited by your visit. Jeremy, please show our guest to the door."

Leopold glared at his host, then cast a final pleading look my way. With his finger, he stabbed once again at the Teufel card.

That hadn't gone very well, I thought as I followed the page back out. I wished once again there was more I could do for the kindly old nobleman. But I'd been told even magical healing can't restore a failing mind.

***

Back at Camburn Manor, another upsetting surprise awaited. As I trudged my dejected way across the threshold, I encountered Toby (the king's page, Toby). He stood waiting in

291

the entryway, holding a package. Lord Camburn was addressing him even as I entered.

"It should only be a few minutes now. She's just finishing up with another suitor."

"Hello, Sir Lucas. Back from your visit, I see. I take it the Steins are in good health?"

"Not so much, your lordship. In truth, the visit went rather poorly."

"Oh?"

"Don't concern yourself, my lord. I wouldn't want to speak out of turn. Lord Darrington seems to have the matter well in hand."

Just then, from the sunroom, Sir Nolan emerged. He was escorting a morose-looking Sir Wulfric.

"So, you see, the lady hasn't time for a leisurely stroll. The coronation is nearly upon us, and she must prepare."

"But I thought, perhaps..."

"Buck up, man; the lady's word in this matter is final."

I stepped aside as the knight protector hauled the woeful Sir Wulfric by the elbow and showed him the door. That's one more down, I thought hopefully. Alas, sometimes hope is but the first step on the road to disappointment, and it can be a short trip indeed.

The baron soon emerged, followed by Megan.

"Are you here for Lucas again?" he asked of Toby.

"No, indeed, your lordship," replied the page with a courtly bow. "The prince would have me convey this gift to your daughter and extend to her an invitation to join him for afternoon tea."

The baron took the package from the boy and offered it to Megan. It was getting rather crowded in the small entry foyer, so I used the distraction to back into the trophy room, there to lurk just beyond its arch. As one would expect, the invitation was promptly accepted. As the page hustled off, I heard Megan remark that the prince must be eager indeed. Then the baron confessed his curiosity.

"Let's see what his highness has sent you as a token of his affection."

"Yes, miss," said Sir Nolan. "I confess to some curiosity myself."

Despite my *own* curiosity, I shuffled off to allow them some privacy. Did I really want to know what I was up against? I got the tale later from Toby (my Toby), who'd pried it out of Lynette. It was a pair of elbow-length white lady's gloves from LaShalts. They were made of fine silk embellished with lace. In the note, Henry said that he'd heard her gloves had been tragically dropped in a mud puddle. He didn't want this to stain the honor of Fairglen in the lady's estimation. He was a clever one, my rival - and quite thoughtful too, I begrudgingly admitted.

Seeking relief from my agonizing worry, I made my way to the yard out back. Weeding was a wonderful way to while away a dreary day. And though the Camburn yard beyond the well was no formal garden, I felt sure I could improve it with some tender loving care. Retrieving my spade, I dug in.

I found some begonias growing naturally. I dug a few up and helped them form a more orderly row. I wish I'd thought to bring along some seeds. For now, I'd just work with what was at hand and take out my frustrations on the weeds.

But even as I bent to my relaxing chore, I writhed in the throes of dread, imagining Megan in the arms of the prince. It didn't help at all that I actually respected and liked the fellow. That only made it worse. I finally knew the torment Royland must have felt when he saw love blossom between Megan and me. Even then, he knew. He knew it well before I could acknowledge it myself.

I told Megan that I would respect whatever decision she made. I'd put it in writing just yesterday. But envy was indeed a soul-crushing beast, one that I hoped I would not have to slay.

"Good evening, brother," came the rumbling speech from deep within my psyche. "Once again, it's time for the sun to be setting. Get you to bed if you're done with your fretting."

Startled, I glanced up. It was indeed almost nightfall. The edge of the lawn now looked like a mad florist had waged all-out war on the unruly hedges, tamed a weed rebellion, and launched a floral *coup d'état* on the otherwise natural border. It had been a long time since I'd so lost myself in my work.

"Rockytop?" I said, knuckling my bleary eyes to clear them. "Do you think we stand a chance?"

"If it is meant to be," said he (and by him, I meant me), "then it will be. And if it is not, then we'll always have our weeding."

Sometimes I detested my own fatalistic sense of humor.

Standing erect, I made for my room and the gentle release from care that was sleep.

***

"Well, where are you taking her, then?" Lynette asked yet again.

"I told you it's a surprise," I impatiently repeated.

"Then how am I to prepare my lady? How should she be dressed?"

She was wearing me down. It was a fair point, I conceded.

"Ordinary everyday clothing is appropriate for the day. But if I tell you more, then you'll tell her, or your face will give it away."

"So..."

"That's all you're going to get from me. Begone, you pestersome imp. I've my own preparations to make."

At that, she finally departed (after sticking her tongue out at me).

Closing the door, I turned to my servant.

"Is everything ready, Tobias?"

"The mule is hitched. The weather's fair, and the girl has promised to meet you there."

I gave him a penetrating look.

"*What?*" he exclaimed. "I thought we was rhyming. *You* do it all the time."

I couldn't deny it. I, too, had noted that penchant creeping into my patterns of speech. It had started on that fateful day when first I'd met the woodland fey. Had they somehow cursed me to think in rhyme? I'd ponder on it later, when I had more time.

"Alright, then," I told Toby. Go and wait outside Megan's room. Come back and let me know when she's ready."

"Yes, master," he said, rushing off down the hall.

Since coming to Fairglen, I'd accumulated a dizzying variety of outfits. But for this outing, I selected some of my plainest clothes. The cloak I donned was an old one of mine that I'd owned e'en before I'd left home. Though patched and worn and somewhat threadbare, it reminded me of a very special day.

When Toby returned and informed me that the lady awaited my visit, I slipped down the hall to collect her.

There was something to be said for the bucolic look. Dressed as she was in a simple woolen kirtle, my lady could almost be any maid of the land. I say almost, because there was no mistaking the poise of a noblewoman. Even bereft of the fashionable dresses she'd been wearing since making her debut, Megan was still quite a delightful sight.

My lady would look stunning in nothing at all, I mused to myself. Aye, splendid. (I censored that thought before it could proceed to an image I hadn't intended.)

She looked me up and down, saying, "Well, don't we make a nice, matched set?"

Lynette stood nearby, scowling.

"I thought my lady might appreciate a day where we could let our hair down, as it were."

Her gorgeous ebony locks were gathered into two loose braids. These cascaded gently down to rest beyond her shoulder blades.

"I pray that where you're taking me, there'll be no chance of encountering Lady Katherine," she remarked.

"Unlikely," I remarked in turn, "but should we do so, the baroness might finally be made to realize that a woman's true beauty is not dependent on her attire."

My lady smiled at that. I offered her my arm.

"Come, my lady; your chariot awaits."

On viewing the conveyance I had rented for the day, Megan was amused. The two-wheeled gig had seating for two. It didn't require a coachman. The reins were managed by the passengers themselves, seated side by side. It was a delightful way for a couple to enjoy a leisurely buggy ride.

"Alright, it's a chariot, just as you promised. But what's that you've got pulling it?"

"Surely you remember Feckless, my lady. He's the mule I rode to the benefit ball. And unlike this gig I rented for the day, Feckless is mine now to keep. Come and befriend him. He'll be hauling us to our rendezvous."

I produced a carrot from a pocket of my cloak and offered it to the lady. With a bemused grin, she accepted it and approached our unpretentious steed. Feckless tossed his head in that way that he had and turned upon spying the treat. His lips curled back as he stretched his neck to reach it. His ear twitched back from a buzzing fly.

"Don't be afraid. He's gentle," I said to encourage her.

Soon the gray monstrosity was munching on the morsel while a laughing Lady Megan stroked his soft muzzle.

I helped Megan up the mounting steps, and soon we were off. On reaching Broadway, we turned south.

"Would my lady like to take the reins?" I offered.

"I'm not sure I... I never..." she wavered.

"It's easy," I assured her. "Feckless knows not to run into anything. And I'll help if you get into any trouble."

She took the reins. She soon started playing with them, veering left and right. Fortunately, the traffic on Broadway this morning was rather light. I leaned back and interlaced my hands behind my head. The weather was clement, just as Toby'd said. The morning sun was shaded by the buildings to our left. It peeped out to dazzle us each time we crossed a street.

"Do you hear it?" I asked. "I've come to like that sound."

"To what sound are you referring?" she asked while steering a steadier course. "I hear sounds from all around us."

"It's almost like a melody. The lullaby of Broadway in all its majesty. I hear children laughing, smithies ringing, and vendors hawking their wares. And the shuffle of the merchants attending to their affairs. Even Feckless adds the clop of hoofbeats to this chaotic cacophony that proudly announces all the city has to offer."

"Oh, that," she said and smirked. "Some people call it noise."

Soon we were approaching the city gates. I relieved Megan of her driving duties and reined Feckless in before them.

"Ho! Sir Lucas!" shouted Wally. "That's a sharp little buggy you're drivin' there. And where might you be taking our lady of the well?"

"It's a secret, Wally. Need to know."

"Well, I suppose it's no business of mine. But I think I might hazard a guess. Seein' as the hospital's done been built already, I suppose slaying a dragon is all that remains."

"Not on my list for today, Wally. I'm with a lady friend. But if I see one, I'll be sure and send it your way."

"You may pass then, Sir Lucas," laughed the guardsman at the gate.

And out we rolled into the countryside.

***

Why had I become so flippant, relaxed, and nonchalant? The nervousness of yesterday lay dormant underneath. But it lay in a dungeon beneath my joy to be spending the day with Megan. The girl was my anchor in a sea of doubt, keeping such demons at bay. I grinned as we approached the lake. Megan just affected me that way.

I'd scouted out the site two days ago. It was perfect for what I had in mind. I recalled the answer I'd given the prince. 'Just be your own true self,' I had told him. I'd be a fool not to follow my own good advice.

"My lady, we've arrived."

Megan simply inclined her head in silent acquiescence.

It wasn't a large lake, more of a pond that had gotten too full of itself. But its gently rippling waters reminded me of my youth. Some shade trees grew around it - strange ones they call weeping willows. And on its surface, paddled ducks in formation with their fellows. I helped the lady down and bade her follow me to its eastern shore. This put the morning sun behind us, where its flashing reflections wouldn't likely blind us.

Stepping down the grassy bank near the water's edge, I found a peaceful spot and spread my cloak. We sat. I fished within my pack to retrieve a stoppered bottle. Long empty, its glass was tinted green. Megan's eyes widened when I offered it to her, and she plucked it gently from my hand.

"Once I was plagued by nightmares," I began softly. "and you sought to ease my pain. The elixir you provided gave me many a good night's rest. Your parting gift to me that day meant more than you can know. It sustained me through some troubled times."

Megan glanced down at the bottle. I stretched forth my finger and lifted her chin. When her eyes met mine, I continued.

"It let me know that someone cared and gave me the strength to continue, sometimes against ridiculous odds. 'Come back to us,' you said. And I have, and always will. And yes, the elixir was appreciated too."

"Our first kiss," she breathed.

I quirked a grin and winked at her.

"I'm glad you said it *that* way, my lady, for it implies there will be another."

She pursed her lips in mock offense and punched me playfully on the shoulder.

"Don't get ahead of yourself with brazen inferences, Sir Harper," she said. "I'm only here to hear you out."

"Fear not, Lady Arenson. There's another interpretation that would leave the purity of your thoughts unimpugned. It was certainly the first time I'd ever been kissed. And if this was true for you as well, it was indeed 'our' first kiss, with no unseemly implications."

She seemed mollified by this. That was one of the things I treasured about Megan. She was a woman who would yield to logic.

"So, how many *other* kisses have you shared in your travels?" she asked abruptly.

"Uh... " I wanted to deny *any* such, but when I thought of the dryad's kiss, I knew I was well trapped. Megan could perceive any prevarication I might attempt. "I once was kissed by a dryad lass. She kissed me on the back of my hand to confer the mark of the fey. I wrote to you about that."

"You didn't mention a *kiss*. And I can see from your guilty feelings there was more to it than only that."

"Well, dryads are quite lovely. It was one of the troublesome times I was telling you about, through which your gift sustained me. And what about *you?*" I asked defensively. "Have you let any of your other suitors kiss *you?*"

Megan scowled, then her face relaxed, and she said most casually, "Only Sir Wulfric."

And there she was, peering over at me to see what I'd make of it. She let me stew for a moment before relenting.

"Relax, Lucas. It was at our first meeting. He took my hand and kissed it, as gentlemen sometimes do. It was right in front of father at the ball. It was *you* who set the precedent that hand-kisses should be counted."

"Well, that makes it better, but not by much. I'm still sad you had to suffer his slobbering touch."

"At least I don't have a tree-hickey," she shot back indignantly. "Is that the only kiss you have to confess?"

"Well," I admitted, teasing her back, "I confess there was one other. It happened a couple of weeks ago at the prince's grand unveiling."

It wasn't a lie, so to Megan's eye, I might just pull it off.

"Oh?" she said frostily.

"Yes. Behind the church before the event, I kissed the archbishop's ring. If, by our rules, hands are to count, I wanted to come completely clean."

She stared at me for a moment, then burst out laughing.

"Lucas, apart from making me laugh, why should I marry you? A prince has offered to make me a queen. Why should I become a mage's wife instead?"

I sensed it was time for honest words, not that with Megan there could be any other kind.

"It's true I can't offer you a castle. A comfortable estate is what you'd get with me. But your life would be unfettered, free from royal responsibility. You could make fine friends with no secret agendas and no currying of your favor. Your life could be adventurous, not locked away in a palace, but underneath the open sky. We could do great things, together, you and I."

Her eyes misted over at my words, and she locked her gaze with mine.

"Best of all, it'd be with me, a man who will always adore you. It's why I chose this venue for our date. Here, we are free of the pretentious masks we are so often forced to wear. Sitting side by side and speaking heart-to-heart is how couples are meant to be. Not you, and I, but you *with* me."

Megan paused.

"You're right about the royal life being a cage of sorts. I felt it from Henry when we spoke the other day. He's a decent and honorable man, and I wish him good fortune in finding a proper bride. But *my* heart now belongs completely to another."

"I accept your proposal, beloved, for all your words bear the ring of truth."

Could this be happening to me? I thought I might explode from the joy that blossomed within me. And Megan, with her talent, must feel every bit of it. Color rose to her cheeks as she refused to look aside. How could a fellow be so fortunate as to have this blushing beauty for his bride?

"We must seal it with a kiss," she said, "a proper kiss. That means you must return it and participate this time."

Her eyebrows arched, and she leaned in close. (The lady would get no argument from *me*.)

I considered which way I should tilt my head. I wouldn't want our noses to collide. Sensing my dilemma, she narrowed her eyes and leaned a bit to the right. Taking this as an unsubtle clue, I contrived to do so too. And when my lips met hers, so soft and warm, my nervous tension vanished. All awkwardness was banished, and my fear to breathless wonder did transform.

As when dancing, I'd been keeping a distance between us, so as not to besmirch the lady's honor. But as the kiss progressed, our bodies closer pressed, and I dared to tighten up my grip upon her. She clung to me as well, and for a time, there we did dwell, with shivers running up and down my spine. In bliss, I was cocooned within her loving arms, the racing of her heartbeat matching mine.

And when at last we came up for air, we found a youngster standing there.

"Am I too early?" asked Bonnie shyly. "I can come back later if you like."

"Uh, no, miss!" I said, a bit too loudly. "You're right on time. We were just sealing a promise. We're done now."

"Is *that* what you city folk call smooching? Anyway, I brought you the victuals you asked for and the bread to throw out to the ducks. I'll just leave it over here and mosey off in case you two want to... seal that promise some more."

With that, the girl went on her way, leaving a picnic basket. Within it was a bottle of wine, some roasted mutton, cheese and bread, and a checkered tablecloth. Megan discovered an apple as well. She held it out to me.

"Can I tempt you?" she asked.

"Get a fig leaf, and we can discuss it," I replied.

This left her blushing furiously once she had sussed out my meaning.

The ducks were angling toward us already. Well, they could just wait their turn. We tucked into the mobile feast and shared the wine without glasses.

"Lucas, how do you feel about children?"

"I love 'em. I *was* one once. We can have dozens if you like."

"Good to know, but probably we should have one first and see how it goes."

"What do the mage's wives do in Conclave?"

"All sorts of things. Some of them are mages themselves. It's like I wrote you in my letters. Conclave is quite progressive."

She was quiet for a while. Later, when we were tearing off bits of bread and throwing them out to the ducks, I started feeling talkative again.

"I can't wait to tell everyone."

"You must tell *no one*, Lucas, not until I speak to the prince. I owe him an answer before he hears about it from someone else. Only you, I, and father must know."

"How shall I act, then? Crestfallen? Otherwise, Toby will know, Lynette will know, Trenton will know --"

"You're right, of course. Can you simply forget it, like with my birthday surprise?"

"I don't *want* to forget it! How about this instead? If you plan to tell him tonight, I can stay at the refugee camp. Or maybe I could go to the quarry overnight."

"That won't work. Everyone will want to know why you didn't return."

"Alright, I'll do it, but I don't have to like it one bit."

"Tell me how it works..."

After Lady Megan grasped all that was involved, she bade me to come and spread my cloak once again beside the lake. We prepared to enact the farce with which I'd disappoint myself.

"Rockytop," I said, "if you lose so much as one precious moment of that kiss, I'll carve you into masonry blocks and build from them a garderobe. Then I'll come and do my business in it every single day."

"A hollow threat, my brother," he rumbled, "for how would you even know? But fear not, Lucas. I love her too. After all, I am part of you. One day, when we are one, she will be my wife as well. So, listen to our lady and play your part. Quiet ourself, it's time to start."

--------Take II--------

"... Best of all, it'd be with me, a man who will always adore you," I recited dutifully. "It's why I chose this venue for our date.

Here we are free of the pretentious masks we are so often forced to wear. Sitting side by side and speaking heart-to-heart is how couples are meant to be. Not you, and I, but you *with* me."

Megan paused.

"Lucas, you're a decent and honorable man, but Henry is as well. I'm sure that life as a princess wouldn't be half as bad as you make it out to be. I cannot accept your proposal just now, not without further thought. I'm uncertain where my future happiness lies. Your words bear the ring of truth, but you could be mistaken. I must speak to Henry once more. If you will wait, I'll give you my answer this evening."

Could this be happening to me? I thought I might explode from the anxiety that welled up within. And Megan, with her talent, must feel every bit of it. Color rose to her cheeks, but she refused to look aside. There was still a chance, perhaps, to have this lovely lady for my bride.

"I hired that shepherdess girl to bring us some food."

"Oh," said Megan, pointing. "I saw her wander up and leave it over there. Though, in truth, I've not much of an appetite, anyway."

Strangely, I didn't either.

"We could feed the ducks. You used to *like* that."

"I think I'll pass on that as well. Why don't we head back to the city?"

"As my lady wishes," I said.

As I harnessed up Feckless, I thought to myself, 'That could have gone *much* better.'

We returned to the Camburn estate. I had Toby return the carriage. He rode back on Feckless, who had a rented stall just up the street. Megan was soon off to meet with her prince again. I was glum, but I took heart from the fact that she hadn't yet said no. Had I detected a slight hint of promise in her eye?

When I saw her returning that evening, Rockytop said he had some interesting news to share.

I was certain my whoop of joy on hearing it aroused half the residents there!

***

On Friday, I awoke with joy. I was affianced! I threw back the covers and leapt from my bed, hastily making ready for the day. My mind was clear, despite the fact that Trenton had kept me up drinking last night. A hearty breakfast awaited me, where all in the house had gathered. They sat me in the seat of honor beside another empty chair. I sat there blushingly, waiting. Then, suddenly, *she* was there.

I arose and held out the chair for her (as any true gentleman should). And after fussing with the seating, I sat beside her and started eating. We had no ring to show them, so abruptly had the arrangement come upon us. But congratulations abounded, and many toasts were made to me and my lady fair.

"Of course, it will perforce be a long engagement," the baron was saying to Count Camburn. "I told him the nuptials must await the day he's officially made a master mage."

"Well, that should give the lad some strong incentive," returned the count jovially.

Megan would return to Meadowfork with her father, and I must return to my master. I'd certainly take to my studies with a vengeance. I knew this first blush of ecstasy would eventually fade and be replaced by a more comforting contentment. But for now, I reveled in the thrill of its exhilaration. I could endure any separation just knowing that there'd come a day when she'd be beside me ever more. Stone is patient.

The day was fine as, all around us, the blessings of summer abounded. We spoke of our plans for our life together in eager and hopeful voices. I wanted to spend every minute with my wife-to-be while I still could. But all too soon, my lady and I (my fiancée, I corrected) were separated by the necessity of preparing for tomorrow's coronation.

I was back in my chamber that evening when there came a rapping at my door. Was it someone else coming to offer me best wishes? But no, it was the baron, looking rather grim.

"Lucas, there are some men downstairs. They've come for you from the royal palace."

Hastening after his lordship, I descended. Two familiar men in black chain mail stood in the entry hall. Both made the sovereign salute as I approached them. So there was *that*, at least.

"Lucas," said Guardsman Willis without preamble, "once again, you are to come with us. The prince has a task for you."

I knew from experience that he would say no more until we were well on our way. The baron stood nearby, worry and curiosity in equal measure written on his face. Toby peeped down from the top of the stairs. He plucked up his courage and descended. The second guardsman moved to intercept the lad, barring his way with a raised hand.

"Just the mage," he said.

As Toby darted around the guardsman to arrive beside me, I saw the man's hand stray to the hilt of his sword. But then my faithful servant unslung my pack. After offering it to me, he retreated quietly.

"Ah," said I. "All ready to go, then. Lead the way, and I shall follow."

A familiar long, black, windowless carriage was pulled up in the lane, barely a dozen steps from the front door. I followed the men, who ushered me in and bracketed me between them on the bench.

"I don't suppose there's any point in asking you about this task."

"The prince will tell you what you need to know," one replied with eyes straight ahead.

As we started down the lane, I recalled the conversation I'd had with Megan the prior night.

"So how did he take it?" I had asked after her visit with the prince.

"Outwardly, he took it well," she had replied. "He offered his congratulations. But I sensed in him an inner turmoil. There was an ugliness within him when I spoke of our love."

"Ah. That was envy, my lady. One of the deadly sins.. I know that demon well. I wrestled with him just last night when I thought I might be losing you."

"I'm sorry we made you feel that way, beloved. It was a nasty, if necessary, trick."

"Fear not, my lady; I'm sure he'll get over it in time."

But would he? I recalled how envy over Megan had driven a wedge between Royland and me for the better part of two whole seasons. And my cousin and I have a much closer relationship than my budding friendship with Henry.

I was also reminded of the cautionary tale of King David from the Bible. On seeing Bathsheba and finding her fair, the king sent her husband off to war to be slain so that he might have her. I hope the task Henry had in mind for me wasn't something like that.

But what was I thinking? Just as Megan had said and I'd seen for myself, Henry is an honorable man. Of course, so should King David have been. For that matter, I'd also heard it said somewhere that *Brutus* was an honorable man. I'd gotten my wish regarding Megan. But perhaps I'd need to slay that envy monster after all, not in myself but in another. That made it harder, actually.

Such were my thoughts as the royal coach slid up once again to the palace's rear entrance. Once more, I was hustled through its door and down its echoing hallways. I was let into the royal audience chamber and was marched into the presence of the prince. Henry was seated on the high-backed chair at the chamber's very center. When the guardsmen knelt a dozen paces from him, I joined them in good order.

I noticed that a tall stepladder had been set up over by the hearth. But there was no noose hanging from the rafters above it. So, there was *that*, at least.

"Well, well," declared Henry, not granting me leave to rise, "if it isn't the heartbreaker himself."

I hoped this was meant to be humor. When you have power over people, you shouldn't toy with them so.

After studying my face for a moment, Prince Henry spoke again.

"You may rise, and you guardsmen are to withdraw. I would have private words with this man."

We arose. But before turning and leaving, Guardsman Willis briefly rested a comforting hand on my shoulder. The gesture was not lost on Henry. When they'd left, Henry stared pointedly after.

"As I said, he's getting quite cheeky, that one."

Henry stood from the throne (let's call it what it was) and stalked over to stand just before me.

"Given our situation, I couldn't help but take that jab at you. I'm told it's how friends often behave. But I noticed the disappointment that crossed your face when I did so. Most men would respond with anger. What say you to that?"

"I wasn't wroth with you, sire; it's just..."

"Just what? You have my leave to speak freely."

"A man in your position oughtn't dabble with dark humor. One who wields power over others must be careful lest he be feared. Teasing is indeed how friends sometimes behave, but not when one friend has the power to consign the other to the black tower."

He considered this for a moment and took another tack.

"You have such an honest face, reared as you were outside of the nobility. Tell me, how was it possible for you to fool Manny? He swears you knew nothing about that ball outside the city, despite the fact that it was you who were hosting it."

Time to come clean. They say contrition is often easier than obtaining permission. Let's just hope contrition doesn't come at too great a cost.

"I am in a delicate stage of my journey toward mastery, your highness. My mind is split in two. This is perhaps an oversimplification, but you can think of it this way. Sometimes my left hand doesn't know what my right hand is doing. Literally. I'm told this ability will gradually recede, but I'm trying to nurture it. Sometimes it's beneficial to keep secrets."

The prince's neck stiffened as I spoke of this, and finally he exclaimed, "You'd make a passing good spy with such a talent."

I hope that wasn't the task he intended for me. I would hate it. Cozying up to people while intending to betray their secrets would rot my very soul.

"Not to your taste, eh?" Henry half-asked rhetorically.

"Then there's the unnatural charm you seem to possess. I wish you could bottle some of that up and sell it to me. You have even won over Lord Gaulle, who had been your greatest detractor. And I'm told his clergymen now treat you as one of God's chosen."

"I wouldn't go so far as that, your highness. We've become friends; that's all."

"Well, I'd certainly like to know just how you do it. Is this, too, part of your magic?"

"Not at all, sire. I'll tell you how I answered Royland once when he posed me a similar query. Persistent politeness and empathy for others can often work wonders."

"Still, you seem to have twisted the noble ideal and stood it upon its head. The commoners see you as one of them, and the noble folk marvel at your deeds. I was angered when Lady Megan chose you over me. I thought you must have mesmerized the lady somehow. But now I must reluctantly acknowledge that it may have been an honest choice."

Strike quickly, strike true, Sir Trenton had been teaching me. I sensed that now was the proper time. I'd try to slay the envy-beast in one sure stroke!

"It's good of your highness to say so, but she found no fault in you. It is more of an unfortunate condition of your station. I've known Megan for years now, and when she told me you were a kind and honorable man, it only confirmed the opinion I had already formed.

"You have no lack of charm yourself, highness. You won my friendship even before I knew you were royalty. I would risk my very life for you, not because you are a prince, but because you're a kind prince. And that's a rare combination. You will need a queen to share your burdens and be your other half.

"I see why you thought Megan might be the one. She has many qualities to recommend her. The two of us are perfectly matched. But your highness can do better for himself and for the kingdom. You will find the right one. She's out there."

He let me run on without interrupting, curious to hear my thoughts. But there were limits to the patience of a prince. I thought I'd best conclude and simply hope my words had been enough to mend our friendship. I'd even dared to *use* the 'F'-word in there somewhere.

"And if you think this is mere flattery," I said with a grin, "just look at this honest face."

The prince stared at me impassively, noncommittally saying, "Indeed."

Alright. I hadn't slain the beast outright, but maybe I had wounded it a bit. Trenton would correct my form and have me try again. Later, perhaps I would attempt it. I'd done enough for now.

"I hope Megan's decision doesn't mean her father won't be raised up to duke."

"He won't," said Henry dryly.

"But --"

Henry's eyes hardened.

"The king has made his decision on that matter. We will speak no more of it."

I fumed to think the good baron's prospects might suffer for something I had done. Had my courtship of Megan rewritten the balance of power in the entire kingdom?

"When summoned," I said, daring to speak again without leave, "I was told you had a task for me. Might I ask what it might be?"

Henry shook his head.

"Are you aware that you often speak in sing-song rhyme? Do you do this on purpose?"

"I am aware, and no, your highness."

"As to the task, come with me."

I followed Prince Henry again to the table near the hearth. Rather than refreshments, it was littered with books. Among them, I spied the tome I had gifted the Prince at his ball - the work by Cicero I'd commissioned.

"Have a seat, Lucas."

I selected one and sat.

"Tomorrow, I will be made a crowned prince," he began. "There are many ritual components to this august ceremony, the culmination of which is the crowning itself. I've been fasting since this morning to purify my body. All this afternoon, I've been studying the kings of old to clarify my mind and will and purpose.

"I've read about all their triumphs and their failures, that I might emulate the former and avoid the latter. And in my reading, I came across an interesting tidbit. It seems my grandfather, King Edward, took his quote from Raymond the first out of its proper context. Edward was seen as a rather weak monarch - a bit of a bully, really.

"Regnum meum et praecepta mea, my kingdom and my rules. That saying always struck me as a tad tyrannical. Here is the full quote."

I scanned down through the treatise he presented to me until I spotted the text in question.

"I see," I said, nodding. "So you want the engraving enlarged?"

"I didn't have the time to bring a master mason up here to expand the quote. I must soon leave for my vigil."

"Your vigil, sire?"

"Yes. Tonight, I must stand an all-night vigil of prayer, cloistered in the labyrinth beneath the castle, to purify my soul. I must stand it alone. I must remain awake, contemplating my sins and renewing my connection to the divine."

"I confess, I never knew there was so much to it, highness."

"Did you figure they'd just drop a crown on my head and call it done?"

"Something like that, perhaps with a few speeches thrown in."

"Many do picture it that way because that's the part they see."

In any event, Lucas, I thought of you and your strange gift for stonework. The book you gifted me tells me you've a passing grasp of the old tongue as well. Not to knock the masons, but I suspect some of those fellows wouldn't know how to 'componere' a proper 'sententia.' So, I sent for *you*. I hope the guardsmen weren't too abrupt. I told them to hurry. Can you do it?"

An eager expectation edged the prince's voice. I could see his excitement rising. I knew Henry had a scholarly side, but I might have underestimated his passion for such things.

"Of course, my prince."

I climbed the stepladder and pressed my forehead against the stones just to the left of the existing inscription. Rockytop was eager for some exercise. He'd been energized by my furious bout of weeding the other day, and I hadn't had occasion since to use very much of this. He would shrink back down to his standard size in a week or so. But until then, he was crackling with power just waiting to be released.

I concentrated on matching the new letters to the size and calligraphy of those already present. It was delicate work, like my art. Once I'd traced them out, the stone just crumbled away, and half the new letters were formed. Henry nodded appreciatively as I moved the ladder to the other side. And soon, the tail end of the message was complete.

Standing back, I surveyed my work by the light of the fire below. The completed message now read:

POPULUS REGNUM MEUM ET PRAECEPTA MEA PRODERUN EIS

(The people are my kingdom, and my rules are to benefit them.)

"That's much better," said Henry, clapping me on the shoulder. Well done, Lucas, ...my friend.

A Final Interlude at Sea

Dark. It was dark, down in the belly of a shark. How I came to be here is a tale of woe and dread.

Fully provisioned, we were only setting out when, down from the crow's nest, there came that fateful shout. "I see a tempest comin' from the north!" the lookout said.

"She's a doozy, by God's teeth, with rogue waves underneath!"

This caused the pirates all to quake and shiver in their boots.

I saw the lightning flashing as the lookout's fears were soon confirmed. It was some ugly weather coming down upon us. The wind whipped up. And at our feet, the deck began to tremble, buck, and heave. Stormclouds rolled in overhead. The sky grew Stygian dark. It was a devil storm like none had seen since Noah sailed the ark.

Not being, originally, a man who sailed the sea, I didn't know what orders I should issue. I therefore turned to Hugo, a man I often used, to discipline the others in the crew. Taking charge, he quickly set to rallying the men.

"Strike the mainsail and furl the jib. Batten down the hatches!" he bellowed.

That small bit of trust in another was my first mistake in a place where any blunder might prove fatal. Betrayal was just the pirate way. There were rules of sorts, but these were flexible as only the victor could enforce them. Loyalty was something owed only to oneself.

Hugo was a scoundrel, disloyal to his core, who secretly hated having me in charge over him. But for all that, he was a steady hand, eagerly obeying every command, and anticipating my merest fiendish whim. Unbeknownst to me, he had planned a mutiny, and enlisted several others in his plot. Sharing many a furtive glance, they'd waited for just the right circumstance, and now they deemed the time was ripe to take their wicked shot.

As I watched the men prepare, I failed to mark the signal - the signal that began their base betrayal. One man cut the lashings free and sent the boom swingin' 'round at me. The force of it, as intended, knocked me tumbling o'er the rail. Overboard and falling free, I plunged into the deep blue sea. With dismay, I wondered how well cow parts floated. Not very well, as it turned out. In panic, I flailed my arms about (and hooves make piss-poor paddles, I desperately noted).

I resigned myself to my sorry fate, knowing already it was far too late to rejoin the foul flotilla I'd amassed. My plans had failed; those ships had sailed. My struggles were to no avail. To Davy Jones' locker, I was sinking fast. My eyes began adjusting to the murky depths in which I failed to swim. I almost wished they hadn't, for as my vision cleared, I made out a horrid sight surpassing grim.

'Twas a shark bearing down on me, predatorially, so large as to make me tremble the nearer that he drew. Enormous was he, a leviathan to which I would be but a tasty morsel. And he must've thought so too, for he swallowed me whole, not even botherin' to chew. (When Hugo, that mutinous scum, once bethought to call me his 'chum', I hadn't known he'd meant it literally.)

'How long could one survive in the belly of a fish?' Three days and nights at least, if you believe that Jonah story. 'Prophet or not, how did he even breathe?' I thought. Surely it was only allegory. No, I could feel the burning of my borrowed flesh already. And stewing there in vile digestive juices, I doubt

I'd last an hour more ere giving up the ghost (though it might seem like much longer while I suffered such abuses).

Ah, well. I'd had a good run.

Man plans. God laughs. But the devil laughs much louder when he calls his servants home. My old friend, death, was coming for me, this time with finality. No longer in this mortal realm, I'd roam. I thought we had an arrangement! I'd sidestepped all of his tricks! I resented the reaper's betrayal now. I'd be sure to stiff him his paltry fare when he oared me across the Styx.

CHAPTER TEN

The Hero

"Great occasions do not make heroes or cowards; they simply unveil them to the eyes of men."

~ Brooke Foss Westcott ~

What could have disturbed my slumber? It had been going rather well. I was cozy, nestled there beneath my bedspread. But something was amiss - a nagging feeling I couldn't dismiss. My heart was racing from some unnamed dread. Then I heard it once again - a baleful baying from the hounds, the ones from next-door who harassed us when we sparred. But this was more aggressive, the howling more impressive. It suggested something out of place was creeping through their yard. I doubt it was a deer or some other natural creature. Such visitors were too common to complain so about.

"Rocky, do you hear it?"

"It's why I woke you, brother. Dress swiftly. Let us go and check it out."

What was with this rhyming? It was getting ever worse. I did it now, despite not even trying. I hurriedly dressed and took up my bob, while contemplating why the hounds were crying.

As I crept down the stairs and made my way out back, I heard the mastiffs yelping out in pain. Then, one by one, each voice was stilled after sounding out its mournful refrain. Then all was silence.

I peeked around the corner, fearing what I might see, when a hand came to rest on my shoulder. I made a fist and whirled about, stifling a startled shout, only to find Sir Trenton standing right behind me. Beside him was Grindal Cain. Both were in their nightgowns - a testament to how hastily the two must have arisen. In the stillness of the night they were quite a rumpled sight. But given the frightful howling we'd just heard, I thought perhaps such sins could be forgiven.

Trenton's brow lowered o'er his flinty eyes. He pulled me back and bade me to be still. Then he peered around the corner for himself. It was then we heard a rustling, and out from the hedges there strode another knight. At first, I was unsure for the lighting was poor, but when the moonlight fell upon his face, I recognized the man. It was the younger Stapleton, Sir Charles, whom I had met last autumn escorting the prince.

"Ho. Sir Charles," hailed Trenton, stepping out into the open. "Why were your hounds raising such an ugly racket? And what do you seek over here?"

He whirled around to face us, wild-eyed. And I saw he had a shovel he was wielding like a spear. He cast his gaze all over the yard before turning back to regard us.

"Intruders visited us this night," he said in a hollow voice that was half a sob. "The blackguards slaughtered our hounds when they raised the alarm. By the time I ventured forth, the foul deed was done. Shadowy figures were all I saw, fleeing this way."

I gulped.

"Well, they're not here now," said my brother-in-law-to-be. "But let's see if we can pick up their trail. Such a foul deed mustn't go unpunished."

"Indeed, not," said Sir Charles emphatically. "They'll not kill my dogs and get away unscathed. Old Goliath didn't go down quietly either. On his cooling corpse, clenched there in his teeth, I found a strip of cloth. He must have bitten into one of the craven, cowards ere they fled. Alas. If I still had even one good hound, we could soon sniff them out."

He held up a torn strip of cloth for us to see. I produced a flame from my finger to give us some light. The ragged swath was as black as the devil's heart, and its fine weave bore a stain from what appeared to be blood.

Trenton turned his regard to Grindal, and they exchanged a look. Grindal scowled but then slowly nodded to his knight.

"Give it to my man here. You remember my tracker, Grindal Cain, who helped us on the hunt? I must ask an oath of thee, Sir Charles. If you will promise to keep his secret, Goodman Cain can be of help to us this night."

Sir Charles nodded, and Trenton seemed to accept it. I suspect a more abbreviated oath had ne'er been sworn. When he handed him the scent rag, Grindal started changing. It was a familiar transformation I'd seen some years before. I thought I'd broken the Cain family curse when I shattered the witch's heart. Hadn't several from that clan even thanked me for doing so?

I was learning only now that, although the curse was broken, some of the Cains still bore a remnant of it. I was later informed that Grindal and some others could still transform, into beastly boars just as they had before. The difference was: the process wasn't governed by the moon. They could do it any time they were so inclined. Better still, rather than descend into savagery, now they could keep their minds . The former curse had instead become a strange talent they commanded. But they still contrived to hide it from all the goodly folk (who mightn't understand it).

His snout grew longer, his tusks thrust up, and bristling fur now abounded. Sir Charles and I were stunned and stood there... dumbfounded. Pressing the cloth to his muzzle, the pig-man took a sniff. Then he snorted, cocked his head, and took another, deeper whiff.

"Alright," he grunted, gruff and deep. "I've got the villains' scent. Where did you last see 'em?"

"They came through just over there," I chimed in, surprising the others.

I lit the way and pointed.

"*You* didn't see them, Lucas," said Trenton in confusion.

I hastily explained how I had come to the conclusion. With my verdant sense, I had scanned the yard. All local greenery I'd sampled. And thus, I quickly noticed my begonias had been trampled.

Shrugging, Grindal trotted over to the place I'd indicated.

"Yep. They came through here, alright."

(I felt vindicated.)

He crouched down low and snuffled all around. Nearly to all fours he descended.

"Oooh, a truffle," he happily snorted. "I'll have to come back later and dig it up."

"Three of 'em," he then reported. "One has a limp. They scurried off this way."

And creeping along with his snout to the ground, he led us toward the well. I quickly fished a lantern from my pack. Pressing my burning finger to its wick, I lit it, bathing the area in a swath of golden light. By this time, others from the house began arriving, their shining lanterns banishing the darkness of the night. Count Camburn stood in front, barring the others from approaching any closer.

"The trail ends here," grunted Grindal, standing erect once more.

His bestial features had, for the most part, receded, and he stretched once again to his more usual height. Had any marked his eerie transformation, they would likely deem it merely a trick of the light.

Had those dastardly men paused here to obfuscate their scent? I doubted that such was the case. No, that couldn't have been their intent. I puzzled over the mystery. Where had the intruders gone? But then, from the many clues I'd had, an answer began to dawn.

Reaching out with my earth sense, I peered straight down the shaft and spied what I had begun to suspect. There was a series of indentations spaced at even intervals, hidden among the stones. They put me in mind of the handholds I had once carved into Oberon's spire.

"I think our prince is in grave danger!" I shouted out aloud.

This caused an alarmed muttering from the nearby, frightened crowd.

"How do you figure that?" asked Sir Trenton, "He's holed up in the palace, surrounded by his faithful royal guard."

Ignoring him, I stalked over to confront Count Camburn, who was looking rather stricken. "Your lordship," I snapped, "what was Javier Lewis really doing here? Is it true, perchance, that this well connects to the labyrinth beneath the palace?"

He looked even more distraught but squared his shoulders before giving his hesitant answer.

"I was sworn to secrecy, but I take your meaning, sir. The king once bade his architect to engineer a way that he might flee the royal palace should it ever come under assault. Just as you have surmised, there's a tunnel from the maze beneath - a bolt hole, if you will. It leads from the maze beneath the castle to emerge here at my well."

I nodded; my horrified suspicions now confirmed.

"And tonight, our prince stands all alone, a prayerful vigil keeping, unguarded in that very maze, while his people are all sleeping. I know not what these sinister men intend, but we must follow them inside at once to thwart any threat to our prince."

"But we have no weapons," objected Trenton, "and our armor isn't donned."

"There's no time for that, I'm afraid," said I. "We must strike quickly and strike true, as my instructor in the sword is so fond of saying."

I fished around in my bob once more, retrieving from it my father's sword.

"I trust you will know better than I what to do with this," I said, handing him the blade.

"I have my magic. It will have to suffice. I can see in the dark, so that should help. I will lead the way. Grindal must accompany us to follow them through the maze's turnings. Let any other follow who is stout of heart and loves his prince!"

At this, I gripped the lip of the well and hauled myself over its edge. Feeling my way most carefully, I began my descent into the damp, dark pit, my sense of urgency tempered only by my fear of falling. Above me, I saw Trenton's boots, seeking for the same toe holds I had used. Down we climbed thus on the slick stone ladder before being engulfed entirely by the blackness below.

***

"I can't see a blasted thing," said Trenton from above me.

I couldn't really either, despite all my boasting. But with my earth sense, I detected an opening below just to one side of our make-do ladder.

"Be of stout heart, Sir Trenton. We're almost halfway there."

"Since when did you become so commanding?" mused the knight. "I don't believe I've ever seen this side of you before."

"I've seen my share of crises in recent years. And if there's one thing I've learned, it's that necessity can bestow leadership even on the timid."

"Mind your grip," I added. "The next groove is awfully shallow. I'd hate to have to fish you back up with the bucket."

When I'd drawn up alongside the opening, I carefully stepped across. It was a tricky bit of sidestepping. I wondered how the king was meant to manage it. The stone hatch had swung inward to reveal the gap in the well's lining. I pressed my hand to its cool surface and made a light that the others might have an easier time of it. I reached out and steadied Sir Trenton as he made the same traverse. He, in turn, assisted the others while I peered down the narrow tunnel, which ran off into the distance.

It was an earthy tunnel, shored up every ten feet or so by timbers. It was cool down here, so far beneath the earth.

I gave way for Grindal to pass me by. He was even now transforming into a beast. It made me wince. I'd been gored by a pig once - an awful ordeal. But I set aside such feelings for the sake of our good prince.

"They definitely came this way," he grunted, confirming what we already knew.

I retrieved my shuttered lantern and lit it once again. I followed close on Grindal's heels (um, hooves?). I was followed by Trenton, who was wielding my father's blade. Sir Charles brought up the rear, still brandishing his spade.

"The moment may be inopportune," said Sir Charles nervously, "but does anyone else have difficulty in tight, confining spaces?"

"Keep the faith," said Trenton. "Does not the code enjoin us 'To serve the liege lord with valor?' Besides, you're with an earth mage. Lucas won't let you be buried alive. And failing that, you've got a shovel, haven't you?"

"Though doubtless your words are meant to inspire, they're doing little more than putting ugly images in my head. Please desist from your attempts at comfort, sir. I'll do better to face my fears alone."

How far had we come? I should have been counting my squishy steps. At least five city blocks separated the Camburn estate from the high quarter, and the royal palace was some distance beyond even that. Call it another two. Depending on how extensive this labyrinth was, it might still be some time before we reached it.

"We should hurry," I said. "Perhaps we can catch them up before they do any harm. But let me take the lead. Architect Lawrence mentioned traps, and I can scan for such."

As my cousin Royland often said, 'Prudence is the better part of wisdom.' It wasn't very long afterward that Rockytop all but shouted in my mind.

"Deadfall dead ahead, brother! It is triggered by plates cleverly hidden in the floor."

I halted our hasty advance.

"I know not how our adversaries safely bypassed this trap; But I'm beginning to suspect they have a confederate within the palace itself. Step only where I step if you value your lives. There's only one way to safely navigate through here."

And calling on my gift, I pushed a spell out through my soles, causing glowing boot prints to appear. Cautiously, I stepped ahead until the way was clear. The others scrambled after.

"From the weight of the walls above," said Rocky in my mind, "I think we are now passing from under the lower city into the high quarter. It shouldn't be too long before we reach the palace grounds.

"Quietly now," I ordered.

Several minutes later, I thought I saw a light, dimly shining way off in the distance. I shuttered my lantern, lest it give us away. A stealthier approach was the order of the day. I prepared myself for whatever we might encounter. I really had no idea what this labyrinth might contain. We all stood still and listened.

"Their smell is fresher now," reported Grindal. "We've almost caught them up."

'Almost' could be too late for our prince. As silently as we could, we hustled toward the light, my earth sense ever stretching out ahead. Three of them, well-armed, and four of us, less so. Would our rescue be successful? Whatever our odds, we would cast the dice. But did the venture have to be so stressful?

And then we were out of the narrow tunnel and blinking in a lighted corridor. I recognized the candles empowered by magic. They would light on command and burn for a month or more. Of course, the king would have access to such wondrous things. Ensconced on the walls, they lined the halls.

"This way," said Grindal, brusquely brushing past me.

With his nose to the floor, he led us to the right. At a side passage, he turned again (left this time). Following the trail was his only concern. With little or no hesitation, he led us boldly forth at every turn.

Occasionally at first, but with greater frequency the farther on we went, large murals adorned the walls we passed. They were mosaics, made from tiny, colored bits of glass, sparkling in the steady candlelight. They depicted various scenes. Many had seated rulers and even some angelic forms. I suspected they commemorated significant events from Osten's past, but we couldn't spare any time for sightseeing.

Instead, we hustled past, barely gaining an impression of one before the next was upon us. But I could imagine Henry taking his time to contemplate each scene.

"Stop," I said. "Do you all hear that?"

But Grindal ignored me, as if he hadn't heard. He was hot on the scent, paying no heed to my command. Then I tugged at his protruding, curly tail. At that, he turned and damned near bit my hand.

Then he heard what we all heard. It echoed down the halls. It was a muted thumping from the hallway just before us.

We crept ahead more cautiously and peered around the bend. And there we spied two men in black. Between them, they held a stone bench. They were using it as a battering ram to bludgeon a large wooden door. Though the bench was in a sorry state, it looked like the door was taking the worst of it. What in the world were they up to? And where was the other one? Then I spotted him. He was lurking in the shadows, some distance back from his bench-wielding brethren.

"Hurry," he was saying. "We're making too much noise. The castle guard will soon arrive. We must get to the prince ere that, or all will have been for naught."

Unfortunately, he spotted us then and hissed to his confederates.

"Beware, servants approach. Slay them quickly."

I suppose it was the way we were dressed. Three men in their nightshirts and a pig wouldn't seem like such a terrible threat. The two knights exchanged a glance, and an understanding passed between them. They went charging down the hallway straight toward the dark-garbed men. The two with the bench quickly dropped it, stepped back, and drew their bows. Knocking arrows to string as quick as thought, they loosed at the unarmored knights.

I'd often had occasion to envy my cousin's shielding spell, a disc so bright and blue. It had saved many men at Westarbor Keep, stopping arrows from piercing them through. I'd tried to learn it several times but never got the knack. So instead, I used the geomancer way of thwarting such an attack.

With a rumble and a quaking, flagstones rose from the floor. They formed a solid barrier before the charging knights. Against this, the arrows shattered, terminating their flights. I knew I could simply crush them, bringing down the ceiling on the men we fought. But I thought that we should take them alive to find out who authored their plot.

Then a tragic thing happened. Just as the astonished miscreants had been beaten back, what remained of the door swung wide revealing the prince who was standing inside. He was draped in white robes and had prayer beads hanging around his neck.

I struggled to raise another barrier. But ere I could manage it, the third man loosed. He was the one with the limp, but his aim was sound enough. Would Henry be skewered after all? But then Trenton was there, interposing himself and shielding the prince with his own body. The arrow slammed home. Spinning around from the force of it. Trenton sagged against the wall. Then he crumpled to the floor, insensate.

A moment later, Sir Charles was bringing down his shovel on the foul offender's head. The blow rang out loudly. But Sir Trenton... Was he dead? He couldn't be. It was too soon. We'd only just started respecting one another. As Henry cradled Sir Trenton's head in his lap, his white robes now stained red, I turned on the two other fiends.

"Terreno tenaci," I said.

And from the earth that lay beneath the flagstones I'd unsettled, erupted earthy arms that bore them to the ground.

And that is how they found us, the prince's loyal men. They'd arrived a little late to prevent their prince's death. Fortunately, we had stopped it in their stead. And though badly wounded, thankfully, Sir Trenton still drew breath.

***

I was weary to the bone. Yet I had to get cleaned up. The prince's coronation was to proceed just as planned. Too many preparations had been made to postpone so momentous an event.

Sir Trenton had been spirited away to the royal physician, whose tender ministrations he was 'enjoying' even now. I couldn't help but recall the haunted look on the baron's face when the chaplain had been let in as well. We were soon assured that the young knight was resting uncomfortably and should fully recover given time and the grace of his creator. The arrow had pierced him just below his right shoulder, coming straight out through the back. We were told he'd been lucky it had missed his lung. He hadn't *looked* so lucky when they'd carried him away.

The king was determined not to reveal the incident to the populace. He'd prefer not to lend any credence to the notion that anyone might oppose his son's worthiness. He'd not bow to an assassin's blade. It was a strange word, 'assassin'. I suppose that whoever invented it viewed them just as I do (each being doubly an ass). The men we'd captured had been hauled away to the black tower, there to be questioned about who had sent them. The king had men there with the proper skills to attend to that unpleasant task.

So here I stood, winding up water from the well for my bath. My nighttime muddy slog through the underbelly of Osten, the subsequent battle and sleepless night had left me a frightening mess. And no one could haul up water as quickly as a winder. I handed the full bucket to Toby, who had just arrived for another.

"I reckon we got enough now, master," he reported. "That should be the last one we're needing."

I was relieved. Although my winding didn't require much magic, Rockytop was somewhat depleted, having burned through his impressive store in the battle we'd waged the night before. My shoulders slumped as I made my way back wearily to our room. The house was all abustle with various preparations. I knew I must make haste if I wanted to be ready to attend the celebrations.

Sigh. This rhyming was getting wearisome, even if it did come unbidden.

Back in our room, I found another unexpected blessing. It seemed Toby had already laid out my best outfit on the bed. I wondered how he'd even managed to fish it out of my bob from among all the other clutter that swirled around in there. Not only that, but there on the floor stood my boots. They were polished and shining as if new. This contrasted sharply with the sorry, mud-encrusted state in which I'd left them.

I scratched absently at the back of my hand.

"Good job shining up my boots, Tobias," I praised, stepping into the bracing water of my bath.

"That wasn't me," said the lad blushingly. "One a the other servants must'a done it."

But what was that peeping out from beneath the sole of my left boot? It looked to be a dried-up leaf.

"Toby, bring me that leaf that's sticking out from underneath my boot at the foot of the bed."

"This leaf?"

"Yes."

He retrieved it.

"What d'you want it for?" my servant said.

I ignored his question and examined the leaf. And just as I suspected, it was marked by a crescent moon and the capital letter 'T.' I summoned up my magic to shed some light upon it - the deep purple hue that had worked before for me. This caused glowing letters once more to appear. They read simply, 'I M HEER.'

"Terwilliger?" I cautiously uttered.

And from out of thin air in the room's far corner, there came a laughing reply.

"You may say my name till yer tongue turns blue, and no longer must I appear! The queen's forgiven my indiscretion and lifted that burden from off my merry soul. Just as I wrote ye, I've traveled quite far to be greeting Sir Lucas here. Have ye some milk? I must confess, the journey has taken its toll."

Toby had leapt up onto the bed and scrambled back until his back met the headboard. With eyes as wide as saucers, he was scanning all around the room.

"Master," he said nervously, "Mum told me there was no such thing as ghosts. But there's *some* kinda spirit in here. It's askin' for milk and the like."

"I heard him, Toby. Have no fear. I know this spirit well. Though, if, as he says, he's been freed from his geas, perhaps someone should fit him with a bell."

At this, the laughing brownie shimmered into view, unsettling my nervous servant anew.

"Toby, please go to the kitchen. Fetch a saucer of milk for our uninvited guest. Put a drop of honey on the side. For he fancies such, he once confessed."

"A... saucer?"

"Aye, lad, and be quick about it," snapped Terwilliger with his eyebrows arched. "I'd fancy that wee bit of honey and confess to bein' downright parched."

Once Toby had gone, Terwilliger hopped up on the bed and reclined. I splashed some water on my face and began to scrub at the dirt and grime. Propping his head up on one elbow, Terwilliger began making small talk as if speaking so to a naked man was the very height of civility.

"I've heard ye been up to some mischief, merry mayhem befitting even one of my folk. Ye've come up in the world as well, I hear, since the days ye was Lucas the Bloke. But high station be no excuse for muddy boots, as surely ye must know. What've ye been up to to soil your footwear so?"

"I'll tell you the tale, but only if you'll answer a question of mine in return. There's something to do with the fey that's been vexing me, of which I yearn to learn."

I knew fairies were close with their secrets and enjoyed teasing you by withholding their knowledge. But they were also curious creatures, and if you struck a bargain with one, he'd be sure to follow it to the letter. After considering for a moment, the brownie nodded his agreement. So I told him of my adventures since arriving here in Fairglen. Fairies love stories.

When I mentioned my engagement, Terwilliger grew excited, offering to throw a bachelor party for me the like of which no human had ever seen. I blushed when I envisioned the bacchanal fairies might consider appropriate for such a celebration. I was just finishing up my recounting of last night's frantic sojourn beneath the earth when Toby returned, carefully balancing the saucer so as not to spill it.

Without so much as a 'thank ye lad', the brownie started lapping it up as soon as Toby rested it on an end table. By this time, too, I'd finished my bath, emerged, and was drying myself off.

"Ah. That was refreshing," said the tiny man. "Ye've hosted me proper; ye have. Now, what's this troublesome matter that vexes ye so? Inquirin' brownies are itchin' to know."

"A curious compulsion has gripped me," said I, "causing me to spout rhymes. It's almost a curse. I even *think* in verse. And people are starting to notice, since it's gotten even worse. What do you know of this compulsion to rhyme? Has it aught to do with faerie kind?

Terwilliger leapt back up on the edge of the bed. He puzzled for a moment as he settled there and said:

"Have ye noticed people liking you a wee bit more than ever they had before?"

"Uh... maybe."

"And have your words become more measured with a rhythm more aesthetic, all lyrical and lovely and waxing all poetic?"

"Yes, I believe they have."

"And do ye often choose words that are similar in sound, their beginning letters matching, like 'dreary drunkard drowned?'"

"Alliteration, we call it. And yes."

He danced a little jig on the edge of my bed. Then the brownie tipped his pointed hat to me and said:

"By Oberon's teeth and the pink gums underneath! I'd wager me old mum's eleventh rib, that to you, my lucky friend, fickle fate did bequeath, that fey power we call the gladsome gift of glib!"

"The gladsome what now?" I asked, pausing in pulling my doublet on over my head.

"Ye've not heard of it? Hmm. How to explain. Ye know ye are fey-touched, right?"

I was aware that on the day I received my fairy mark, I had joined the ranks of that sodality. Moreover, since I'd been fostering a changeling since the moment of my birth, perhaps I even had a double dose.

I nodded.

Toby, meanwhile, had seated himself in the corner and sat, wringing his hands and absorbing it all in quiet fascination.

"Well," continued Terwilliger, "occasionally, and over time, a fey-touched human may develop one of the blessings of the faire folk with whom they've had contact. 'Tis wonderful that ye've done so, Lucas lad."

"And this giddy glamour of garrulousness..."

"The gladsome gift of glib," he quickly corrected.

"Yes, that. It causes one to spout rhymes?"

"No, lad," said the brownie, waving his hand in dismissal. "That be only a side effect. The gladsome gift makes one likable. It causes others to hear yer words in the kindliest way they can. And it can do even more impressive things; I've been given to understand."

"But I'll soon sound like a ninny if I'm rhyming all the time, and I must attend a ceremony just this afternoon. Likable or not, my friends will think my nerves are shot. Is there any way to stop myself from babbling like a loon?"

Terwilliger grinned and considered this before saying in a confidential tone:

"I'll let ye in on a secret we brownies sometimes use when we're feelin' grumpy and dinna want to rhyme. We think of a word that has no match and ponder it for a time."

"You mean a non-rhyming word? Which word do you use?"

"*I* think of the word 'oranges,'" he said proudly, "to which no other can be paired."

"What about 'door hinges?'" I asked without delay.

"Ach! Now ye've gone and *ruined* it," he fumed. "I can't use it now that a match be known. For that, I think I'll leave ye here to figure it out on yer own!"

And, hopping to the floor and striding toward the door, an irate Terwilliger vanished once more.

"Master, is he mad at you?"

"He'll get over it, Toby. Come help me strap on my sword belt. Faeries are temperamental. I'll show you how to tie a proper peace knot."

I resisted for as long as I could before blurting out the rest.

"I hope your hands will be gentle."

***

Again, I was seated in the great colosseum, this time with the Westarbor contingent. Megan and I sat to the left of her mother. To the baroness' right was Sir Nolan, filling in for the baron. At least we were down in front. But the sky had grown overcast. Storm clouds were sweeping in from the west, and soon the skies would open up to put a damper on the festivity. It was a most dismal day to be crowned.

I furiously sought for a way to suppress, the impulse to in rhyme express, our joyous celebration being 'drowned.'

I needed a touchstone - a word that had no rhyme. I considered several such, on which the bards had given up. 'Silver' was no good, for although it showed some promise, 'pilfer' matched it closely enough. 'Purple' likewise wouldn't do. For it was sad but also true that the forgiving nature of my curse, would allow near misses like 'circle' and 'verbal', to complete an awkward verse.

I stayed quiet for the most part, speaking less and less, despite the many feelings that I wanted to express.

"Cease your squirming, Tam," said Lynette, who sat on the bench just behind us. "You promised to be on your best behavior at this august ceremony."

"I did," he shot back. "But this bein' only June, I reckon it ain't no August ceremony."

My servant, always an endless source of amusement, had confused the rare adjective with a month...

"?"

"Month," I said aloud, and the urge to rhyme was stymied for a time.

"What's that, love?" asked Megan.

"Ah, just a stray thought, my lady," said I, taking up her hand in mine.

"No. Tell me," she wheedled. "What has you smiling so? It looks like we're about to get drenched, after all."

"I'll explain later, my love. But for now, suffice it to say, 'April is a dangerous month.'"

It was then that the trumpets brayed and the royal guard marched onto the field. The royal platform had once again been set up on the southern end of the arena. This time, however, there was additional seating in the field's center. This was set aside for the high nobles who would swear fealty to the newly crowned prince. That was also where Lord Westarbor and the other barons of Northford were seated, confirming the notion that there would be a new duke raised up from among them.

The stands were filled and overfilled. Despite the threatening weather, no one wished to miss the ceremony on coronation day. They'd slog through whatever moisture the clouds cared to throw down upon them just to tell their grandchildren they'd been there. When the royals appeared, the crowd roared out its approval.

And then it happened.

Just as the royal procession made its way up to their seats, the rising wind suddenly abated. Their cloaks ceased flapping, and a soft light appeared as the clouds began thinning above.

This drew my eyes upward to where gray masses swirled and parted, allowing the sun to peek through. A shaft of golden light pierced the gloom, coming to rest directly at the center of the field. It grew wider by the minute until it encompassed the entire colosseum, bathing all in its effulgent glow.

All around, the thunder still grumbled, and flashes of lightning were seen. But directly above us, all was peaceful, balmy, and serene. The crowd had grown quiet as this progressed, but now a hushed muttering arose as people began remarking to their neighbors on the marvel they were witnessing. This soon transitioned to oohs and ahhs as further wonders unfolded.

Arching across the sky above, a ribbon of color presented itself, growing thicker and more intense as its hues separated. Bands of brilliant color, ethereal but true, painted the sky above us, a rainbow like no other I had ever seen. The red was redder, the blue was better, as were the yellows, oranges, and greens. And the purple was ('circle'? 'verbal'? Ha!). Anyway, it was delightful.

From over the rainbow came streaking a shimmering ball of linden green. And finally, I began to ken what was happening. It was how Titania, the fairy queen, liked to travel about. I'd met her once (well, almost) and had seen her briefly another time. As she was now our ally, I doubted her intentions would prove hostile (as if the rainbow hadn't made her good will clear enough).

My fey mark began to tingle and throb as the green comet descended to hover over the center of the stadium. In its wake, it trailed a tail of glittering sparkles. It was as if the rainbow had decided to fragment and swirl overhead. These soon spread out to circle about. And when some drifted nearer, I realized it was a swarm of pixies in our midst, the sun's glinting rays refracting from their delicate wings.

The crowd's murmuring grew louder, and some cheers burst out when, drifting down from on high, there came a rain of flower petals. I could barely tear my eyes from the dazzling display, but when I heard the herald, I did so anyway.

"The king would have his envoy come forth. Your services are urgently needed."

What?

I felt Megan's elbow dig into my ribs. Not the ribs again, I moaned.

"He means you," my lady prompted. "Best you move swiftly to heed the royal command, beloved."

The 'beloved' lessened the sting somewhat, but I wondered whether my next doublet should include some kind of padding. This being only my second visit, I was unsure of the quickest route down to the field, and I didn't want to make his majesty wait. So I hauled myself bodily over the lip of the wall, intending to hang and drop. But though twenty feet didn't sound like much, it seemed much farther when looking down. I clung to the lip, looking silly.

Taking command of myself, I decided just to make my own handholds and climb down lower. Yes, that would be much better for my knees (and dignity). On reaching the arena floor, I turned and sprinted toward my king, his faithful envoy, heeding his command. At my approach, fully twenty royal guardsmen gave me the sovereign salute. Not looking so silly now, was I?

I silently intoned my new mantra: April is a dangerous month.

"I am here, my king, and yours to command," I said, falling to my knees.

"Am I thinking correctly, Sir Lucas, that this ball of light is foreign royalty?" muttered the king, *sotto voce*.

"Yes, sire. I believe it is Queen Titania herself, although faeries prefer their true names not be used. She prefers to go by the sobriquet Queen Tinatia."

"Strange," said King Raymond. "Then it falls to us to welcome her. You must do so on our behalf, envoy."

What? Um. Okay.

Get a grip, Lucas, I exhorted myself as the herald handed me the staff. I rose to my feet. My head swam as I turned to face the thousands of expectant citizens in the crowd. My fey mark was throbbing with the beating of my heart and tingling to beat the band. I had no idea what to say.

But when I looked up at that nimbus of light hovering above, something inside me came unstuck. Waves of tingling ripples cascaded up my arm and crept over to my throat.

"King Raymond of Osten would like to thank your majesty for the honor of your visit to the crowning of his son."

What was this? Those were the words I was hearing, but the throbbing of my throat bespoke a different tale. A series of gurgling bell-like tones were tripping off my tongue. Later, I would learn that everyone in the colosseum heard my speech in his or her own native language.

"His majesty would have it known that you and your entourage are most welcome. We call this, our capital, "the Fair City", but it has never been more fair than when graced by the presence of Tinatia, the fair one herself. Your gift of clement weather is appreciated and will forever be recalled with joy in the annals of our people.

While I was talking, the king dispatched a man to retrieve another chair. I stepped down and moved closer to the hovering ball. Recalling that faeries considered rhyming to be polite, I let loose.

"As your majesty can see, the event is well attended, to the point of having no seats left at all. But as hosts of this affair, we can't leave you in midair. And seeing as your folk are rather small, we would be delighted for your beautiful attendants to enjoy front-row perches right up there on the wall. They can rest their pretty wings while the business of kings is conducted to the wonderment of all."

At this, I bowed my lowest bow and froze in that position. My throat felt raw, and I doubted I could croak out another syllable. Is this what Terwilliger meant when he said the gladsome gift might do more impressive things? The green nimbus slowly descended, and upon touching the arena floor, it burst like a soap bubble.

The lady certainly knew how to make an entrance.

And she wasn't alone. Oberon was there with her. I was a little worried because I'd battled him once. Or, rather, a changeling posing as my former non-homunculus had battled him while in possession of my body. (It was a little complicated.) He was a tall, muscular man with curly brown hair and a regal face. All but one of the blemishes that had marred that face were now absent.

The queen, too, was much as I remembered her. She was a tallish woman with dragonfly wings sized up to suit her stature. She was garbed all in green, right down to her boots, and wore a conical silk hat atop her head. The queen stepped right up to me, took my chin in her hand, and peered into my eyes. She had the most beautiful sky blue eyes, the pupils of which were vertically slitted, like those of a cat.

"We are pleased by your welcome," she said.

Even without the staff, her melodious words rang out to fill the amphitheater.

Straightening, she approached our king, followed closely by her consort, and addressed him.

"It was our wish to look upon this Prince Henry. We understand that he will be your leader one fine day. And thus it behooves us to know his mind since soon he will be managing the affairs of the fey."

Smiling and nodding to King Raymond, she added, "Not too soon though; we fervently pray; I am told it might be polite to say."

She stepped even closer to our mystified monarch, right up to the edge of the platform itself. Then her wings blurred into motion, and she rose until she met his eye like an equal.

"We fey have some complaints against you mortal men of Osten, with whom we are so recently allied. These are matters our ambassadors will soon become engrossed in. But let us set such grievances aside. Eschewing all such accusation, let us join in jubilation to enjoy this joyous celebration upon the happy occasion of the crowning of your son."

I was glad I wasn't the target of that lyrical litany. The blushing king only nodded pleasantly.

Soon the faerie queen and her consort were seated at the platform's far end, the archbishop having quickly vacated his own seat in the latter's favor. I wasn't sure what to do with myself, so I wandered over to stand beside them. As the envoy, I figured I could help if they had any questions or needed anything. Oberon shot me a quick glance and a smirk when I did so.

"On with the ceremony!" announced the herald.

***

"It is our good king's intent, as all here know, to see our good Prince Henry crowned on this happy day. Being of age and cleansed in body, mind, and spirit, Henry now stands ready to receive the coronet. The peerage is assembled and has had ample time to ponder this grave matter. As custom dictates, I must ask. Are there any who object or would voice a reservation? If so, stand and do so now."

All remained seated.

"Then we shall proceed," said the herald after a suitable amount of time had lapsed.

He handed the speaker's staff to King Raymond, who remained seated.

"I shall now call upon my dukes of the realm to swear fealty to my son and heir. His grace, Lord Brax Steelaxe of Echo Hills, will be the first to offer such an oath. Step forward, your grace."

The Dwarven Lord traversed the arena from his seat at its northern end all the way up to the royal platform. By this time, Henry was standing just before it. Brax knelt and removed his coronet. He laid it on the ground before the prince. With his head bowed, he gave his oath.

"I, Brax Steelaxe, duke and laird of the Echo Hills, renew my pledge of fealty to King Raymond Andrew Osten, rightful ruler of our realm. I vow to provide my arms in times of war, my art in times of peace, and my service in times of need. I promise to defend our fair kingdom against any who would work her harm by my word, deed, and force. I will continue to be faithful, holding honor and courtesy above all. Additionally, I pledge this day my support for Henry Roderick Osten as his legitimate son, heir, and successor."

The audience remained quiet to hear Prince Henry's reply.

"Let all here bear witness that I, Henry Roderick Osten, Prince of Osten, hear and accept your oath, given in good faith. In turn, I vow that upon my ascension, the crown will continue to defend and support you and yours with word, deed, and force. Those who keep and hold this oath true will be rewarded with my favor. Those that forget this oath and break faith shall be repaid with my judgment and dreadful wrath."

At this, Henry took up the coronet and placed it on the Dwarven lord's head.

"Now, arise and go, keeping honor and courtesy above all."

Each duke or duchess of the realm was called forth and bent the knee before their prince. All, that is, save for Lady Brighton of Lorédon. In the Great Accords of Osten, the elves had made a special arrangement with Raymond the first that no Elven ruler would be made to kneel before a king. It was a curious exception. Nevertheless, she took the same solemn oath as the others.

After all nine dukes had sworn their oaths, it was finally Henry's turn. As a mere duke regent, Manny hadn't been summoned. Nor was there a Duke of Northford. Otherwise, the full count should've been eleven.

The vows Henry made were no less solemn. His golden circlet looked much plainer than the elaborate bejeweled crown of the king. It was scarcely weightier than the coronets worn by his dukes. It had a few majestic arches that I later learned were known as "dragon scales." Henry looked most regal indeed when the archbishop rested it atop his head.

And up from the masses there arose a mighty cheer, a wall of sound comprised of all manner of congratulatory shouts. The roaring din continued unabated for minutes on end as Henry panned his gaze over the celebrating crowd. The shouting grew more rhythmic, and a chant came to dominate it, growing ever more distinct.

"Hen-ry! Hen-ry! Hen-ry!"

And on and on, it went.

When it finally started to settle down, the king himself arose and strode forth to embrace his son. And the cheering grew even louder than when it had first begun. He raised his hand for quiet and retrieved the speaker's staff.

"Then on to other business," said the king with a hearty laugh.

(April is a dangerous month.)

"My other son, Richard, too, will be honored on this fine day. Step down here, Richard, and kneel before your monarch and your monarch-to-be. It is time that you assume your new station. Give us your oath, then."

Richard knelt before the king with Henry by his side.

"I, Richard Raymond Osten, hereby accept my duties as duke of the province of Fairglen under the auspices of Raymond Andrew Osten, its rightful ruler. I vow to provide arms in times of war, my art in times of peace, and my service in times of need. I promise to defend our fair kingdom against any who would work her harm by my word, deed, and force. I will continue to be faithful, holding honor and courtesy above all. Additionally, I pledge this day my full support for my brother prince, Henry Roderick Osten, as the legitimate son, heir, and successor to our lord and liege."

At this, King Raymond passed Henry a coronet, which he, in turn, placed on his brother's head.

"Arise, brother, and go, keeping honor and courtesy above all."

"And may your hunts be ever joyful," he said more quietly, patting his sibling's shoulder.

It was at this time that the fairies departed. Queen Titania was courteous but resolute. She'd seen all she cared about. Any further intrigues involving our petty nobles were of no concern to her. She left the same way she had arrived, after promising to leave her sylphs to keep the weather calm. After that, I stood idly by, unsure what to do with myself. I was glad enough for the front-row seat. I felt undeserving of it, but no one was chasing me off.

***

"And now, for the *crowning* achievement of the day. Ah. I am informed by my herald that we've had that already."

The king looked around expectantly, but no one laughed. Rolling his eyes, he continued.

"It has been quite some time since the kingdom of Osten has been whole. Forty-seven years, to be exact. But today, I intend to remedy that by appointing a new duke of Northford."

An excited murmur answered the king. It occurred to me then that speaking before a crowd was a lot like having a conversation with one big, very stupid individual. The barons of Northford, seated on the field behind the dukes, shifted about restlessly. I spied Baron Westarbor who was sitting far more placidly among them.

"I'll spare you any further suspense," declared the king. "Leopold Stein, arise and stand forth."

The murmuring of the crowd grew louder and more chaotic, with exclamations ringing all about. "What the heck?" the consensus seemed to be. Nonetheless, Lord Leopold stood shakily to his feet and faithfully ambled toward his beckoning monarch. He arrived at the base of the platform and stood silently before his king.

"It is my intent to have this man made duke, filling the final vacant slot and healing the decades-long absence that has marred our rule. I deem that Leopold Ludwig Stein stands ready to receive the coronet. The peerage is assembled and has had plenty of time to consider this appointment. As our custom dictates, I must ask. Are there any who object or would voice a reservation? If so, stand and do so now."

It was too much to hope that all would stay silent. Several lords looked ready to pitch in their two farthings. But they sat for many moments staring around at one another as though deciding who would be first. *My* money was on Downham, and nor was I wrong. I only wish I'd had somewhere to actually place that bet. The man soon stood up from the chair where he'd been sitting to loom above the others in the row.

"Ah," said King Raymond, pleasantly enough, "I see at least one who would second-guess the crown. As a gentle monarch, we welcome all advice. Bring forth your objection. Let us hear your thoughts on the matter."

All eyes tracked the self-styled "Hawk of Northford" as he prowled up the aisle in his checkered livery of black and red. Everyone knew he'd prefer to be the new duke instead. What might he say to bring pressure to bear to dissuade the king from his choice? He soon arrived by Lord Leopold's side, towering above the old wolf. He bent the knee before the king and accepted the staff from the herald.

"Your Majesty," said he most deferentially, "I must first acknowledge the solemnity of this appointment ceremony and the wisdom that typically guides our sovereign's decisions. Lord Leopold Stein has indeed been a venerable figure in our realm. We are all aware of his history and achievements."

I sensed there'd soon come a 'but'.

"However, I wish to raise several concerns regarding this appointment."

Alright, it was a 'however' (tomayto; tomahto).

"Not to be indelicate, but due to the baroness' barrenness, this man has no heirs to continue his line. And as your majesty is well aware, this can lead to uncertainty where stability is desired. Your majesty has many other fine choices, with dynasties fully intact.

"Exacerbating this situation is the matter of the good lord's health. From reports I've heard, he's not the man he once was. In fact, he's not expected to live to see the spring. Why make such an appointment knowing this, my king? I would humbly request that our sovereign provide clarity on the reasoning behind this appointment."

Raymond stared at Downham, (who stood taller than him by a head).

"Let us hear from the man himself. Give Stein the staff," he said. "What say you, Lord Stein? Have you an answer to this?"

Lord Stein's face transformed as he accepted the staff. His jaw no longer hung slack. There was a spark of mischief in his eyes. And his cunning smile was back.

"Setting aside your unfair and ungentlemanly affront to my wife, the mother of my child, and the love of my life, I'll be happy to answer your objections, sir."

His sudden loquaciousness caused quite a stir. (And April is a dangerous month.)

"Your chief objection seems to hang upon my health, which is, indeed, a matter of *grave* concern. I freely admit that my mind drifts in and out, but I'm feeling quite *lively* today. I think I've found a way to preserve the Stein legacy. With his majesty's blessing, I should like to adopt as my son and heir a man who all here already honor and revere."

That was interesting.

"Will you, Baron Vincent Arenson, Lord Westarbor, eschew your lands and titles to become the heir of Stein?"

"I will," came a shout from the back.

"This is all very irregular," sputtered Guy Lord Downham, whose face had grown pasty and pale. "In our realm, we've long valued the established order of succession and the adherence to established norms. Deviating from tradition should be done only with careful consideration."

"I have considered," said King Raymond. "I will allow it."

The big man's shoulders sagged. He could recognize a set-up when he witnessed one. The whole thing smacked of prearrangement.

"By your leave, then, my king, my objection is withdrawn."

And so it came to pass that Leopold Stein was made the new Duke of Northford. His new 'son', Vincent, became his heir and would one day soon replace him. All the barons of Northford swore their fealty to Leo. None of them dared to raise another objection. Wilhelmina could live out her life as the dowager Duchess Stein. And all was - *but wait!* There's an important part I oughtn't skip past.

"Who will take over in Westarbor?" I asked with sudden suspicion.

No admonishment was forthcoming for my speaking without permission. The king looked over and winked at me. And at his signal, all the trumpets sounded. Throughout the great arena, gladsome fanfare rebounded. A lone figure was revealed when the northern doors spread open wide. His arm was in a sling, but a bounce was in his jaunty stride. At his approach, every guardsman made the sovereign salute. And up in the stands, a silence descended, becoming absolute.

"As I am now a duke," said Leopold, "I have the great pleasure of appointing a new baron to a land that's lacking one. Who better knows the barony than the former baron's son? I present to you Trenton Arenson, now Lord Westarbor, and hero of the realm!"

Epilogue

The sunroom was no longer as neat and tidy as it had once been. Boxes and crates lay strewn about, and four women were sorting through a clutter of gowns and other garments. I hesitated at the threshold. The baroness... I mean, Lady Chamille, the former Baroness Westarbor, was grousing to the others.

"That man never seems to *tire* of changing my name. First to Lady *Arenson* when I agreed to wed him, then to Lady *Westarbor* when he was raised up to baron. Now it's to be Lady Stein, and one day, 'her grace, Lady Stein.' Once again, it seems, I have an enormous pile of embroidery to undo."

"Lucas," said Megan, dropping the dress she'd been folding and stepping over to greet me with a hug.

Rolling her eyes, Lynette took up the dress Megan had abandoned and began folding it neatly.

"Save some for the honeymoon, you two," said the newest Lady Stein, clucking her tongue in mild reproach.

In truth, I was uncertain how to address her now, since *both* Lady Steins were present here today.

Belatedly, I bowed.

"It is good of your grace to visit," I said, addressing the elder of the two. "I trust from this that your husband is recovering well from his risky foray into alchemical stimulants?"

"He's resting now at the palace. Vincent is sitting in for him at the king's council. Thankfully, Brother Wallace was able to administer the antidote before it stopped his foolish heart. As the royal physician, the good friar strongly advises against any more such nonsense. The poor dear is sleeping it off. He's a brave one, that man I married."

"He is indeed," said Megan's mother, pausing in her stacking of linens. "It's just the sort of thing my Vincent might do. Never mind that it causes his poor wife to age a year for every such capricious caper. I suppose it's just part and parcel of being married to such amazing men - and why we love them so."

"Sir Lucas," said the Duchess Stein, "here in private, you may address me as Lady Wilhelmina. We're nearly family, after all. Though I don't favor being made a 'granny' so soon, I'm technically your grand-mother-in-law-to-be."

"Yes, my lady," I replied.

I filed 'granny' away with 'willy' to use later if the duchess and I ever became close enough to exchange such barbs. I was all too aware of the imminent threat from my fiancé's eager elbow to dare any such monkeyshines yet.

"Have you heard if they've discovered all the traitors in our midst?" I asked instead.

"We believe they've all been rounded up. Leopold named several ere he succumbed to his medications. I was shocked to discover that our host, Lord Darrington, had a hand in it. Theodore was always a fool, but I never thought he would take part in such a heinous plot."

"How did Lord *Leopold* learn of this?" I asked in puzzlement.

"He overheard them talking one night when they thought he was asleep. He was having one of his listless days, but he retained awareness enough to hear them speak unguardedly. That's what he was trying to tell us with the cards. But even *I* didn't understand his warning. I'll never underestimate that man again."

The lady promptly sat and dabbed a kerchief at the corner of her eye. Chamille rushed over and sat beside her.

"As to the conspirators," continued Wilhemina with a sniff," they're in the Black Tower awaiting the king's displeasure. I hope to be well gone from this place when his judgment falls upon them. Leopold and I are staying at the palace now while all of the former Lord Darington's staff are being questioned."

Hoping to lighten the mood, I posed another question.

"Where's Trenton, anyway? Shouldn't he be helping to pack up all of this?"

The baroness made an exasperated grimace that soon turned wistful.

"That boy is *another* one who refuses to acknowledge his limits. He should be resting peacefully, but would he deign to miss sword practice this morning? Never. 'Tis an ideal opportunity to practice swordplay with my left hand,' he insisted. And now I believe he's off courting half the eager young maidens of Fairglen."

It is true that the ladies of the kingdom now viewed the heroic, young, unattached, and newly arisen baron as a surpassingly eligible target for their ambitions. It aligned well with his motto of 'strike quickly and strike true' to capitalize on such pursuits at once.

"Actually," put in Megan, "Derrick told me he would be calling on Baron Nicolás Nimble of Navarra and his daughter, the Lady Jaquelyn, this afternoon."

A worthy pursuit indeed, I thought. I wouldn't mind in the least having Jackie as a sister-in-law in-law.

"To be fair," added Lady Wilhelmina, emerging somewhat from her dismal mood, "the young buck might be *wise* to move so quickly. He needs to get started producing heirs for both the duchy and his new barony."

"Still, I wish he'd learn to pace himself," fretted the man's mother. "Well, back to work. Lynette, did you find that bracelet you were looking for?"

We left the others to proceed with their packing. Megan and I wanted a few more private hours to bask in one another's presence before our long separation was to commence. Arm in arm, we slipped away to the rear of the estate to enjoy what remained of the day in companionable bliss.

That evening, the baron returned, or perhaps I should now say Sir Vincent. It had been getting hard to tell the knights without a herald these days.

He plopped down in a chair, looking exhausted.

"There's my poppet and the audacious journeyman mage who dared ensnare her."

"Hardly that, father," objected Megan". I entered into the arrangement willingly. If anything, 'twould be more apt to say that *I* ensnared *him*."

We were once again in the sunroom. The clutter had all been packed. Over in the corner stood the boxes, neatly stacked. The baron had only just returned from an all-day council with the king. And April still remained, I thought, a dangerous month.

"How went the council with the king and his dukes?" asked my beautiful bride-to-be.

"Grueling," replied Sir Vincent. "I thought running a barony was demanding, but there seems to be no end to the matters urgently requiring a king's attention."

"Are the pirates still causing trouble over on the coast?" I asked.

"Strangely, no," said Vincent. No one's seen hide nor hair of them for several weeks now."

"That's good to hear," said Megan. "The people of Indigo Bay deserve a respite."

"You would think so, but it seems they have another problem now. There's a great white shark capsizing fishing vessels and causing all manner of grief. It's a monstrous leviathan never before seen in those waters."

"Oh, dear!"

"Oh dear, indeed, poppet. Not to worry though. Lady Cynthia has dispatched one of the finest captains in her fleet to hunt it down - a fellow named Ahab. He and his men have sworn to put an end to the threat."

"Did anything else exciting come up?" I asked.

"Not that I can tell you about, Lucas. But everyone is still going on about how you greeted the faerie queen in her own language. That was quite an unexpected and impressive feat. There's a betting pool among the dukes over what you might get up to next. It's a shame you have to leave us tomorrow."

Sigh.

"It is, but I've put it off for as long as I can. Master Balderas and the other mages will be setting off this afternoon. He insisted that I accompany them. I promised him I would leave at first light and catch them up by tomorrow evening at Sleepy Hollow."

"Is that rascal of a servant going with you?"

"No. Toby's mother and father are staying here to run the almshouse, and he's too young to strike out on his own."

"I thought as much. You know, at council, an interesting topic was brought up. It seems that as a crowned prince, Henry will require a page of his own. Henry added the name Tam to a list of other candidates. With a proper letter of recommendation, your servant might just find employment at the palace."

"Really? I'll get right on that then... Vincent."

"That's still Sir Vincent to you, Lucas. Not only is a duke's son owed that honorific, but I retain my knighthood, after all. Perhaps one day you may replace it with 'father'. But until then, pay proper respect where it is due."

Megan gave my hand a squeeze and smiled demurely. Another wave of gratitude washed over me to be part of this loving family. I could scarcely contain it. Turning to Megan, I said, "I still have trouble believing in my good fortune. I will forever bless the day when you agreed to be my bride."

"Well," said she, playfully, "I couldn't very well leave you to 'wander about the land as half a man' now, could I?"

I rolled my eyes as her father laughed. I would never live that letter down.

Nor, I thought with a mental shrug, would I ever *want* to.

***

My heart was heavy as I steered Feckless along the busy lane. It would be my final ride for quite a while along the thoroughfares of Fairglen. I'd given my goodbyes and made my fond farewells. Now all that was left was the leaving. I summoned a stoic smile to my lips (but inside, I was grieving).

For how many months must I greet each day without the joyous sight of my lady's winsome face? How long before I next heard the ringing of her laughter? In melancholy, I'd dwell for now, sustained but by our solemn vow that one day, should the fates allow, we'd live in bliss thereafter.

By the hallowed halls, that was a long one. Such a somber stream of verse felt like letting loose with a sneeze. I was learning to control it better now. I could rhyme whenever I wanted, but I could revert to more ordinary speech when I didn't. Every once in a while, though, it came bubbling up to take me by surprise. I blinked hard and shook myself to clear my head.

In the distance, I made out the marquee of the Silverlight Grand Theater. A man was just taking down a ladder that had been resting against it. As I drew closer, I saw that the lettering had changed. It now read:

Tonight's Feature:

"Lucas and the Prince"

A tale of friendship and rivalry

Fancy that. I suppose our recent escapades would indeed make for a fun, action-packed, romantic play (or a comedy). If experience were any guide, it would likely be an exaggerated tale bearing little resemblance to actual events. I wondered whether it would have a long run. The royals would doubtless have it shut down if it proved too uncomplimentary to his highness. Let the people have their fun. At least I got top billing, I smugly mused.

Soon, Feckless and I were beyond the city gates. In the glorious morning light, we approached the well. But what was this? In front of it were a dozen people standing in a line. Each held flowers and appeared to be waiting their turn before the statue, where one old woman knelt. Next to her stood a boy, addressing the others.

"Step right up and bring your offerin'," said the ragged boy. "'Tis said that if you make her a gift of flowers and tell the lady of the well your heart's desire, she might grant it."

I smiled, prepared to move on.

"What about you, mister?" the boy shouted up to me. "Got a wish for the lady?"

"She's granted mine already," I replied as I rode past. "If it's of any help, I found the lady prefers gardenias."

I felt my stoic smile soften and become more genuine.

Reaching the outskirts of Refuge itself, I marveled at the changes that had been wrought since my first arrival. There was the hospital, standing proudly beneath a newly thatched roof. Beside it was the smokehouse, emitting gentle puffs from its stout brick chimney. Beyond even that, I saw yet another building. In front of it, men were queued up in a line. And emerging from it came the very rascal I'd come here to see.

"Master!" cried Tobias upon sighting me.

He was carrying an empty bucket, which rattled against his leg as he made his excited way over. I dismounted and awaited his approach.

"I'm no longer your master, Toby," I said as the lad drew near. "You can call me Lucas if you like."

"Oh, I couldn't do that," he exclaimed. "How about I call you journeyman instead?"

"Whatever you're comfortable with. Say, what's that new building you just came out of?"

"That's the new bathhouse, journeyman. Remember when I told you they sawed that tun in half? Well, they built the bathhouse around it, and we're all usin' it to get cleaned up. It can service three at a time!"

"Three men in a tub, eh? What did they do with the other half?"

"Oh. It's just down the street. We're usin' *that* one for laundry and the like."

I thought the lad was being rather generous to refer to this bare dirt path as a 'street.' The residents of Refuge seemed to be taking a little more pride in their nascent village. It made me glad to see it.

"Before I forget," I said, "this is for you."

I withdrew the sealed envelope from the pocket of my cloak and presented it to him. Toby frowned.

"Master, you know I can't read," he said, accepting it nonetheless.

"It's for you to give to the prince," I explained. "He needs to hire a new page boy. I think you'd make a fine candidate for the job. The pay is much better than that of a standard servant, and you'd get to live at the palace."

The lad looked stunned.

"Of course, it's not a sure thing," I added with a smile. "There are many other fine candidates for the post. Some of them are the sons of nobles. But I think you made a good impression on Henry at our several meetings, and my word might carry some weight in the matter. If it does come about, it won't be easy. You'd have to learn to read, among other things."

"Ma!" he shouted, dropping his bucket in the middle of the 'street' and running back toward the bede house. Then he pulled up short, turned, and flashed me a smile.

"Thank you, master!" he shouted before hurrying on his way.

So, I remounted and rode on, trusting that the good folk of Refuge could look after their own. As the miles slid by, I became lost in my thoughts. Even Rockytop was silent. At the crossroads, I turned west toward Donovan's Rise.

A lot had happened since I'd last ridden up this path.

I had seen a righteous monarch crowned and danced at a royal ball. I won the heart of my lady fair (the sweetest thing of all). Though it saddened me to be leaving, I knew it was time to depart. And though April may be a dangerous month, June will forever have a very special place in my heart.

Author's Afterword

Dear Reader,

I hope you've enjoyed the magical land of Osten and its many colorful characters. I have certainly enjoyed writing about it. This series was my first attempt at creative writing, but I now suspect it won't be my last. Among all the epic fantasies floating about, I believe there's room for a bit of humor and an uplifting tale that doesn't take itself too seriously. Some comments I've received from readers just like you have been downright heartwarming and confirm this notion.

I've said before that it helps to write from personal experience. I have never attended a royal ball, of course, nor flown upon a griffin. But it's the little things that make a story entertaining. For example, I once went on a land tour of Alaska for a family vacation. At one stop, my youngest son, Eric, was invited to feed a reindeer by holding a carrot out to it in his teeth. The smelly old thing peeled its lips back and took it from him. What a great photo-op that was! I picture that reindeer every time I write about Feckless.

Another time, we visited Williamsburg, Virginia. Among many other fun activities, they rebuild colonial buildings from historic architectural renderings using native materials. There, my family was invited to stomp around in a clay pit and work clay into bricks for the drying racks. Although we didn't get our feet dirty that day, observing the fun left quite an impression on me. The only thing that would have made it funnier is if dwarves were doing it.

And, of course, there's the fact that Luanne, my wife of thirty-seven years, and I shared our first kiss at a pond after feeding the ducks. She was a very strong candidate for my dedication. She inspires and supports me. But I've decided to save *her* for some future novel.

Instead, for this last novel in the Osten Chronicles, I am choosing to honor a friend who has been with me from the project's beginning. He beta-reads the chapters as I post them and has helped keep me from going too far down the rabbit hole. On one occasion, his feedback caused me to back up, reassess, and rewrite an entire chapter.

We worked together at several I/T shops over the last thirty years or so, most recently for the banking industry. But I first met Roger Anderson as part of a gaming group. In fact, he ran a Pathfinder campaign in the fictitious land of Osten he created. The books I write bear little resemblance to the rules or swashbuckling adventures Roger ran. But I take great pleasure in using the name of his kingdom, its rulers, and many of its geographical features in my writing. I suspect he gets a chuckle from it as well.

So here at the story's end, I applaud my creative friend,

as I pen my author's afterword in the gentle light of dawn.

I've a sense of satisfaction

and would love to know *your* reaction.

(So don't forget to review this novel out on Amazon!).

Still Feeling Feisty and Ready to Rhyme,

Daniel Thorman

Appendix I

(Dramatis Personae)

For your enjoyment and to help you keep track of the many characters populating this novel, I've provided the following reference. It's a short summary of the characters encountered. Reference with care as a few of these passages may contain spoilers. Otherwise, enjoy.

Main Characters

Lucas Matthew Harper (aka Lucas the Just) - Once again we find our humble hero intent on setting things to rights. This time, he's rushing to his lady's side to fulfill the oaths he swore. Alone and friendless, he makes his way to the kingdom's capital of Fairglen. But is Lucas ever truly alone for long? He tends to make friends wherever his wanderings may take him.

Rockytop - Rocky is Lucas' inner voice. He is a portion of Lucas' awareness we might call the unconscious mind. The mages of conclave call this a homunculus. They are useful mental constructs every journeyman mage must discover and train.

Tobias Antonio Moss (aka Tam) - Formerly of Gretchford Gulch in the southern part of Eagle's Keep Duchy, this scrappy young fellow is struggling merely to get by. Fate was unkind to his homeland, placed as it was directly in the path of an escalating conflict with the dark druids. With his mother and his father, he fled toward safety in the north. But what a cold reception they received on their arrival! To what lengths would *you* go in such a situation to insure your family's survival?

Megan Irene Arenson (aka The Lady of the Well) - The daughter of the baron has finally come of age. It is time to make her debut and officially take her place among the courtly nobles of the kingdom. Megan shares her father's gift to sense another's thoughts by touch or by making eye contact with them. She must uphold the honor of Westarbor and present herself at court. As a nobleman's daughter, she is also expected to receive suitors. Will she find among them someone with whom she might find happiness?

Truman Huber (aka The Demon of the Sea) - In this kingdom of goodly men, how's a dishonest necromancer supposed to get by? I'm done with it; I am. I've got some plans of my own - big plans. Just you wait and see...

The Royals

King Raymond Andrew Osten III - The convivial monarch of all the realm of Osten, named for his forebear, Raymond, the first. King Raymond is seen as a fair monarch, but is not counted among the great ones. He was crowned when he was but a boy and relied on his mother's advice long into his reign (some say too long). He means to see Prince Henry crowned.

> ***Tobias of Ghent*** - A merry lad who serves the king as his page.

> ***The Royal Guardsmen*** - This elite force answers directly to the king. They are responsible for the royal family's security. Usually dressed in distinctive black chain mail, each of them is said to be worth ten ordinary soldiers. Guardsman Willis is 'the cheeky one'.

Queen Audrey Osten - Formerly Audrey Blount of Galliwick, she is mother to Prince Henry. She is a kind woman and loves her husband despite his indiscretions.

Prince Henry Roderick Osten - As the son of King Raymond and Queen Audrey, Henry is the heir presumptive to the crown of Osten. As his eighteenth birthday approaches, he prepares to be made heir apparent. Henry is very intelligent and likable in his fashion. He's been protected for most of his life from the brutal truths of the kingdom's governance. He is scholarly and well-read.

Prince Richard Raymond Osten - Richard is the result of a dalliance King Raymond had with one of the maidservants in his youth. He is eight years Henry's senior. But his birth and royal standing weren't acknowledged by the king until he was in his teens. As the eldest son, he might have a claim on the crown, but he purports having no desire to rule Osten. Richard enjoys hunting.

Queen Titania "The Fair" - She and her court have ruled over the seelie fey for centuries. Titania is a tallish woman with dragonfly wings. She recently concluded a bitter rivalry with the unseelie fey commanded by her former husband, Oberon. Oberon is now her consort and hopes to regain what he lost while possessed by the vile artifact, Rhea.

The High Nobles

Duke Phillip Gaulle - Rules over the duchy of Eagle's Keep, sometimes referred to simply as 'The E.K.'

Lady Brighton - Elven duchess of Lorédon.

Duke Brax Steelaxe - Dwarven Laird of Echo Hills.

Duke Sean McAlister - Ruler of Ironhill Duchy, a mountainous northern land.

Duchess Cynthia Farax - Lady Cynthia rules Farax Duchy, a northern coastal land dominated by pirates in times past. She also commands Osten's naval forces.

Duke Conner Deerfield - Rules over Deerfield Duchy wherein the conclave of wizards lies.

Duke Charles Nelson - Duke over Indigo Bay.

Duque Mateo Batron Cuevas - Ruler of the southern duchy of Freemark.

Duchess Teresa Tetchin - Rules a loose confederation of islands known as the Indigo Isles which is technically Osten's eleventh duchy.

Duke Regent Harold Manford (aka Manchester Kidder, and many other aliases) - Many forget that the province of Fairglen itself is a duchy. The post is somewhat symbolic because the king directly oversees it. When the former Duke of Fairglen retired a few years ago, Lord Manford was appointed as Duke Regent for Richard Osten.

(There is no Duke of Northford) - There hasn't been for decades. Not since the Northford rebellion was put down. The king takes a more direct hand in the affairs of the barons there.

Some Other Nobles (in no particular order)

Lady Katheryn De Kuttleston - Daughter of Lady Cynthia of Farax, she considers herself the leading debutante of the season. Blonde and attractive, she likes to flaunt her wealth with fine outfits.

The Marchioness Victoria Castleberry - Widow of the former Marquis Castleberry. Her husband governed multiple counties and parishes in the province of Fairglen itself. As a dowager, the Lady Castleberry still commands great sway in the king's council. She is very cunning and intelligent. She also enjoys gardening.

> ***Leonard Wexely*** - Lady Castleberry's porter and majordomo.

Count Edmond Camburn - This widower is an old friend of Baron Westarbor. He owns an estate near the high quarter and has offered lodgings to the baron and his entourage.

Baron Stanley Stapleton - Owns the estate adjacent to the Camburn estate. Lord Stapleton enjoys hunting and has a kennel of hounds.

> ***Sir Charles Stapleton*** - First encountered escorting the prince on his grand tour of the kingdom, the younger Stapleton is a knight who has made quite a name for himself on the tourney circuit. Sir Charles can be a little bombastic and suffers from claustrophobia.

Baron Theodore Darrington - An acquaintance of Lord Leopold from his younger days, this lord owns a manor house two streets up from the Camburn Estate. He has offered to host the ailing Lord Stein and his lady wife during the upcoming festivities.

Lord Everette Winthrop - This Earl of Hamelinshire is Megan's escort to the prince's ball. The Earl despises faerie folk due to an unfortunate encounter with a pied piper in his capital city of Hamelin. The sorrowful place is missing an entire generation!

Sir Alfred Wulfric - The handsome Sir Wulfric is looking for his bride. Self assured and from a good family, he believes his prospects are quite good. He has set his sights on Megan.

Sir Arthur Murray - This dapper old gent owns a dance studio known as Castle House. He enjoys instructing the nobility in all the courtly dances, from the latest to the more traditional.

Thane Ewen MacLaren - Distinguished thane of the Citadel Deep. This Dwarven lord is known for his generosity and for being a bit soft spoken.

> ***Lady Felicity MacLaren of Dalriada*** - Thane Ewen's daughter and the apple of his eye. Felicity is one of this season's debutantes. She speaks her mind. In addition to her father, this Dwarven maid has six other protectors.

Baron Nicolás Nimble of Navarra - A baron from down in Freemark.

> ***Jacquelyn Beatrice Nimble*** - One of the season's debutantes. She is a skilled dancer and is purported to be brave (and very nithe).

Some Barons of Northford

> ***Lord Leopold Ludwig Stein*** - His symbol is the wolf. Once an amazing innovator, Baron Stein is in sharp decline due to a strange malady that robs him of his memory and awareness. It is a progressive condition that is steadily worsening. His wife, Lady Wilhelmina Stein actually runs Barony Stein with the help of his loyal knights.

Guy Lord Downham - The self-styled 'Hawk of Northford' governs a farming barony. It has prospered, but he drives his tenants rather hard. According to Lucas, he exemplifies much that is bad about the nobility.

Vincent Arenson Lord Westarbor - Once a humble knight at the capital, Sir Vincent led a force north to repel a goblin invasion. This won him the new barony he named Westarbor. He has been steadily investing in the barony and its people. Only recently has all this hard work and dedication begun to bear fruit. His symbol is the dove.

Chamille Arenson Lady Westarbor - Wife to Vincent and mother to Trenton and Megan, Lady Westarbor is a brave and respected leader in her own right.

Lady Megan Arenson - (see 'Main Characters').

Lynette Powel of Sommerset - Lady Megan's companion and handmaiden.

Sir Trenton Arenson - Westarbor's heir and brother to Megan, Sir Trenton earned his knighthood two years ago after battling a gryphon (that's what we call the wild ones - the tame ones are griffins). The young knight and Lucas got off to a rocky start, but he's mellowed a lot since then.

Derrick Lester - Sir Trenton's squire.

Taylor Allen - The archer for Trenton's lance. Taylor formerly served in the king's spy network, the Brotherhood of the Board.

Connor Dawson - The cook for Sir Trenton's lance.

Grindal Cain - The new tracker for Sir Trenton's lance.

Sir Nolan - An older knight serving Lord Westarbor.

Jay Harvey - Sir Nolan's squire.

Rupert Cain - A griffin trainer and now a griffin rider in his own right. He serves Lord Westarbor, bearing messages around the kingdom.

Nellie Cunningham - This griffin rider is married to Rupert Cain. She's been hiding in the carriage house with her broody griffin, Blynken. They are keeping

Blynken's egg a secret as it is to be a birthday gift for Prince Henry. Nellie has a secret of her own. She suspects she is with child.

Other Folk

Cliff - Proprieter and bartender at the Wayfarer's Rest in Cheapside.

Clem and Wally - Two of the duke regent's soldiers typically stationed at the gates. They wear green livery depicting the black dragon of the realm.

Benjamin - Owns a barber shop on Fleet Street above the meat pie shop. (Nothing scary going on there... yet).

Nora Moss - Toby's mother living in the refugee Camp. She tends to the sick and elderly there.

Aaron Moss - Toby's father has been conscripted to work at the king's quarry downriver.

Javertimus Stoneheart - A dwarf in charge at the king's quarry. He's a bit greedy and known to have a temper.

Caesar Hollander - An elderly rancher from the western E.K. He fled north with all the others when his ranch was overrun by foul abominations sent by the dark druids. He now ekes out a meager existence at the refugee camp.

Cedric Monroe - An account clerk at the Bank of St. Matthew.

The Fiddlers Three - Once a famous group of minstrels that traveled around the kingdom in master Cole's caravan, the group split up over creative differences and has only recently decided to band back together. They are:

   Liam Gordon - first fiddle.

   Julian McGee - second fiddle.

   Renny Labeau - (the heartthrob of the group).

Guildmaster Bennet - A master mason and guildmaster of the Fairglen Masons.

Sir Archibald Lawrence - The Royal Architect.

Benedict - Archbishop of the Church of Fairglen.

Bonnie Sheppard - A shepherd girl from a nearby ranch.

Enoch - A friend of Toby's. Enoch runs a ragtag gang of youths at the refugee camp.

Master Balderas - Headmaster of the conclave of mages. He is a loyalist originally from Freemark.

Appendix II

(Spells)

Fun Fact: The 'old tongue' I use for the spell verbalizations is simply Latin. You can usually plug a spell name into a Google translation to find its literal meaning. Lucas and his cohorts have learned quite a few since their apprenticeships. Below is a fairly comprehensive listing of Spells used in my novels to date. The ones with asterisks denote spells new in this novel:

```
Old Tongue (Means)
  ambulare interitus (Withering Stride)
  aqua exstinguit (Water Quenches)
  aquam claram (Clear Water)
  arescet et mori (Wither and Die)
 *aurea lux mollis (Soft Golden Light)
  ave cantus et flores (Birdsong and Flowers)
  calidus ignis ardentis (Blazing Hot Fire)
  capturam petram (Catch Rock)
  cogitationes liberare (Liberate Thoughts)
  digitus flamma (Flame Finger)
  exorcizo spiritus (Exorcize Spirit)
 *flammas auget (Intensify Flames)
  frigus metallum in perpetuum
  (Permanently Cool Metal)
  geas silentii (Geas of Silence)
  gloriabitur securis (Force Axe)
  iactare spheara (Spinning Toss)
  ignis loquela (Fire Speech)
  Impedimente (Shield/Protect)
  inexsuperabilis permanens lignea
  (Permanently Impregnable Wood)
 *inter guttas (Between the Drops)
  internum calorem (Inner Warmth)
  levare et colligentes (Lift and Pull)
  levare et conicere (Lift and Throw)
  lumina in (Lights On)
  lumina quell (Kill the lights)
```

manent vigilate (Remain Alert)
miscere cogitata (Combine Thoughts)
motis cessabit (Calm of the Grave)
omnino siccis plantis
(Completely Dry Plants)
personalis zephyris spirantibus
(Personal Zephyr)
podagra flammae (Gout of Fire)
Praefundo harenae (Dampen Sand)
Praemium (Explode)
pulver in ventis (Dust in the Wind)
quaerite mihi amans (Seek my Love)
*quaerite mihi ovium (Seek my Sheep)
quaerite nuntius flammae
(Seek the Messenger of the Flame)
quomodo probatur in conflatorio mortis
(Crucible of Death)
radet ovium (Sheer Sheep)
repellere insectorum (Drive Away Insects)
scripturam vim extermina (Erase Writing)
spacium girabit (Rotate)
sphera de incineratio
(Sphere of Incineration)
sternetur tinea munda (Maggot Cleanse)
suspendium tenaci (Choking Grip)
tenera pluviam (Tender Rain)
terram aratro (Earth Furrow)
*terreno tenaci (Earthy Grip)
ut reflectum speculum (Glass that Reflects)
viburnum pugna (Snowball Fight)
visio tenebris (Darksight)
visus aquilae (Eagle's Sight)

<<<<>>>>

9 781963 913286